FIONA MITCHELL

The Maid's Room

HODDER &
STOUGHTON

First published in Great Britain in 2017 by Hodder & Stoughton
An Hachette UK company

1

Copyright © Fiona Mitchell 2017

A CIP catalogue record for this title is
available from the British Library

Hardback ISBN 978 1 473 65956 8
Trade paperback ISBN 978 1 473 65957 5
eBook ISBN 978 1 473 65958 2

Typeset in Plantin by Palimpsest Book Production Limited,
Falkirk, Stirlingshire

Printed and bound in Great Britain by Clays Ltd, St Ives plc

Hodder & Stoughton policy is to use papers that are natural,
renewable and recyclable products and made from wood grown in
sustainable forests. The logging and manufacturing processes
are expected to conform to the environmental regulations
of the country of origin.

Hodder & Stoughton Ltd
Carmelite House
50 Victoria Embankment
London EC4Y 0DZ

www.hodder.co.uk

For Mike and Olivia,
who were there through it all.

Prologue

This is where she sleeps. A cupboard. A bedroom. A windowless box.

She flicks the light switch and there is the bucket speared with mops, the washing machine and the mattress on the floor. The room is so packed that only a few of the floor tiles are visible. Sweat drips off her nose and splats onto one of them. The tumble dryer has fattened the heat; it's been churning sheets and now there are clods of dust everywhere like she's running a wig shop in here. She struggles to breathe in the hot, scarce air. The smell of boiled vegetables from the nearby kitchen makes her feel sick.

There's a tiny table beside the mattress, clogged with photograph frames and drawings, and something small and beige and swirly. Her conch shell. If she stares at that shell for long enough, she can transport herself to some place far away. Beside the sea, the surf lapping and frothing over the pebbly sand, a child's chubby fingers pressed into her hand, her feet soothed by the cool water. She keeps her eyes on that shell and her aching back starts to ease; her tight chest starts to loosen and she just breathes.

The sound of shouting slices into the silence then and she's back in the room again, the pressure building in her head and the walls closing in on her.

She opens the door, and in the hallway mirror she sees a woman with lines around her eyes and grey-flecked hair. The voice grows more urgent now: 'Girl!'

She feels the cold coil of the shell in her hand. She pushes it into her pocket and hurries down the corridor towards the voice that carries on screeching.

Chapter 1

Greenpalms Condo, Singapore

Jules clips along the condo pathway, smoothing her fingers over the puncture wounds in her stomach. Music thumps through the 35-degree heat. *Doof-doof-doof.*

'Maybe this time it'll work,' she says to her husband David, whose forehead is beaded with sweat. He glances at her, then his eyes find the concrete.

'Let's just wait and see. Anyway, at least this party will be a distraction.' He grabs her hand and pulls her along more quickly.

Tightly packed white apartment blocks tower around them. They look like City of London offices dominated by glass, except that there are balconies on these buildings. There is a woman on one of the balconies, sitting beneath a green canvas sun umbrella pressing a cigarette to her lips. On another, a pink towel is folded over the glass balustrade. There are purple-flowered shrubs on some balconies, garden furniture on others. The ten-storey blocks are punctuated by columns of smoked glass lift shafts, softened by clusters of lipstick palms with their slim red trunks.

The blocks encircle two blue-tiled swimming pools, one of them Olympic-sized, the other for the kids, shallow and triangular. There's a splash pool too, edged with statues of frogs and snakes that fountain water, the constant rush of them accompanied by a chorus of tweeting birds. A child's blue bike has been set down on the crazy paving path that frames the pools, its back wheel still spinning. Along each length of the big pool, there's a wide decked area with sun loungers and tables and rattan chairs. A pair of goggles lie abandoned on the top of one table; a chair beside it has fallen onto its back. Flower beds line the pools at intervals with bursts of white spider lilies nodding their heads. At the bottom of each apartment block, there's a town house with tall sliding glass doors, the upper half of them covered by horizontal metal bars. The party is in one of these.

It is starting to go dark and the air is violet. Bats are flickering overhead. A raucous laugh hacks the air and there it is, number 16. People are standing around a table in the yard, and through the open glass doors there are shadowed bodies, moving, twisting, dancing, pressing champagne flutes to lips. Here goes. Jules' mouth gets ready to lift a smile. There's no point in knocking, the music's too loud, so she pushes the plain oak front door which she knows will be open. Hardly anyone locks their doors.

Their American neighbour Amber teeters towards them on navy patent wedges, her face sharpened by a pointed chin.

'Hi there,' she drawls. She air-kisses Jules near one cheek then goes to pretend-kiss the other one, but Jules has already pulled back. Their lips collide.

'Girl snog,' says Jules and raises an eyebrow, but Amber doesn't laugh. Her long brown hair is tied into a ponytail pulled forward over her shoulder.

Jules follows her through the open-plan ground floor into a sea of dresses patterned with colourful squares, beaded appliqué and blue birds flapping across silk. David has gone in ahead of her and is already digging in to the crisps on a side table, tapping his foot to the music. The room is bright white and minimal, with globe-shaped lights hanging on metal wires from the double-height ceiling.

'You'll need a drink,' Amber raises her voice over the music.

I *wish*, thinks Jules. 'Something soft,' she says.

This isn't the first time Jules has been in this house; two weeks ago, Amber had invited her to a book group. Jules had read *We*

Need to Talk About Kevin before, so she went along. But it was like she'd lost her voice that night. She was tight-lipped, her throat tight too. The other women were all so controlled, especially Amber; it made Jules want to say something outrageous. But maybe it was just her; everyone else seemed to be enjoying themselves, marvelling over the chocolate cake that the helper had made. Not that Jules had seen the maid. 'Oh no, she hardly ever works evenings,' Amber had said, and flicked her ponytail onto her other shoulder. Perhaps it was just that Jules didn't fit in – most of them had about three kids each, and only one of them worked, and their faces were made up, their hair shiny and tame, perfectly neat like this town house. Wooden stairs lead to a glass-balustraded landing, beyond which are the bedrooms. Another set of stairs lead down to the basement area. Amber gave Jules 'the grand tour' of the three-storey house during the book group meetup. At the back of the living room, there's a kitchen with sliding glass doors. The two rooms are separated by a marble-topped island unit.

Amber takes a champagne glass from the maid who's carrying a tray of them; she pushes it into Jules' hand. Amber's forced smile is packed with strong, even teeth.

'Oh, no, I'm not—'

'It's a party!' snaps Amber.

Jules opens her mouth to say something else, but Amber's already walking off towards the maid with the tray.

The maid's face is an oval of porcelain skin, but it's her ears that Jules can't stop looking at, pincushioned by gold hoops. That must have hurt. Jules touches her nose and the tiny hole that's never disappeared. She went through agony for that ruby stud, but then she'd been a different person back then. She plonks the glass of champagne on a side table brimming with crisps and dips.

David is talking to Amber's husband, Tor, a slightly crumpled Norwegian with a lone privet of silvery tufts on the front of his balding pate. He always seems to be in linen. He towers over David, who's challenged in the height department with his spiky hair and red cheeks. Tor has to stoop to hear what David is saying, his steel glasses slipping down his nose. He must be at least ten years older than his wife.

The maid passes, carrying a new round of champagne glasses. There's a frenzy of grabbing, of bubbles sloshing. The tray tips until there's nothing left but liquid on chrome. She sees Jules' empty hands. 'Let me get a drink for you, ma'am.'

'That'd be great, thanks. A lemonade, or, well, whatever you've got.'

The maid walks into the kitchen. She's dressed in a knee-length black skirt, scabbed with pastry, a safety pin jutting from the side. She returns with a glass and an open can of 7UP.

'Thanks,' says Jules. She scans the room.

A man is staring at the maid, compressed features and a once broken nose, his eyes going up and then down. He should be so lucky. He catches Jules looking and strides over.

'Lovely pair of pins,' he says to Jules. He's Australian.

The maid moves away.

'What was that?' asks Jules.

'I've seen you in the pool and you've got a bloody gorgeous pair of legs.' His tongue peeps out and glosses his lips with spittle all the way round.

Jules resists the urge to look at her knobbly knees. 'Right, erm, thanks,' she says.

She spots the dining table, which is packed with plates of beef-topped vol-au-vents, smoked salmon blinis and folds of red meat. There's her excuse to escape.

'I think I'll just get something to eat,' she says and hurries away from him. She picks up an olive and puts it into her mouth. The man slots himself into another group of people, but carries on ogling Jules. She looks away. The maid sets more bowls of food on the table.

'What's your name?' asks Jules.

The maid smiles at her, says nothing.

'I'm Jules, and you are?'

'Dolly, ma'am.'

'Hello, Dolly.' Jules smiles; the name suits her pretty doll-like features.

Amber is beside them then. 'We need more drinks over here,' she says, an edge to her voice.

'Yes, ma'am,' says Dolly. She heads back into the kitchen.

Jules chomps on a handful of ready salted crisps and peers at a lidless jar of jam.

'Lingonberry preserve,' says Amber. 'Tor just has to have a taste of Lillehammer.'

Amber snatches up Jules' wrist, crisps scattering. 'I want to introduce you to someone.' She drags Jules through the crowd.

A woman with brown eyes is dancing on the spot, making rhythmic up-and-down movements and puckering her lips. Her hair is done up in a chignon, but the kirby grips aren't doing their job.

'This is Maeve,' says Amber.

'Hi,' Maeve says, continuing to dance.

'Oh, and I'm Jules.'

'Short for Julie?' asks Maeve, a cockney lilt to her voice.

'Just Jules. That's what everyone calls me, apart from the other things.'

'Oh? What's that then?'

Twig. Professional worrier, she could say, but if Maeve is anything like the other women, her face will stay frozen and the tumbleweed will roll.

Jules touches her hand to her neck to choke the quip. 'Oh, this and that,' she says instead.

Maeve stops dancing and introduces her husband, Gavin, the lech from earlier. His eyes scope the room then he starts thrusting to the James Brown track playing in the background.

'Jules is the newest recruit to the book group,' says Amber.

'Oh, yeah?' says Maeve.

'You weren't there for Jules' first time, Maeve.'

'It's *The Help* next, isn't it?' asks Maeve.

'Yes,' smiles Amber.

Jules is halfway through the book, but already she's trying to think of reasons not to go. The music beats on. Jules gazes out at the dancers, taps her sandal.

'So, where are your kids?' Maeve asks her then.

Amber answers for her: 'Jules doesn't have kids.'

'Lucky you,' Maeve says in a blurt of a laugh. 'Still, there's time enough for—' The end of her airy sentence is snatched by the rising beat of 'Sex Machine'.

'How many do you want?' Amber asks Jules.

'What do you mean?'

'Children, of course,' laughs Amber.

'None,' says Jules.

'Oh, you say that now . . .' continues Amber. 'I didn't have my second until I was forty-one.' A wide smile splits her face.

Gavin slides away.

'How long have you and your husband been together?' asks Maeve, a V deepening between her sculpted eyebrows.

'Eleven years,' says Jules.

'Oh.' The V gets deeper still.

Jules starts jabbering over James Brown's increasingly desperate entreaty to get on up.

'David and I met at some crappy club in the London suburbs originally. We were just kids really. Both went off to uni and it petered out. Thank God for Google, eh?'

'What do you mean?' asks Maeve.

'David tracked me down, the stalker!' Laughter bursts from Jules' mouth.

Maeve and Amber remain stony-faced. Still, at least Jules didn't swear. Someone turns off the music briefly and jumbled voices rise. Another song booms from the sound system then.

Amber clears her throat. 'Jules is in healthcare.'

'Me too,' says Maeve, holding her glass with both hands as she takes a gulp. 'I'm a cafeteria assistant in a hospital – well, was. You know.' She chuckles, leaning into Jules' left ear to make herself heard. 'Lady of leisure now. So what was it that you used to do?'

A small blond boy, a red blotch on his forehead, pulls on Amber's arm, distracting them. The ice rattles in Amber's drink as she moves away with him.

Maeve raises her eyebrows. 'That's Amber's youngest. He's probably complaining about his older brother, The Feral Child. He's a real nightmare, punched my daughter in the mouth once.'

Another woman comes up to Maeve and they start talking. Jules zones out, taps her foot harder. Oh, how she misses her real friends, and the hospital in London where she used to work, with all those new mums holding their precious bundles for the first time, joy stirred into their eyes. She thinks of all the discarded IVF syringes in that yellow bucket in their new apartment here, and sighs.

In the kitchen, Jules drinks a glass of water while gazing at the wreckage of half-eaten hors d'oeuvres. The party has thinned out, but there are several people sitting in the front yard deep in conversation.

There's a blue curtain at one end of the kitchen. Presumably, if it's anything like Jules' apartment, there will be a small passageway behind it which leads to a narrow toilet, and a cupboard with reinforced concrete walls and a thick metal door.

The estate agent, who showed Jules around the apartment they're now renting, pointed at the cupboard, and said, 'When you get your maid, she'll sleep in there, the bomb shelter.' Jules had said things like, 'But there's no window,' and 'There's no hot water.' And the estate agent had replied, 'They don't need things like that.' Echoing that awful blog that Jules came across yesterday, by someone called Vanda. She'd listed all these ridiculous rules for having maids, like confiscating their passports and forbidding them boyfriends. Things are different here, that's for sure.

A man's Australian voice booms beyond the curtain now. 'Oh go on!'

The curtain bulges and someone gets tangled there. A hand fumbles the fabric aside. Jules recognises the man's weathered face. He is rubbing at his eye, and shaking his head. She tries to summon his name.

He notices her and shrugs. 'Women,' he says.

He drifts out to the yard and sits among the remaining group of people. It's only then that she remembers his name is Gavin.

Chapter 2

Dolly's stomach constricts as she walks towards the shop that sells the illegal pills. The date for her health check is on the calendar at the town house where she works. *Thursday 13th – Dolly's clinic visit.*

That's eight weeks away. Ma'am Amber penned a red bubble around the words with a huge exclamation mark as if it was something to look forward to. But Dolly will have to take a test there like she always does every six months. And when the employment agency finds out she's pregnant they'll deport her, just like all the others.

She blows a clump of black hair out of her face and paces on past the shops – a tattoo parlour, and a store selling wigs.

There are shoppers everywhere in the brightly lit mall, plastic bags and mobile phones in hands, and men filling their faces with sotong balls. There's a greasy circle on that man's T-shirt; his chin glistens. The air is thick with the smell of steamed dumplings.

Saliva rushes up into Dolly's throat, but she can't see a ladies toilet, so she stops for a moment, tries to gather herself, sucking in the warm air and swallowing. The urge to vomit passes.

She tucks her bright yellow T-shirt, with the black line drawing of a smiley face, into her shorts and starts walking again, flip-flops smacking. The shop that sells the drugs is up ahead on the left.

Dolly wants to get it over with, so she strides faster, past a souvenir store selling Merlions trapped in glass globes that fizz with glitter when you shake them, and drink mats shiny with

Singaporean flags. A Katy Perry song pounds from the open doors.

There it is, looming with the poster outside dancing in the air con: *Reflexology, Indian head massage and Tui Na.* Rows of teapots decorated with Chinese letters, and packets of pills and jellies line the shelves on one side. On the other, there are bouquets of rubber gloves and checked carryalls covered in flowers.

'You like?' the woman shop assistant, with cropped hair, asks. A sharp hair sticks out of her nostril like a bristle.

Dolly digs into her pocket and touches the 100-dollar note that Gavin gave her, with a mumbled, 'There's no way my wife can find out about this.'

'I've got gastric problems,' says Dolly, keeping her eyes fixed on the torn linoleum floor.

The woman looks outside, but there's no one around.

'Follow me.' She swivels on her high heel.

The checked overall strains across her back. Dolly kicks the woman's ankle by mistake and the woman tuts. They dodge a pallet on the floor brimming with floral soaps. On the shelves above, there are pots of vitamins and herbal teas, but nothing as strong as what's behind the steel door that the woman is pulling open now.

The room is dark inside. The woman flicks a switch and the light flashes on then off until the room's blazing. The steel door closes with a click. There are no windows. Dolly's heart vibrates like a trapped fly. Nameless glass bottles, some with their lids off, are stacked on a cabinet.

'So, how far gone are you?'

'Six weeks.'

The woman's brown eyes bulge towards Dolly; she has to look away. She's been so damn stupid, but she had her reasons, and it's not too late to fix this mistake then things can go on as they were.

The woman sighs, pulls open a drawer and pushes two chalky white tablets from a blister pack, the word *Cytotec* printed across it twenty times over. She scrapes the tablets across the metal table towards Dolly.

'Seventy-five dollars,' says the woman.

Dolly puts the pills into the pocket of her shorts and passes the woman the money.

The woman riffles through the pocket of her apron and gives Dolly the change. She turns off the light. Dolly stands there in the dark before the woman pulls open the door and the light from the shop threads its way in. Dolly just wants to be out of here.

She doesn't look back. She walks so fast that she's breathing hard by the time she gets to the escalator. She pulls her purse from her beaten handbag and opens it up. A small photograph of her daughter stares up at her. The black pigtails, the whole of her chubby face beaming with gappy teeth, and the brown eyes taking everything in. It's been two years since Dolly saw her last. She pushes the red notes into the slot at the back of her purse then shuts her bag. She's going to have to be more careful in future. Her daughter's depending on her; she can't afford to make any more mistakes.

She climbs off the escalator and passes a ride-on car swaying beside the open door of a toyshop. A little girl is clutching the wheel of the car, a moon-faced Filipina standing over her. The shop window is furnished with *Despicable Me* characters – a Gru and a group of yellow Minions. Dolly goes inside and grabs a Minion from the window. She uses the change from the pills to pay for it. A rare gift for her daughter.

She goes out of the mall then, and the heat swallows her up. On the other side of Orchard Road, there's a huge shimmering shopping mall that looks as if it's covered in a sheet of diamonds. She turns to the mall she's just left. The 'Plover Plaza' sign above the open doors burns bright green. Filipina, Indian and Indonesian women surge up and down the steps. *We're all here for the same reason*, thinks Dolly. *Looking after somebody else's kids to give our own a future.*

⌛

When Dolly first arrived in Singapore, Ma'am Amber was pregnant with Sam. When he was born three and a half months later, Ma'am brought him home and put him into Dolly's arms. Dolly's heart grew heavy as he cried. Ma'am Amber sat in a chair, plastic cones on her bare boobies. 'Don't look at me,' she said. A yellow machine droned and the cones pumped, and milk spurted into a small plastic bottle beside her. 'What a racket!' Ma'am Amber said. 'So goddamn stressful.' And Dolly looked at Sam with his peach skin and his heart-shaped mouth. Was it the baby that was stressing Ma'am Amber out, or the machine? Dolly wasn't sure.

She opened her mouth to ask, but instead of speaking, Dolly took a deep breath and held it. Then she sealed up her mouth like one of those Ziploc bags that Ma'am Amber buys in bulk from Ikea, and she carried on swaying Sam in her arms.

Two days later, that machine was in a plastic bag by the front door. And Ma'am Amber told Dolly to sleep up there beside Sam because she was 'a bit beyond all this nonsense'.

And so Dolly cradled baby Sam during those sleepless nights, him with his skin all Nivea cream and her desperate to be in the same room as her own baby again. She put the bottle into Baby Sam's mouth and watched him suck, and willed herself back home.

Sometimes she'd hear Ma'am Amber snoring through the wall, and it was like a hand closing around her throat. 'Keep breathing,' she said to herself. And so she did. In and out through sinking-mud mornings, and grey afternoons despite all that sun. And now Sammy is five years old and he just about fills up Dolly's heart with that smile and his eyes different sizes, and his hair as silver as water in the light. He follows her around, jumping into her little-me shadow.

⧗

Dolly had her daughter, Mallie, ten weeks before she left for Singapore. She gave birth in an almost silent room full of women on trolleys. Their faces were red and screwed up as they pushed.

Others held new infants in stained towels while a midwife rushed between them. The pain pressed Dolly's insides, threatening to break her open, but she bit down and braced herself. 'I can do this,' she whispered.

Mallie's father Nimuel had gone by then, so it was only Mama and Mallie who Dolly had to say goodbye to at the bus stop. She closed her hand around Mallie's tiny, clenched fist and kissed it. She kissed her nose, and her mouth, and she breathed in her vanilla smell. She collected each of Mallie's little features in her head and told herself she'd take them with her across the miles she was about to travel.

She tried not to think about how she'd never see this baby face of her daughter's again, never smell that new skin, but it punched her in the gut. There might be Skype calls and photographs, but the next time Dolly was with her daughter, the girl would be different.

It was as if someone was wringing out the cloth of Dolly's face, but she swallowed down the tears. Because all the other women who'd left on the bus before this one had cried, but the bus had carried them away from their kids anyway.

She climbed on board, found a seat. The window got fogged with her breath, so she wiped a hole and stared. Mallie's brown eyes, her button nose, that stupid woollen hat that Mama had insisted Mallie wear even though it was 33 degrees out there.

The bus started; the engine roared, matching the noise contained by Dolly's skin, her ribs. And Mallie got smaller and smaller through the glass, until she was nothing at all.

⧗

All over that living room, Ma'am Amber goes now, her finger furry with dust. The phone is pressed to her ear and she rolls her eyes backwards.

'No, Mom, four weeks is not going to work in July. I mean, we've got a trip to Siem Reap planned then.'

She walks over to Dolly, points her dusty finger in her face and shrugs, her forehead crinkling into an angry frown.

'Yes, we'll have to think about August, though I'm not sure it'll—'

Ma'am Amber paces then stops and cups her hand over her head. 'Anyway, I'm real busy right now, Mom . . . Yes, okay.'

She makes a kissing sound into the phone and hangs up. She lifts the framed photograph of her family then – the stern, seated father with the beard sashed around his chin and no moustache, the sparrow-bodied wife standing beside him, along with Ma'am Amber's elder brother, now a multi-millionaire living on Long Island. The young Ma'am Amber is spotty with tightly braided plaits and a sad smile.

'Goddamn it, Dolly, why do you keep putting this one back on display?' She shuts the photograph into a drawer.

Dolly keeps rubbing the butter into the flour. The kitchen counter is already piled high with cupcakes. Ma'am Amber comes into the kitchen and stops. *Is she looking at Dolly's stomach?* Dolly turns herself away. Ma'am starts writing on the list of jobs stuck to the fridge.

'Stupid pen.' She shakes it and tries again.

She's all worked up about the playdate she's arranged today for her ten-year-old son, Colby. Some of the Western women in the condo call Colby 'The Feral Child', but Ma'am Amber won't admit there's anything wrong.

Her breath is fast like when she comes back from running in the condo gym, her cheeks red like the raw beef Dolly buys for Sir Tor. Ma'am Amber's lost weight over the past few weeks, her cheeks hollower than they were before, her frown line more gouged out. Short grey hairs spiral up from her parting like the leaves on top of a carrot. But she fancies herself up every day. Make-up on as soon as she rises, hairdryer humming. Designer clothes. The wardrobe door barely shuts with all the dresses she has, and she's got more pairs of shoes than Imelda Marcos. She's two sizes bigger than Dolly, who always tries on Amber's new pairs – the flat bejewelled sandals, yet another pair of wedges, the latest ones red.

Ma'am Amber's like so many other white women, doing her best to make herself glamorous in rainforest heat that she wasn't made for. Maybe that contributes to Ma'am Amber's stress. Maybe that's why her lip goes tight over her teeth when Sammy Bean says, 'Play catch, Mommy,' and Colby says, 'I hate you,' and Sir Tor says, 'I'm working late again.'

Ma'am Amber spots the cakes on the counter.

'You can't keep baking all these cakes. I don't want to get f— I mean, I don't want the children to get fillings.'

She fans herself with a magazine. 'You people, I don't know how you can stand this heat.'

She picks up the air-conditioning control and switches it on. In front of the mirror now, she moves her head from side to side examining her teeth. She pulls back the skin on her face and stares at her tighter reflection. She sighs.

The house is bright white around her, not a thing out of place. The living room is tall, with no wall at one end, just sliding glass doors and through them palm trees and the largest of the swimming pools. It's like the Fullerton Bay Hotel with its marble floors and wooden stairs.

The family go to the Fullerton every other weekend for an all-day brunch. Ma'am Amber drinks champagne and laughs harder than she usually does. And the children lean into their elbows on the table, until Dolly takes them to the playroom. As the computer games churn out gunfire and electronic music, Sam sometimes sits on Dolly's knee and she examines the labels in his clothes. Ralph Lauren; Armani Junior. When he grows out of them, she'll make sure Mallie gets them. Mallie's six months older than Sam, but she's much smaller.

Dolly opens the oven door now and pushes in the next tray of cakes. At the end of the cramped kitchen, a curtain hangs.

Behind it is a short hall that leads to her closet-sized bathroom with its concertinaed plastic door. Inside, there's a toilet and a broken showerhead fixed to the wall above it which spews cold water only. When Dolly turns it on, the water covers everything – the disinfectant bottles on the floor, the mop and the toilet.

Dolly's cupboard room is the next room along. It's a bomb shelter, with no windows, and a poster stuck to the thick metal door. *This room is a civil defence shelter provided under the Civil Defence Shelter Act 1997.* The room is stuffed with Dolly's things, a narrow bed pushed against one wall. A thin cupboard where she keeps her clothes and books. Cardboard boxes under the bed, and photographs on a corkboard. Overhead shelves run the length of one wall, and despite the air vent close to the ceiling, the cramped room is stifling.

The oven pings and someone knocks on the front door. Ma'am Amber opens it and Rita is standing there with her hands on a boy's shoulders.

'Oh, yes, hi there, Roy,' says Ma'am Amber, a rictus grin on her powdered face.

The boy, his hair shiny black, walks in with a big box clutched to his chest like a shield. Rita manages a wave before the oak door slams shut in her face.

'I'll help you with that,' says Ma'am Amber, tugging at the box.

The boy tugs it right back.

'Colby, honey! Roy's here!' shouts Ma'am then throws out an airy laugh.

Footsteps pat the stairs.

'Sam!' shouts Roy and runs towards the stairs, the plastic counters rattling inside the cardboard.

The strained smile on Ma'am Amber's face has gone now and she turns to Dolly.

'You'll have to take Sam out, take him swimming or something,' she hisses. 'I mean, Roy's meant to be here to play with Colby, not Sam.' The veins in Ma'am Amber's neck are standing to attention.

'Roy, he's closer in age to Sam,' says Dolly. 'Those two, they quite often—'

'Just take Sam swimming!'

Ma'am Amber's eyelid flickers and she's breathing hard and fast. Dolly puts a hand to Ma'am's bare arm, but Ma'am bats it away and strides towards the stairs, taking them two at a time.

Dolly follows. She stops at the door of Colby and Sam's room, her nose full with the smell of sweaty sneakers. The air con's at refrigerator levels, its slats tilting up and down. The window stretches the width of the room and has a ledge underneath with a long red velvet cushion on it. There are posters of cartoon faces all over the wall, and that picture that Dolly bought of a little boy kissing a rabbit that says 'Be Ye Kind'.

Ma'am Amber is kneeling on the floor, her white dress rising up her squashed thighs. There is a dark fur of hairs on them. Colby is sitting at the end of the room on the bottom bunk. The fringe of his brown hair is wonky, his face showered with freckles. The birthmark on his nose is the shape and colour of a dollar coin. He glowers at Sam who is unloading the counters from Roy's Connect Four box. Colby's scabbed knees dance about.

'I need a wee,' says Roy, hopping from foot to foot.

'Colby's got a Wii, Roy,' says Ma'am Amber. The sore smile is back. 'A Wii with Mario Kart and everything. Haven't you, Colby?'

'It's coming!' says Roy.

'Come, Roy; I'll show you where the toilet is,' says Dolly, stretching out a hand.

Roy walks quickly towards her, but doesn't take her hand.

'No, no, I'll show him,' says Ma'am Amber.

She pushes herself up and goes out of the door, bumping Dolly sideways. 'You just get Sam's swimming things ready and take him out.'

'But I want to play with Roy!' says Sam, his eyes swirling with teary anger.

Colby glares at Sam.

'Are you all right, darling?' Dolly asks Colby. He carries on glaring. 'Colby?'

'I'm staying here,' says Sam, folding his arms, legs akimbo.

'Sammy Bean, we don't have to go swimming. Let's try the playground instead. Just for a little while,' says Dolly.

She takes his hand; he takes it back again. She walks out, hopes he'll follow. The door slams behind her, the handle rattling. A high-pitched scream gores the air.

'Dolly!' Sam shouts through the wood.

Dolly touches her hand to the oak, tries the handle, but it doesn't give.

'Do-lly!' Sam's voice is broken by a sob.

Ma'am Amber is beside them then, her body stiff, her head jerking. 'What the hell's the matter?'

'It's Colby, ma'am, he's locked the door.'

More screams. The landing is a gathering storm of Ma'am Amber's panic.

'I want to go home,' says Roy, who has just returned from the toilet. A strand of his hair has fallen into one of his eyes.

'Just wait!' snaps Ma'am Amber. Her feet are broad on the marble floor. 'Open the door immediately, Colby Moe.'

'Mommy!' cries Sam.

'Now!' shouts Ma'am.

'Colby, darling, just open the door, let me in,' Dolly says in her loud voice, which isn't that loud at all.

They stand there, silent, suspended, waiting. Then Sam starts to scream.

'Just open this fucking door!' shouts Ma'am Amber. The loose long sleeve of her dress has fallen off her shoulder and a bright white bra strap has made a red incision.

'I want my auntie,' says Roy.

'All right, darling,' says Dolly. 'Just give me a minute and I'll take you home.'

'Do something, Dolly,' says Ma'am Amber, her eyelid twitching.

Dolly heads down the steps, opens the cupboard under the sink and brings out the big wallet of keys. She pulls one out with the label underneath that says 'kids' bedroom' then goes upstairs again, her feet carrying her towards the sound of Ma'am Amber's muttering.

'Hurry,' says Ma'am Amber, her voice hoarse. She snatches the key from Dolly's hand and wiggles it in the lock.

But she hasn't pushed it in far enough and the key fails to turn. 'Son of a bitch!' she snaps.

Dolly glances at Roy who bites his top teeth over his bottom lip. Exasperated, Ma'am Amber puts her head into her hands. Dolly pushes the key right into the lock, turns it, and pulls it out; noisy air gushes out of Ma'am's throat.

Dolly opens the door then and there is Colby with his hands in Sam's hair. Sam is kneeling on the floor. Ma'am Amber's bare feet slap across the marble, her whole upper body lifting and swelling. She pulls Colby off and raises her hand like she's about to serve in her twice-a-week tennis lesson. She slaps Colby's face. He groans and runs towards the bunk beds.

'You little shit. What is wrong with you?!'

Sam runs to Dolly and clings to her leg. 'All right, Sammy Bean.'

She lifts him into her arms and hugs him, touches his hair for blood, but there's none. Ma'am Amber is reaching for him and he clings harder to Dolly. She is wrapped with his crabbed legs, his arms.

'Come to Mommy,' says Ma'am Amber.

'I want Dolly,' he says.

'I want to go home,' says Roy again, pulling at Dolly's shorts.

'Yes, yes, Dolly needs to take Roy home, Sammy,' says Ma'am Amber, moulding her mouth into a neck-clench of a smile.

Dolly unlocks Sam's arms from around her neck and tries to put him into Ma'am Amber's arms. He kicks his way to the floor and runs off. Ma'am Amber rushes after him, the hem of her dress folded up on itself.

'I don't like it here,' says Roy, clinking the Connect Four counters back into the box.

Colby is face down on the bottom bunk, a pillow squashed over his head. Dolly goes over to him, lays a hand on his shoulder. 'Colby?'

She smoothes her hand over his back and lowers her face to his. Heat radiates from his sweaty neck and some emotion strangles Dolly's stomach, but not just for him. It's been too long since she last saw her daughter and when she did go home, the girl didn't seem to understand that Dolly was her mama.

'You're okay, Colby,' Dolly says.

'I'm going,' says Roy.

'Wait!' Dolly sits up, takes her hand away from Colby's shoulder.

Roy marches down the stairs, the counters in the box scraping like pebbles in a cup. Dolly keeps pace just behind. He pushes on his blue Crocs at the front door and goes outside, walking faster, the distance between them stretching. He trips, but rights himself just at the condo entrance where she manages to catch him up.

He's out of breath, his twisted mouth preparing to cry.

'I'll call Auntie Rita, tell her to come and get you.'

Roy stands there sniffing his snotty disappointment back in and mashing a bare foot on top of his Croc.

Dolly pulls her mobile phone from her pocket. There's an unread message on it.

Let's meet tonight.

She ignores the message and dials Rita's number, pressing the phone to her ear.

Essential House Rules for Foreign Domestic Maids
Rule 1. Security: Maids can be a real security issue. That's why it's essential to keep your maid's passport locked away, especially if she is looking after your children.

Chapter 3

Tala is sitting on the single mattress on the floor of the utility room which doubles as her bedroom. She eyes the whizzing fan suspiciously, her bare back hunched. She's been asking for air conditioning in here for the past six years, and yesterday her landlady Mrs Heng finally gave her a second-hand fan. It barely makes a dent in the thick humidity. The tumble dryer, next to the separate washing machine, spins and drones. Sweat bursts on Tala's forehead. A strand of her glossy black hair is matted to her cheek.

Her beige bra sags under the weight of her pendulous bosoms, her bread-dough stomach spilling over her pleated orange skirt. It doesn't help that her younger sister Dolly keeps on baking those cakes and Tala can't stop eating them. Thank God for elasticated separates.

She lifts her old black laptop onto her considerable thighs. One of her former employers gave her this years ago and though it's slow, and sometimes whirs like a plane at take-off, it's loaded with Skype, so she can speak to her two sons twice a month, and keep tabs on the venom that Vanda blogger spouts on a daily basis.

Tala types in the address and the Vanda blog papers the screen with red butterflies. *Life as the Employer of a Foreign Domestic Helper.* All this flowing writing like the title page of a historical novel. The way Vanda goes on, she does a good impression of someone living 200 years ago. There's a new post: *Essential House Rules for Foreign Domestic Maids.*

Tala delves into her gadget-filled bag – and there amid the

tape measure, miniature scissors and screwdriver are her glasses, a gold chain dangling from the shut legs. She unravels the chain and pushes the specs on, oversized black frames that curve into exaggerated points at each side of her face. She stares at the computer screen.

> Keep a logbook of your maid's mistakes. Get her to sign it, acknowledging that if she repeats a mistake, forgetting to lock the front door for example, you'll have to fire her.

Just who is Vanda? Tala's been asking herself that question ever since the blog went live eighteen months ago. It's someone with a lot of time on their hands, that's for sure; Vanda posts almost every day, opinion pieces about how easy it is to sack a maid as well as interviews with annoyed employers. But the worst posts are the ones Vanda dedicates to bad maids, putting up their photographs, their names and their work permit numbers and listing all their mistakes. Tala has made it her mission to find out who Vanda is. She's been snooping around the houses of all the women that she cleans for to work out whether it's any of them, but she's still no closer to discovering Vanda's true identity.

Tala clicks on her hotmail and there's an email from her eldest son, Ace, with an attachment called 'Your First Grandchild'. She clicks and in front of her, like a fleshy hot-air balloon, is an oversized photograph of a stomach that belongs to Ace's pregnant girlfriend. Tala's first grandchild is probably going to be a whopper; Tala's boys, Ace and Marlon, were both around the ten-pound mark when they came out. She looks at her bulge, silvery with stretch marks, then slams the laptop lid shut.

Riffling through her bag again, she brings out the pot of Pond's and starts rubbing it in circles over her neck. There is a small canvas propped on the table beside her bed. Stripes of sand and sea, the paint built up and rough in places. There's a passport-sized photograph of the artist, which has blown face down in the breeze of the fan. She turns it over. Her youngest son, Marlon, looks her straight in the eye: the cleft chin, the sparse scattering of freckles over the nose, and the height – though, of course, this head-and-shoulders picture doesn't show that. Marlon – the artist of the family. He draws and paints on any available space: bits of old wood, the inside of cereal boxes.

Oh, but it's hot. She presses the high setting on the cordless fan and the gale force sends her hair spinning, a chunk of it sticking to her face like a beard. She peels it away and switches off the fan.

Something doesn't feel right about that fan. Just why has Mrs Heng given it to her after all this time?

The 'I love Singapore' sticker on the side of the fan is so worn away that what it actually says is 'I love por'. Well, poor is top of the list of things Tala doesn't love – followed closely by cooking. She digs into her handbag again. There's the yellow savings book, now containing four figures, alongside that special metal pendant which gets rid of the garlic smell from hands. Shame it only works for garlic. She glances accusingly at her feet. Then her hand finds what it's looking for, the little screwdriver.

She fiddles and creaks and the fan ends up in two parts in her lap, a mess of wires spewing out of it. She slaps her hand to her chest. There, staring up at her is a miniature security camera. She sits taller, sucking in her stomach, the gold crucifix glinting on her chest. My God, Mrs Heng has been watching her for the past hour. The pieces of the fan clatter to the wooden floor as Tala hauls herself off the mattress. She shimmies over to the stained wood door, the camera shut firmly in her hand.

'That woman!'

She opens the door and a drift of fried fish fills her nostrils. She takes two steps backwards, picks up her T-shirt from the bed and yanks it over her head. Her stubby fingers, the veins in relief, are itching to point through the air at Mrs Heng and give her what for.

Tala strides along the hall, passing three badly painted terra-cotta tiles on the wall depicting warriors with big hair in various stages of a punch-up. Mrs Heng is a budding yet terrible artist. Tala clenches her fist tighter.

Her heart's beating too fast, the sweat dripping out of her, down her back, her thighs. Her feet squelch across the marble tiles and arrive on the brown living-room carpet. She sniffs the burn of sandalwood incense, her eyes filling with the darkness of mahogany-stained furniture and the wallpaper patterned with green fleurs-de-lis.

Mrs Heng is standing in front of a bureau with her satin pink back to Tala, banging the top of her silver Apple iMac. Tala's angry heart fizzes, but she needs to keep this place to live, so she'll have to zip it. Then again she's taken the miniature camera which Mrs Heng will find out about soon enough. Tala pushes the camera into the pocket of her skirt.

'Stupid thing!' The bureau trembles with Mrs Heng's wrath. '*Ta ma de* computer!' she shrieks.

Tala clears her throat and Mrs Heng spins around on the heel of her elasticated knitted pink slipper. Her mouth, a graveyard of yellow teeth, falls open when she clocks Tala. She shuffles sideways like she's doing a warm-up in an old people's exercise class, her eyes darting.

'Look at that!' She lifts her bony arm, the short sleeve of her shirt riding up, and points at the spread of darkened windows. 'They're dirty!'

Her grey hair sits bushy on her shoulders, her face speckled with age-spots. Her matching shirt and three-quarter-length trousers are covered in large brown flowers.

'Well, what are you waiting for, girl?' Her nostrils flare in her snub nose.

Tala retreats to her bedroom to get the bucket and ladder.

She stumbles back into the living room, sets the ladder up and climbs it, going through the motions with a wet sponge.

'Make sure you get that huge stain there!' shouts Mrs Heng.

'There's no stain there, ma'am.'

'Right there!' Mrs Heng points a gnarly finger.

With her other hand, she prods at the brown spot in the crevice of her teeth. She climbs up the ladder behind Tala. Mrs Heng rips the sponge from Tala's hand and throws it at the pane, drips scattering.

'Are you blind, girl? There, like a big greasy cloud!'

Tala retrieves the sponge from the now damp carpet and tries again, wetting the glass that's already shiny. All around them, on little round tables, there are jade feng shui dragons and trees. A battery-operated gold cat waves its arm backwards and forwards, filling the room with clicks. There are three easy chairs patterned with red velvet flowers and leaves.

'No, no!' Mrs Heng shouts. 'Go right!'

It's time to bring out the big guns. Tala climbs down the ladder and heads into the tiny kitchen. She pulls a bottle of vinegar from under the sink and douses a cloth with it. The stink makes her eyes water, but she pins a smile to her face and climbs the ladder again.

Mrs Heng's face is frozen in wrinkled contempt, unaffected by the vinegar stench. Just like her selective hearing, her nose doesn't seem to do the job it was made for. Tala slides the cloth in circles like her arm is riding a bike.

'No, there's still that bit there,' says Mrs Heng.

Tala's smile is as limp as a week-old lettuce leaf left out of the fridge, but at least this is giving her flabby upper arms a bit of exercise. She stops and climbs down.

'It'll do, I suppose,' says Mrs Heng.

Tala heads back down the corridor, the ladder clacking on her shoulder.

Mrs Heng and Tala have got an illegal arrangement. In Singapore, foreign domestic helpers are meant to work for a single employer, but Tala got sick of earning so little doing that, and Mrs Heng agreed to help at a price. Tala cleans and cooks for her, lives with her and cleans at eleven other homes where the people pay cash in hand. Mrs Heng has told the Ministry of Manpower that she's Tala's only employer, and in return Tala pays her a percentage of her monthly earnings. 'Mutually beneficial,' Mrs Heng said. Mrs Heng makes a fat profit from what Tala pays her. But who else is going to pretend for Tala?

Inside her bedroom, Tala drops the little camera to the floor, pushes on one of her diamanté sandals and crushes it underfoot. She goes to sit on the mattress, but it's lower than she thinks, and her legs shoot into the air like an upside-down turtle's.

'*Ay nako!*'

She scoops up the computer, opens Vanda's blog post again and starts to type in the comments box. She stops, takes a deep breath then deletes what she's written. Vanda hasn't put up a single one of Tala's comments. There must be some other way to get her point across.

She does a bit of research, googling the words 'maid' and 'Singapore'. She clicks and she reads. There are more than 200,000 foreign domestic workers in Singapore. The majority of them are from the Philippines and Indonesia. Tala can't find specific figures, but smaller numbers of women come from Sri Lanka, Myanmar, India and Bangladesh too. That's a lot of women for Vanda to shame, and where can they tell their stories?

A thought takes hold, something thin and insubstantial. Tala clicks on Vanda's blog again. It's one of those free ones on WordPress.

Tala clicks on the WordPress home page and reads up about how blogs need a theme – *Hemingway; Independent Publisher; Relief* – she could do with some of that. She sits there, reading about how to set up her own blog. Then stands and paces, tapping her mouth with her finger, sweaty footprints patching the floor. *Maid in Singapore. Maid Trouble. Maids for You.* No, no, none of those are right. They sound like a bunch of employment agencies. *Voice of the Maid. Help for Helpers. Maidhacker.*

Maidhacker – that's something, isn't it? *Maidhacker.*

She types the title. She creates a menu too. *I'll show you.* She keys in her first post. It takes her a long time, using a single thick finger, but out the words come.

MAIDHACKER'S BLOG:

What It's Like to Be a Domestic Helper

Lights, Camera, Action!

I love a good nosy at other people's lives, don't you? That's what doctors' surgeries are for. When little Agamemnon (expats choose even weirder names for their kids than us Filipinas) has a drippy nose, I take advantage and dive into Woman's Day, or Simply Her! J-Lo with a sliver of olive wedged between her two front teeth; Madonna tripping up a stair – it's all there.

But it's not just the rich who are stars.

Look up at the ceiling where you live and you might just see a little red light flashing in the corner. That light's unlikely to be part of a security system – I mean, you're in Singapore, where the worst thing that could happen to Mrs Fawcett-Smythe is chipping a nail, so who needs a burglar alarm? No, that light could be your boss spying on you with a hidden camera.

This isn't me – Maidhacker – trying to be as sensationalist as those glossy magazines. A survey has revealed that one in five employers in Singapore uses surveillance cameras to sneak a peek at their maids while they're in their own rooms (slash cupboards, slash the sofa in the lounge). And with more than 200,000 of us maids here in the Lion City, that's a whole lot of spying going on.

So next time you're using the sponge for the toilet seat to give the toothbrush cup a once-over, stop and get batting those eyelids because bosses don't always put cameras in the most obvious of places.

A new ornament in the shape of a budgerigar in little Araminta's playroom? A camera – you mark my words! Kitchens, toilets, bathrooms – nowhere is off limits.

Think before you take a squidge of Ma'am's Aveda shampoo, or scrub out the wok with Clorox, because Big Boss is probably watching.

Be watchful, ladies. And wave.

She presses 'post'.

Take that, Vanda! The thought pumps through her veins alongside another one. If anyone finds out it's her who wrote that, there'll be consequences. There always is for people who criticise Singapore. And there'll be questions. The Ministry of Manpower might discover that she's working illegally. She'll be thrown out, or worse still, she'll go to prison.

She snaps her computer shut and gives her feet a dousing with her Scholl Odour Control Shoe Spray. She sits there in the fog of it, wondering how she's still managing to breathe.

Tala is dusting Ma'am Maeve's guest bedroom when she notices the silver laptop open on the desk where there's a packet of red Marlboros, and a shiny box with the words 'Sonic Purifying Brush For Men' emblazoned across it. She gives the mouse a little shake and the screen comes to life. Ma'am Maeve's voice drifts in from the living room. *Should she?* She pulls the bedroom door shut, the smell of Pledge sifting through the air. *She should.*

She clicks onto Firefox and moves the cursor around until she finds the browsing history. *Commodity Trading Prices. Daily Mail. Vanda's Blog.*

She clicks the Vanda blog link and peers at the screen, her smudged glasses in need of a bit of Pledge themselves. The editing function on the blog is closed; no one's signed in, but that doesn't mean Ma'am Maeve isn't the author. She might just be signed out.

There's a grinding of wood on wood and the door to the en-suite bathroom slides open. And oh, there is Sir Gavin with a folded-back magazine in his hand, pictures of tanned, muscled men on the page. Tala turns away, presses the nozzle on the polish so that it foams the desk. The smell of the natural shine formula mixes with another more powerful pong.

'Oh, have you been there the whole time?' asks Sir Gavin, slamming the bathroom door shut behind him.

Tala looks up at him; he is dressed in a short-sleeved white shirt, sweat circles forming in his muscular armpits, an electric blue tie.

'I, erm . . .'

Sir Gavin goes over to the desk, picks up a square bottle of aftershave and sprays it onto his thick neck then into the air between him and Tala.

'Having a surf on the interweb, were you?'

She sends out an overenthusiastic laugh, more of a shriek really. 'I don't know anything about computers, Gavin.'

'Sir'll do, thanks all the same.'

'Yes, yes. I mean, sir. Sir Gavin.'

He looks at her copper wedding ring and winks at her. 'That husband of yours is a bloody lucky man.'

'What?'

'Bit of make-up, bet you scrub up all right.'

He turns away and starts examining the thinning crown on his tiny head in the full-length mirror, the white shirt stretched across his back.

'Don't want to keep you,' he says, twisting towards her again, a smirk plastered on his pale face.

Tala bails out of the room and down the corridor. She heads into the main bathroom and locks the door behind her. Everything's gold in here. Enormous mirror framed in gold, gold taps, even a gold flusher on the toilet, and marble this and that. She stares at her reflection.

Her hair's slick, black and long, her mouth bracketed by lines. Not that she's old. She's forty-eight, but doesn't look her age. And her front teeth, wide and white and straight, well they're something to smile about. Oh, but now she's boasting. Still if a woman can't give herself compliments . . . Her husband Bong rarely gave her any, that's for sure. *The machine gun*, that's what he used to call her, nodding that head of his, eyes drifting to some place over her shoulder. But whatever he said about her talking, God threw the listening gene into the bargain too. Listening to all her friends like she does. Drinking in every detail of their troubles then writing everything down later in her logbook.

Her friends call her 'the rescuer', but she shrugs it off. She just tries to help women who are domestic helpers like her, that's all. She's been here longer than most. She knows how to play the system, to speak up and out. She warned off Rita's obsessive ex-boyfriend who kept following her after she'd finished with him. And Tala's got lots of passports back from employers who locked them away – putting on her best skirt, knocking on their doors with her glasses perched on the end of her raised nose as if she were someone important from a charity that stands up for domestic workers' rights. She held that clipboard to her puffed-out chest, her shaky voice reaching pneumatic jackhammer levels.

Just like it did when April Joy fell to her death from the window of the apartment she worked in. Nine floors up. April Joy had been complaining to Tala for months about her employer forcing her to teeter on a ledge so she could clean the outside of the windows. 'Just refuse, girl!' Tala kept urging. But April Joy didn't.

After her death, Tala took the logbook, with April Joy's details, to the police station, but the man behind the desk rolled his eyes and said that no, of course he wouldn't photocopy the pages. That hasn't stopped Tala trying to get April Joy's employer arrested, though.

So many women. Some are like Tala and Dolly, and have left their children at home. Others are the family cash cows, their fertile years melting away like an ice lolly in the heat while they're maiding.

Tala's boys have been far away for the past eighteen years, but she's held them right here in her chest, their roars and their running.

Ace and Marlon were ten and eight when she left. She's a talker, but in the days leading up to her leaving Tagudin, she was a woman of few words. She packed that canvas bag then turfed everything out of it. She couldn't do it; she couldn't leave her boys. She tucked three photographs of them into her purse and tried to memorise their faces. Taking hold of their cheeks, tracing the surface of their noses, their lips, with her fingers. The truck pulled up outside and Marlon hugged her. 'I want you to stay,' he said. 'There's no other way,' she replied. She stepped towards Ace who let her hug him then she heaved her bag into the back of the truck.

As she climbed into her seat, Marlon put something into her hand – a shiny, beige conch shell. 'It's my best thing,' he said. They looked at each other then – him with his thick eyebrows knitted together in a frown and his eyes empty of light, her with a throat full of river stones. She touched his young face one more time and slammed the door, and the truck juddered away.

She takes a card from the back of her shorts now: it arrived for her yesterday. Smudges of pink and green charcoal. She has to stare at it for a minute before she sees herself – her hair tied back in a thick pink band, the stretch of fields behind. Marlon has stitched white thread around the edges the way he's come to do lately. *He could have been someone.* The thought sucks away her smile.

She pushes the picture back into her pocket then sprays Clorox onto the his and hers sinks. Oh, there goes another empty bottle of it into the bin. The smell of pretend lemons fills the air.

She heads into the living room, gold-rimmed glass coffee tables here and there with wooden figures on each of them; it's as if Ma'am Maeve's in competition with Mrs Heng's feng shui specials. Ma'am Maeve and her friend sit with their legs crossed, facing each other, muttering words Tala doesn't catch. They look so overdressed for drinking tea. Gold bangles decorate Ma'am Maeve's wrist, her hands laced together on top of her puffball skirt. The other woman scratches her face with a diamond-encrusted finger, her lashes so false and long it's like a couple of redbacks have climbed onto her eyelids. Tala collects the women's plates, dabbed clean of cake crumbs, but the women don't say a word.

'Bird's Nest', that's what Tala calls Ma'am Maeve, her hair all done up in that bun with bits sticking out. Ma'am Maeve often has her hair in rollers when Tala is around, but that hair is not for taming. It's as wild as that open-mouthed lion statue standing on its hind legs outside the front door. Sitting there, in her leopard-print top and leopard-print pumps, she wouldn't look out of place at the Singapore Zoo. Tala dusts off one of the pictures hanging on the walls, a heart made from locked-together red and pink English words like 'kindness' and 'family' and 'children'.

Tala's mind ticks away as the women talk. She worked for seven families, living backstage in their homes, cleaning and cooking for twelve years, before she had her big idea. That's when she took the room at Mrs Heng's and started to make a living by doing illegal part-time jobs.

Ma'am Maeve gets hold of her own face and pulls the skin back until her lips turn into a stretched flat line.

'Just eat more. Putting on half a stone's better than surgery,' says her friend.

Sir Gavin saunters into the living room in his slip-ons. 'I'm off.'

He leans down and kisses Ma'am Maeve's cheek. Her face sucks tight like she's peeled a lime and eaten it whole. She wipes her scarlet fingernails over the place where he kissed her. The varnish wouldn't be that pristine if she was tapping on computer keys every day, but Tala's not ready to rule her out of being Vanda just yet.

The front door slams. The two women exchange looks.

'What was he doing home?'

Ma'am Maeve keeps her voice low. 'His irritable bowel is playing up again.'

'Oooooo.' The woman shakes her head. 'Things any better between you two?' she asks.

'Could you do the bedroom?' snaps Ma'am Maeve. 'We're talking here.'

'Yes, ma'am.'

Tala heads into the main bedroom, a marble square with a bed against the wall and this gold carved board where they put their heads. There's a big light on the ceiling, gold too of course, with all these little lampshades. It's the ugliest thing Tala's ever seen. Even the bedside cabinets are painted gold. The place has got more gold than Australia.

Tala sets to, folding and tidying the clothes on the floor. The bra, so small Tala wonders why she bothers, the dresses – a strapless black one and a short thing with thin red straps. Tala sniffs cheese. A stilton or a camembert melting. She should have put the Scholl Odour Control Shoe Spray into her bag.

Ma'am Maeve's voice filters into the bedroom.

'Black hairs all over the floor when she's gone. I caught her using the en-suite once. I was so annoyed. I mean, I don't want her minge anywhere near my loo seat.'

Echoes of laughter.

Ma'am Maeve continues: 'She should come with subtitles. Tell

her to do something and it's all "What?" "Disgusting", and Gad
this and Gad that.'

'Gad?' says the other woman.

'Gawd,' says Ma'am Maeve.

'Gawd?'

'You know, Gawd.'

'Oh, God, yeah!'

Tala picks up a photograph beside the bed and buries Sir
Gavin's head in a dollop of polish. She tries saying 'God' the
way Ma'am Maeve did.

'Gad.'

'Gud.'

'Gourd.'

She tucks her gold cross into her T-shirt and pats it. There's
loose change on the bedside cabinet and she dusts around it,
picking up a photograph of Ma'am Maeve in a white dress and
Sir Gavin, with his crushed, twisted nose. They're both smiling,
though neither of them looks happy, even then. She sprays polish
onto a photograph of the children. The tall teenage daughter and
the much younger son.

Tala goes to get her duster from the living room. She feels their
eyes on her and the silence smacks the walls. Where has she put
that thing? There it is on the table, yellow, worn and filthy.

'Oh Christ, stuff this,' says Ma'am Maeve. 'Shall we start on
the vino?'

The other woman looks at her watch. 'Well, it is a quarter to
twelve,' she says.

And credit to Bird's Nest, she doesn't ask Tala to do the
honours. She gets the wine from the fridge herself. All she has
to do is screw the lid off after all.

Tala moves on through to the bedroom again and the women
murmur.

'She looks like a Filipino Barbie doll,' Ma'am Maeve says.

Tala listens hard.

'Well, Dolly is rather beautiful.'

The bedroom can wait; Tala goes into the hall and starts polishing a window that's already clean, her ears expectant.

'Aw no, I wouldn't say beautiful; pretty in a little girl sort of way,' Ma'am Maeve says, in a voice that curls at the edges.

'Yeah, but would you trust your husband with someone like that? If she was living in, there'd be plenty of opportunity,' says the other woman.

'I bet he's a randy old goat, that Tor,' says Ma'am Maeve.

Ay nako! They're talking about the man Dolly works for. Is she having an affair with him? If Ma'am Amber finds out, she'll sack Dolly for sure.

There are shrieks of laughter from Ma'am Maeve and her friend.

'Want another glass?'

'Oooh, yes please.'

'Taylor!' Ma'am Maeve calls.

Even after all this time, she hasn't got Tala's name right.

Chapter 4

Jules is working as a receptionist at the doctor's surgery, propped behind the counter in her white scrubs. A woman with a stretched-smooth face peers across the top, her French-manicured hand pressed flat to the Formica. Jules clicks the mouse and spots the woman's name on the computer screen.

'Oh, here you are. Just take a seat and Dr Wong will call you in.'

Jules puts a hand on her stomach. During the last round of failed IVF, she spent three days lying down, so this time she's decided to carry on as normal. There are two fertilised eggs inside her now. *Two.* Two small chances. She closes her eyes. Can she feel something bedding in? Bubbling? Oh, stop.

The woman, with rectangular diamonds glinting on her earlobes, sits beside a teenage girl on the cream leather bench that lines the surgery walls like a stripe. The girl, dressed in flowery shorts, takes a glossy magazine from the rack on the wall. The woman clenches her jaw, stroking her hand up and down her neck; Dr Wong deals with all the facelifts.

A little boy zooms a car across the rug patterned with buildings and roads. The helper looking after him sits nearby on another bench, twisting a red and yellow friendship bracelet around her wrist.

Even doctors' surgeries are in shopping malls here. This one is in-between a nail bar and a bakery. Jules digs into the jar of Ferrero Rochers on the counter, unwraps one and pops it into her mouth.

'Ooo ambassador, you're really spoiling us with these Ferrero Rochers,' she says under her breath.

The other receptionist is on her break and there's nothing much to do, so Jules logs on to her Instagram account. Five likes on that latest photograph – a coiled incense stick hanging in front of that Buddhist temple. A monk, folded in robes, happened to be passing, which put an orange blur into the background.

A photographer she follows has posted a picture of a foreign domestic helper balancing on a fifth-floor window ledge, a squeegee in her hand. There is a caption: *New blog tells the truth about maids #Maidhacker*. Jules googles 'Maidhacker' and clicks on the link.

MAIDHACKER'S BLOG:
What It's Like to Be a Domestic Helper

Why Maids Need a Day Off

There are posters plastered all over this country aimed at raising the plummeting birth rate. Well, ladies, apparently the lack of babies is all down to us maids. That's what Vanda reckons anyway.

'If we had better maids, it might push the dwindling birth rate of this country up,' Vanda says.

But don't make the women who work in your homes the scapegoats for your choices. If you really want to have kids, go ahead and have them, and we'll do our very best to look after them. Although we'll do it a hell of a lot better when we have a day off thrown into the bargain. I don't mean the kind of day off where you demand that we're back by 6 p.m. After all, we want to make the most of our freedom and sit down for a while. Rest has a fringe benefit for you employers too

– we'll be able to concentrate more, which is useful when we're looking after your children. Safety is better than slave labour, wouldn't you say?

Jules joins the hundreds of people who've already starred Maidhacker's post.

'My face is so sore,' says the plastic surgery woman in a cut-glass English accent. Her teenage daughter rolls her eyes.

Doctor Zainab emerges from behind a sliding oak door, her baby bump straining against the fabric of her red satin dress. She hands a file to Jules.

From the leather bench, Jules hears the well-spoken voice again. 'I don't know why you look at all those gossip magazines. Most of those actresses and models are completely Photoshopped.'

The teenage girl shuffles along the bench, putting distance between herself and her mother.

Jules' mobile phone vibrates. She delves into her handbag.

Since you're too busy to pick up calls, perhaps you could let me know whether you're coming to the book group!

The text is from Amber. *Bloody woman needs a job*, thinks Jules.

She drops the phone back into her bag, but the text needles her. She wonders what Amber's problem is.

Just working, that's all, types Jules. *I'll be there.*

Dr Wong wanders out in her silent moccasins.

'Mrs Woods for Dr Wong,' Jules calls.

The woman with the sore face rises and her daughter follows.

'No, just stay here, darling,' the woman says, and the girl picks up her copy of *Grazia* again.

Fuck it, there's no one in the waiting room now apart from the teenage girl, who's absorbed in her magazine, and the little boy on the rug, and his helper. Jules opens the large metal door to the side of the surgery and steps into the labyrinth of shelves where the files are kept. She runs her fingers along their papery ends. *M, M, M,* she finds it on the third shelf down and opens it.

There, in black script, is the name: *Amber Moe*. Jules takes furtive glances around the surgery, but still no one's looking her way. She shouldn't be doing this; God knows she's no snoop, but this is for the common good, right? Or at least for Amber's good; if Jules learns more about her, she might even grow to like the woman.

Jules flips through the file. Two years ago, Amber suffered from kidney stones. She's had mycoplasma too. And there's the word LUSTRAL in capital letters. She's on them now, Jules sees: antidepressants. Maybe that's why Amber's sending desperate texts even though Jules has only known her for four weeks.

'Next patient, please,' Doctor Zainab calls to Jules.

Jules walks out from the shelves and calls the name of the boy playing on the rug. His helper stands and takes his hand, and they follow Doctor Zainab into one of the consulting rooms.

The other receptionist comes back from her break and dumps her bag beside Jules.

'You off home now then?' she asks.

'Yeah, guess so,' says Jules.

She grabs her bag and pushes her hand into the chocolate jar again on her way out.

She takes the lift to the ground floor. The doors spring open and she walks out into the sun. People sally past, umbrellas up to shade their heads. Cabs zoom along the curved road, but she doesn't want a cab, she just wants to be outside. Never feeling cold, that's really something, isn't it? Because she's always felt the cold. Turning up the thermostat in their draughty Balham flat, David coming home from work, complaining that it was too hot and turning it down again. Hot water bottles stuffed under her jumper until June. Oh, she'd felt low during those grey days and cold winter nights. Her whole life had gone dark, it seemed as the years ticked by with no sign of getting pregnant. Most of her friends had become parents; they didn't want to go dancing any more; no one met for drinks. There was just her and David venturing out to the same spots – pubs and restaurants, an occasional club where she'd watch people ten years younger than her throwing shapes on the dance floor. She couldn't even bring herself to tap her foot. She felt flattened out after the first IVF attempt failed, then the second. She phoned friends, but they shared only half-listened-to conversations since their young kids usually demanded attention. Jules didn't belong there any more. But how could she move on from this when there was nowhere to move to?

So when the Singapore posting for David had come up, Jules had pumped her fist through the air. 'An adventure,' she'd said. 'An escape more like,' David had shot back.

They have a list of places they want to go and see in Asia: Angkor Wat, Hoi An, Bali. Forget Puerto Pollensa or Fuerteventura, this is where it's at. And yet . . . She walks towards the cream curves of Tanglin Mall now, with its terracotta finial. She could be lying on a beach, the sun beating down, having just won the lottery and she wouldn't feel right because she doesn't have the baby she so desperately wants.

Inside the mall, she takes the escalator to Cafe Beviamo. People are slotted together on the square tables. Mahogany pillars jut to the ceiling; murmured conversations spill from the open sides. A waitress with a small apron tied around her waist moves between the tables, a pencil stuck behind her ear. A chef in a tall white hat works behind the counter with a smudge of flour on his face. There's a woman totting up bills at the cash register.

Jules looks at the colourful lines of cupcakes inside the glass display cabinet. There are swirls of icing piled high.

'I'll have that one, please,' she says, pointing to one dotted with marshmallows.

There's a stack of free magazines in a cardboard holder to the side of the display cabinet. She pushes one into her bag.

Women in sunglasses glide up the escalator next to her while she glides down. Strapless silk dresses, fingernails shiny with varnish. She looks down at her surgery whites, the badge still pinned to her chest. *Jules Harris.*

She goes out through the sliding doors and dips into her bag for her sunnies which aren't in a case. She blows off the dust and puts them on. She's going to walk back to the condo.

The green man beeps and she crosses the immaculate tarmac. This place, with its pristine shops and chandeliers and its endless warmth, is a long way from Westminster Bridge Road, the crisp packets in the gutter, the low, dull sky.

She pulls the cake out of the paper bag and sinks her teeth in. Mmmm, all that sugar. She probably shouldn't be eating this, but it's the healthy option compared to what she's done in the past. Binge drinking when she went clubbing, and dropping pills. Still, over the past few years, she's notched up enough clean-living points to rival Gwyneth Paltrow. The gluten-free diet, the dairy-free one and now she's a vegetarian, all in the pursuit of motherhood. So stuff it – she chews the cake a bit faster.

She heads up the long straight pavement, the cars on Holland Road whizzing by. She opens the magazine as she walks, its glossy pages packed with adverts. There's a photograph of a woman with an ice pack on her head. Underneath it is a question: *Is your maid giving you a headache?* It's an advert for an employment agency that places domestic helpers.

She carries on flicking through, walking slowly and glancing at the pavement every now and then in case she trips.

Could you foster?

This one's a feature – about the only one in the whole magazine. There's a photograph of a woman pushing a pram. Her name's Sue and she's got three kids and she looks after babies whose mothers can't look after them for different reasons, none of which the article mentions. Sue has looked after ten babies, ranging from between three weeks to two years old.

Jules stumbles and rights herself. She puts her hand to her stomach then pushes the magazine back into her bag. Her heart hammers. She is wet in all her crevices, under her breasts, in her armpits, in her knickers. She didn't even bring any water. This won't do her any good. No wonder she's never gone running here – just the odd twenty minutes on the cross trainer in that downstairs gym, tiny and mostly empty, apart from when David pounds away on the treadmill next to her. And that bloke who's often in there, sizing himself up in the mirrors. What was it Amber had said about it? 'Oh, the mats are just disgusting. It's a disgrace.' But a swish facility in the basement of your apartment block, it's hardly Brixton gym. Amber and her sense of privilege; she makes Jules want to pull her own hair out. But then the woman's on antidepressants; Jules should probably try to be more tolerant.

Not much further. There's the high-rise Housing Development Board blocks which frame Ghim Moh market with its huge metal roof, hawker stalls underneath with circular stools and tables. She gets the smell of chicken curry rice. Around the edge of the market, there are other stalls with white awnings, some displaying mobile phone covers, others selling plants, and fruit and vegetables. A pile of spiky green durians under one, baskets of rambutans and oversized papayas and pineapples under another. Static bursts from a radio.

She walks on by, pumping her arms up the hill, stepping over the concrete, lined by a length of open drain, and everywhere greenery, orange hibiscus, purple Singapore rhododendrons and yellow stem fig trees. There's a school which looks like a massive white multi-storey car park. She passes houses with pillared terraces behind barred gates, and long, thin swimming pools in their front yards. She pulls a purple-pink flower from a burst of bougainvillea. A zebra crossing beeps as a woman pulling a trolley presses the button and the green man comes out.

Jules turns into the condo and stomps past the swimming pools. Both of them are empty, the water as smooth as blue glass. She slips off her sandals and walks towards the water, breaking the surface with a toe. A gentle breeze pulls through the palm trees then. She looks up and scans the balconies, but the only movement is a large sheet folded over one of the balustrades. The sheet swells and settles.

She walks towards the lift and goes up. Inside the two-storey apartment, she inches off her uniform, and leaves it in a heap on the marble floor of the open-plan living room. Floor-to-ceiling windows fill one side of the space. There's a flat screen television mounted on one of the grey walls, and a beige leather sofa faces it. Four wooden chairs are set around a glass dining table close to another wall. The adjoining kitchen has pristine white cupboards and a thin sliver of marble counter where a kettle stands along with a line of jars filled with rice and cereal.

The heat of the apartment is almost unbearable and she runs naked through a longer hall, past the spare bedroom at the end of it, and up a flight of wooden stairs to an upper floor where her stark bedroom is. There's another small living room up here too, with sliding glass doors that open onto a decked balcony. She opens a door of the expansive wooden bedroom wardrobe and searches the drawers inside for a swimsuit. She doesn't find one, so goes into the slate-tiled wet room and grabs the one that's draped over the shower tap, dripped dry from yesterday.

She pulls it on, takes her goggles from the side of the sink, along with a towel.

Downstairs, she stands on the edge of the pool and jumps into the deeper end. She plunges beneath the surface and swims underwater. A leaf dances on the bottom. She breaststrokes one length, freestyles another, her measured breath soothing away the worry that's been fizzing through her during this two-week wait. Have the embryos taken? She kicks her legs harder, water smacking in her ears, hearing the gasp of her breath. Everything else falls away apart from the motion. She takes a mouthful of chlorinated water and coughs, but carries on swimming anyway. She loses count of her lengths after twenty-five, but ploughs on. Out of breath, she stops at the edge and rips off her goggles.

There's a young boy at the side of the big pool now. A bird *hoo-hoos*. Another replies with a distant squawk.

That white hair – it's Amber's youngest son, Sam, isn't it? Jules looks around the pool, but no, there's no one here watching Sam. He stands in the shallows then jumps in, his head going right under the water. He bobs around submerged, and Jules swims over.

'Hello, Sam. Are you out here on your own?'

Sam laughs, climbs out then jumps back in. His face beneath the water is a magnified smile. Jules looks around, but still there's no one. Where the hell is Amber?

Then Dolly is rushing towards Sam, peering into the water. She nods at Jules and smiles, her earrings flashing in the light. Dolly sits on one of the seats and pulls out her mobile phone. Jules looks at her then back at Sam. Jules should say something to Dolly about keeping a closer eye on the boy, but she doesn't. She just pulls herself out of the pool and folds the towel around herself.

Back in the apartment, Jules drinks a glass of warm tap water. She looks down at her shrivelled fingers. She presses her hands together, points a prayer at the ceiling.

'Please,' she whispers.

She thinks of her dad telling her to kneel at Sunday six o'clock mass, but she left that God alone years ago. No, she's sending the thought out to the universe instead.

Just this one small thing.

She rips off her swimsuit and showers, then pulls on a maxi dress and her leather bracelet with its silver heart charm.

She grabs her camera and takes the lift to the ground floor again. She passes Dolly then stops. Sam is still swimming underwater, and Dolly is still on her mobile phone. Oh sod it, thinks Jules, and she zooms in on Dolly, capturing the side of her face and all those shimmering earrings. She quick-fires the camera then walks on. Dolly doesn't notice.

A luminously white man in black Speedos – *isn't that Gavin?* – stands on the shallow ledge of the swimming pool, rubbing lotion into his hairy chest. His arms are thick with muscle, but his legs are twig-thin.

There are four other maids gathered at the front of the condo, sitting on the low wall, chatting. A small waterfall trickles over the stacked rocks behind them. One of the maids smiles at Jules. She's talking to her friend.

'Mind if I . . .?' goes Jules, tapping her camera, and one of the women giggles.

Her friend however loops her arm around another woman and makes a peace sign with her fingers. Jules snaps and looks at the shot. The shutter speed's not quite right, so it's too blurry. She tries again and the camera focuses on their eyes, sharp with pins of light.

'Thanks,' Jules says.

She walks out of the condo and onto Mount Sinai Road. Detached flat-roofed houses sit side by side, all of them behind metal-gated yards, bamboo leaves fanning the windows outside. A Filipina woman in battered black espadrilles wheels a floral shopper up the hill towards Jules. A blue cab happens to be passing and Jules flags it down.

She climbs into the back; it's one of the few manual ones, the suspension just about gone.

'Dempsey Hill, please.'

The driver cracks his knuckles; the car creaks and bumps along. She tunes the noise out by flicking through the pictures on her camera. That one of Dolly is good, only the side of her face in focus and the earrings. There's a blurred tattoo of a butterfly on her shoulder. She really is quite beautiful. Jules thinks back to the party; *just what is Dolly doing with a bloke like Gavin?*

Jules gets out in the car park and pays the driver. The sun is starting to set. There are cars in every available space, bars and restaurants all around. She makes her way over the tarmac to a bar called The Woods. The air smells of cement and spices, cinnamon.

She walks through the side entrance to the garden at the back. The trees close together above her. David is sitting at a round table, his mobile phone pressed to his ear.

He sees her; his eyes flit away. He covers his mouth and speaks quietly into the phone: 'I can't talk about that now; I've got to go.'

He clicks the phone off, puts it on the table as far away from her as possible.

She sits. 'Who was that?'

'No one,' he says in that high-pitched voice he uses when he's lying.

'Is there something going on?'

'No.'

He brushes some invisible dust off the table and she notices that he's been biting the skin at the sides of his fingernails. The man on the next table lights a cigarette; she fans herself with a hand.

'Do you want to move?' asks David.

'No, you're all right.' She fixes his beer with a stare.

'The alcohol police are out on patrol again,' he says. 'Anyway, I've already done the business.'

She smiles.

'Maybe it won't work,' she says.

'Then again, maybe it will.'

'What if it doesn't?'

'What if it does?'

'Oh, stop.'

The waiter arrives and she orders a Lemon San Pellegrino. All the tables outside are taken. Pizzas arrive for a group of women. The place is full inside too, lots of people seated behind the copper-rimmed panes of glass. And, hang on a minute, isn't that Tor inside? He throws himself back in a chair and its front legs tip. A woman in white stilettos beside him has her back to the glass and Jules can't see her face. There are three other men in the group. Jules gets up and makes her way to the toilet.

Mosquitoes buzz around her head as she pushes open the door. She tuts at the shower of piss on the seat. It's the only toilet, so she goes in. On the way back, she trips on a ridge in the ground.

Tor is sitting at the table beside David. 'Hello there,' says Tor, standing and kissing her on both cheeks.

'Oh, hi, Tor.'

He's overdone it on the aftershave. They sit.

'You must try the 1989 Pouilly Fumé,' says Tor, flicking through the wine list.

'I'm okay with beer,' says David, raising his glass.

'Where's Amber?' asks Jules.

'The kids have got a busy day tomorrow. Craft classes, a party. She's taking it easy.'

'Mmm,' says Jules, her eyes searching inside for Tor's friends. The table he was sitting at is now occupied by a woman in pink taffeta and a man in a suit.

'So, David, how's the job?' asks Tor.

'Go to work in my flip-flops, fifteen-minute drive. It's pretty good,' he says.

Jules hasn't asked all that much about David's new job; he provides database support for the traders.

Jules pours herself some more lemonade then holds it up and looks at her blurry husband through the murk. She guzzles it down in one go. David talks about football, reeling off the names of some notable Scandinavian players.

'Do you play?' he asks Tor.

Tor clears his throat, gives a gentle laugh. 'Cross-country skiing was more my thing back in the days when I exercised.' He pats his belly, its size invisible beneath the outsized crinkled shirt. Jules can hear the shape of Tor's Norwegian accent in some of his words.

'Do you miss Lillehammer?' she asks.

'I haven't lived there for many years. I moved to Chicago in my twenties.'

'Is that where you met Amber?'

'Yes – though, of course, that was years later. We used to work together – hedge fund management.'

'Oh, right.'

Tor shuffles in his seat. 'Funny, thinking back. Some of the other analysts used to call Amber "The Smiling Assassin".' Tor laces his huge fingers together under his chin.

David's cheeks swell and he gulps his beer down noisily. Jules' face pinches with confusion.

'She was the boss, quite the career woman,' explains Tor. 'She's very different nowadays.' He finishes the last of his drink then sets the glass down on the table.

'I don't know how she does it, to be honest. The other week when she went out, Dolly had a day off and I was left with the kids. Amber was at one of those all-day brunches – champagne on tap, eat as much as you like. Have you ever been?'

David shakes his head. Tor looks only at him.

'Well, the boys were behaving so badly. I had to call Amber and tell her to get herself back super quick.'

David and Jules lock eyes for a second.

'Don't ever get tempted,' Tor says, planting a hand on David's back.

David looks at Jules again. 'Well, we'll have to see what the future brings,' he says, his smile disappearing before it's fully formed.

Tor's phone beeps. He pulls it from his pocket and reads the text message. The colour drains from his face.

'Jesus,' he says.

He puts his trembling fingers over his mouth.

'What's wrong?' asks Jules.

He's hyperventilating, his hands shaking even more now. Jules takes his wrist. 'Have you got a pain in your chest?'

Tor shakes his head, sinks lower into his seat. He coughs and slides a hand over his balding scalp. David is sitting forward, puzzled. He catches Jules' eye.

'What's the matter, Tor?' he asks.

'I'll be fine. Low blood sugar or something. Oh, my Lord, this is embarrassing. Obviously haven't eaten enough.'

'You're sure you haven't got a pain in your chest?' asks Jules.

'Nor pins and needles in my arms,' says Tor. 'It's not a heart attack. I'll have another drink. That'll sort it.'

Tor gestures to the waiter.

'A whisky, double,' says Tor.

David orders another beer. It's dark now, stars sprinkling the black sky above them. When the drinks arrive, Tor gulps his down and orders a second. The trembling in his face has disappeared, but the glass quivers in his hand. Some of the whisky slops over the side.

Tor orders a third drink and when the waiter puts it down in front of him, he says, 'Another of the same.'

Tor pulls his chair into the table and ends up with his thigh pressed against Jules. She crosses her leg away from him, catches David's eye and mouths, 'Let's go.'

David texts a request for a cab and gestures to the waiter that he wants the bill. When the waiter brings it, David hands him three notes and stands. Jules picks up her handbag from the ground and stands too. Tor opens his mouth to speak; he blinks slowly. David cuts him off.

'Come on, Tor, we've got a cab coming. Jump in with us,' he says.

When the cab arrives, three women rush to the driver's window, but David has already opened a back door. 'This is ours I'm afraid, ladies,' he says.

Jules gets into the front and slams the door. The men climb into the back. She turns to see Tor, his head bumping against the glass, and David leaning in to fasten his seat belt for him.

They pass a fountain, the square full of restaurants and cars. The driver switches on the radio and violins sing out a tune Jules recognises from some war film.

'Aaaaah,' Tor slurs, 'Adagio for Strings.'

A nearby car toots its horn and their cab speeds along through the bleary light. Tor's eyes are closed. David is daydreaming. The cab smells of rancid breath.

The pair of them struggle to pull Tor out of the cab when they arrive at the front of the condo with its white concrete columns, square glass covering and the guardhouse. The cab driver looks in his rear-view mirror. With one last heave, Tor staggers out and sways in a circle. The trio reel along the pathway around the pool, stumbling left, so that David ends up tramping among the flowers. Could there be snakes in there? Jules thinks. She tries Tor's front door and it gives.

'Thank God for lax security,' she says.

David pushes Tor in and follows. Jules stays outside, her back against the smooth white wall. It's eleven o'clock at night and still it's boiling. She blows air into her face and twists her wedding ring round. *Harris. Jules Harris.* It's only now that she's using her married name. At the hospital, she was always Kinsella. So she's trying something new, so what? Her old identity sure as hell doesn't seem to fit any more. Going to her mother-in-law's for Sunday lunch once a month and laughing off Beryl's ill-chosen words as she served up the roast potatoes. 'Having children, it's what life's all about really.' Attending the christenings of her friends' babies. Swallowing a kernel of pain when one of her patients asked, 'So, who looks after your children while you're working here?'

When David emerges, he gives a thin smile. The oak front door clicks closed behind him.

'What was all that about?' she asks as they walk.

'Maybe it's got something to do with his wife being a complete ice maiden.'

'She's not that bad.'

'Isn't she? The only time she melts is when she's showing off about what wonderful parents she and Tor are.' David puts on a plummy American voice. 'Oh, Tor spends hours talking to the children in Norwegian. And we usually hire a Norwegian nanny for extra lessons during the summer vacation.'

'Is that what she said?'

'Yeah.'

'Mmm, well, maybe there are reasons for the way she acts.'

'Like what?'

She thinks of the Lustral. 'Colby's a flipping nightmare for starters.'

'At least we'll never have that.'

'We might do though.'

'In that case, I'd rather not have any, thanks all the same,' says David.

There are lights dotted along the pathway, the shadows of sunbeds on the parallel decking, the pool water bright blue. Jules strides on ahead and David only manages to catch up with her when she stops to call the lift.

'Are you all right?' he asks.

'I'm fine,' she says, her voice clipped.

She can feel his eyes lingering on her face, but she doesn't look at him. Instead she presses the lift button again and again until her fingernail bends back with a twinge of pain.

Essential House Rules for Foreign Domestic Maids

Rule 2. Boyfriends: Your maid must not have a boyfriend. After all, if she gets pregnant, she'll be deported and you could be forced to pay her airfare home.

Chapter 5

Mallie is sucking her thumb, looking tired, her shoulder-length hair pushed behind her ears.

'So, what are you doing now?' asks Dolly.

She moves her face closer to Sir Tor's computer screen, as if by doing so, she might see the finer details of her daughter, the lines beneath her eyes, the little fingernails.

Mallie pops her thumb out. 'I'm talking to *you*, Auntie,' she says, a twisted front tooth in her smile.

'She's not your auntie; she's your mama,' Mama's voice thunders from some place unseen.

Mallie giggles. 'When are you coming back?' she asks.

'Well, I have to work, but maybe later in the year.'

'The girls at school say you're a big shot,' says Mallie.

Mallie's friends think Dolly is a high-flyer because she works overseas. Dolly laughs.

'That's what they say.' Mallie's voice is insistent. 'I said to them that you're small, not big.'

In a minute, she and Dolly will have to say goodbye to each other because it's Mallie's bedtime. Dolly tries to keep Mallie in front of the screen for a few moments more; her bony arms, the colourful characters smiling across the front of her swimming costume.

'Mallie, look!' Dolly lifts the yellow toy in front of the screen.

'A Minion!' shouts Mallie, jumping.

'I'm going to whisper some things in his ear, and when I send him, he'll tell you them, okay?'

Mallie's crooked smile freezes on the screen.

'Mallie!' calls Dolly.

But Mallie is completely still, then the computer pings and it's clear that the Skype call has been cut off. She waits there anyway then tries to Skype Mallie back, but the call won't connect, so she trudges up the stairs from the basement, just as the front door slams. Ma'am Amber must have gone out, and Sir Tor's working late.

Dolly goes up to the first floor where Sam is asleep on the bottom bunk in the bedroom he shares with Colby, droplets of sweat on his nose. She climbs two rungs of the ladder, and Colby's eyes are closed too, freckles over his nose. Their school uniforms, white polo shirts and navy shorts, are folded over the arms of a chair. Dolly goes downstairs into her cupboard room and takes off her clothes. She puts on a clean pair of shorts and a T-shirt.

She steps out of the front door and there, just two metres in front of her, is the largest swimming pool. The spotlights dotted around the sides throw sickles of light onto the surface. A mosquito buzzes in her ears. Hundreds of white apartment blocks surround the swimming pool, some of their rectangular windows lit up. She can see the shadows of a potted palm on one, a huge sun umbrella on another. Canned laughter from a television rumbles through an open window. She pulls the band from her hair. The reflected light swirls as she climbs into the water.

She tries to swim, lifting her arms and splashing them down. When she takes her feet off the bottom, she sinks, the water up her nose, burning her throat. She pushes her head up and out and coughs, her watchful eyes scanning the dark grounds, but there's no sign of anyone.

She'd thought she was alone when she tried teaching herself that one time in Tagudin. She pushed her arms out, tried to float, then put her feet down to steady herself. There were three young men on the shore. She stood up, her clothes dripping, and they were laughing at her. One of them came into the water, big grey teeth and a purple cap twisted backwards on his head. He reached out and ran a rough thumb over her face as if he was trying to wipe away the traces of her personality. He left his hand there. If she could swim, she could have got away. She stood there thinking her face had let her down; that if she was plainer, he wouldn't be standing there smiling at her like that, or touching her. She looked at the others on the sand, then the man's hand moved to her booby and this sick feeling came up her throat. There was the sound of water; they were coming for her.

But it wasn't them; it was Tala. 'Get your hands off my sister.' The man-boy in the cap took his hand off Dolly's chest. He walked away quickly and they all left. Tala held Dolly's shoulders. 'What did they do?' she asked. 'Are you hurt?' Dolly shook her head. And Tala held Dolly against her, and Dolly knew then how much she was loved. She never did learn to swim.

She walks forward now and circles her arms in the warm water. 'Hey you!' a voice shouts.

The security cameras must have given her away. The security guard puts his hairy finger in the air and waggles it about. He stands on the edge of the pool staring down at her. His badge, his clipboard, his white shirt.

'Domestic staff not allowed to use facilities unless looking after employer's children,' he says in broken English. 'I have told you this many times before.'

She climbs up the ladder and the guard puts his pen to his clipboard and writes.

'I'm going to have to tell your ma'am,' he says and walks off.

Dolly stands there dripping; she's forgotten the towel. She slaps away a mosquito that's landed on her arm. It buzzes away. She heads downstairs into an enclosed courtyard with a large square pond in the middle bubbling with koi.

She goes inside the gym with its steamy windows, and a camera in the corner. She writes her name into the steam then wipes over it. 'I ♥ Mallie', she writes instead. She goes out and sits on the bench. It's like a room down here, walls all around, the glass doors of the gym along one side and an office where the manager sometimes sits. Then there's the communal toilets.

That skinny British woman is coming down the stairs now. She puts a coin into the drinks machine and a can bangs down. She's even thinner than Dolly remembers from the party, silver thread running through her loose vest top. Her face registers surprise as she turns around and sees Dolly, a bright white smile breaking across her sunburnt face.

'Oh, hi,' she says. 'Did you enjoy your swim?'

She puts her head back and drinks the Diet Coke, though she doesn't need to diet as far as Dolly can see; she needs one of Dolly's cakes all to herself. She's all twigs: arm twigs, leg twigs – even her face is long and thin.

'I'm not allowed to . . . Oh, it doesn't matter, ma'am.'

The woman starts laughing then. 'I'm sorry, it's just . . .'

Dolly bites her lip.

'You calling me "ma'am". I've been called some things in my time, but "ma'am" isn't one of them.'

Dolly fidgets on the bench, glances at the stairs.

The British woman takes another drink and sits beside Dolly. 'Do you want a can?'

Dolly swallows.

'Iced lemon tea, Sprite, Coke?' She jangles her hand in her musical pocket.

'No, no, it's okay, ma'am.'

'Seriously, I'm Jules. We talked at that party.'

'Yes, ma'am, I remember.'

'You were rushed off your feet.'

Dolly lifts her head, looks at the woman properly. Her nose as pink as ham, and peeling; the forehead crisp. And to think of all the trouble some Asian women go to, slapping whitening cream onto their faces.

Ma'am Jules picks at the orange nail varnish on her thumb. 'How long have you been here?'

'Five and a half years.'

'Whoa, that's a long time. Do you like it?'

'I have a nice room, good employers.' Dolly crosses her leg away from Ma'am Jules.

'Where are you from?'

'The Philippines.'

Ma'am Jules takes another drink, slumps in the seat, thighs splayed. 'What's it like there then?'

'It's very green, not too many buildings where my home is. How many kids have you got, ma'am?'

Her right eye twitches. 'Oh, none.'

The fish slap through the silence. Ma'am Jules gets up, kicks two abandoned fish-food pellets into the murky water then sits back down. The bench trembles.

'So are you going back for a holiday any time soon?' asks Ma'am Jules.

'There's nothing planned, ma'am. Besides, when I go back, it's expensive.'

'The flight?'

'I don't earn anything when I go home. And my family, my neighbours and friends all expect me to buy gifts for them.'

'Oh, oh right. Amber said you've got a daughter.'

'Yes, ma'am. Mallie.'

'How often do you see her?'

'Not very often.'

'That can't be easy.'

'I need to work to keep my daughter in school.'

'So what does Mallie want to be when she grows up?'

'An astronaut.'

Ma'am Jules laughs. 'Setting her sights high then. Ambitious.'

Dolly smiles. 'Yeah.'

A fish tail whips the water.

'I'm looking for someone to do a bit of cleaning.'

Dolly's eyes flip to the stairs. 'Maybe I could help.'

'Well, yeah. If you're up for it, you could do it on your day off. I mean, God, I'm sorry to ask.'

'I meant I can ask my sister, Tala.'

Ma'am Jules frowns. 'What?'

'My sister, she's a good cleaner, the best. She's better than me; she's shiny.'

Ma'am Jules smiles, her eyes taking in the different parts of Dolly's face. Dolly looks away.

'Great,' says Ma'am Jules.

She takes her phone from her pocket. Dolly takes hers out too and scrolls down to Tala's number. The only number Dolly knows by heart is Gavin's. She can't type it into her contacts list in case someone discovers it. She says Tala's number and Ma'am Jules types it in.

'Amber says you're a bit of a Mary Berry.'

'What?'

'Brilliant at baking.'

Dolly peers at the clock through the gym window, but can't see the time. She stands abruptly. 'I've got to go.'

'Oh, okay. Well, you'll tell Tala I'll call, yes?'

'Yes, ma'am.'

'Jules, just Jules.'

Dolly runs up the stairs fast, dripping all the way.

She goes through the front door, past the kitchen clock which tells her that she's got back just in time. Gavin should be here any minute now. Back inside her dark room, she rips off her wet clothes. She towels herself off and pulls on a clean T-shirt. The metal door to her room creaks, and fingers touch her shoulder.

'Shit,' she says. Then Gavin's fingers are cupping her bare buttocks, pulling her towards him. He laughs into her ear. 'It's me.'

'You gave me a fright.'

'I'm about to give you more than that.'

As usual, he's come in through a side door that no one in the house, apart from Dolly, uses. She leaves it unlocked on the nights he visits. He flicks on the light switch. His eyes have lines around them, like he's been squinting in the sun. He's too old for her, but she pushes the thought away and forces a smile. He presses his lips against hers, licks the inside of her mouth.

She pulls away. 'Wait.' She closes the door and the heat swells. He kisses her again. He tastes bitter like Ma'am Amber's coffee. He takes a condom packet from his pocket and rips it open with his teeth. She can feel herself grimacing as he shuffles his trousers down and smoothes the rubber sheath over his veiny hardness. She switches off the light, goes to the bed and lies down. He's on top of her then, his mouth against her neck. He nuzzles his nose against hers and she turns her face away, trying not to breathe in his smoky stench. She tries to think of someone else's face – Mallie's father, or the attractive dockworker who she's chatted to on her occasional days off. She fills her head up with the dockworker, and that dilutes the grunting discomfort of this man on top of her.

Her affair with Gavin started one night when she was in the condo swimming pool. She put her hands out in front of her in the water. She sank, came up coughing with her hair over her face. A dot of orange light curved through the dark air. 'I could teach you,' a nasal voice said.

Dolly waded over to the side and sat on the edge beside the smoky stranger. His chinos were rolled up to his dunked ankles, his face blue in the pool lights. 'The name's Gavin,' he said. He put the cigarette into the pucker of his thick lips. 'Me and you, we should . . .' He blew a rope of smoke from his mouth and smiled. She stood there in the water, the taste of disgust on her tongue like chewed aspirin. She started to wade away; he tried another line. 'We could have some fun together.'

She stopped, the blood roaring in her ears. An opportunity had presented itself, but was she going to take it?

She didn't turn around straightaway. A storm heaved in her stomach. She couldn't, could she? Even that one small look at him had revolted her. But this could be a way to help Mallie . . . She turned around and faced him; she swallowed hard.

'You can take me to dinner,' she said.

Laughter burst out of him. Stony-faced, she held her ground.

'You must be bloody joking,' he said.

She made her way to the pool ladder, climbed out and started to walk off.

'Oh, bloody hell,' he muttered. She got further away. 'Wait!' he shouted.

She stopped.

'I suppose we could go out,' he said. 'What's your number?' He pulled out his mobile phone.

A week later, he started giving her presents. A scarf with turquoise spheres bleeding into a red background. The label read 'Real Silk'. A fortnight after, he gave her a silver necklace from Tiffany & Co. That's when she let him in. He came in through the side door to her room where she opened her legs. And later, when he was asleep, she sat there with his wallet in her hand, assessing how much she could take without it being missed. He's become her work on the side, her extra, so she swallows her disgust along with her voice and when she speaks to him, she says things he wants to hear. 'Oh, yes'. 'More'. 'Where shall I touch you?'

She feels the urge to spit, but his tongue is circling her mouth. He moans with a drawn-out 'Oh', then pulls out of her and slings his sweaty thigh over her leg. She pushes it off. Her head swims with her daughter and this unwanted pregnancy that happened because of a split condom.

The metal door creaks open, and light from the corridor window seeps into the room.

Dolly gasps. 'Who's there?'

She pushes herself to sitting. Footsteps scamper away. Things are bad, but they'll be a whole lot worse if that was Ma'am Amber. None of the family have ever come into her room during the night before.

'Wake up!' she hisses.

Gavin moans, yawns. 'What?'

'You fell asleep.'

He sits up. 'I need to go.'

Dolly climbs onto her knees, picking up his trousers and shaking them the right way round again. She pushes her hand into the pocket where there's a screwed-up tissue and something papery like money. She slides the papery thing under the bed and he puts on his clothes. He touches his finger to her shoulder, and makes shapes there, following the lines of her butterfly tattoo. Then his mouth goes there and he kisses it softly.

The door clicks closed behind him, and Dolly listens hard in the dark.

Tala is late, so swishes across the road, with an extravagant swing of her pelvis, the crucifix bumping against her chest. This is a rare afternoon of freedom for some of the maids, and they're going for a picnic together. The cars roar and whine beside Tala, and she keeps walking, every part of her moving, hips swinging, arms pumping, bag tapping. Who needs exercise DVDs when you use as much energy as Tala to move from A to B?

By the time she's on the arching white bridge in the Chinese Gardens, she's as hot as a chicken in a rotisserie oven, albeit a better dressed one. Her T-shirt's cerise and her skirt is flowered with large red poppies. A bandy-legged Western woman, stuffed inside a white shirt, walks on by. Tala smiles, but the woman doesn't smile back. Tala's feet are already squelching in today's flip-flops, a pink plastic bow on each one.

She heads over the grass, her hand shading her eyes against

the sun, searching. And there they are, her friends, her women, variously spread out on colourful mats – pink and blue squares, some with tassels on. A guitar lies on one of the mats, and voices rumble. There's a rattle of laughter.

'Eh, Tala!'

One of the women, with pink glitter smudged on her eyelids, gets up and wraps her arms around Tala.

The nearby pond is flat and green with a red bridge over it like an upside-down smile. There are lots of pink lanterns on it, big stones around the sides and a lamp post too. In the distance, a red and white pagoda reaches towards the sky.

Tala spots Dolly on her knees offering around a plastic box of cupcakes. Her sister is thirty-five years old, but could pass for a woman of twenty-five. Today she's pale in her buttoned black dress, the cotton straining around her cleavage that looks even more ample than it usually does. Her lips are painted red and there's the pink wrap folded on the mat which Dolly always drapes over her shoulders later at these get-togethers, lending an air of sophistication to her slightly washed-out best dress. Around her, there's a rainbow of T-shirted women, a woman having her nails filed, another pressing a plastic cup to her lips.

'Hi, Tala,' says Dolly.

'Oh, you're looking bloated.'

Dolly puts the box of cakes in front of her stomach, looks into the distance then down at the mat.

'Are you ill?'

Dolly pushes her hair behind her ears, clacking her earrings.

'I'm fine. Anyway, it's not me you should be worried about.'

Dolly jerks her head sideways towards Rita who's sitting there with another box of cakes on her lap, that one tooth missing from the side of her mouth. Crumbs are stuck to the corners of her lips. The speed she's eating at, there won't be any cakes left. Tala hotfoots it over, kicks off her slippery flip-flops and plonks herself down. Rita's eyes are red-rimmed.

'How many of those cupcakes have you eaten, Rita?'

'Four.'

'Well, these hips don't need any more bulk.'

Tala takes hold of her sides and squeezes then digs her hand into the box. As she does so, Rita picks up the cake she's going for and starts munching.

'Nothing but rice for dinner for the last four days,' Rita says through churned sponge.

'Really?' Tala grabs a cake and eats.

'And they've got me getting up in the night with the new baby.'

Rita works for a family who live in the same Housing Development Board flats as Tala. A thirty-storey-high block in a housing estate, with a supermarket, a clinic and a hawker centre in the middle of the grounds.

'You've got to stand up to them, Rita – say you can't work without proper food.'

'I say anything, they say I'm rude. I'm already on a final warning.'

'*Ay nako!* I'll come to the employment agency with you, explain the situation.'

'And if things weren't bad enough, that Vanda is writing stuff about how employers need to watch what maids are eating in case we cost them too much money. Like we're all a bunch of gluttons or something.'

'Disgusting!' says Tala, and takes another bite of her cake.

Tala eyes Dolly, whose forehead is covered with pearls of sweat. 'Have you got a temperature?'

'I'm fine, really?' says Dolly, turning the statement into a question as if she doesn't believe her own words.

Tala carries on staring and frowning. Dolly bites her nails. There's thirteen years between the women, but they can read each other like twins. Perhaps it would have been different if their mother hadn't miscarried all those babies in-between.

Caroline arrives then, her hair newly short.

'Hi, everyone,' she says and shakes her hips. There's laughing and then some. She pulls six cans of Red Horse beer from an orange carryall. The plastic cups on the mat fall sideways as she pours the beer in. Rita grabs one. Dolly offers Tala a cupcake from one of her boxes.

'I shouldn't be thinking about cake, not when Rita's suffering like this,' says Tala, helping herself to two. 'These are good enough for that bakery you're going to open one day, Dolly.'

'Paper bags on a hook on the wall. Cakes on shelves. In my dreams!' Dolly winks at Tala.

'A bakery!' Rita says, beer spraying from her mouth. 'People like us don't open bakeries!'

'Hey, have you seen that new blog? Some outraged Filipina on her soapbox,' says Caroline.

Tala coughs into her hand. 'How did you hear about that?' she asks in a voice ten octaves higher than her own.

'Everybody's talking about it. I can't wait to see what she writes next,' says Caroline.

Beer runs down Rita's chin.

'This Maidhacker person's risking her life,' says Dolly.

'Is she? He?' says Tala. She fiddles with the strap of her yellow suede handbag.

'Well, look at what happened to the guy who wrote that book about the death penalty,' says Dolly.

'What?' asks Caroline.

'He accused the government of mainly hanging poor people and leaving the rich ones alone,' says Dolly.

Caroline frowns. 'Maidhacker's not exactly criticising the government though.'

'Yeah, but she's criticising some of their policies. Writing about how we need a day off written into our contracts, about people spying on their maids. She's rocking the boat.'

'Well, I'm glad she is,' says Caroline.

Tala's eyes are just about bulging out of her head. She tries to make her voice sound vaguely normal. 'And, er, what happened to this man you mentioned, Dolly?'

'He ended up in Changi Prison.'

So help Tala, she sits on her right hand to stop it from blessing herself.

'Oh, Dolly, you're exaggerating!' says Rita, taking another slug of her drink.

'People who say the wrong thing here can end up in court,' says Dolly.

Caroline shakes her head.

'It's true,' says Dolly. 'It'll be so easy for the authorities to find out who Maidhacker is. All they need to do is trace her IP address after all. And if she doesn't end up in prison, they could take away her work permit.'

Tala zips open her bag, pulls out her paper fan with the daisies on it, and gets wafting.

'Who do you reckon it is?' asks Rita.

Tala looks up; Rita's staring right at her.

'How should I know?' shrieks Tala. She gets more brisk with her fan.

'Because you know everyone!' says Rita.

Dolly turns to Tala then. 'You wouldn't give her away even if you did know, Tala. But seriously, if you do know who's writing this, tell her to stop.'

'I have no idea who's writing that stupid blog.' Tala sniffs hard. 'Vanda though, I've got my suspicions about that one.'

'Really? Who, Tala?' Rita turns her can of drink upside down and shakes it. It drips. She crushes it in her hand, reaches for a carrier and pushes it inside.

'Well, your ma'am and her friends are my prime suspects,' Tala says to Dolly.

'What, Ma'am Amber?'

'Well, why not?'

'No, I don't think so,' says Dolly.

'Oh, I bet it's her,' says Rita. 'Can tell by that face. That face has suffered things – those lines and that long, thin chin.' Rita sucks her cheeks in. 'A face only a mother could love, that one.'

'She's okay, Ma'am Amber, she's just a bit, well . . . Oh, look, she's a decent woman in her heart,' says Dolly.

'Decent?!' says Rita. 'She hardly ever gives you a day off.'

'I'm here today, aren't I?'

'All I'm saying is, all of us need to keep our eyes and ears peeled,' says Tala. 'That's the only way we're going to get closer to finding out who Vanda is.'

Rita grabs another can of Red Horse.

'She's been at it again,' says Caroline. '*Don't let your maids out. It only takes a free afternoon for her to get pregnant.*'

Dolly drops her cup of lime juice. It spills. She reaches for a piece of kitchen roll and starts dabbing the mat.

'Remember Florence Torres?' says Caroline. 'Vanda put her name and work permit number up on her website after she got pregnant. Florence got deported two days later.'

Dolly drops the kitchen roll into the rubbish carrier, bites her nail then looks at her hand. There's a droplet of blood in the quick.

'And her with two other kids to support at home,' says Tala.

'"No boyfriends!"' shrieks Caroline. 'That's what Charmaine told me in one of her lessons at the employment agency.'

'Well, Rita didn't listen!' says Tala.

Rita laughs. 'How about you, Dolly? Have you met anyone lately?'

Dolly clamps her fist shut then shakes her head. Tala stares. Dolly turns a plastic bag upside down. Lots of hairbands fall out, pink ones, purple ones, yellow ones and ones with little jewels, hairs and crumbs caught up in them. She gets up and sits behind Rita, starts plaiting her hair.

'Well, Charmaine, Vanda and my bitch of a boss, they've all met their match in Maidhacker,' says Caroline.

Maidhacker. Tala's heart is racing so fast it's like she's about to have a cardiac arrest. She takes a drink of her lime juice. Rita picks up her guitar and starts singing some rural Filipino song. Her fingers hit bum notes and twangs. They eat and they sing. They do each other's hair, and the hours slip past.

Rita's eyes are closing; she lolls forward, her hair in two neat plaits. Tala sits beside her. Alcohol fumes seep from Rita's skin.

Tala looks at Rita. 'Oh my Gad,' says Tala, slipping into English. Sometimes she thinks in English rather than Tagalog, she's been speaking it for that long.

Rita splutters with laughter, spit spraying. 'Where did you learn to speak English like that anyway?'

'At school for a while,' says Tala, reverting back to Tagalog. 'Through cassette tapes after that.'

'Well, you ended up absorbing some weird accent,' says Rita.

She pushes herself up and it's like she's on a boat on rough sea. She staggers towards a bush, Tala following. Behind it, Rita leans forward and vomits.

'You're in a state. How much did you have to drink?'

'Leave me.'

Rita falls into a heap on the grass. Her knee thwacks a stone. 'Ow!'

'I'll do no such thing! I'll get you something to drink.'

'I never wanna drink Red Horse again.'

'I don't mean alcohol!'

Tala wiggles away, fills a cup with lime juice and grabs their stuff. Loaded up with her own handbag and Rita's guitar on a strap over her shoulder, Tala heads back to the bush.

Rita drinks the juice down then Tala pulls her up. She's heavier than Tala tonight even though she's all bone and bosom. They start to walk, Rita's arm cabled around Tala's neck.

'I'm taking this one home!' shouts Tala over her shoulder.

Dolly blows Tala a kiss. Some of the women wave. Tala and Rita take faltering crunches along the pavement.

Tala manages to get Rita into the lift and the pair of them stumble along the thin balcony to Mrs Heng's red front door. There's no way Rita can go home in this state, thinks Tala, especially with all that talk of final warnings. Those people don't need any more ammunition to get rid of her.

'What am I going to do, Tala? I can't live like this any more,' Rita slurs.

'Shut your big mouth, Rita, Mrs Heng's home!'

She turns her key in the lock and the heat of the dark hall wraps itself around them. They lurch through it to the utility room, every footstep turned to full volume in Tala's ears. She switches on the light and Rita slips onto the single mattress on the floor, a dry morsel of cake stuck to her chest like a brooch.

'You need to sober up, girl.'

Tala glances at the cupboard where her computer is, but Rita's not in any fit state to climb up there and start snooping. Her eyes are closing.

Tala tiptoes through the dark to the kitchen and fills a mug with water. She stubs out four ants on the metal window frame.

Rita's dribbling on the pillow when Tala gets back. Pope Benedict, Blu-Tacked to the wall above, gives Rita a hard stare. Tala lifts Rita's head and presses the mug to her mouth. It drips down her chin, but she manages to swallow some of it. Her burp rips through the air.

'Holy mother, will you keep quiet?'

It's only then that Tala sees the cut on Rita's knee. She scrambles through her bag, takes out a wad of cotton wool and presses it to the cut.

'Ow, ow!' Rita sits up.

'It's not deep, what are you making all that fuss about?'

'It hurts.'

'You keep seeing all these men of yours and it's not just your leg that's going to be sore; you get yourself a baby inside and your undercarriage will never be the same again, you mark my words.'

Tala sits on the mattress, getting her breath back and counting in her head how many of her friends she's sent to that Plover Plaza shop that sells the illegal pills. Not that any of them need to ask her any more; they all seem to know where it is.

'You can stay tonight, but you must be quiet in case Mrs Heng hears.'

Wry amusement travels across Rita's tired face. 'Why have you never found yourself a man, Tala?'

'I'm married, remember. Besides, lots of employment agencies tell us we aren't allowed boyfriends.'

'How many rules have you broken, Tala?' Rita's smile widens.

Tala touches the cross on the end of her necklace. 'Rules are there for a reason,' she says.

If Rita ever found out Tala is working illegally for all those other people, the whole Pinoy community would know too. Everyone's got a nickname in Tala's head. And Rita's is *Salamin* – that's a best-selling newspaper back in the Philippines. Tala's eyes flit to the cupboard again.

'Always listening to other people's problems and being the funny lady, but when you think about it, we hardly know anything about you at all.' Rita's voice is a slack thing.

Tala tucks her T-shirt into her skirt, straightens her back and looks at Marlon's canvas landscape amid the gallery of photographs on her bedside table.

'There's not all that much to know, apart from the fact I've got two sons at home and they're strangers to me.'

'At least you've got kids, Tala. I wish I did, but time's running out for me.' Rita slouches and stares at her cut knee. 'I'm stuck here earning money to put my two sisters through college. They're clever, not like me. This is all I'm cut out for. By the time I get to go home, it'll be too late for me to have a family of my own.'

Tala rubs a circle on Rita's back then gets up. She puts some towels on the thin slice of floor, layering them up for a bit of cushioning. The amount of cushioning Tala's got, it should be her on the floor, but oh no, she's tired. Rita peels off her orange dress. Tala stands there and pulls off her skirt then swishes along the corridor to her little toilet cubicle where she cleans her teeth.

When she gets back, Rita's arms and legs are spread out like a big bony starfish on the mattress. Her mouth, with its oversized teeth, drops open and she's snoring.

Tala shakes her shoulder. 'Rita!'

Rita stays still, her throat honking and bubbling. Tala looks at the magazine on the end of the bed. The open-wide smile of her favourite astrologer, Russell Grant, stares up at her like he's about to eat a doughnut. Oh, please, Russell, make her shut up, thinks Tala.

She fumbles for the toilet roll beside her mattress, screws bits of it into pellets and pushes them into her ears. She switches off the light and lies down, squashing herself into the space on top of the layered towels. The toilet roll doesn't do any good. My God, Rita can make some noise.

Tala's beeping alarm pierces the silence. She thumps the clock. Rita doesn't move, her mouth gaping, her arm curled over her head. The room is a compressed box of body odour. Wooden cupboards with silver handles line the wall on one side. There's a collection of mops leaning in a corner and black mould clings to the ceiling. Tala heaves herself up and opens the door a crack to let some light from the hall filter into the windowless room. The fan is still in two parts on the side table. She pushes her legs into some clean knickers and throws her T-shirt at Rita's head. The dust from the dryer tickles Tala's nose. Her bladder is full enough for a leakage if she sneezes, so she bustles to her toilet, pressing one hand to her nostrils, the other to her saggy bare breasts. That's the problem for big-breasted women across the globe; for years, your bosoms are your trophies, then they're rocks in wet socks.

She sits sideways on the pan to avoid the cleaning fluid bottles that line the side of the cubicle. A cracked floor tile cuts into the sole of her foot. On the way back, she hears the squeak of Mrs Heng's elasticated slippers on the marble tiles. She's standing, her outsized ear pressed against the closed door to Tala's room. She jumps when she sees Tala.

'Don't think I don't know what's going on, girl!' she says, shaking her hair-netted head.

Tala stiffens, empty of excuses, wrapping her arms closer to her slack chest.

'Enough, Tala. Women, *ta ma de* women, all the time in my house, every one of them lazy like sloths!'

'Sorry, Mrs Heng.'

'No more sorry, Tala.' She waves a finger in the air. 'This isn't some women's shelter. Tidy yourself up.'

Mrs Heng turns on her heel. Tala fingers the sleep in her left eye and watches Mrs Heng go, her nylon housecoat fluttering around her like wings.

Chapter 6

⧗

Dolly traces her finger over the broken skin on her shoulder where Colby bit her this morning. There he goes, running through the sand towards the line of zip wires, Sam following. They're both still dressed in their school uniforms.

Colby punches Sam, but Ma'am Amber and Sir Tor, who are standing metres away from Dolly on the playground pavement, don't notice. Sam rubs his arm and looks towards Dolly who gives a smile and nods encouragingly. She watches his forehead unfold itself, his mouth lifting at the edges. It's enough for him that she's seen.

Colby takes the wire, straddles the seat. 'Mom!' he shouts.

Ma'am Amber is glaring at Sir Tor, his balding pate shining like a silver globe.

Sam wanders to the climbing frame made from different coloured ropes. Around it, there are plastic things to climb into like trains and planes.

'I don't want this any more,' says Sir Tor.

Dolly holds her breath, so her ears can do their work.

'Don't dictate to me,' Ma'am Amber says. She has on wedged shoes that don't match, one of them blue, one of them dark green. Ma'am must be even more stressed than usual to have mismatched her shoes, thinks Dolly. She concentrates harder on hearing the couple's conversation. Sir Tor says something else, but Dolly doesn't catch it. Ma'am Amber grinds her fist into an eye socket, creating a panda-patch of mascara.

'This isn't a marriage,' says Sir Tor.

Ma'am Amber mutters. Dolly steps from the concrete pathway into the sand.

'Stop shifting this,' Sir Tor says.

'Screw you, Tor.'

'Keep your voice down.'

Ma'am Amber starts to cry, her face a squashed pink cloth.

'You can't leave me,' she says. 'I'll take the children. They won't be part of your life. You'll see them for days during a vacation, hardly at all.'

Sir Tor shakes his head. Ma'am Amber walks towards the car park, going over on a heel. Sir Tor rubs what's left of his hair backwards with a hand.

A boy jumps off the zip wire; it sways empty in the middle of the line. Dolly runs towards it, grabs the line and speeds up. She jumps on and her flip-flops slap into the sand below. She whizzes to the wooden platform where Sam and Colby are waiting. Colby is jerking around, putting his eager arms out towards Dolly, who jumps off. Colby jumps on and shoots away.

'Go for it, Colby!'

He gets stuck in the middle of the wire, and Dolly jumps down into the sand and rushes to help. She grabs his feet and runs him along, the air breezing past, her heart thumping. He jumps off and Dolly looks at him, his freckled, smiling face slick with sweat. She brushes her hand over his wiry brown hair. His smile fades.

'I saw you and my dad.'

Dolly frowns.

'The other night,' says Colby.

'What do you mean?'

'Dad had no clothes on; he was in your bed.'

'That's not what you saw.'

'I did.'

'That's not what you saw, Colby.'

'It was.'

'Shit.' She glances at Sir Tor, whose hands are on his head.

'I just had a friend over, that's all.'

'A naked friend.'

His words stay suspended in the heat. She wants to grab them, stuff them away, but she can't.

'I take care of you, right?'

'Yeah.'

'Do you want me to keep looking after you?'

He nods.

'Then, darling, you can't tell anyone about what you saw.'

'Why not?'

'Because your mama will sack me.'

'But—'

'Please, Colby, you just have to trust me. I don't want to leave you; I don't want to leave Sam either.'

His eyes swing to his father and back to Dolly.

She folds him into a hug. 'I love you,' she whispers, but Colby pushes her away and runs towards the climbing frame.

Dolly massages her forehead, her heart punching her ribs. She walks back towards Sir Tor, whose trouser hems are caught under his Birkenstocks.

'She's driven off,' he says. 'Oh, Lord.' He wipes his mouth with a hand. Dolly's eyes dart about. Colby's climbing, but there's no sign of Sam.

'Where's Sam?'

'I don't know,' says Sir Tor.

He runs towards the zip wire, his legs flapping. Dolly runs and overtakes him. She looks under the wooden blocks, but Sam isn't there.

'Sam!' shouts Sir Tor. 'Sam!'

'Where's Sam?' Dolly calls up to Colby.

He looks down at her, shrugging. Dolly's mouth is as dry as the day she lost Sam in Lion Plaza. She'd run around calling, past the employment agency who'd given her her training. She hoped the agency boss, Charmaine, wouldn't see her – not much of a recommendation, losing a kid. She found him ten minutes later, in a musical instrument shop, watching the assistant banging sticks on a drum.

'Sammy!' she shouts.

'Where is he?' asks Sir Tor. His face is flour-white.

She runs towards the play car. Sam isn't there. He isn't on top of the balancing logs or inside the castle either. Sam is gone. The light is dim; it'll be dark soon. Dolly turns in a circle; a blur of kids, and people in sunglasses.

'Sam!' Sir Tor shouts.

'Sam!' Dolly screams it this time. People stare.

And that's when she sees him. His light hair blowing in the breeze, two steps up the climbing wall.

'He's there!' she shouts. She runs to him and lifts him kicking.

'I want to go up,' he says.

'We thought we'd lost you. You just disappeared,' says Dolly.

'Like Mommy,' he says.

She kisses the top of his thick, silvery hair, the soapy smell of it. And her mind drifts to Mallie and the smell of the soap they use back in Tagudin.

'Where is Mommy?'

'She had to go home.'

'Why?'

Sir Tor is beside her then, clearing his throat. 'Thank you, my dear.'

He puts his arms around them both. Dolly's shoulders relax and she leans into him, so that it's as if he's holding her up. She turns her head slightly and there's his large hand, a thin line of white on the finger where his wedding ring used to be. It's hot in his arms; there isn't much air, but she doesn't push him away.

She looks into the distance, and her eyes meet Colby's. They are green and angry and staring right into her.

⌛

'Mop the floors, Dolly, then do those quiches,' says Ma'am Amber. Her eyes are red. Has she been crying?

The pastry cases are already lined up on the kitchen counter. Dolly slides the mop across the marble floor. Ma'am Amber is in the living room, plumping up the cushions on one of the white leather sofas. When she's done, she bites her lip. Her right eyelid is flickering. She looks at the clock and starts pacing. She's not usually this worked up when she's hosting the book group.

Dolly stabs the mop into the basket of the bucket then slides it again, erasing two manic ants. Ma'am Amber stretches her arms wide. She has on a big white cape dress, arms like wings.

'Miu Miu,' she says.

Dolly frowns then gives an uncertain smile.

'It's new,' says Ma'am.

Dolly raises her eyebrows and nods. Sam emerges from the kitchen, still in his school uniform, his hair tousled.

'Can I do painting, Mommy?'

'Where have you been?'

'In Dolly's room.'

'I told you, you're not to go in there.'

'But I like it in there.'

Ma'am Amber tuts.

'I want to do painting!'

'I don't want the place messed up, or your school uniform. Just stay clean until everyone gets here.' Her voice is full of hard edges and sighs.

Sam flops down on a sofa and starts playing his DS. Electronic music jingles out; his fingers tap. There are loud, uneven footsteps on the stairs then, and Colby slams into the living area in his Crocs, and bangs on the television.

'Colby!' shouts Ma'am Amber.

He turns the television up and a cartoon boy with spiky hair jumps through the air, snarling. Colby sits on the other sofa then twists round, so that his feet are hanging over the back.

'You'll have to turn that off when the ladies get here,' says Ma'am Amber.

Colby's eyes are fixed on the screen. Ma'am goes upstairs, a billowy sack of quick white cotton.

'Colby, darling, I could use your help putting out the crisps,' says Dolly, leaning now against her mop. She takes a big breath. He turns to her and sneers.

'Colby, come on.' She can hear the false authority in her own brittle voice.

He puts his freckled face into his hands and shakes his head hard. She steps towards him and his fingers claw his cheeks.

'You told me not to tell.'

Dolly's eyes go wide; she looks up at the stairs, but they're empty. She looks back at Colby, forcing her face to stay smooth as a pebble. She lets her eyes glide to Sam who is still pressing on the little console.

'Sam, come on,' she says. 'I've got a job for you.'

'What's that?'

'Cracking eggs.'

She risks a look at Colby again; there are scrapes down his cheeks. He stares at her as she goes into the kitchen, Sam following.

She ties an apron across Sam's back. He cracks the eggs into a bowl and beats them. Soon he starts slamming the fork into the mixture, flecking his hair and polo shirt.

'Shit, no, Sam.'

'Shit. Shit. Shit,' he says.

'I mean, sugar.'

She takes the fork from him, pours the mixture into the pastry cases and slides them into the oven. The door goes then, two half-hearted knocks. Colby is gone from the living room now, and Dolly lifts the remote control and turns the television off. She pulls open the oak front door.

Ma'am Jules is standing there in a pair of ripped denim shorts, a pink T-shirt falling off her shoulder. There's a gift wrapped in red spotted paper in her hand. She thrusts it towards Dolly.

'I'll just get Ma'am.'

'That's for you.'

'Me?'

'Yeah, I don't know; I just went into this shop in Holland Village and thought of you. It might make a good recipe book.'

'What do you mean?'

'Amber said you've got all these papers with cake recipes on; just thought you could stick them in there.'

Dolly looks at the package then back at Ma'am Jules. From the corner of her eye, Dolly can see Ma'am Amber on the stairs.

'Jules. How nice,' says Ma'am Amber.

Dolly says a quiet 'thank you'.

Ma'am Jules bends down to Ma'am Amber who starts kissing the air. They look like opposites, Ma'am Jules all torn up and Ma'am Amber dressed as if she's about to leave for a wedding.

More women arrive. Hellos and kisses. One of them has on a green dress with silver bangles on her wrist. Dolly remembers that her name is Ma'am Kathryn. The other woman, in a long flowery dress, is called Ma'am Yi Ling. Ma'am Jemima arrives. She has on a catsuit that's not the right size and the black fabric strains and moulds around her crotch. She opens her bag and puts a book onto a coffee table. *The Help*. Maybe it's like that book that Tala gave Dolly to read. *The Secret*. It's supposed to solve all your problems, but it hasn't made any of Dolly's dreams come true so far. She glances up the stairs, but there's no sign of Colby.

'What did you think of it?' asks Ma'am Amber, her eyes grazing the book.

'Marvellous,' says Ma'am Jemima. All the women, apart from Ma'am Amber, have sat on the sofas.

'A thing of the past, thank God. All that fuss over the toilets. Just awful,' says Ma'am Amber. She sits on the arm of a sofa.

'Well, that's just how it was,' says Ma'am Jemima.

'That's just how it is,' says Ma'am Kathryn.

'What do you mean?' asks Ma'am Amber.

Ma'am Kathryn looks up at Dolly. Dolly goes into the kitchen, puts Ma'am Jules' gift on the counter. Sam is nowhere to be seen.

'Well, all the maids here have a separate toilet,' says Ma'am Kathryn.

'It's hardly the same,' says Ma'am Amber.

'Of course it is,' says Ma'am Kathryn.

The label on the gift says, 'Love Jules'. Dolly pulls the quiches out of the oven and puts them on the table with the salad. She fills glasses with elderflower cordial and passes them round on a tray. The sound of something falling and breaking apart comes from upstairs. Ma'am Amber goes up, sighing.

'I liked it more than the last book, anyway,' says Ma'am Jemima. '*We Need to Talk About Kevin*. Not my thing at all, really.'

'We need to talk about Gavin, more like,' says Ma'am Kathryn.

Dolly walks slowly back to the kitchen, listening. Ma'am Jemima sniggers.

'What do you mean?' asks Ma'am Jules.

Just then Ma'am Amber comes back down the stairs, and sits again. 'To go back to the book, it's just not the same as here. I mean that was the Deep South in the sixties.'

'I'm just saying it's comparable.'

'But *The Help* has a whole backdrop of lynchings and stuff.'

'Who needs ropes when you've got that awful Vanda?' says Ma'am Kathryn.

'You can see her point though,' Ma'am Amber says.

'Can you?' asks Ma'am Kathryn, her mouth falling open.

Dolly comes out of the kitchen, starts rearranging plates on the table. Ma'am Jules gets up and goes towards the table where she takes a piece of quiche and bites. Crumbs fall onto her chin.

'Well, I mean, the boyfriend rule. It's a good thing,' says Ma'am Amber. 'I don't want my maid getting knocked up on my watch.'

Ma'am Jules rolls her eyes. Dolly looks down at her stomach straining slightly against the waistband of her shorts. She pulls out her tucked-in T-shirt and lets it fall baggy around her hips.

The woman in the flowery dress, Ma'am Yi Ling, says, 'It's not right though, putting women's names up there like that. It's their livelihood.'

'I wonder who Vanda is,' says Ma'am Amber with this smile on her face.

There's no way Tala can be right; Ma'am Amber isn't Vanda, surely.

'She's probably some bored housewife with nothing better to do,' says Ma'am Jules. She puts another piece of quiche onto her plate, and for the next minute the only sound is her chewing.

'Yes, well . . .' says Ma'am Amber eventually.

'I agree, too much time on her hands,' says Ma'am Yi Ling.

'Vanda may seem a bit prescriptive, but you do have to spell everything out for these girls,' says Ma'am Amber. 'I mean, they're just village girls, from the middle of nowhere, uneducated.'

'Well, at least this other blog is giving Vanda a run for her money,' says Ma'am Jules.

'What blog?' says Ma'am Yi Ling.

'Maidhacker. Sending Vanda into a right old spin,' says Ma'am Jules.

'Oh, that won't last. It's just some maid with a chip on her shoulder,' says Ma'am Amber.

'I wouldn't be so sure about that,' says Ma'am Jules. 'Have you seen the comments section? She's obviously striking a chord with people.'

Dolly passes round some slices of quiche. Something slams to the floor in the direction of her room. The women snap their heads round to hear. Dolly goes to her room. Inside its claustro-phobic walls, Sam is on his knees beside her bed, searching inside her shoebox.

'Sam, what are you doing?'

'Jewels,' he says.

Mallie's Minion toy is in his hand. Threaded through his other fingers is the white gold Tiffany necklace with the heart pendant, a gift from Gavin. The $50 note she took from his pocket the other night is folded on the bed, and that homemade card from Mallie with a cupcake drawn on the front.

Dolly takes the necklace and drops it into the box. She closes her hand around the money, the papery reason why she has sex with that man every second night. The reason she puts an emotion she doesn't feel into her eyes when she looks at him, and wipes away the wet slide of him afterwards. He's only once mentioned the money that goes missing from his wallet every time he visits her room. 'I know you took something from me,' he said with a smirk on his face. But the next time he visited her at night, his wallet was still tucked into the pocket of his trousers, so she carried on stealing from him. Gavin is a small profit, that's all, a way to make a little extra. She puts the note into the box and lays Mallie's card on top of it.

'Come on,' she says to Sam. She puts the lid on the box. 'I need your help.' She inches the Minion away from him and lays it on the bed. It's impossible to keep anything private when there's no lock on her bedroom door.

In the kitchen, she puts some crisps into a bowl and Sam helps himself to one mouthful after another.

'Offer them to the ladies.'

She peeps around the door and sees Ma'am Amber's eyes raking Sam's messed-up clothes, his face.

'You still haven't got a live-in maid?' Ma'am Amber asks Ma'am Jules then.

'Er, no.' Ma'am Jules takes a stack of crisps from Sam's bowl.

'I don't know how you do it.'

'Well, there's only me and David.' Jules shrugs.

'But you work and there's all those floors. I mean it's just part of life here,' says Ma'am Amber.

Sam's bowl crashes to the floor, and splits into shards and scattered crisps.

'Oh, Sammy, you stupid boy!' Ma'am Amber shouts then laughs and covers her mouth. Gentler then, 'Such a dingbat!'

She gets up and takes his hand. He pulls it back again.

'Dolly, just take him out. He's bored.'

'Yes, ma'am.'

Dolly gets the dustpan and brush and sweeps up the crisps, the broken pieces of the bowl.

'Let's go swimming,' Sam says.

She walks into the kitchen and lets the shards slide into the bin. Sam yanks at her loose T-shirt.

'Please.'

Dolly takes Sam's hand and leads him upstairs, past the women who are all talking at once now; a laugh, a chink of a cup.

Inside the boys' room, Colby is pulling a book from the shelf unit pushed against the wall. He opens the book then drops it to the floor and pulls out another.

'Colby, do you want to go swimming?' asks Dolly.

'He had no clothes on,' says Colby, books in both his hands.

'Darling, I . . .' starts Dolly.

'Who had no clothes on?' asks Sam.

Colby drops the books one by one to the floor.

'No one,' says Dolly.

'Who?' says Sam, his chin tipped towards her.

'Leave me alone!' shouts Colby. His face reddens as he tumbles more books to the floor, faster now.

'Don't be cross, Colby,' says Sam. The younger boy lets go of Dolly's hand and touches his brother's back. Colby spins around, lifts Sam's hand and bites it. Sam screams.

'Stop it, Colby!' says Dolly.

She examines Sam's hand. There's a semi-circle of teeth marks on it. She rubs and Sam starts to cry. She picks him up, rocks him. The books continue to bump to the floor.

'It's all right, Sam,' says Dolly.

Colby mutters. She pulls Sam's swimming trunks from a drawer and walks out, Sam still in her arms. Dolly puts him down and they take the stairs.

Ma'am Amber is sitting on the edge of a sofa, back straight, a glass balanced on her thigh. The women stop talking, angling towards Sam whose crying is quieter now.

'Colby bit me!' he says.

Dolly touches her stomach. *Don't mention the word 'naked'. Just don't.*

'He's tired, that's all,' says Ma'am Amber. She pats Sam's hand then rises, picks up a plate of sliced quiche and offers it around.

Sam marches into Dolly's room and Dolly follows. They strip and get changed into their swimming outfits.

'That's my sister,' says Sam, pointing at the photograph on the pinboard screwed to the wall at the end of her bed.

'That's my Mallie.'

The girl is a baby in the picture, sitting inside a blue basin of water, a gummy smile on her face.

'You're my mommy, so she's my sister.'

'I'm your auntie, Sammy Bean, not your mama.'

'Mommy.' He hugs his little body against hers and she crouches and hugs him back.

'You're fat,' he says.

'No,' she says.

He puts his warm hand to her belly. 'Yes, you are.'

They go outside. The swimming pool is deserted apart from Ma'am Maeve sunbathing in a black bikini beside her teenage daughter, and the son who keeps jumping into the pool then climbing out. Ma'am Maeve must have declined the invitation to this month's book group.

Sam runs and jumps in. Dolly goes down the ladder, the water closing over her. She walks along the bottom, making circles with her arms and Sam swims away.

'Shit,' says Dolly.

He goes right to the end of the pool near to Ma'am Maeve's boy who tries a dive, narrowly missing Sam. Dolly gets out of the water and walks around the edge to be closer to him. He swims back towards the shallow bit, so she returns there and climbs back in.

'Just do your arms like this, Dolly. Take your feet off the bottom.' His separated eyelashes are wet triangles.

Dolly stretches out her arms, and lifts her feet just like Sam said. And for one perfect moment, she floats. Then her nose goes under the water and she sends her feet to the floor and coughs. Sam laughs.

'You did it, Dolly!'

She pulls him against her and turns him, his head going backwards to meet the water again. She lets him go then catches hold of his feet and makes a circle with him in the water.

'You're a mer-boy.'

At the end of the pool, the security guard is standing beside Ma'am Maeve whose wet hair is tousled and spiky. She is pointing towards Dolly and shaking her head. The security guard walks over to Dolly.

'Get out now!' he says in a protrusion of teeth.

'But I'm looking after the kid.'

'You need the swimwear.'

'I have.'

'You got on shorts. Shorts not allowed!'

Dolly sighs, climbs out and sits dripping on the side. Sam somersaults in the water.

The security guard goes back over to Ma'am Maeve and nods.

She says something to him then lies back on the sunbed and picks up her book.

⧖

Later, the book group women have left; it's only Ma'am Jules that remains. Dolly puts a plate of cheese sandwiches in front of Sam at the table. Ma'am Amber picks up Dolly's gift and reads the label.

'Thanks, Jules, I didn't realise this was for me,' she says.

Ma'am Jules says, 'Oh it's . . .' She looks at Dolly, and Dolly shakes her head.

Ma'am Amber rips off the paper. 'How lovely!'

The notebook is covered in little squares of different material, glitter, stripes and golden swirls. Ma'am Amber offers her cheek to Ma'am Jules, who kisses it.

'Oh,' says Ma'am Jules. 'You're welcome.'

On the way to the door, Ma'am Jules stops in front of a side table covered in the large books Ma'am Amber usually keeps in a cupboard: *A Hundred English Interiors*; *New York in Pictures* . . .

Ma'am Jules puts her hand on one of them.

'Oh, you must borrow that,' says Ma'am Amber.

'No. It's just, I've got one of Avedon's books at home.'

'At home? In a box somewhere, you mean. You must.'

'No, honestly.'

'Really, I insist.'

Ma'am Amber pushes the book into Ma'am Jules' hand and they start that awkward kissing all over again, then Ma'am Jules leaves.

Dolly picks up the dirty plates and watches Ma'am Amber climb the stairs with the notebook in her hand, Dolly's notebook.

When she's finished tidying, Dolly goes upstairs. Through the crack in the door to the master bedroom, she sees Ma'am lying down with a wet flannel over her eyes. Dolly goes into the boys' room. Colby is sitting on the floor, scribbling furiously on a sketchpad. The shelves are empty, books scattered all over the floor. Dolly sits beside him, takes the sketchpad from him.

There are grey pencil lines scored into the paper.

HELP ME.

She flips to the next page. The same words are printed there. She turns another page and another. The entire book is filled with the same plea.

She puts her arm around the boy. He leans his head against her shoulder and starts to cry.

Chapter 7

The doorbell is ringing. Jules reaches for the alarm clock –
10 a.m. There's a pain in her stomach; her knickers are wet. It
couldn't be, could it? Maybe the eggs are bedding in. She was
going to do a pregnancy test today. The bell rings again; they'll
go away. She heads into the toilet, pulls down her pants. The
gusset is red, sodden. There's no mistaking it; the IVF hasn't
worked. All $10,000 of it; the third and final time.

'Fuck,' she says, then grits her teeth.

They can't afford to do this again. Hell, they couldn't afford
to do it this time either. All their savings are gone. What a waste.

She pulls a Tampax from the drawer and pushes it in. The bell
continues to chime.

'Oh, fuck off!' she snaps then realises who it is. Her part-time
cleaner starts today. She grabs a pair of pants and some shorts
from an overflowing drawer. Pulling on a top, she rushes downstairs,
just as her mobile phone starts to go. She opens the front door.

'So sorry, ma'am. I didn't know whether you were in,' Tala
says, mobile phone in hand.

Jules steps back to let Tala in. Tala kicks off her flip-flops, a
faux diamond glinting where the straps meet, and lays her yellow
handbag on a chair.

'Thanks for coming,' says Jules.

Lines gather around Tala's eyes as she smiles. Her dress is
covered in sunflowers.

'Oh . . . Here, I bought some cleaning things,' says Jules,
gesturing towards the carrier bags in the kitchen.

Tala wanders into the small corridor off the kitchen. 'I'll change in here,' she says, pointing to the bomb shelter where Jules has propped the empty cases, half-unpacked boxes and a vacuum cleaner held together with tape.

'Okay, although it's hellish in there.'

Jules thought she might be different here with her belongings pared down, but she's still a calamity. She opened some of those boxes, pulled out her camera and its lenses then closed the boxes back up.

It hasn't worked. The thought thuds through her.

When Tala emerges again, her dress has been replaced by a brown vest and beige shorts. She is carrying a bucket and dusters. Jules bites an apple and pulls up one of the floor-to-ceiling blinds on the wall of windows that look out over the grounds and swimming pools. Tala, dusting the wall-mounted television now, stops.

'Erm, ma'am, I don't want anyone to see. Please.'

Jules stands still, the apple in mid-air.

'I could get into trouble if anyone sees me.'

Jules swallows the chunk of apple and pulls the blind back down. It unreels, the base of it clattering onto the floor.

Tala picks up one of the photograph frames and wipes. When she dusts down the photograph of Jules' parents clinched together on some Lake District hill, Jules has an urge to go through the house, hiding personal items: the face mask by the bed, the used panty liners in the upstairs bin. And that tub of discarded syringes; what a complete waste of time. But then there are worse things. So having kids isn't for her; she'll find something else. But what? She can't see herself going back to midwifery, delivering other women's babies when she knows that she'll never have one herself. If she goes back to being a midwife, it'll destroy her, won't it? But if she doesn't go back, all that training, everything that made her who she is, will be gone.

She runs through the corridor, past the spare room and upstairs. Dropping the apple core into the bin, she picks up the bucket of syringes and throws them with a clatter to the back of the cupboard.

'Bastards!' she hiss-whispers.

She goes into the adjoining wet room, and stands in front of the mirror that covers the whole of one wall. She pulls the pregnancy test out of its plastic cover and tries to snap it in two. It doesn't break, so she tries again, gritting her teeth and snarling. It splits apart, rectangular plastic and white fabric pinging out. She drops the pieces into the bin, creases up her face for crying, but nothing comes. Her hair is straw and she pulls at it, pulls hard, and it feels good hurting herself like this just for a moment. She could do with some chocolate, a whole bloody bar of Galaxy. Or a bottle of Sauvignon Blanc all to herself. But she did that the first time it failed. Self-pity just left her with a hangover. She smiles to herself – an apple this time around, my God, she's being restrained.

She walks into the upstairs living room with its thin marble table against one wall, an L-shaped grey fabric sofa against another. Her surgery uniform is heaped on the sofa, her name badge on the table. She clicks on her MacBook Air laptop. Images of singers and bands in David's iTunes collection cover the screen. She shuts it down and opens her Instagram account. The picture of that dockworker in an orange boiler suit, staring and holding his hard hat, has been liked fourteen times. She uploads her best pictures into the Cloud, and shares her favourite one: that close-up of Dolly and all those earrings, the tattoo on her shoulder.

She adds a caption: *#HelperSingapore*.

She goes out onto the decked balcony and pulls one of the wooden chairs into a thin slice of shade. Amber is lying beside the swimming pool, face down, her bikini unclipped so that her striped back glistens in the sun. Maeve is at the other end of the pool engrossed in a magazine. Jules is surprised the women are seated so far apart. Aren't they meant to be friends? Sam is playing in the shallows, unwatched. Jules stares at them, Amber twisting her ankle in the air, Maeve blotchy and still.

She goes downstairs where Tala is standing on the kitchen worktop wiping a cloth along the overhead dish drainer, the contraption that Jules bashes her head on whenever she washes up. Tala shuffles along and starts polishing the expansive sliding window.

Jules imagines the window opening, Tala slipping and toppling and crashing to her death. Oh, Christ, she can't stop herself.

'Be careful up there.'

'So sorry, ma'am.'

'Don't be sorry; just don't fall.'

Tala turns and laughs, her smile bright white. It makes Jules want to smile too. What is it about the woman? She's only been here for half an hour and something in Jules feels a bit better, despite the ache in her gut, despite another failure. Fertility Friends. Just Get Pregnant.com. Why did she even bother looking at those sites? Why did she pretend to herself that she might just get lucky? She checks the window is locked, starts to walk away then rechecks it.

She goes into the downstairs bathroom and rearranges the bottles around the white sink. She paces.

After a while, she goes down the corridor and finds Tala in the guest bedroom with its double bed pushed against a wood-panelled wall. There is a photograph of Jules' niece as a baby in Tala's hands, and a series of nonsensical sounds are gurgling out of Tala's mouth.

She looks up and smiles. 'Is this your daughter?'

'My niece,' says Jules.

'You have children?'

Not today. 'No.'

Tala's eyebrows shoot up. She carries on dusting. Jules stands there trying to level out her breathing. Thank Christ for David's older sister, Rach, who's a veritable baby-making machine. Jules' niece and three nephews have relieved some of the pressure from Jules' clucking mother-in-law, Beryl. Jules' parents, on the other hand, bought her insistence that she didn't have time for a family. They didn't press her, even though she was their one hope for grandchildren – the only thing Jules' younger brother Steve would be adding to the family tree would be more reptiles to keep his snake and two tortoises company.

'When are you going to get yourself a baby?' says Tala with her back to Jules.

'Oh, we . . .' Jules takes a shallow breath. 'We're happy as we are.'

'Better not leave it too long.'

'Listen to you.' Jules laughs, but she's not smiling. 'Do you have children?'

'I've got myself two boys, but they're all grown up now. I'm about to be a grandmother. And there's my sister's daughter too.' Tala pushes the duster into the grooves of the panelled wall.

'Oh, right. Yeah.' Jules nods then walks out of the room.

She goes upstairs, back out to the balcony, and takes the free expat magazine out of her bag.

Amber is gone from the side of the pool. Maeve is still there, now in a wide-brimmed straw hat. There are several empty sunbeds arranged at jaunty angles. A woman walks barefoot along the path, cut-off white shorts, with a tassel of frays, making her legs look browner still. Clouds billow across the blue sky.

A man's laughter cuts through the air. It's David down there in his work clothes. What's he doing back so early? He's dragging his feet, loping along with his head bowed. She watches him pass Dolly who is pulling her fingers through her long black hair. Dolly keeps her eyes on David as he passes.

Jules steps inside and rereads the article about the babies who need foster care. Fostering isn't something she's considered before, but adoption is. She requested information from three adoption agencies after her second IVF failed. She scoured the pages of those adoption brochures – all those photographs of sibling groups and children over the age of five, but it was a baby that she craved. She'd helped deliver hundreds of infants, all that maternal effort, all that fatigue, then, later, the wild-eyed jubilation. She wanted all of that: the unconditional love, the cradle cap, the sore and leaky breasts. She'd do anything for a baby of her own, yet her body kept letting her down. 'There are other ways,' David said more than once. After each failed IVF, they spent hours talking about other possibilities: surrogacy, donated eggs and always, finally, adoption. Maybe all of this was pushing her to that place. Maybe fostering could be a trial run.

She's going to do it; she's going to volunteer. It would be nuts, wouldn't it, to look after a baby, especially in this aftermath? Then again it would be another distraction, like the photography. She picks up her mobile phone and dials.

'Kids' Refuge!' says the voice on the other end of the line.

'It's . . . erm, I saw your advert, I mean, article in the *Finder*. And I'm interested in volunteering.'

'We're always looking for volunteers. Have you seen our website?'

'Er, no.' If this is a test, perhaps she's failed on the first hurdle.

'Well, all you need to do is fill out the application form. Just click on the downloads icon.'

'Okay.'

'Can I take your name?'

'Yeah, it's Jules, Jules Kinsella,' she says, then blurts, 'Well, Jules Harris actually. And, er, I'm a midwife.'

'Oh, that's great . . . Most of our volunteers don't work though.'

'I don't work, not really.'

'Well, put your number on the application form and we'll take it from there.'

'I'd like to do it as soon as possible.'

'Right, okay, well I've taken down your name, and I'll note that.'

Jules ends the call and pushes the phone into her pocket. She types the web address into her computer. David is coughing downstairs. On the home page is a pair of tiny feet enclosed by a man's hands, which are bent into a heart shape. Phrases flash up: *Pregnant and alone. You don't know how to care for the baby* . . . She downloads the form and begins to type. She proofreads it six times then hits send. Her mobile phone vibrates. She scrabbles around in her pocket.

Are we still meeting for coffee on Wednesday? Please reply ASAP!

It's Amber again. What a control freak, but then what with Colby and her depression, Jules should give the woman a break.

Of course, types Jules, even though she's a tea girl all the way.

She picks up her camera and heads downstairs. David is sitting on the sofa, leaning forward and typing into his phone.

'Oh – Jules!' he says and starts scratching his head.

'You're home?'

'I thought . . . I thought you were working today,' he says.

'No.'

'It's, er . . . There wasn't that much to do at the office, so I thought I'd come home early.'

'Oh, yeah?'

Tala starts humming a tune from another room in the apartment. The melody filters into the room.

'Who's that?'

'Our cleaner. She started today.'

'Oh.' He sighs.

She sits beside him. 'What's going on?'

'What? God, Jules, you don't look well at all.'

She sighs loudly. 'It hasn't worked.'

'Shit.' He folds his arms then unfolds them, covers her hand with his own.

'You were so positive, but I knew it wouldn't,' she says.

'So we'll try again.'

'We can't go on like this.'

'It'll work . . . eventually.'

'I'm finished. Done.' She moves her hand away from him, balls it in her lap.

'Then we'll try something else.' There's a note of hysteria in his voice. David, who's always so careful to shield her from what he really wants.

'You're going to think I'm nuts,' she says.

'What?'

'I've volunteered for this fostering charity.'

'Oh?' His eyes widen. 'To do what exactly?'

'To look after a baby.'

'But why would . . .?'

'Apparently unmarried mums don't get the same benefits as married mothers here, so if you're poor and unmarried and you don't have the support of your family, you might have to give the kid up.'

'Oh, God. When's this going to happen?'

'I've just put my name down.'

'And could we adopt a baby?'

'I'm not sure.'

'Because you know, we said we'd think about adoption; that was going to be our next step.'

'I know . . .'

'I mean, we'd be capable of loving a child that wasn't actually related to us, wouldn't we?'

'But adoption could well be full of disappointments and stress. They could turn us down, then what?'

'Or they could approve us.'

'I just keep hoping a miracle will happen, that we'll get lucky, that we won't have to go through all of that.'

'And what about all the kids that are going through hell? Parents who can't care for them, people who abuse them; I bet they're hoping for a miracle too.'

She feels the despair squeezing her chest. Tala walks into the room then.

David gets to his feet. 'Hi, I'm David.' He puts on his upbeat radio DJ voice. He stretches out his hand.

Tala shakes it, looking up at him with a big smile on her face. 'Tala, sir.'

She chortles, points to the kitchen then wanders off out of sight.

David turns to Jules again. 'This could be the start of something else, Jules.'

He stands there looking at her with a face full of sympathy.

She manages to raise a smile. 'Well, I'm sure we'll have to jump through loads of hoops before they let us do this fostering thing anyway.'

He pushes a strand of hair behind her ear, kisses her then heads out of sight down the corridor, his footsteps on the stairs. She picks up her camera and fiddles with it.

When Tala comes out of the bomb shelter in the sunflower dress again, her shopping bag is on her arm, glasses on a chain around her neck along with a gold cross catching the light. Jules doesn't ask; she fumbles with the lens then shoots. The camera takes about twenty photos in a row.

'Oh my Gad!' shouts Tala, smacking her hand to her chest.

'Sorry, I didn't mean to give you a fright.'

'What are you taking pictures of me for?'

'Because . . .'

'Well?'

Tala puts her hand on her hip, stands there with her legs wide apart. She pushes her hair behind her ear, lowers her shoulders, touches that cross. 'Not that it's such a problem,' she says and forces a thin laugh.

'You just look so, I don't know, so happy.'

'Me, happy? Oh my Gad.' Tala throws her head back and laughs a real laugh of mostly white teeth, a couple of black fillings at the back.

'I'll see you next week,' she says, shaking her head.

The front door closes behind her and it's as if all the light has been sucked from the room.

Essential House Rules for Foreign Domestic Maids

Rule 3. Food: Your maid should keep her food in a separate cupboard to yours, so she doesn't get confused about what she can eat. For example, I drink Illy coffee which is far too expensive to share with my maid.

Chapter 8

Ma'am Jemima's blind dog, Malcolm, skids towards Tala, barking. Ma'am Jemima strides through the hall.

'Oh, Tala, you're here. Look, I've got a business meeting in thirty and Malcolm, my poor bubba, is desperate for a walk.'

'Yes, of course, ma'am.'

Tala pins the pretend smile to her face so hard her cheeks hurt. Maybe Ma'am Jemima's what you call glamorous, but Tala has never seen an outfit like this before. A white suit with red volcanoes at the hem of the sleeves. Ma'am Jemima's staring face is a question mark, and Tala realises her own eyebrows are flying in the air.

'You look like Michael Jackson,' says Tala.

Ma'am Jemima is quiet for a long time after that.

In the utility room, Tala changes into her beige clothes. Armed with her cleaning arsenal in a black bucket, she shuffles around Ma'am Jemima who is still standing in the hall gazing down at her failed haute couture.

Ma'am Jemima walks away then, zips open her make-up bag and starts a frenzied application of mascara at the gilded mirror.

The dog, floppy brown ears flapping, tongue wagging, wraps its legs around one of Tala's and starts rubbing.

'Disgusting!' says Tala then adds, 'Oh, Malcolm, darling, I'll take you for a walk soon.'

Bad things said about Malcolm are bad things said about Ma'am Jemima, and Tala mustn't pour salt into an already stinging wound. Ma'am Jemima turns to Tala and smiles, a thick black line around her lips. *My God.* Tala hopes she hasn't said that out loud. Tala shakes the dog free, trying and failing to cover up its yelp with her own high-pitched laugh.

He scampers over to Ma'am Jemima who bends to him, puckering up. He jumps and touches his black nose to her lined lips.

'Ooooh, my baby bubba. Mummy's going to miss you. See you next week, Tala!' she says. 'Oh, by the way, there's a box of things there that I don't use any more. Take whatever you like from it.'

The heavy maple door shuts behind her, Malcolm howling. Tala's cash is already there on a side table. Underneath the table is a cardboard box. Tala crouches, knees cracking, and opens it – just out of interest. It's bursting with colour: a green bag with white dots, a high-heeled pair of white sandals. A yellow shirt with a bow, and other things. She leaves everything inside and closes up the flaps.

The house is like a black and white film. Photographs, white walls, white fabric and enormous windows. Ma'am Jemima's got some high-flying job that involves words like 'bottom line' and 'securities'.

Tala isn't sure why anyone would want to look at so many photographs of themselves, but there she is, perched on the end of a rock in some canyon, hiking boots on. In another, she's soft focus and snuggling Malcolm. Why that lady ever got the dog is beyond Tala. She spends most of her time working and that little mutt – what is he, a shih-tzu or something? – is cooped up in here all hours. Tala's never been much of an animal lover, if the truth be told. They had a dog on the farm when she was a child, but cats and dogs like this excuse for a canine were never her thing.

She passes a photograph of Ma'am Jemima cross-legged on a stool, airbrushed to the point of lifelessness. The smooth-skinned lovely in this picture doesn't bear any relation to the real thing with her thinning hair and lined face. Despite this, she oozes a confidence Tala admires. 'I'm a single gal,' she told Tala when they first met. Cradling Malcolm in her arms, and cooing, 'My bubba,' she had kissed his nose and whispered, 'Mummy loves you,' into a pricked-up ear. Then there was that time when she told Tala how she lets Malcolm sleep on her pillow. 'Aaaah,' she said, 'his little lipstick pops out in the morning.' *My God, that woman's in need of a man.*

Tala goes into the study with its two computers. She doesn't risk switching either of them on, but fans through some of the papers on the desk. Vanda's bound to write notes for her blog posts after all. Numbers, and bills; old copies of *TIME* magazine. A folder marked 'Private'. Tala flicks through that one, but there's just more paper containing numbers.

She spots a notebook with a big 'J' on the front of it and opens it. *Ideas for holidays.* And what's this here? *The Help. Hilly. Vanda.*

Vanda? Could Ma'am Jemima be the one? When Tala finds out who Vanda really is, and gathers enough proof, she intends to expose the person by posting their name on her blog perhaps or writing a letter to a newspaper. That would shut the person up for good hopefully.

There's a scrape of claws at Tala's calves and she gasps.

'Get down now!' she shouts at Malcolm. He tilts his head, a fringe of fur in his redundant eyes.

She refocuses on the papers, trying to remember how they were arranged. She moves them about a bit.

Ma'am Jemima, could it really be her?

Tala marches into the kitchen and spoons jellied meat from a tin. It doesn't smell so good. The dog guzzles. She fills a metal bowl with water and sets it on the floor. She ties her hair back and cleans. She polishes and sprays, but the smell of dog persists. She lays a plastic poop bag on the counter and clips the leash to Malcolm's neck.

She needs to get herself a glass of water, so traps the handle of the leash under her foot and reaches up. She stumbles, takes her foot off the handle and it shoots towards the dog with the force of a cord being sucked back into a vacuum cleaner. Malcolm does a little gallop through the air on impact.

They go outside, walk past gates with steel flowers climbing up them. Over a fence, Tala sees a swimming pool, a statue of Buddha and a porch lined with plastic chairs. Malcolm pulls on the lead and there's a wham as he collides head first with a tree trunk. They step along pavements, cars parked on the edge, and places where bricks spill onto the tarmac. They walk through the heat of the day.

Tala's cheeks go pink when she thinks of Caroline reading her blog. Caroline said other women were looking at it too. Tala smiles, then remembers what Dolly said about how easily the Ministry could find out who Maidhacker is. Her stomach starts to churn.

A Western woman in a fat black stripe of sunglasses holds her mobile phone towards Tala and makes it click.

Oh my, someone from the Ministry has come for me already.

'That should do it,' the woman says.

Tala stands there, bracing herself for the plastic cuffs.

'Because it is just appalling,' the woman continues. 'And I've got the photographic evidence here.'

The woman, in her Jesus sandals, moves closer to Tala now, her yeasty breath on Tala's face.

I'll just delete my blog posts. No harm done.

The elasticated lead pulls at Tala's arm. Looking down, she sees hard brown pellets underneath Malcolm. The toenail on the woman's big toe is sinewy and speckled with a fungal infection.

'No, I'm sorry, I'm fed up with this. Who do you work for? I want their name and address.'

'I'm going to pick it up.'

Tala pokes her hand into her pocket, but the plastic poop bag isn't there.

'Really? With what exactly?'

Tala takes a step backwards, so the woman can't breathe on her any more.

'I've seen it so often, you girls letting dogs foul the pavement. Well, this one's going into the rogues' gallery.'

'What?'

'The Vanda blog. You girls never listen and it's just unacceptable, so bad.'

The word 'bad' floats there and takes aim.

'I'm good,' says Tala. It's as if someone has turned the gas of her anger up to full. She is pointing a stiff finger towards the woman's face.

'Well, it is bad,' the woman says.

'Don't call me bad.'

'I want your address.'

Tala stares into the sunglasses. She sees her own trembling yet defiant face reflected back at her. She turns and walks away. The dog unmoving, pulls her backwards.

'Well, someone will recognise you when I send Vanda this picture. You people.'

Tala jerks on the lead and trudges up the hill, feeling the woman's eyes on her every step.

Later, Tala finishes up in Ma'am Jemima's house. Malcolm jumps up at her, whining. Poor little ball of fur. She goes out of the front door and manages to close it without sandwiching Malcolm between it and the door frame. How many hours will he be in there alone?

Tala walks up the road and the bats swoop low around her head. Her size fours in the flip-flops are wide, but so pretty with that 'Ignite the Night' nail polish on them. Appearances can be deceiving though. People have been complaining about the smell of her feet her whole life. She's tried everything: talcum powder, witch hazel; she even plunged them in bleach once.

Just accept yourself for who you are. Russell Grant's astrological voice drifts into her head. And he's right because her feet are not for changing. Although he did say she was heading for a big change with her moon opposite Venus. God, she wishes her moon were anywhere but here. Change. Maybe her blog can make changes. Showing people that domestic helpers are not all like Vanda says.

Tala gets on the bus and snoozes, but her head falls forward and jerks her awake. The cars are thick across the four-lane highway. A woman in white clogs crosses the road. Tala rubs at the goosebumps on her arm from the overactive air con then gets off and trudges through the grounds of the tall yellow Housing Development Board blocks.

That budgerigar is flapping around in the outdoor cage. And here comes Rita with her ma'am's new baby.

'Things any better?'

Rita shakes her angular head. Tala's nostrils flare. She looks into the pram.

'How old now?' she asks, putting her hand to her mouth to stop those ridiculous sounds she makes when babies are around.

'Six weeks, so cute,' says Rita.

'And the name?'

'Angel.'

'Oh, the poor child.'

Rita laughs through her gappy teeth.

'At least she didn't call her after a country,' says Tala. 'I mean, India, I ask you.' She reaches her hand in to the wide-awake baby and gives her cheek a gentle squeeze. 'Hello there, Philippines. How are you doing in there?'

The toothless baby yawns.

'Sssssh,' says Rita, smiling. 'I'm trying to get her to sleep.'

She wheels the pram away. The woman's like a walking skeleton with teeth to match.

Tala takes the lift and opens the door, releasing a fug of

day-old pork-rib soup. The house is silent apart from the hum
of the fridge. Mrs Heng will be staying late tonight at her
daughter's apartment, a forty-minute drive away in Pasir Ris,
something she does every week. Tala climbs onto a chair and
gropes for her logbook and computer on the high-up cupboard
shelf. She adds Rita's name to her logbook of maids' complaints.
There's Marifé Mendoza whose ma'am slapped her face four
months ago, and Lydia Ramos who left her first job after the
husband of the house pinched her bottom. And all the others;
there are pages of names and gripes. She closes the book now
and switches on the computer.

The Skype opens automatically. A few seconds later, chimes
sail into the dusty room: Ace is calling. She clicks and there in
front of her is his smiling pockmarked face. Someone is moving
around in the background.

'Hey, Mama!'

'Did you get the job?'

'More than twenty other people went for it. What were the
odds?' shrugs Ace, his arms out at either side.

Tala tries not to think it, but it gathers inside her anyway: he's
Skyping to ask for money, and how can she refuse when her first
grandchild's so close to being born?

'You did go to the interview?'

'I'm trying.' He looks away. 'Really.'

He leans back, puts his palms behind his ponytailed head. His
T-shirt has a face on it with angry eyebrows and a speech bubble
that says 'POW!'. Her nostrils flare; he could have been top of
the list of twenty if he'd stayed on at school.

Before Tala has a chance to speak, he gets up and moves
towards the person in the background. He pulls her into view.
Alice. She is blinking rapidly, refusing to look at the screen. Her
nose is an arrow pointing downwards.

'Alice,' says Tala. 'How are you feeling?'

'I'm fine, Lola, thank you.'

Lola? What the . . .? Tala won't be a grandmother until this baby is born.

Ace moves his girlfriend sideways. 'It's a girl, Mama.'

'What?'

'We had the scan, and—'

The screen is fizzing with black and white specks. Tala bangs hard on the top of the old computer, but it doesn't make any difference; they've been cut off. It's probably another one of those Tagudin power cuts. It certainly can't be a fault with Ace's computer, which she bought for him six months ago with her savings.

She tries Skyping his number, but it cuts off, so she logs on to her blog instead. Oh my. Her first post about spy cameras has been liked 307 times. There are five comments waiting for her approval before they go up on the page.

The heat rushes to her face, and a silly smile swells. Then she thinks of Rita, stops smiling and starts typing.

MAIDHACKER'S BLOG:
What It's Like to Be a Domestic Helper

Let Them Eat Cake!

Singapore women with their size 0 clothes and feet the size of a Barbie's are enough to give Western women expat-orexia.

As any Filipina who's gone shopping with her Western Ma'am knows, the question, 'Do you have this in my size?' is often met by the answer, 'We don't do XXXL.'

Here's what follows:

– Silence.

– The creaking of weighing scales behind the closed bath-room door.

– Your ma'am complaining about the too-large portions you serve (I get these complaints all the time, but that's another story. Let's just say, I won't be doing a recipe special on this blog).

– And, if you bake cakes, you'll become enemy number one.

Mind you, there's no such thing as Filipina-orexia. We may have backsides and guts of various sizes, but most of us come in extra small.

And, let's get physical – all that cleaning and shining, vacu-uming and washing of cars, well you're going to need a whole lot of calories to keep on going. You'll turn as thin as the paper your contract was typed on if you don't.

The other week, Vanda featured a post about just how much food an employer should give a maid. Well, boss ladies, a bowl of rice for dinner is not enough.

If that's all you give her, your maid will end up having to see a doctor and you might not be too happy about paying that medical bill. Your maid's miles per hour will plummet. Clean the house top to shiny bottom in four hours flat? Forget it. And it'll be impossible for your maid to keep that wash-ing-powder-white smile stretched across her face.

Helpers need protein. Nuts, cheese, meat – you name it – to keep that smile real. Remember, flat moods can catch (not mentioning your peri-menopause, ma'am).

And since you've probably gone right off those Bread Society
specials all because of that upsetting Orchard Road trip,
there's no point in letting those yummy delicacies go to waste.
So, boss ladies, let your maids eat cake.

She hits 'post'.

☒

There's a noise in Dolly's ears like she's sinking in deep water.
She clicks off Maidhacker and swallows. Her mouth is parched.
That's Tala, a badly disguised Tala. Dolly should have worked it
out before.

She heads up to the ground floor, her pulse jabbing her neck.

Ma'am Amber is in the kitchen area, filling a glass with water.
The bottom of her nose is shiny with snot, her cheeks patched
with red clouds. She is muttering a mantra over and over again.

'I am not my mom. I am not my mom.'

She's wearing a dark green silk nightdress, an eye mask in her
hair like an Alice band. She pushes a pill out of a blister pack,
puts it into her mouth and swallows.

'Ma'am, are you all right?'

Ma'am jumps. 'Oh, you gave me such a fright.' She shuts her
hand around the pill pack, shakes her head and walks away, up
the stairs.

Dolly grabs her pink handbag from her room and goes out of
the front door, past the swimming pools, and into the hot, dark
street. Bats flicker around a lamp post as she climbs the hill. A
bus spins past. She breaks into a run, her flip-flops slapping
against the concrete. She makes it to the stop just in time.

She climbs on the bus and sits. She can't see anything out of
the window, just her own worried face staring back at her, her
earrings glinting. A woman with false eyelashes holds a silver
compact up and applies some bright red lipstick. Dolly takes her
mobile phone out of her bag to distract herself.

Have you taken care of it yet?

It's him again. He hasn't come to her that often this last week. She deletes the text message. The journey seems to take forever. She bites her nails then presses her hand to the glass along with her nose. Eventually, she dings the bell and gets off, runs through the HDB gardens, and raps on the window of Mrs Heng's apartment.

It's in darkness. Is Tala out? Dolly knocks harder on the glass then walks towards the yellow wall with the air vent in it, behind which is Tala's room.

'Tala! Tala!' Dolly says in a voice that's far from loud. Footsteps are muffled through the front door. It opens. Dolly recoils. Mrs Heng stands there, a pair of pink pyjamas sagging around her skeletal frame, a yellow hairnet pulled low over her forehead.

'This is *ta ma de* ridiculous. It's eleven o'clock at night, girl!'

'I'm so very sorry, Mrs Heng.' Dolly bundles past. 'It's just, well, I need to speak to my sister.'

Dolly doesn't bother to knock on the utility-room door. She goes into the hot, dark room, fumbles around for the light switch and shuts the door behind her. Tala is asleep on the mattress in a long grey T-shirt with pink toilet paper sticking out of her ears.

Dolly shakes her shoulder, and Tala sits bolt upright, her eyes blinking in the shock of light.

'My God, Bong!' Tala shouts.

Dolly pulls the toilet roll out of one of Tala's ears.

'You're Maidhacker!' hisses Dolly.

'WHAT?'

'You're the author of that damn blog.'

'Keep your voice down!' Tala bellows.

'Sssh!'

Tala fights with her other ear. The tissue ends up in her hand. 'I don't know what you're talking about.'

'Do you realise what a risk you're taking?'

'Oh, my sweet God, you woke Mrs Heng?'

Tala leaps out of bed then, practically cartwheeling. She opens her bedroom door and peeks out. She stays there for some time then closes the door again.

'You mustn't mention this to anyone, Dolly.'

The two women stand facing each other. Dolly takes hold of both of her sister's hands.

'I'm not going to tell anyone about this, but Tala, no one else can find out. The Ministry can't be looking for you yet because with their power, they would have tracked you down by now. But you've got to stop this.'

Tala folds her arms. 'I'm not stopping.'

'You always have to have the last word in an argument. Why can't you just keep quiet for once?'

'Someone's got to stand up to that Vanda.'

'But Tala, you could get thrown out.'

'Girl, the way that stomach of yours is expanding, I'm not the only one who's going to get thrown out.'

Dolly opens her mouth to speak then closes it again, looks away.

'You *tanga*! My God, whose is it?' Tala blesses herself not once but twice.

Dolly shrugs. 'I've been seeing someone, but he doesn't mean anything to me.'

'You're sleeping with someone you don't even care about?'

The colour drains from Dolly's face. 'He's . . .'

'What?'

Dolly grimaces, shakes her head. 'I don't want to talk about him, Tala.'

'It's Sir Tor, isn't it?'

Dolly's chest fills with air. 'Of course it's not Sir Tor! I've been seeing an expat man from the condo. Gavin.'

'Gavin? Australian Gavin? Ma'am Maeve's husband?' Tala's face screws up. 'Oh, my God, are you going to tell him you're pregnant?'

'I already have. Anyway I'm getting rid of it.'

'What are you talking about?'

'I've bought some pills.'

'You should have been more careful.'

'It's too late; it's done, but what are you going to do about this blog?'

Tala sniffs.

'They could put you on the first plane out of here when they find out. You have to stop, Tala; you must.' Dolly glances around the room. 'Where's your computer?'

Tala finger-combs her hair, looks at the high-up cupboard and shrugs. Dolly climbs onto the chair and reaches up. There's a scrape of books, then it's there in her hands, the battered black laptop.

The two women sit on the bed and Dolly switches it on. She clicks onto the internet, and *Salamin,* the Filipino newspaper site, is the home page.

Who is Maidhacker? We are offering a cash reward to anyone who can reveal the identity of bolshy blogger Maidhacker.

'Shit!' says Dolly.

'What?' Tala squints.

'You're front-page news.'

Dolly retches, covers her mouth with a hand. Tala reaches for her glasses and puts them on.

'Oh, my heavens and hells,' she says.

'You've got to delete that blog.'

Tala logs on to Maidhacker's statistics page and the two women look at the screen then back at each other.

'My God, I think it's too late for that,' says Tala.

The number of blog visitors rises before their eyes like a stop-watch.

Chapter 9

Jules loads her latest pictures onto Instagram. That bloke flying a kite at West Coast, a black and white snake tattoo coiled around his arm; the close-up of that Filipina woman at the market, two of her bottom teeth missing. The woman had laughed when Jules showed her the image on the little camera screen.

And here's me with my luminous gnashers. Jules had the braces put on two years ago. None of those Invisalign whatsits, she'd gone for the full-on train tracks followed by whitening. When they were removed, David kept shielding his eyes when she smiled. 'That bright white Colgate smile,' he'd said.

'I'm off.' David comes into the room now, birds chittering beyond the window.

She doesn't look up, her back slouching into a curve.

'Jules?'

He crouches, takes her face in both his hands. 'How are you doing?'

She takes a long, slow breath. 'Yeah, oh, I don't know.'

'I could stay.'

'It won't change anything.'

Someone raps on the front door. David goes downstairs, answers it. She follows.

Amber is standing there in an orange shift dress, a splodge of mascara underneath her left eye. 'Hello, David.'

'Oh, hi.' He turns to Jules, hugs her, whispers into her ear: 'I'll come back early.'

'Don't be daft. You don't want them giving you the elbow this early on.'

Lines go into his forehead, his Adam's apple bobs. 'Right, yeah.' He laughs, but it's forced. He goes outside and presses for the lift.

'Come in,' Jules says to Amber.

Amber steps inside. David and Jules stare at each other. He walks back to her, smoothes her hair away from her face. The lift doors spring open, and he leaves. Jules goes inside.

'A coffee would be nice,' says Amber.

'Instant?'

'I'll have herbal tea.'

Jules flicks the switch on the kettle.

'We don't have to do this,' says Amber.

Jules coughs into her hand.

'What I mean is, if you don't want to see me, it's fine. I have plenty of friends.' Amber twines her finger around her ponytail then flicks it over her shoulder.

'I'm not sure what you mean,' says Jules.

'You've been avoiding me.'

'I haven't.'

'It's obvious. You saw me the other day waving at you. You went the long way around the pool, so you didn't have to speak.'

'Did I?' asks Jules.

She thinks back. The stork painted on the window of one of the town houses. The woman who lives there has just had a baby. Jules chose the longest route out of the condo, so she wouldn't have to walk past.

'There are ways of handling it when you don't feel like talking. You could just say, "Hi." You don't have to be rude.'

Jules' third and last IVF has just failed, and this woman is clinging to her like a life raft. Then Jules thinks of the Lustral.

She clears her throat. 'Well, I'm sorry if you thought I was rude.'

Amber's palm is flat in the air. 'No matter. I'm not one to bear grudges.'

'The thing is, I'm . . .'

Amber is shaking her head, her face taut. 'No, I won't hear any more about it. How have you been, anyway?'

Jules plasters a smile across her face. It fades.

'What's wrong?' asks Amber.

'I'm . . . it's . . . I thought I was pregnant.'

Amber's mouth opens, her eyes go wide. She takes two steps towards Jules. 'And?'

'And, I'm not.'

'Oh, oh goodness, Jules, I'm sorry.'

Jules nods, waits.

'Have you been trying for long?'

'Years.'

'Oh.' Amber stares, opens her mouth to speak again, but decides against it. Jules could let the silence hang, but there's such a hopeless look on Amber's face that she doesn't.

'I was doing IVF.'

'You could try again,' Amber blurts in a breathy voice.

Jules shakes her head. 'We've tried it twice before. It doesn't work. For us.'

'Well, take it from me, children aren't all they're cracked up to be. And they're expensive. I dread to think of all the money we'd be spending if we had to pay the school fees.'

Jules slings a chamomile teabag into a mug and pours in the hot water. She hands the mug to Amber.

'Anyway, thankfully Sam seems to like school, whereas Colby . . . Maybe he's like me – I didn't fit in at school really.' Her eyes drift.

She looks at Jules again then. 'Oh, but I am sorry it's not happening for you. Maybe if you just relaxed, tried not to think about it for a while. You hear of all sorts of stories like that.'

Jules kneels on the red woollen rug to retrieve Amber's

photography book from under the sofa. 'Look, I don't want to talk about it any more. Here's your book.' She brushes off the dust.

'I love the way Avedon shows the rawness of people,' says Amber.

'Not so keen on the bare willies though,' says Jules.

Amber's laugh cuts through the thick atmosphere. She sits on the sofa and sips her tea.

Jules' stomach growls. 'Oooo, excuse me.' She presses her hand there.

Amber smiles. 'You're hungry.'

'Well, maybe a bit.'

'Don't let me stop you.'

Jules moves across the open-plan living room into the kitchen area where she pulls open a cupboard, takes a paper bag from on top of a pile of plates. Inside is a hard doorstep of bread. She opens the fridge. Three discarded grapes lie saggy in a tray. A tipped-over jar of pesto sauce sits in a greasy puddle on a glass shelf. She didn't bother eating anything yesterday, and David must have used up the last of the salad. She needs to go to the supermarket. She sits on the sofa, but her stomach won't let up.

'Why don't we go for lunch?' says Amber.

'What about your herbal tea?'

Amber puts it onto the floor and stands. 'We'll get something at PS Cafe.'

How bad can having lunch with Amber be? thinks Jules, grabbing her bag.

Inside Amber's four-by-four, the smell is musty, as if an orange is gathering mildew, hidden and forgotten. A crisp bag lies empty and wrinkled in the corner of the footwell. A string of banana is stuck to the space behind the shifter stick. In the back of the car, a child's seat is peppered with crumbs. Amber climbs in, picks up a glass bottle and sprays a mist of lemon air freshener.

'Forgive the mess,' she says, hauling the door shut. 'And the smell for that matter. When you have boys, you have to put up with sneaker rot.'

Amber pulls off her wedges, lets them topple onto the floor in the back. She turns the key and swings the car out. The roof of the car park presses down on them. They climb the steep hill to the road then turn on to the highway.

Jules sees a child climb from the back of a silver Mercedes into the front seat beside his mother, who doesn't have her eyes on the road. A blue cab speeds over the black and white stripes of a crossing just as a woman in outsized black shades steps into the road. She shakes her fist at the driver as he passes.

Amber's painted toenails are splayed on the accelerator. There are no gears to change. She indicates to pull over and the car in the parallel lane speeds up to stop her crossing.

Amber turns her car into Dempsey Hill. She sighs; the car park is full. She tries another one lower down the hill, and reverses into a narrow space. When Jules gets out of the car, she has to squeeze herself flat, pressing against the steel for freedom.

They walk over a pathway towards a large white concrete box of a building, with floor-to-ceiling windows, and trees clustered around it. Jules and Amber sit at a square black table outside.

A waitress sets down a jug of water and two glasses. Amber pours. The table tilts, making the two glasses of water scrape towards Jules who catches them both. How her stomach aches.

'We should ask them to put something under here. It's that leg,' says Amber.

Jules can think of nothing to say, so stares into the distance, the slanting hills of trees, the blue sky. Inside, the restaurant is all copper counters and stripped wooden floorboards.

'You have to make instant friends here,' says Amber. Her smile is strained.

'Yeah,' Jules says, thinking about the embryos bleeding out of her still.

'You need to have at least ten friends, so that if one goes, you've still got other people.'

'Sounds like stock control.'

The lid of Amber's eye is twitching. There are grooves in her cheeks that weren't there before. Has she lost weight?

Amber orders a bottle of white wine. When it arrives, she swills her glass and sticks her nose in. She drains half the glass on her first swallow. The table wobbles; Jules wedges her knee against its leg to hold it steady. She looks at the menu and chooses the quinoa salad.

'So, erm, have you seen much of your friend?' asks Jules. It's coming to her, she thinks. 'Maeve.'

'I don't see that much of her.' Amber forces a smile.

'Oh, I thought you two were as thick as—'

'I beg your pardon?'

'Good friends, you know.'

'Who are your friends?'

'Well, there's David . . .' Jules contorts her face, and Amber laughs raucously.

Jules forces a smile.

'And me,' says Amber.

Jules puts her hand around her wine glass then reaches for a tumbler of water and drinks that instead. 'So do you like living here then?'

Amber thinks for a moment. 'It's hard being away from family, but it's easier with the children. You know, with the help.'

Square plates of food arrive and Jules presses her elbow on the table to stop it tipping. She pushes the salad around her plate, watches Amber load tuna into her mouth. Amber fills her glass again. Jules sips at her own.

Two eggs, thinks Jules, *just two. No wonder it didn't work.*

Amber's fork chinks on the plate. For the first time, Jules notices that the top part of Amber's little finger is missing.

'Oh, my amputation,' says Amber. She balls her hand. She

pushes the food into the corner of her mouth and chews with exaggerated nods of her head.

'What happened?' asks Jules.

'King William, that's what happened.'

Jules narrows her eyes.

'My older brother. We used to fight like cat and dog. He slammed a door shut on my hand when we were arguing. Valerie popped the top of my finger into a plastic bag with ice, and called the paramedics.'

'Valerie?'

'Our Mexican live-in. Anyway, my poor little pinky didn't make it, and William didn't even apologise.'

'God.'

'Oh, shoot, it all happened a long time ago.'

They both carry on eating. Jules presses a hand to her stomach. So much for running away from London, thinking she could escape the longing for a child of her own. Her desperation is stronger than ever.

'So what brought you here?' asks Jules.

'Tor's job. Colby was just a baby – he's never known anything else. Lord help us if we ever have to go back to Chicago.'

'You must get bored though.'

'I do quite a bit for charity. And Tor doesn't want me to work.' She breaks into a smile. The mascara splodge is still there under her eye.

'So . . .' ventures Jules. 'How did you two, you know, get together? You worked at the same place, didn't you?'

The laugh again. A woman in a green satin dress, sitting at a table further along, turns to look.

'It was a works night out. An Elton John concert. I kept on thinking how uncomfortable Tor looked, shuffling his feet, clicking his fingers.'

Elton John? Jules can see David throwing his eyes to the ceiling about that one.

'At work, Tor always had his head buried in papers. He seemed terrified of me to be honest.' Amber gives an airy laugh.

Jules swallows hard.

'I'd drunk quite a lot that night and the moment took me,' continues Amber. 'I could feel him behind me and I turned around and hugged him and . . .' She straightens her knife and fork on the plate.

'And you knew he was the one?'

Amber takes a large gulp of her wine.

'Well, there wasn't anybody else!' says Amber.

'Oh,' says Jules. 'But he's a good bloke, Tor. Kind,' says Jules.

Amber screws her face up, the lines gathering around one eye. A triangle of disagreement cuts into her top lip then she looks away.

⌛

Dolly climbs onto her bed, feels along the overhead shelf. She picks up the pills, wrapped in foil, and sits.

The photographs pinned to the corkboard on the wall at the end of her bed smile down at her. Mallie in a pink dress, her eyes looking skywards, her mouth open with laughter. When the midwife had put Mallie into Dolly's arms for the first time, the love had been instant; the years they'd spent apart had only thickened it.

Dolly has been nursing fantasies that she wouldn't have to take these pills, that some miracle would happen like finding a big wad of cash on the ground or someone walking out of a crowd and saying, 'You're going to be the Next Top Model.' She kept waiting, willing, but nothing did. She's left it until the last moment to do something, and here is that last moment.

Her health check is weeks away. It's this or be deported. It's this or giving one of her kids a life that's second best, a life she doesn't want either of them to have.

She's hungry, the way they used to be sometimes before Tala left to work overseas all those years ago. The way Mallie might feel if Dolly were to lose this job. And there's no knowing what's going to happen to Tala now she's writing that damn blog.

No, this is the right thing, the only thing. Dolly pushes down like she's trying to give birth; if she'd just start to bleed. She pushes the pills out of the foil, two white circles in the palm of her hand.

'I'm sorry.'

She puts both the pills onto her tongue. They start to disappear.

Somewhere in the sky there are the strains of thunder. Jules runs towards Amber's four-by-four. The car lights flash. Jules gets in, already soaked through. Amber slams the driver's door, face flushed, and starts the car.

The rain patters against the windscreen, hesitantly, then insistently until the wipers can do nothing to clear the deluge.

Amber doesn't see the river of water collecting in the road; either that or she doesn't care. She speeds through it, spraying glassy arcs of water. Her car soaks two pedestrians, one woman fighting with an inside-out umbrella, the other with a plastic carrier bag on her head.

The rain raps against the car. The wheels whoosh and turn over the flooded road. Amber doesn't slow down. Jules imagines skidding, the car catching the kerb and ploughing into the open drain lining the road.

She holds tighter still.

Tala picks up the notes that Ma'am Maeve has left for her on the side of the kitchen worktop and lets the front door close behind her. The rain lashes through the lobby grilles, soaking her feet.

Tala takes the lift to the ground floor then she's out, sopping and sliding around in her flip-flops. There's a river of water gushing along the pathways, chopping at the swimming pools. This won't do. She's got to get to the front of the condo, so takes a right and goes down the steps into the underground car park. She'll walk this way, so she doesn't get any wetter. She pulls her T-shirt away from her skin; it sounds like a noisy kiss.

Rain spills through the air vents on the ceiling of the underground car park. A cab clunks around the corner, its sound bouncing off the low ceiling. Tala steps into a wide driveway, walled by pillars, where there's a table tennis deck and stacks of toys, a bike, a doll and a playpen. The cab passes and turns behind a wall and she steps out again and under another leaking vent. She wipes at her dripping forehead.

She looks at the numbers on the doors: 37, 38. She's lost. God knows how she's going to find her way out.

⧖

Dolly drinks from a water bottle, but still her mouth tastes bitter from the pills. A chair scrapes along the floor in the nearby living room. She stands and goes towards the noise.

Colby's cheeks are red; he's wearing swimming trunks, shorts with seahorses, and a toggle at the front.

'What are you doing?' she asks.

'I'm looking for my towel. I left it here,' he says.

His school uniform is heaped on the floor. He drags the squealing chair.

'Just be still, darling.'

'I'm not your darling. I just want my towel.'

'But your mama said you can't go swimming when there's a storm.'

'You're not my mom.'

'No, but she said.'

Sam is watching, cross-legged on the marble floor in the corner of the bright white room.

'I'm going,' says Colby.

'Not on your own, not now.' She stands against the oak front door.

'Yes, I am.'

'But it's raining.'

'I saw you and my dad, so don't tell me what to do.'

He runs at Dolly. The back of her head bumps the door and she falls. There's a warm smell up her nose. Sam starts to cry.

'Stop!' Dolly shouts.

Colby pulls at her hair. When he lets go, he looks at her and shakes his head.

'Do you love my dad?'

'No,' she says.

She gets up off the floor to go to Sam, but he's gone from the room. The whole house is silent until Colby screams his brother's name.

Jules holds tight to the car door as Amber negotiates and fails to take the sharp right into the Greenpalms underground car park. The car's too close to the bollard.

'Honestly!' Amber snaps as she reverses and tries again. It is the first time either of them has spoken during the journey.

Red capillaries weave across Amber's cheeks; her nose is flushed. They twist through the clean, concrete walls of the car park, right underneath the swimming pools, paths and condo apartment blocks. The rain finds its way down here too, gushing through the grilles in the ceiling, gathering in puddles on the ground.

'I could drop you back at yours, save you walking in this,' suggests Amber.

'No, it's okay,' says Jules, already knowing she'll lose her way in this underground labyrinth with its mailboxes and lifts, but she's eager to get out of the car. The journey has made her edgy, her neck stiff, her shoulders hunched. She just wants to be on her own for a while.

Amber turns off the wipers just as another waterfall surges onto the car. She pushes the stick into reverse without looking back as if she's made this manoeuvre a thousand times before.

'We should do this again,' Amber says, her eyebrows raised in request.

Jules zips up her bag.

There's a thud. The car has hit something.

The white car pulls forward again. There's a blurred blue shape on the ground behind it. Tala moves as if through tar, and sees it clearly then: the T-shirt, creased and rising over the little belly on the ground. My God, it's a child.

And Tala is roaring and slamming on the windscreen with all the force of someone trying to shatter it into a thousand pieces.

Time is long and slow. The grey eyes of the driver stare at Tala, skin sucked tight over her jaw. Tala thinks that, in a moment, she'll take two steps back and look at the damage. 'A broken blue toy,' she'll whisper and apologise, and hope that she never sees this woman again because her mistaken panic will be so embarrassing. Yes, she's made a mistake; that's why the woman in the passenger seat looks so puzzled and the driver is frowning at Tala with barely concealed fury. But it slices through Tala's head again: there's a child back there knocked to the ground.

The driver's hand twitches at the dashboard. She must have turned off the engine, but Tala is deaf to the pitch change. Tala moves sideways, sinks to her knees and reaches her right hand towards the bare flesh of the small still boy. The heat rises from his skin. His bloody face is twisted against the wall. Tala clutches her outstretched trembling hand with her other one.

A woman with long brown hair drops to her knees beside Tala now, pushing her head down towards the boy. It's as if someone switches off Tala's mute button and the sound comes back.

'No, no, no,' the woman wails. 'Don't die.'

The front door of the car is open, and with a jolt Tala realises that this woman screaming is the driver. High-pitched screaming like an animal trapped in wire. Then she notices the passenger, her hands now pulling on the woman's shoulders, but the woman stays put. *The passenger is Jules.*

Jules is whispering soft words to the woman on the ground then she says, 'I worked in a hospital back in London, remember I told you? Let me take a look at Sam.'

Sam? Dolly's Sam? Jules catches hold of Tala's upper arm and pulls her to standing, then Jules climbs onto her knees beside Sam. That's when Tala realises that the driver is Ma'am Amber; a shrivelled-up, grey version of Ma'am Amber.

The boy is too still and Tala cannot look at him any more in case some negative thought flies out of her and snuffs out his last chance. She pulls her eyes away from him, and there is the back door that he must have come out of, painted grey and patterned with white scratches. The back door that opens straight into the basement of Ma'am Amber's town house. The boy must have seen his mother returning in her car yet she didn't see him. Dolly is standing on the steps in front of that door now, horror animating her blotchy face. The seconds slow and stretch on and on, and Dolly stares at the car, a tear spilling over the rim of her eye and drawing a line down her cheek.

From under the car, Jules says, 'Tala, phone an ambulance, please.'

All the things inside Tala's handbag clatter to the concrete. She fumbles with her red metallic phone, but there's no signal down here. She runs past Dolly, through the door that opens too slowly and up stairs that take too long to climb.

Chapter 10

Blood is pumping from Sam's forehead. Jules touches his neck.

She had thought they'd scuffed a supporting column, or hit a pet perhaps. Inside Amber's car, the bump had been a small one, yet Jules had felt it all the same.

The smell is like split raw meat. She hears Amber's voice, a sudden battery of noise as if Jules has been underwater and now come up for air.

'Just make him all right,' says Amber. 'I'll do anything.'

Jules bends her ear to the boy's blue lips. His eyes are closed.

'Sam, can you hear me?' she asks. There is nothing, but the sound of Amber's hoarse sobs.

'Sam, can you feel my hand?' asks Jules, touching his face.

Nothing comes back, so she pinches his cheek hard between her fingers and the boy quivers with a faint gasp.

She glances at Amber beside her, then clambers backwards. She pulls her T-shirt over her head then climbs under the car again, pressing the white fabric against the blood on the boy's forehead. Establish baselines, she thinks, and tells Amber to press the fabric instead of her. But Amber is shaking so much that when she tries to apply pressure, her son's head begins to tremble too.

'It's okay,' says Jules, lifting Amber's streaked fingers from the blood.

Jules presses the T-shirt against Sam's head herself. With her other hand, she pulls open first one eyelid then the other to check the size of Sam's pupils.

'Amber, have you got a torch?' Jules asks. She wants to see if Sam's eyes react to light.

'I don't know. Maybe,' mutters Amber.

'You need to get it,' says Jules, but Amber doesn't move.

'Now!'

Amber stumbles away, her orange dress smudged dark in places, and the basement door clatters behind her. Jules fingers the boy's scalp, the hair wiry and white. There is a soft, jelly-like pad behind his right ear. She takes the boy's unsteady pulse. Seconds become heavy. Has Tala called the emergency services, summoned them to the right place? Jules wants to trust Tala, but still the ambulance doesn't arrive. Jules stands, looks up and down the car park, but there is nothing.

The ambulance will be here any minute, she tells herself. It's like that recurring dream of hers where she keeps dialling the emergency services, but can't get through. Jules kneels again and examines Sam's still bleeding forehead. She feels cold, yet the heat in the air has started to build again. The boy's right ear is burning red, a terrible contrast to his icy skin.

'Everything is going to be all right, Sam,' she says.

Minutes stretch. Jules is numb with the waiting. Her heart batters. Then a siren blares around a corner, just at the moment Amber returns, the torch in her hand.

Jules takes the torch and shines it into each of Sam's eyes. Amber kneels on the ground beside her and whimpers.

The ambulance grinds to a halt. A paramedic climbs out, a woman in a navy uniform. She takes the T-shirt from Jules' hand.

'What happened?' she asks.

'That car hit him,' says Jules. 'He's breathing, pupils equal, severe cut to his forehead, swelling behind the right ear.'

The woman speaks in Mandarin to her partner, a man whose hair is standing on end like a fibre-optic light. He drops a canvas bag to the ground.

'What's his name?' the woman asks.

It's Amber who answers in the smallest of voices: 'His name is Sam.'

The male paramedic pulls a pad from the bag and fixes a swab to the boy's head. The paramedics, both with gloves on, exchange more words. The man holds his fingers against Sam's neck then unleashes a rigid cervical collar. He takes a stretcher from the back of the ambulance. Together the paramedics and Jules move Sam onto his side. The woman touches the beads of his spine.

They lower him to the stretcher then and hoist it into the back of the ambulance. Amber is on her feet now, her arms outstretched and trembling. Standing on a step just below the ambulance doors, Jules hovers her hands beneath the stretcher in case the boy falls. Then she gets out of the way and pushes Amber hunchbacked into the ambulance, slamming the doors in her wake.

The ambulance roars away, then grinds to a stop. It reverses to negotiate a pillar then drives off at speed. Jules hears the siren stir in the not too distant road.

Her fingers are shaking. It makes her think of the way David steadied her hand as she lit the candle in the church the day they married, the Catholic church even though neither of them had been since they were teenagers. And all that stuff the priest had said about going forth and multiplying. Christ.

Pipes line the low-down ceiling. Her bloody T-shirt is scrapped on the ground. Blood is pooled behind the car. Dolly is standing on the concrete, staring at the four-by-four, Tala behind her on the steps leading to the basement door of the town house.

The lunch weighs in Jules' stomach like guilt. Everything should be left as it is; the open door of the car, the blood.

She walks towards Dolly, turns the woman, stiff in her arms, and they walk up the steps as Tala stands aside. Jules tries to think of something to say, but her head is muddy with questions.

Dolly refuses to go through the door. Jules' arm strains and falls as the woman walks two steps back down and plants herself there, resting her head on the wall. Tala sits beside her then, their shoulders touching.

The air catches in Dolly's throat. 'Is he dead?' she asks.

Jules paces the floor. She is wearing a T-shirt Tala found for her, two sizes too small, its multicoloured stripes straining across her chest.

Colby is sobbing, his mouth open, tears and snot glossing his face. He sits on the sofa then gets up and paces.

'It was an accident.' Dolly puts her hands on both his shoulders, but he turns his head away from her.

Tala has a hand on her hip, and fiddles with the gold cross around her neck. Colby shakes Dolly off and bashes his head against the wall. The energy leaves him then and he sinks to the floor, his crying quieter.

'Come on now,' says Dolly. She looks up at Jules. Her eyes are red.

Jules goes towards the boy and crouches. 'Can you copy me, Colby? Breathe, okay? Slowly in.' She fills her chest with air. 'Then slowly out.'

The boy follows her movements over and again.

'Better?' asks Jules.

Colby gulps at the air then gives a vague nod. There's a scab on his knee that's slightly septic. He stands, his swimming shorts falling down, revealing the crack of his backside. He's as pale as milk. Dolly leads him up the stairs, holding his hand.

Jules sits on the sofa. *Of all the shit days.* The sofa sinks; she turns to see Tala sitting beside her.

'You're a nurse, ma'am. I mean, what do you think?' Tala's voice is so quiet, it's like someone else is speaking.

'I'm not a casualty nurse, Tala; I'm a midwife. I just deliver babies, that's all.'

'Just? My Gad, you're a midwife.'

Sitting this close to Tala, Jules can see the lines around her hazel eyes, the different tones, the flecks of light.

'I so hope he's going to be all right,' says Jules.

'Dolly's looked after that boy his whole life.'

Tala's touching that cross, her eyebrows knitted together. Feet pad down the stairs. Dolly stands over them then, her hair in a tangled knot at one side. Tala presses on her own thighs to heave herself out of the seat.

'Sit down there, Dolly,' she says.

She takes Dolly's arm and Dolly ends up doing a sort of run. She falls backwards into the sofa.

'How are you doing, Dolly?' asks Jules.

'Ma'am Jules is a midwife,' says Tala.

'Just call me Jules.'

Their eyes are fixed on her. When she mentioned what she did for a living, it had that effect sometimes, but it wasn't like she was anything special.

'You saved his life, ma'am. She saved his life, Dolly. Still, I expect that's all in a day's work for someone like you,' says Tala.

They stare. Jules gets up, fills a glass with warm tap water and turns to them. 'Want anything?'

Tala shakes her head. Dolly keeps staring at Jules without saying anything. Tala goes to sit beside her sister, loops an arm around her shoulders.

'What happened, Dolly?' she asks.

'Colby gets so angry,' says Dolly. 'He was hitting out at me. And Sam was crying. He just ran off. I've tried talking to Ma'am Amber about Colby before, but she won't listen.'

The phone shrills. Jules walks across the marble floor to it and freezes. She's scared to pick it up. It rings six times before she does. Colby is standing on the landing now, on the threshold of tears.

'Hello,' Jules says into the receiver.

'He's got two linear fractures in his skull.' It's Tor's voice, deep down the line.

'He's going to be okay though, right?' ventures Jules, looking up at Colby who has paused, halfway down the stairs.

'Lord, I hope so. The doctor says the fractures, they're not putting pressure on the brain, so Sam won't need surgery. They say they'll heal.'

Jules is nodding towards Colby.

'He's going to be okay,' calls Jules, edging her mouth from the receiver.

'Is my mom there?' asks Colby.

'Can you put Amber on?' says Jules.

Colby patters down the stairs. Dolly shakes silently on the sofa, Tala squashed in beside her. Colby cries, the phone pressed to his ear. He pinches his nose, shakes his head.

'He's there because of me,' he says.

Jules puts her arm around him. He's crying even harder now. Jules takes the phone from him.

Amber is sniffing. 'Would you stay with Colby tonight?' she asks, a voice full of phlegm.

'I will, of course, but Dolly's here.'

'If she'd been looking after them properly, none of this would have happened.' Her voice rises in waves.

'Something happened, Amber.' Jules looks at Colby standing there, and Dolly bent over. 'It was no one's fault. Sam just ran out.'

'I didn't even see him,' Amber wheezes. 'My little boy.'

'Don't,' says Jules. 'He's going to be all right.'

'God, I really hope so.'

'We'll speak to you tomorrow,' says Jules. 'But just call my mobile in the night if you need me, okay?'

'Thank you.'

Jules puts the phone back into the stand. Tala wiggles over to Colby.

'Come on, boy,' she says. 'Let's go upstairs and find a book for you to read. Take your mind off things.'

Colby doesn't argue and the pair climb the stairs.

⧖

Dolly can't sleep. She started to drop off once, but then there was the concrete with the blood on it, and the car. And Sam might die. What if Colby mentions what he saw? What if Ma'am Amber sacks her? And, what about all her plans for Mallie's future?

She gets up and goes out to the hall where the washing machine is. It's loaded with unwashed clothes and she pulls out some things, underwear and tops, and socks. She finds a sock of Sam's, sits and sniffs. She breathes it in then stuffs it down her top, so it's a comfort to her heavy heart.

She holds it there.

This feels like when she was a girl. A few blades of rice stuck up through the water. She and Tala took what little they had, all wrapped in canvas, and they walked up hills, along thin tracks. They walked until their feet were sore, the dust up their noses, inside of them. There was something heavy about Tala. Her hand was clenched around Dolly's, short fingers, rough palm. She was stooping.

They walked into the shop and the owner didn't smile when he looked into the canvas bag. He shook his head. 'I've dropped the price I pay,' he said. 'You've got to be joking, man!' Tala said and put a hand to her hip. But her fire went out as she stood there. Her sparky eyes and her high-pitched voice turned to smoke.

When Tala left for Hong Kong a few weeks later, Mama told Dolly to stay inside, but she watched as Tala hugged the boys. And she wished Tala was her mama, strong and young and funny.

Tala wrote. Pages scored with loopy letters, the lights, the smells, the sounds. She'd been good with words since she'd been at school, which was where she'd learnt English. Back then, Tala's parents could afford to send her, but when she was twelve, money became scarce and Tala had to leave school early. She carried on writing anyway, filling notebooks with stories and dreams. Dolly didn't go to school at all and when it came to Tala's sons, she had to choose which one to send. Since Ace showed promise in languages just like her, Tala chose him. Dolly took one of his books from his bag once and hid it at the bottom of a katmon tree. His foot was hard on her backside, the air over his head fat with all those words he was learning.

Then when Tala came home, Dolly's eyes went to her bag and took in the T-shirts and sweets. And she thought about the places Tala had been, Hong Kong and Singapore, and all the things that she could do, the freedom. Dolly wanted to open her arms like wings. She wanted something more than sitting in people's houses and waiting for Tala to come back. Was it then that she knew she'd become a maid too? She'd only become one with Tala's help, though, because how could she afford the airfare? She knew that Tala would help. Dolly got distracted however, and instead of fixing her eyes on leaving and getting a job, she fixed her eyes on Nimuel.

She'd walked to the Green Market, took the way through the woods. She heard whooping. She kept still and quiet, and she crouched. Men were splashing around in the water, dunking each other down. One got out and climbed onto a rock then dived in. Dolly was so set on looking at him that she didn't notice the crunching, the steps, then there he was through the trees, Nimuel, stocky and naked with this smile on his face. He walked towards the water looking over his shoulder at her, the caves at the side of his buttocks, the ripple of his sinewy calves. She smiled back. They met under trees, in an empty nipa hut, his place when his father was out.

She got pregnant soon after. Mama slapped her face so hard it turned her head sideways when she found out. 'Stupid girl!' Mama shouted, her plump pink cheeks wobbling, her short black hair bluntly cut. Six weeks later, Dolly couldn't even keep water down. She wanted to lie in the dark and be still; she wanted the time to disappear because all there was was the vomit and the churning. She was thin and dry and emptied out, and Mama said: 'That baby's going to die if you don't get some food inside you.' And Tala phoned and Dolly stood there beside Mama in the village shop as Tala shouted, 'The baby's going to die? Dolly's going to die first if you don't get her to a hospital.' It was Tala who paid. Dolly clutched the man on the scooter as he drove her to the hospital.

Dolly was on a drip for two weeks, but her mouth was metal until Mallie came out. Tala came home for a week when Dolly was six months gone. 'No way you're going to give birth at home,' she said. 'You're going to hospital.' 'But the baby is the right way round; there's no complications,' Dolly said. And Tala said, 'What kind of crazy person are you? I've already paid the bill. And I'm not cleaning all day just to throw money into the wind.' Tala eyed Nimuel, smirking in the chair. She gave him some aftershave and patted his hand, but it didn't do any good. Four weeks before Mallie was born, he left. Mallie arrived in a room with other women pushing beside Dolly. And it was quiet and much sorer than Dolly thought it would be, and she had imagined the worst kind of pain.

It was a good beginning, but then it was payback time, so Dolly left and joined her sister because it was Dolly's turn. It still is; Tala shouldn't be here now. And she needs to leave before someone finds out about Maidhacker.

Dolly's glad she's taken those pills. They should be working. But she hopes this baby is the only one that loses its life today.

'She didn't even see him,' says Jules. 'I didn't see him.'

David takes the cushion from behind his back and puts it beside him on Amber's white sofa.

'I'll stay; you go up to the apartment, get some sleep,' he says. 'The last thing you need is spending the night on someone's sofa.'

'I'm all right, David.'

He smells of shower gel; his hair's still wet, standing on end.

'I wondered what was going on. Police tape all over the car park, and you weren't back. God, I had a really bad feeling about it.'

Jules hears a creak upstairs.

'This is a total mess,' she says. 'You might as well go back up to the flat; no point in you losing sleep too.'

'I'm not leaving you here.'

'But the child . . .'

'What, Sam?'

'Colby. I just don't want him kicking off again.'

'Shall I bring anything else down for you?'

'No, it's okay.'

She looks at the pale stripe of her belly underneath the too-small T-shirt. She takes it off and reaches into the carrier David has brought. She pulls a vest top on. Something falls upstairs.

'Well, I'm going to keep my phone on,' says David. 'Just call and I'll come back.'

They both stand; he hugs her hard and plants a dry kiss on her cheek, but she tugs him by the arm towards her and grinds her mouth against his. He pulls away, avoiding her eyes.

Some part of her sinks when he leaves without a goodbye. She stands there staring at the door. Things between them had been better; they are better, but something's off with David. Lights leach through the blinds. Just what is Jules doing here? Dolly's perfectly capable of looking after Colby. It's like Jules is keeping guard, and none of this is Dolly's fault.

But whose fault is it?

Amber had drunk about half that bottle of wine at the cafe; she must have been over the limit. She'd driven erratically on the way home, silent and concentrating, keeping her foot on the accelerator, unworried about skidding on the flooded road. Had Jules been speaking to her as she reversed into the parking space beneath the town house; had she done something to distract Amber? Had she upset her? Amber had a lot on her mind what with Colby, and the Lustral. She'd called Jules a friend, but she hadn't confided any of this to her.

Women in the ward, Jules' friends, they'd often say she was a good listener. 'You've got such empathy; couldn't do that job of yours if you didn't.' That was David. But she wasn't doing the job any more, so maybe she'd stopped being a good listener. Had Amber tried to speak to her about Colby? Jules had been so caught up in her desperation to be pregnant that sometimes her mind would drift to the possibilities of her own baby's face while people were talking. Everything felt inconsequential compared to that.

If she'd been paying more attention, perhaps she might have done something to stop what had happened. Suggesting Amber lay off the wine. Telling Amber not to drive. Urging her to drive more slowly.

Christ. Her stomach aches. The Ibuprofen is in her bag, still in the car parked on the concrete where the blood is. Blood is smeared across her knickers too. She's never going to have kids. That's it, a future gone. She would have been a good mum; she's sure of it. She'd had enough practice with all those nursing mothers and their babies. And David is never going to be a dad. He's so good with kids, too. When their niece and nephews were round, there were obstacle races in the garden, trips to museums, science projects and pictures, paint smudged on the stripped wooden floors. David has all the makings of a *Blue Peter* presenter, or a dad.

'Stop it,' she says.

There's a child in the hospital on the edge of death and here she is feeling sorry for herself. There are worse things, much worse.

It's different to the first time she tried IVF when she felt like she was entitled to a baby. Everyone else had one, so why not her? All those comments. 'It'll be you next'; 'You must be feeling the pressure'. It was like being stabbed when people said things like that, especially pregnant friends.

There'd been four follicles, not the ten she'd hoped for, but there was still a chance. There were people all over those fertility chat rooms who'd had a small number of follicles and went on to have a baby. She was only thirty-two; she should have had time left. Two of the eggs had fertilised. The doctor, with a craggy scar over one side of his face, had pushed them back in. A fortnight later, she didn't need a test to prove it hadn't worked; the evidence was right there in her knickers.

Of course she and David had argued. She can't remember what he'd said now, but it had been the wrong thing. And she'd picked up one of his Adidas trainers and lobbed it at his head.

The doctor said her egg reserve was low and rage had swelled from her chest to her head. She'd gone home and dropped three glasses onto the kitchen tiles. Good ones from The Conran Shop, ones that David had chosen. He bought *Livingetc*, did the house out in coir matting and Balzac sofas whereas she was more of an Ikea girl. Functional will do; that was her motto. She'd rather spend her money on sunny holidays and going out. The smash of those glasses into pale blue shards was satisfying.

They'd tried a second time and she'd got a single egg. The test had been negative. This was the last time.

She'd been a midwife since she was twenty-two years old. She loved the ward smell – some green kind of soap; the elation in the eyes of most of the women – wide open, electric. Everything raw and beginning. There were stillbirths, and shocked reactions to Down's, but no amount of watching other people's grief had taken hers away, and hers was nothing compared to such things.

Then there was that woman on the trolley bleeding out, miscarrying, crying, the skin around her eyes puffy. And Jules had felt jealous because that woman lying there, at least she'd managed to get pregnant in the first place. From a window of St Thomas' Hospital, Jules stared across the river at the Houses of Parliament and pulled off her rubber gloves. That was an ugly thought, cruel. She didn't want to do this any more, couldn't do this, not when she could think such things. She wasn't upbeat, energetic Jules Kinsella any more, with her empathetic smile.

It's no good, she's going to need to find some painkillers. She goes into the kitchen, opens the cupboards and peers in. Nothing. She tries the drawers, rows of sparkling knives and forks and spoons, silver placemats and tablecloths. No junk drawer, no oddments, no mess.

She goes upstairs and turns into Amber's room. Things are less neat in here. Clothes sticking out of the wardrobe, bottles higgledy-piggledy on top of the dresser. The bed is made; cushions in shades of purple and blue are arranged in angles over the pillows. It all seems a bit designer untidy, like an interiors magazine shoot full of French antique furniture.

'Aspirin; paracetamol,' she says out loud, trying to assuage how weird it is to be looking around Amber's bedroom, but this is a mitigating circumstance.

Then again, with a five-year-old in the house, maybe Jules should be looking for pills in a place out of reach. She goes into the en-suite, decorated in slate tiles just like the bathrooms in her apartment, and opens the mirrored cabinet. It's packed with skin lotions and make-up, tubes of antiseptic, and toothpaste pumps. There are two electric toothbrushes. She smoothes her hand over the top of the cabinet. Her hand gathers dust, and there's a box there. Lustral. She opens it; the blister packs are empty. The date they were prescribed was just a fortnight ago. Has Amber been overdosing?

Something creaks next door and Jules freezes. It's not like she's snooping, though; she's just trying to find some blooming painkillers. She puts the empty packet back where she found it and goes in the direction of the noise.

The door to Colby and Sam's room is ajar. A dim bedside light is on, casting balloon-shaped shadows onto the ceiling. Colby isn't there. On the bottom bunk, there's a tumbled quilt and a collection of haphazard felt-tips. She shuffles through the mound of A5 cards on the bedside cabinet. The top one is covered with black lines. She turns it around to get a better look, but there's no mistaking it, that's Amber: a pointed chin, a sheet of dark hair, a face without eyes.

There's a painted clay figure on the bedside cabinet too. It has a hanging mop of hair, a noose in all its stringy detail around the neck. There's a plastic label at the bottom: *The Forgotten Prisoner.*

Jules looks under the bed, behind the door, then she opens the wardrobe. There he is, Colby, in a pair of blue pyjamas, his feet high against the wood, his eyes bloodshot, clothes dangling on hangers above him.

'He's going to be all right, you know,' she says.

Colby doesn't look at her.

'I didn't mean it,' he says.

'Budge up,' she says and climbs into the wardrobe too, her back against the wood, feet pointing towards the bedroom, some piece of hanging fabric bunched on her head.

A clock is ticking somewhere. Colby starts jigging his leg, adjusts his position then bats an elbow sideways, touches his head.

'It was a pretty upsetting day,' tries Jules.

Colby carries on fidgeting, doesn't say anything.

'The pictures out there, they're good. Did you draw them?'

'Yep.'

'Some of them are a bit scary.'

'I'm scary too.'

'Are you? You don't seem scary to me.'

'I scare me.'

'How?'

'My heart goes fast. I shake.'

Jules nods.

'Don't tell anyone,' he says.

'Well, where I work, there are lots of people who come and see us, saying they feel like that sometimes.'

'It's all the time.'

'But Dolly knows, right?'

'She tries to help me.'

'And your mum?'

He shrugs. 'Don't tell her though.'

Jules squeezes one of his jumping feet.

'Dolly should be my mom. Daddy likes her a lot. One night I opened her door and Daddy was in there on top of her. He had no clothes on.'

Holy shit. Jules tries to arrange her face into something approaching understanding.

'Did you tell your mum about this?'

He shakes his head. 'I said to Dolly that I'd seen the man, and she said not to say anything to my mom.'

'Fuck.' Jules clears her throat. 'I mean, flip, that must have been weird.'

Dolly and Tor; she can't see it somehow. The bloke might have been good-looking when he was young, but he's all Aramis after-shave and stray hairs now, big clumsy feet and legs splayed to the side when he runs. And under those linen shirts is a pair of man boobs. But if he's having an affair, why is it that Jules feels sympathy towards him? Amber is just so bloody icy and controlling. Oh, but stop; the woman's son is in hospital for God's sake. And there's no way gentle giant Tor would be bedding Dolly anyway.

'I'm certain that wasn't your dad in Dolly's room, Colby.'

'It was.'

'Did you see his face?'

'It was quite dark, but I could see his bare back.'

'You can't be sure it was your dad then.'

Colby shrugs.

'It was probably someone else. Maybe Dolly had a friend to stay. Honestly, there's no way that could have been your dad.'

The boy's chest is rising and falling too fast.

'I think you should get into bed, Colby. Try to breathe like I showed you earlier.'

He gets up and climbs into the top bunk.

'I can stay if you like,' she says.

He shakes his head

'Well, I'll be downstairs if you need me.'

Downstairs, she sits in the living room, running her fingers over the smooth heels of her feet. She's wired – the accident, the failed IVF, and now this revelation. Of course, the boy is mistaken. But all that stuff he said about scaring himself. She's going to have to tell Amber and Tor about it, and soon.

She opens the fridge and takes a bottle of wine out. She pours two inches into a glass and drinks. What a mess.

The curtain separating the kitchen from the short hall to Dolly's room hasn't been pulled across. Light spills into the kitchen from Dolly's room. The sisters aren't getting any sleep either then. The house is quiet. She takes another sip, replays the moment of impact. She asks herself the question again: was she speaking to Amber just before the bump? Did Amber turn to hear what she was saying instead of looking back at where she was reversing? Was Amber drunk?

Two linear fractures in his skull.

Jules drinks some more wine. Something patters. Then it comes again, a little louder. She sets the glass in the sink and wanders to the front door. Through the peephole, she sees a man outside, watermarked by the glass.

She opens the door.

'I'm sorry, I . . .' he starts, eyebrows raised.

It's him, that bloke, she thinks, remembering him shrugging

as he walked from Dolly's room on the night of the party, the curtain flapping behind him. Maeve's husband, Gavin, the blond hair sitting thinly on his scalp, the once-broken nose stretched above an uncomfortable smile. He is neither attractive nor ugly, his body a sum of asymmetrical parts. His arrogance holds her gaze.

'They're still at the hospital,' says Jules, even though she knows it isn't Amber and Tor he's come to see, not this late at night.

He must be the man Colby saw in Dolly's room that night.

'She's not here,' Jules says.

Gavin's mouth hangs open; he laughs. 'I don't know what you—'

Jules doesn't give him the chance to finish. She shuts the door, turns the lock and rests her back there against the wood.

Just what is Dolly playing at? And yet, the man, Gavin, is the one creeping about in the dark, betraying his wife, taking advantage.

Her pulse quickens in her ears and when she looks through the tiny glass hole again, there is nothing but hard walls and pathways and the darkness beyond.

Essential House Rules for Foreign Domestic Maids

Rule 4. Looking After Children: Your maid must not scold or beat the children. It's her place to cook, and watch over them, not to point out whether they are right or wrong.

Chapter 11

Tala opens her eyes and the knots of her neck press into the concrete floor. Light from the kitchen window pours through the open metal door. Mallie as a baby looks down from Dolly's wall, all pudgy cheeks and tiny teeth sticking up from the gums.

Tala puts her arms around herself and hugs; her ears ring. Pushing herself up, she dabs at her forehead, slick with sweat. Dolly's lying there, staring up at the ceiling, arms crossed over her chest like she's the one in the hospital.

'Dolly!' Tala whispers.

Dolly doesn't move. Tala gets to her feet and sits on the thin bed.

'Oh, Dolly.' Tala takes Dolly's hand.

'I should have slept on the floor,' says Dolly.

'No, I was fine.' Tala stretches her back right out; it cracks.

'I'd better see to Colby.'

'That boy! He's the one who caused this.'

'He's sick, Tala. There's something not right with him.'

'It's just excuses. Not all naughty behaviour needs to have a name, you know; it's just naughty!'

'If only Ma'am Amber had locked that basement door when she went out. Shit, Tala, Sam could die.'

'He won't die. Put that out of your head.' Tala closes her fist and throws the invisible thought through the air. 'Jules said he's going to be okay.'

'They took him away in a damn ambulance.'

'And they saved him.'

Tala can't stop her hands from blessing. The women need all the help they can get. She scratches at the corners of her mouth, flattens her hair. She pats Dolly's hand and goes into the kitchen, runs her wrists under the cold tap. Cold tap; there's nothing cold about it, warm gushing through. *It could do with a polish-up*, thinks Tala. *Oh, but listen to me, that boy's fighting for his life in hospital and in pop thoughts of cloths.* Cleaning's been her life for that long, thinking about it is just like blinking.

Something swishes and crumples behind Tala and she jumps. It's Jules on one of the sofas, looking like a crushed-up rag. Tala gasps.

'I slept here last night. Amber asked me to. I'm sorry.'

'Is it because she doesn't trust Dolly any more?'

'She wasn't thinking straight,' says Jules. 'I mean, oh, shit, if you hadn't bashed on the window like that . . . The thing is . . . You stopped her running him right over. You saved his life.'

A saviour. A rescuer. It was Dolly who first called Tala that. 'Goddamn Mother Teresa over there,' Rita had said. And Dolly had turned to her and said, 'She's a rescuer, that's all.' They're going to need more than Tala's rescuing credentials to solve this mess though.

'Look, I've got to get to work,' says Jules. 'Do you think Dolly'll be okay?'

'She can't be anything other.'

Jules grabs her bag. 'You've got my mobile number. If you need anything, just call. I'll look in later.'

She leaves. *A midwife, and she's having to use those fertility syringes*, thinks Tala. She spotted an empty one on the floor of Jules' apartment when she was cleaning and looked up the name on the internet later.

Tala sits on a white plastic dining-room chair. She picks up a spoon on the table, looks at her upside-down reflection in it. If Ma'am Amber sacks Dolly, and Vanda gets wind of what's happened here, Dolly and Tala are going to be upside down and inside out too. Tala will be further away than ever from being reunited with her sons and seeing her first granddaughter in the flesh.

When Tala left Ace and Marlon that first time, she didn't see them for three years. There wasn't any Skype back then and she was only able to call them infrequently. When she returned to Tagudin on her first trip home, she sat on the bus thinking, was she different now? Were they? Would they all fit together like they had before?

The Santan shrub had turned into a red tree and the house looked more brittle, the paintwork that her husband Bong had never finished peeling away. Next door, Dolly and Mama's house looked even more broken up. There were displaced boards on the roof of Tala's house, the outside tap dribbling water. A dog Tala didn't recognise lay squeezing its eyes open and closed.

The door shifted back, then Marlon moved into the light. My God, he could have done with a wash, a gash of mud on his cheek, his greasy hair growing upwards rather than down. Tala started to march towards him, thinking it was a good thing she'd bought five scrubbing brushes from Daiso, but then she stopped. She hadn't been around for the past three years; it wasn't her place to start laying down rules like the Commandments.

He stood metres ahead, stooping in a too-big T-shirt; his fat cheeks were gone forever. She wanted to cover him in hard kisses, smell that dirty hair. She wanted to wind the whole thing backwards, so he'd be her little Marlon again, but all she could do was stare at this boy who reminded her of someone she once knew so well.

'My son,' she said, holding her hands out towards him.

His lips shaped a silent 'Mama' and as he walked towards her, he smiled.

'You're late,' he said.

She hugged him and he put his arms around her and hugged her back. He pulled away then and looked at her as if he was trying to place her, to remember who she'd once been. She'd missed so much of him. His tenth birthday when some of his friends put a banner across the main street and let fireworks off in the field. The town running race in which he took second place. My God, he didn't get those running legs from Tala – oh no, everything God could have put into making her muscles faster went into the wiggle of her hips. She'd missed all those milestones, but still her love for him remained strong. Mind you, she didn't love that smell.

'When was the last time you had a wash?'

'Erm . . .'

That 'Erm' was her answer. She took hold of his arm and left-righted him inside. She pulled one of the Daiso brushes from her bag and passed him a lump of soap. All her working to bring the tap inside and her son didn't even wash.

The front door opened and Bong stood carrying the bag that Tala had dropped into the dirt outside. They looked at each other. His skin clung to the bones of his skeletal face. His eyes seemed too big for it. He was the one to look away first, but Tala wasn't having it. She'd birthed two children with the man. Shoulders back, chest puffed, she hurled herself at him and kissed him right there on the lips. His eyes went ping-pong ball. She wanted the weight of the last few years to be gone for a few moments, for it to be carried by someone else, but Bong's arms weren't big enough for her. He didn't kiss her back.

'So how have you been?' he asked and began doing that breathy whistling that wasn't really whistling at all.

'I've got more muscles than you, man. What have you been eating – air?'

He sat, leaning forward, elbows on knees. Marlon started cutting something at the sink.

'You didn't answer my letters,' said Tala.

'Nothing to say. Life here's pretty much the same.'

'And Ace?'

My God, three years away and Tala's eldest son couldn't even turn up for the welcome home party, although party was over-doing it. Bong shrugged again. He circled the room, chewing his gum. He kicked a stone around the floor, took the peelings outside.

'I'll be back later,' he said, touching Tala's shoulder.

Her mouth opened to ask him where he was going, but if he had another woman, well, Tala wasn't about to throw away her dignity.

He left.

Tala couldn't stand just waiting. She picked up a cloth and started rubbing it in circles over the dresser. Then Ace was behind her, his arms clamped around her in a hug. Marlon laughed, and Ace let go and moved in front of her. His spotty face was angular, severe. Even the kinks in his long hair had been ironed flat. 'Who are you?' Tala wanted to say. She wanted to strip away the person in front of her, to uncover the layers like one of those Babushka dolls from the Wan Chai Street Market containing smaller and smaller versions of themselves. The outer doll the most detailed – gold eyelids, red lips – but the inner one, the size of a thumb-nail, had just a line-drawing of a face. It was this Tala wanted to see, the ten-year-old boy inside the teenager, the one she'd left behind.

'So, my boy,' she said. 'I've missed you so much, like an ache right here.' She knuckled her chest. 'Have you missed me?'

'We have Daddy, don't we, Marlon?'

Ace glanced at his brother at the sink, and blew his hair out of his face.

'Yeah, sure,' Marlon said. It was only then that Ace stopped smiling.

Then the handle of the front door shook and there was Mama in the doorway, Dolly just behind. Dolly tried to get through the door, but was squashed and defeated by Mama. Mama took Tala's hands and dragged her into the light.

'Oh, my daughter, you've got so old.'

It was as if someone had put a bowl on Mama's thick hair to cut it. Tala looked past her to Dolly, standing there in a pink T-shirt dress. She was more beautiful than ever, like someone had sculpted her from marble. But Tala was careful not to say anything about being pretty; she knew how Dolly hated it.

'Have you been reading those books I sent?'

'Maybe we can practise,' said Dolly in English.

'You sound pretty good at English already.'

There were more books in Tala's bag. 'You too, Marlon, you can give it a go.'

He nodded, not a trace of annoyance in his eyes. Some children get angry when they're not the chosen one for school, but not Marlon. Tala knelt down and started unloading her bag. Every tiny space in it was filled with clothes and gifts. There were candies, cologne and T-shirts, a booty of two-dollar Daiso buys. Even when the bag was empty, Ace kept on looking into it.

After Dolly and Mama left, Bong came back, fists in pockets. Tala had known every part of that body once – the curl of the eyelashes, the birthmark on his thigh. How they'd laughed back then, sitting on top of the dining table with their feet on the bench, his hand smoothing her back as they looked at the abstractions of colour Marlon had charcoaled onto flat pieces of wood – a blue sky blending with a pebbly shore, rubbings of cream and turquoise in which she found two faces pressed together: her face, Bong's face. But that day she returned, Bong just stood there, keeping distance between them and staring at the floor.

'Are you still playing your kalaleng?' she asked.

'No.'

'But that was something beautiful.'

'Everyone's changed. I've changed,' he said. He was breathing fast like he was about to say something important.

Tala took a deep breath and held it. She walked over to him. He angled his head as if he was trying to get away from her without appearing to move. She pulled his hand out of his denim pocket and saw that the wedding band had gone from his finger. My God, he had someone else. She hadn't seen it, she hadn't thought he could ever be with someone else. All she had kept of him were good memories that hadn't left room for the shouting matches they'd had just before she left. She looked at him, her eyes filling. He didn't look back at her, so she folded her arms and the tut came loud from her mouth.

Voices drift into Tala's ears now, real voices, children's voices. She goes over to the window and watches all the little ones in their school uniforms – green dresses, checked blue shirts. They chatter and drift away. It feels wrong, that time refuses to stop for other people while the women step slowly through this after-shock. Her phone vibrates in her bag. She picks it up and reads.

I need you to clean apartment tonight! It's Mrs Heng.

Tala switches off her phone and throws it back into her bag. She goes into Dolly's room and sits beside her on the mattress, two of them on this bed raft, the water choppy and neither of them able to swim.

'Look, I know this is hard,' says Tala. 'But try to concentrate on what you can do, not on what you can't change. You just look after that boy up there.'

She wraps Dolly in her arms then kisses her cheek.

'And, Dolly?'

'What?'

'You took those pills, didn't you?'

Dolly nods.

'I need to go to work,' says Tala.

Dolly just sits there on the bed when Tala leaves through the side door. Tala inches along an alleyway at the back of the buildings. The thin pathway is sandwiched by the wire fencing of the school playground on one side. On the other, are the backs of the town houses, clothes airers outside them loaded with tops and pants and tea towels. In the school playground, four girls are taking it in turns to shoot hoops at the netball post. The pathway is fringed with white spider lilies that look like Mallie's drawings of the sun with rays shooting out. A maid is on her knees on some nearby steps scrubbing the concrete, surrounded by froth. Tala takes a left past an open-air exercise area, with two metal cross trainers, and out towards the condo entrance.

When Tala gets to the main road, the bus is coming, so she dashes. Then she sees the queue of people waiting to climb aboard and slows down. She's sweated a river by the time she gets there, but then it's sky-high humidity. Like always.

She's out of breath when she falls into a seat next to an old lady who eyes her. There's a child screaming. He's sitting on his maid's knee at the front of the bus where two benches face each other, his cheeks glazed with tears.

The sound makes Tala think of the boy and the car and the mother's screaming that went on and on. She tries to stop looking at the boy with his Mickey Mouse T-shirt and navy sandals. He's trying to buck himself from the woman's knee.

'Hush, little one,' the maid says in Tagalog.

'Mama!' the boy shouts, looking to another woman, the one sitting next to the maid, tapping on an iPhone. She doesn't look at him. The maid carries on whispering in his ear, and the boy continues to cry.

The lady next to Tala gets up and thuds her legs against Tala's knees. Tala turns to the side, trying to make herself smaller, and the woman pushes on past wordlessly. She dings the bell and gets off. Three more people get on.

'Excuse me! Excuse me!' a loud voice says.

An enormous shopping bag is held high, bashing the faces of people with their arms holding on to the crossbar. Someone tuts. The person sits and boofs Tala's side with their bony hip. Rita.

'Oh, Tala. That blogger could have been writing about me a few days ago. She talked about how we need to eat cake.'

'Sorry, what do you mean; what blogger?' Tala's eyes open so wide it's like she's doing facial exercises.

'Maidhacker!' shouts Rita.

'Ssssh, be quiet, for God's sake.'

'Oh, it is you, isn't it, Tala?'

Rita's leaning forward, two centimetres from Tala's nose, staring right into her eyes. My God. Tala doesn't know what she's done to give herself away, but Rita slaps her skinny bare thigh so hard it sounds like the bus has crashed.

'I knew it! All that raw anger. Oh, my God, Tala, are you nuts?'

'Keep your voice down.'

'Have you seen how many people are reading that thing? You've got even more stars than the sky at night.'

'Rita, you can't tell anyone.'

'You know me, Tala.' Rita closes her lips, and draws her finger and thumb along them like they're a zip.

I know you, Rita; I know you only too well.

'Oh, my friend, your secret is safe with me,' Rita says loudly.

Tala says a silent thank you that Rita's talking Tagalog, then looks around the bus. Apart from that woman with the crying boy, there are no other Filipinas on board.

Chapter 12

✈

Jules stands in the hospital shop looking at the magazines on shelves, the starved cut flowers in buckets, the rows of chocolate boxes. She pulls a strand of wilting orchids from one of the buckets, looks at the chocolates then returns to the bucket again and chooses an additional bunch of flowers, pink lilies this time, their petals withered.

Her phone hums. She opens her bag. The screen flashes: 'Caller Unknown'. She thinks about not picking up, but she drops her bag to the floor, lays the flowers on top and pushes the phone to her ear.

'Is that Mrs Harris?' the voice says. It's the woman from the charity.

Jules says, 'Yes,' quieter than she intended to, so tries again and almost shouts it.

'I have good news,' says the woman. 'We have a baby. One of our volunteers has a daughter who needs to go into hospital in two weeks, so she can't continue looking after him any more.'

Jules swallows. This is all she needs. 'Er, right.'

'You sounded enthusiastic,' says the woman.

'I, erm . . .'

'It's not a problem if you've changed your mind.'

'No,' says Jules. 'It's just . . . I . . .' She can't seem to find the right words. 'No, I want to do it.'

Does she? Just what is she saying?

'That's great.'

'Boy or girl?'

'He's a little boy we call Khalib. He's six weeks old.'

'I haven't got a cot or anything.'

'The volunteer has a bassinet, clothes.'

'Hang on a minute. Don't you want to interview me first?'

'Well, you've filled out the application form. We have your Green Card number.'

'But the flat . . . Don't you want to see my flat, so that you can make sure it's, well, you know, baby friendly?'

'It's not necessary,' says the woman.

Surely it is, thinks Jules. She could have towers of newspapers in there, walls infested with cockroaches.

'I'll have to, erm . . .' Jules' job. She's not one for shirking, but what the hell, she does want to do this. 'How long will this be for?'

'A fortnight at most. The volunteer could probably drop the baby off with you, but I'll keep you updated via email. . .'

The woman rings off. Jules stands with the flowers still on her bag, the phone in her hanging hand. She looks at it, feeling the urge to text someone. *I've got some news.* She's wanted to say those words for a long time, to David most of all. Wrapping a positive pregnancy test with spangly paper and giving it to him to open. She dials his number.

'It's happening,' she says.

'What is? Are you all right?'

'The fostering charity just rang. They want us to look after a baby.'

'Huh?'

'That charity I told you about. They have a little boy.'

'Oh.' She hears him swallow.

'What?'

'It's a bit sudden, isn't it? We haven't had an interview. They haven't even checked out where we're living.'

'They aren't as strict about stuff like that here, I guess.'

'Are you sure you haven't got your wires crossed? It just seems really odd.'

'They said we'd be getting him in a couple of weeks.'

David gives a befuddled, breathy laugh. 'Is he okay, the baby?' he asks.

'I didn't ask all that much about him.'

'I feel really weird about this, Jules. I mean, what kind of system allows a random couple of expats to look after a little baby?'

'But you wanted to do this.'

He breathes out. 'I do, it's just . . .'

'What?'

'God, Jules, a baby. How long would this be for?'

'A couple of weeks.'

'And then what?'

'I guess he'll be adopted.'

'I don't know.'

'We'd be doing something good.'

'Yeah, but it's afterwards that I worry about.'

She goes quiet. 'I really want to do this, David.'

'You've been having such a crap time lately. And when you have to give this baby back, I'm just worried it's going to be too much.'

'Look, I'm not some weakling. You know I can cope with this.'

'It sounds like you've made up your mind, but . . .'

'It's just a bit of babysitting, and God knows I'm an expert at that.'

'Well, you've got me there,' he says and laughs.

They say their goodbyes and she hangs up. She feels lifted. But then, the charity worker is bound to change her mind; she knows nothing about Jules and David after all. David's right, it's inconceivable that some woman will just drop a baby off with them and hope for the best. No, the woman's bound to call back and say there's been a mix-up, that she called the wrong person.

A baby, Jules thinks. Here she is with another failed IVF behind her and there could be a real, live baby in her apartment in a few days. She shakes her head, laughs to herself.

She goes to the till to pay for the flowers. And, when she goes out of the shop, Tor is striding past in a pair of light blue linen trousers, the hems under the heels of each of his boat-like brogues.

'Tor!' she calls. 'Tor!'

His jowls sag. He runs his hand through his thin hair.

'You must be exhausted,' she says.

'A bit,' he replies. He closes his eyes, hangs his head.

She puts both her arms around him and squeezes. He is poker-straight. She squeezes a little harder, but still he doesn't respond, so she pats his back a couple of times and withdraws.

'You helped to save his life,' he says, linking his fingers over his chest.

She shakes her head.

'I mean it. Thank you, really, thank you.' His milky blue eyes are looking straight at her.

'I just did what anyone else would have done.'

'Well, we were lucky that someone medical was there. I had no idea you were a nurse.'

'I'm a midwife. Well, was. How is Sam doing?'

'Much better. They've taken the monitors off him.'

'Oh, Christ, what a relief. Are you off home to get some rest?'

'I've got this meeting and . . .'

'You're going to work?'

'I have to be there for it. It won't be for long. Anyway, thank you again,' he says.

He bends towards her and kisses her stiffly on both cheeks, then heads towards the sliding doors.

She takes the lift to floor 12. A nurse shows her the way, her rubber-soled lace-ups squeaking as she walks. Jules follows the nurse into a room with several white dispensers on the walls.

'Clean first, okay?' says the nurse. She smiles and walks out, her ponytail swinging.

Jules washes her hands, pulls plastic coverings over her plimsolls, pushes her hair into a plastic cap. She goes out, looking through the windows of the ward doors. Through one of them, she sees Amber slouching in a plastic chair. Jules opens the door and goes inside.

Sam's hair is matted, patched burgundy with dried blood. Amber looks at her through puffed eyes, grey skin. There's sleep in her eyes. Jules hugs her as if she might break. Her mouth is full of Amber's hair.

'He's sleeping,' Amber says. 'They don't want to disturb him too much.'

'And you? Have you slept?'

'A little. Even after what I've done.'

The springy plastic chair sinks as Jules sits beside her. Sam's slightly purple face is turned sideways on the pillow. There's a long cut on his forehead. Pale veins branch from his closed eyelids, his wrist swathed in bandages. Jules takes Amber's hand.

'The doctors say he's been very lucky,' Amber says. 'That we might be able to take him home in a couple of weeks.'

She removes her hand from Jules'.

'They won't have to operate,' says Amber. 'That's something.'

Amber gets up, pulls the sheet over Sam's protruding toe. She can't stop looking at him.

'The police came to the hospital as soon as we arrived in the ambulance,' says Amber. 'They asked me a whole bunch of questions like I was some sort of criminal – which I am, I guess. I mean, what kind of idiot runs over their own child?'

'It was an accident.'

'They breathalysed me, of course.' Amber shakes her downcast head.

'I was over the limit. The way they looked at me . . . They said I could end up in court. I felt completely sober when I drove, but then how could I not have seen him, Jules? I'm such a goddamn fool.'

'No, you're not, Amber.'

Jules tears the cellophane from the flowers, fills the chipped vase with water from a sink at the side of the room. The zip is down on Amber's puffy blue shorts. Jules should have brought Amber something clean to wear, a toothbrush, a magazine.

'Do you need anything from home? I should have asked before,' says Jules.

'Tor's gone back to get some things.'

Jules nods, doesn't mention what he said about going back to work.

'I can't stop going over it,' says Amber. 'I could have killed him. I didn't even see him, my own son. Tor blames me, of course.'

'No, I'm sure he doesn't.'

'Things weren't good between us, but now . . . Is she still there?' Amber reaches out to Sam, touches her hand to his covered feet.

'Who?'

'Dolly.'

'At the house, yes.'

'She should have been watching him, taking care of him.'

'It wasn't her fault, Amber.'

'Why did Sam run out like that?'

'Colby was having a tantrum. It was pretty physical, he—'

'She should have been watching him. If she had, this wouldn't have happened.'

Christ, Jules should spell it out for Amber; her son needs help. 'Colby was—'

'That's just an excuse. It's her doing, this.'

'No.'

'Yes it is. She's going to have to go.'

There are goosebumps on Amber's arms despite the cloying heat of the room.

'It was a terrible accident,' says Jules. She should say something more about Colby, fight Dolly's corner properly, but not here, not now.

Amber reaches for a tissue beside Sam's bed and blows her nose. She gulps at the air and starts to cry.

Tala opens the red front door. Blinded from the sunshine outside, she tiptoes through the momentary darkness towards her room.

'Tala?' shouts Mrs Heng from the depths of the apartment. 'I want to talk to you.'

'Okay, okay.'

Tala stops in the hall and blinks. She pushes her hair behind her ears and a strand of grey comes into focus. There'll be a clump of the stuff if Dolly loses that job.

Mrs Heng comes out of the living room, in a black silk pyjama outfit covered in white doves. Don't they symbolise peace? thinks Tala. It's like putting a baby in a necktie; it's just plain wrong.

'You haven't cleaned the apartment for over a week. You've been avoiding me, staying away,' says Mrs Heng.

'Oh, Mrs Heng, something's happened, something bad – the child my sister works for, his mother ran over him in the car.'

Mrs Heng's eyes narrow. 'What?'

'It was an accident, a terrible accident.'

Mrs Heng's lips bunch. She regards Tala with an air of suspicion. '*Ta ma de* rubbish! I fill out your forms for the Ministry. And you clean this house, twice a week. It is not many times, not too much to ask. Stop being a sloth and clean today!'

Tala picks up her duster and starts with the photographs. The grandchildren with their fixed smiles, the soft-focus daughter who looks straight through Tala when she visits. Mind you, she always smells nice – taking that glass bottle, with the plastic flower on the top, from her handbag when she comes over, and spraying it. 'Urg, it smells of old people in here,' Tala caught her saying once when Mrs Heng was out of the room. Mrs Heng was unwittingly taking the rap for Tala's feet most probably. Tala's feet look like something out of a painting, but it's true what they say about appearances. Look at Mrs Heng's daughter, thinks Tala. She's like some Hollywood actress, but there's something prickly in the air when she's around.

Tala switches into bionic cleaning mode, brushing the duster over some of the surfaces, scrubbing the paint stains from the bathroom sink, beside which Mrs Heng's paintbrushes are packed together in a chipped mug. She listens out for Mrs Heng, and hears cupboards opening and closing somewhere deep in the apartment. Tala twists the taps on the sink. The water runs hot and she takes a pump of the Jo Malone handwash as a reward; Mrs Heng won't smell it on her since she doesn't have a sensitive nose. *Probably why she lets me and my feet live here*, thinks Tala.

Mrs Heng hurries past her in the corridor, holding what looks like a five-centimetre-thick recipe book close to her chest. She doesn't look at Tala.

Inside her room, Tala slumps onto her bed, wiggles all her bare toes and breathes. She lies there for half an hour staring up at the shapes of light on the ceiling. She brings down the computer then, pushes on her glasses, and logs on to *Salamin*. They're still going on about her: 'Search for Maidhacker Continues'.

She looks at the numbers on her blog. Her pulse speeds up like the out-of-control tick of a clock that needs to go back to the shop. Eight hundred and one people have starred her post about cake. Rita's right, this thing is getting popular.

Tala clicks onto the analytics page. More than 11,000 people have viewed her blog since she started it. That can't be right, surely. She keeps clicking, but the line of that graph stays sticking up like an orange skyscraper. People are actually interested in what she's got to say. Her face goes so hot, she could do with that fan. But there it is, still in two parts with the wires sticking out of it.

She's written five posts so far. There was one about how the agencies deduct all that money from what you earn because of the training they give you. Training, pah! Putting a nappy on a plastic doll, wiping the brown sauce from its bottom. Tala's written about how those and other deductions mean you might not earn anything for almost a year after you arrive. And Tala's talked about how there's joy here: swimming in the sea at East Coast Park; that afternoon tea Dolly set out for Tala and some of the other women at Ma'am Amber's, the one time they didn't take her on their holiday to look after the children – meringues filled with Korean strawberries, tiny scones, macarons in different colours.

Tala brings up Vanda's blog then. Oh, just look at Tala, adding to her audience, but she wants to check that the photograph that woman took of her walking Malcolm the dog isn't up there.

Everything stops for a moment then. Tala goes still, her heart thumping her ribs, the noise spreading to her neck, her ears.

There is Dolly's name and her work permit number on the screen – even the name of the Greenpalms condo.

Vanda can't do this; no one will take Dolly on if Ma'am Amber gets rid of her. But then Vanda's already done it, for anyone to read. A fire starts in Tala's chest.

A child is fighting for his life in hospital after being run over by a car on his maid's watch. The maid, Dolly Pabro Castillo, 35 (work permit number 67894), was looking after the boy when he ran into the car park and the car ploughed into him.

A source said: 'Pabro Castillo is completely inexperienced and lazy. Because of her incompetence, the boy's condition is critical.'

Thirty-two people have given this piece of nonsense a star. *A star, I ask you. It needs a big red line through it.* And there's a photograph too, a close-up of Dolly's face and all those earrings.

Tala's suspicions were right; Vanda must be one of Ma'am Amber's friends. How else would she have got hold of a picture of Dolly?

Tala slams the lid of the computer closed. What are they going to do? She tries Dolly's number, but it switches to voicemail.

She opens up her blog and starts typing.

For your information, Vanda, here are the facts about the terrible car accident you've written of.

A mother reversed her enormous car over her own son because she wasn't looking properly while she was parking. It had nothing to do with Dolly Pabro Castillo. In fact, Dolly was in the middle of looking after the woman's other child who was having a tantrum.

Dolly is excellent at looking after children. She is hard-working and uncomplaining even though she rarely sees her own daughter who lives miles away in the Philippines.

Her girl was just two and a half months old when Dolly left. Imagine that, you imbecile! Imagine not seeing your child for three whole years. Forget about putting your expensive coffee on the top shelf and worrying about which toilet you allow your visitors to piddle in, Dolly has more important things to think about like paying for her child to eat and go to school.

Tala writes more words, a lot more words, the typed-up equivalent of her rants. She hits 'post'.

Chapter 13

Dolly walks along Holland Road, the cars whizzing by. There's still been no blood. She took the pills a week ago, so why aren't they working? She walks harder, faster. She pushes her hand into the leaves of the hedge and drags, her fingers hitting little branches.

Traffic zooms along the tarmac; people surge across a footbridge. She passes an empty bus stop. There's a new condo, a stack of enormous white cubes, and blue plastic over the windows. And further on, another condo flanked by palm trees. She passes a wrought-iron gate, sunshine streaming through its carved leaves. Slow engines are turning over, and she climbs the hill to the hospital. A man in red shoes and a baseball cap walks by. A woman is pushing a boy in a wheelchair with a tube up his nose.

It's as if someone has used an ice-cream scoop on Dolly's insides. All those times she tried to talk to Ma'am Amber about Colby and now it's come to this. Why didn't Ma'am Amber look properly before she reversed?

Dolly goes through the sliding doors into the hospital lobby. The smell of baking hangs in the air. There's a cafe where paper bags crinkle, and people sit on stools, cups steaming. *A bakery, her bakery.* The thought stays lodged in her head. The list of floors blurs in front of her. A nurse squeaks past in white, rubber-soled lace-ups.

'Where is the emergency place?'

The nurse's eyebrows arch.

'Head injury,' says Dolly.

'Floor 12.' The glass doors to the outside open and the nurse goes through.

Dolly presses for the lift. It takes a long time to come and when she steps in, her breath feels constricted. On floor 12, she starts walking along a starched corridor that smells of bleach.

'Hey!' someone calls. 'You need to clean up.'

A man in white scrubs leads her into a room and points at a mound of blue fabric.

'Put these on,' he says. 'But wash first.'

She turns her hands in circles under the gush of the hot tap, the nail on her forefinger broken into a wavy line, her fingertips dry. She puts on a cap, overalls and things that look like plastic bags on her feet.

Sir Tor gets up when she goes into the room that smells of medicine. Sam is on the bed asleep. Dolly puts a hand up to her mouth to stop herself making any kind of sound.

'I'm so sorry,' she says.

Sir Tor pulls her in, pats her back.

'No, no,' he says.

She tries to push him away, but his hand sticks her there to his linen chest. When Dolly steps back, she sees that his eyes are scratched with red lines, his skin looser, older. He has on light grey, crushed-up trousers. The collar of his white shirt is open and stained. There are patterns of light on the sill.

'Come on, sit awhile,' says Sir Tor. 'Sam will want to hear your voice.'

She rubs a fist into her eye socket and sits.

'He's getting better,' says Sir Tor. 'And the doctors say he'll probably be allowed home in a matter of days.'

The name of the hospital is slashed lots of times across Sam's sheet. There is a dressing on his forehead. His scalp is pink like poodle skin showing through the fur.

She licks her lips and swallows. There are rocks in her throat. She thinks of Sam trying to teach her to swim and a smile flickers across her face.

'Keep getting better, Sammy Bean,' she says.

She reaches out her hand to him then takes it away. He's too broken to touch. Sir Tor puts his thumb on Sam's hand and makes circles there. Dolly touches a hand to her own thumb in a bid to conjure up just how hard and round and small that callous on Mallie's thumb is. Mama still hasn't managed to get her to stop sucking her thumb.

Sir Tor and Dolly sit for what feels like a long time.

'Amber knows you haven't moved out yet,' Sir Tor says, pushing back his slipping-down glasses.

'I haven't done anything wrong,' says Dolly.

'I know you haven't, but she's determined to get rid of you. The only reason she's turned a blind eye to you staying is that she's practically living here at the hospital with Sam.'

He looks away, coughs into his hand.

'I've tried to make her see sense, but she won't listen,' says Sir Tor.

Dolly keeps staring at Sam's smashed-up face.

'It's probably best she doesn't see you here.'

'What do you mean?'

'She just went out to grab some lunch. She'll be back any minute.'

Dolly leans in to kiss Sammy's hand, but her face hovers inches away. In the end, she kisses her own hand and lets her fingers rest for a second on the back of his palm. She opens the door and steps out into the corridor.

The next day, Tala is walking towards Greenpalms condo, holding her head high like she always does. The security guard with the buck teeth ignores her. She passes the swimming pools, and detours into a stairwell, which leads down to the car park right under all those swimming pools.

Tala keeps looking around her, like she's doing something she shouldn't. Being here doesn't feel real, like she's hovering inches from the ground everywhere she goes, but let's face it, there's no way she's getting airborne. She needs to see the place where the accident happened; there might be some small detail she missed.

An overhead air vent drips water. Like tears, she thinks, until a child's laughter drifts in through the grilles. The child must be standing at the side of the swimming pool above the car park, pouring liquid through the ceiling. A car judders past and she jumps.

She keeps on seeing the boy under that car, lying there in that T-shirt, the whole thing in slow motion, like they were wading through glue. What would have happened if the rain hadn't sent Tala down here?

The white car is parked in a proper space now. She should get out of here and check on her sister.

The basement door to Ma'am Amber's place opens then and there's the lady herself, barefoot, her hair bouffant like she fell asleep while it was wet. The door slams behind her, sending her into a stagger. Tala stands still with her bag against her chest, but it's no camouflage and Ma'am Amber looks up, so Tala walks towards her, moderating her extravagant sway.

'Hello, ma'am.'

Ma'am Amber's arms are folded against her stomach as if she's trying to keep whole. And here's Tala, ghost of the past. There's a circle of bleach on Ma'am Amber's T-shirt, which is so faded that Tala starts to wonder if she's taken some of Dolly's clothes by mistake.

'I'm Tala, the one who—'

'I know who you are.'

'Your son?'

'I just came back to get some clean clothes, to clean up.'

Ma'am Amber sits on the concrete steps, her bare legs speckled with stubble. She leans her head against the wall. Tala lowers herself, almost sitting on top of Ma'am Amber, there's so little space for her backside.

'Oh, ma'am, I'm sorry about what happened.'

'I just didn't see him and now he's lying in a hospital bed.'

'It was an accident.'

'Dolly was meant to be watching him.'

'But Colby was being very naughty.'

'Oh, no, I'm not having this.' Ma'am Amber puts her hand flat in the air.

'You have to know what happened, lady.' Tala lays her hand on Ma'am Amber's shoulder, but she shrugs it off.

'That stupid car,' she says, looking over at it. 'Bloody expat-mom, oil-guzzling pile of shit.'

Tala touches her cross. Ma'am Amber gets up and goes over to the car, the wheels twisted. She strains her leg upwards and bangs her bare heel against its shiny white body. She tries again, but still her kick doesn't make a dent. She starts to cry.

'How can I go on? After what I've done?'

'But he's alive, my Gad, he survived.'

'I'm being punished,' she says.

Dolly has never mentioned that Ma'am Amber is religious. A car judders past. Ma'am Amber gasps then sits on the steps again. She looks up at the concrete ceiling with all those pipes, and the minutes tick past.

'I'd better get back to the hospital,' says Ma'am Amber.

She gets up and opens the door.

'I'll just check on Dolly,' says Tala.

Ma'am Amber doesn't hold the door open for her, and it smacks into Tala's hands. There's a pile of shoes on a rack in the basement hall that opens into a larger area where three computers are surrounded by wires and the sound of the air conditioning. Ma'am Amber wipes her nose on her arm. The skin glistens.

'Why are you still here?' Ma'am Amber screeches.

And so help Tala, her feet leave the floor she gets such a fright. She clutches her bag, thinking Ma'am Amber's talking to her. Dolly's on the stairs that lead to the ground floor, looking paler than ever.

Ma'am Amber starts jabbing her finger. 'You need to get out!'

'I love Sam, you know that,' says Dolly.

'Love?! You're the goddamn paid help. What would you know about love?'

The chinking of Dolly's earrings is the only sound in the hall.

'Colby was having one of his angry fits, and Sam just ran off,' says Dolly in a level voice.

'Don't blame Colby,' snaps Ma'am Amber.

It's building in Tala, a red fiery heat, but it's important not to make the woman angrier than she already is. Tala takes a big breath and hopes that what she says next will soothe like Kofi Annan.

'It's nobody's fault,' she says.

Ma'am Amber turns to Tala. 'If she'd been doing her job properly, this never would have happened.'

'I was doing my job; I was trying to calm Colby down. Like I've said to you so many times before, he—'

'Where were you? Plugging away on your mobile phone? Chatting to your friends?'

Kofi Annan's clearly not working.

'Get out!' shouts Ma'am Amber. 'The only reason you're still here is because I'm spending all my time at the hospital with my son. But he's coming home soon, and when he does, I want you gone!'

Ma'am Amber bangs against Tala as she barrels upstairs, pushing Dolly against the wall as she goes. There's an unnatural silence then a clattering starts. Tala wiggles past Dolly up the stairs, abandoning Kofi at the bottom.

The vibrations are coming from Dolly's room. Tala arrives at its doorway and watches Ma'am Amber scoop and bump books from the closet. Dolly is beside Tala then. Ma'am Amber rips photographs from the board at the end of the bed. They flutter torn to the tiles. Mallie's face, in pieces, gazes up from the floor.

That's it! Tala pushes her shoulders back, ready to bellow a warning. Tala opens her mouth, but it's not her voice that comes out.

'Leave my things alone!' Dolly shouts. It's the loudest noise she's ever made.

Ma'am Amber goes bright red, and looks around the room. She pulls clothes from the closet and they land in a heap on the floor. A shoebox full of trinkets clatters down, a yellow Minion toy, and a homemade card, one of Mallie's, a $50 note and a turquoise box with the words 'Tiffany & Co.' on it.

Ma'am Amber sees the box and stops, breathless. 'Get out!' she shouts then she raises her hand to slap Dolly's face.

Dolly catches Ma'am's wrist. Ma'am tries to bat Dolly away, but Dolly's knuckles are tight around Ma'am's wrist. Ma'am brings up her other hand, but Dolly catches hold of that one too, pressing, lunging, jerking. The pair of them look like a t'ai chi session that got an electric shock.

'Get off me!' screams Ma'am Amber.

'No!' Dolly shouts. She is gritting her teeth.

'Stop it!' Sir Tor shouts from behind.

He edges past Tala and puts his arm around his wife. Dolly drops Ma'am Amber's arms. Sir Tor pushes Ma'am Amber through the door, his hands cupped around her shoulders.

Tala starts doing what she reckons she's best at. She gathers the torn-up photograph pieces and the books. Dolly starts to help.

'She'll come round, you'll see,' says Tala.

Tala puts her fist up to her mouth then. She sounds just like Mama. *What will be will be. What's for you won't go by you.* Mama counselled herself through Daddy's sudden death with platitudes when Tala was a teenager and Dolly was just two years old. Tala's been putting off telling Dolly what's on Vanda's blog; there's no way Tala can share that with Dolly now. It's been a long time since Tala filled out the forms for Dolly at Maid Easy for You, but they are both going to have to go back there now.

Tala presses her cross and mutters a quiet prayer that the agency boss lady, Charmaine, doesn't read Vanda's blog.

Chapter 14

The dialling tone pulses in Jules' ear. It's like Glastonbury 1999 all over again when she'd phoned in sick to her Somerfield Saturday job. 'Diarrhoea,' she'd rasped. By the sound of her voice, Angie from Produce hadn't believed her.

'Hello,' says a voice at the other end of the phone now.

'It's Jules. I'm not feeling so good.'

'What's wrong?'

'Flu, I think.'

'Well, come in and I'll get one of the doctors to look you over.'

'Oh, no, I . . .' She throws in a fit of coughing. 'I don't think I can face going out,' she croaks. Sweet Jesus, she's always been such a terrible liar. 'I'm so sorry. I'd better go, I'm feeling so rough.'

She sits there, guilt lodged in her chest. She'd never throw a sickie if she was at St Thomas', but she's only a part-time receptionist. And telling them about fostering this baby would raise too many uncomfortable questions. A bird chirrups; a hose sprays. She clicks onto her computer – the baby will be here any time now. Her hand hovers over the keyboard. She won't look at Fertility Friends, no. She logs on to her Instagram notifications instead. That close-up photograph of Dolly has been liked fifteen times now. She uploads the rest of the pictures from her camera and chooses the best three to share. That one of Tala in her sunflower dress is really something: the lines around her eyes, the way the upper part of her face is in sharp focus, a slight blur to the chin.

The doorbell chimes. The baby. Jules forces herself to go slow down the wooden stairs. She opens the front door.

The volunteer smiles. 'Hi,' she says, an American accent.

A plaid car seat hangs from her hand, the baby inside asleep. His curly head lolls over to the side. The woman's body is tilted with the weight of him.

'Come in,' says Jules.

Inside, the woman sets the seat down. Jules drops to her knees, inclining her head to look at the boy better. There are dimples in his cheeks, his legs bent up, chubby. His hair is flat, apart from the patch of curls at the front. Sitting this close, Jules can hear his faint wheezes.

'He's beautiful, isn't he?' the woman says, crouching, hands on her knees.

'Yes,' Jules whispers, then adds, 'Is he a good sleeper?' It seems the most important thing to ask.

'He'll be going through the night before long,' the woman says.

'Do you want to sit down?' Jules points to the leather sofa.

'I'd better not. I've got to get back to my daughter.'

Jules sees the carrier bag in the woman's hands. 'Are his clothes in there?' she asks.

'There's not much. Just two little tops, three pairs of trousers and a onesie. There's a few bottles and not many nappies left, I'm afraid.'

Jules takes the bag and the smell of laundry liquid seeps out.

'What's going to happen to him?' asks Jules. 'In the long term, I mean?'

'They don't tell us that much,' says the woman. 'He's the second baby I've looked after. You get them for a few weeks, sometimes longer, then someone turns up and takes them away. Khalib is going to be adopted.'

'Oh,' says Jules. 'It sounds like it might happen quite soon.'

'Well, you just never know. Sometimes there's complications.'

Jules stands, eyeing the sleeping boy.

'What about a cot?' She asks then.

'Oh, it's outside,' says the woman, turning to open the door.

A fraying wicker basket, lined with once-white cotton, lies beside the shelf of candy-coloured Crocs that belong to next door. The woman presses the button to call the lift and Jules realises she's about to leave.

'He should wake in the next half an hour for a feed,' says the woman. 'There's only a small bit of formula left, so I put it in a plastic box in the bag. You'll need to get more. I'm sorry, I just haven't had a chance.'

The lift swallows the woman. Jules stays in the lobby watching her through the grilles as she walks along the pathway below.

Jules brings the bassinet inside. The front door closes with a thunk and Jules is on her knees again, just looking. She's held hundreds of babies, yet here she is with one, and she's not sure she can remember what to do.

She scoops the contents of the carrier bag out and lays each item of clothing onto the marble floor beside the boy. There's a blanket knotted at his legs, a yellow booklet, which she flicks through, containing graphs and scribbled notes – information about the baby, she presumes, though she doesn't look closely. There are no soft toys, no nappy cream. The paraphernalia that goes with a baby has been stripped down to the bare essentials. Forget all those baby massage classes her friends went to, and the Bugaboo Frogs.

'Khalib,' she says.

His adoptive parents will call him something different. She'd liked so many boys' names: Charlie, Joe, even Sam come to think of it. Sam, poor kid. All that medical training she did and here she is playing at being an expat wife. At least helping Sam was something good. At least this is too.

The baby blinks his eyes open, jiggles his legs. He has the longest eyelashes. She pushes a finger into his fist. He smiles at her – well, it looks like a smile; maybe it's wind. She unclips him from the car seat and lifts him. She walks him around. *So this is what it would be like. Maybe I can keep you.* She hasn't allowed herself to fantasise for months.

She puts him back into the car seat and boils water for the milk. He starts to cry. She tries a bit of peek-a-boo, but it doesn't work.

She makes up the milk, but it's way too hot, so she pushes the bottle into the silver fridge. She picks him up again and jigs him, and still he cries. She's getting her chance after all, she thinks. She walks around with him for a long time and there's an occasional gap in his crying.

Finally the bottle is cool enough and he guzzles it down. She lays him in the bassinet where he falls asleep. She texts the woman at the charity and asks for more formula; she has no idea of the brand that he's used to.

⧗

Dolly's on the landing cleaning when they bring Sam home from the hospital.

'I won't have it!' Ma'am Amber's voice booms.

There are heavy footsteps on the stairs and Sam is floppy in Sir Tor's arms. Sir goes into the master bedroom with him then Ma'am is in front of Dolly, her face grey, the hair dry and tangled.

'I told you I didn't want you here when Sam came home from hospital.'

'But what happened wasn't my fault.'

'There's no way I can live in the same house as you. You need to leave right now; you might as well, I'm not paying you any more.'

'It's not just Sam that's damaged; Colby needs some—'

Ma'am Amber snatches away the Clorox and the duster from Dolly's hands then throws them across the landing; the bottle bursts, churning out a glutinous urine-coloured puddle. Ma'am Amber stands there, sobbing now, her head jerking, a tear dripping off her chin.

Dolly touches Ma'am's arm. Ma'am Amber twists away from her as if she's been burnt.

'Don't.'

'I just meant that Colby needs . . .'

'I can't handle this,' Ma'am mutters.

She moans slightly, then runs downstairs to the front door, opens it and leaves. As the door bangs shut, purple petals from the potted orchid shower down.

Dolly goes over to the Clorox puddle and rubs at it with a duster, going backwards and forwards to the sink. She sets up the ironing board on the landing and starts on the clothes. Is there a pain in her stomach? Perhaps it's starting finally. There's been no blood even though it's been two weeks since she took the pills. If she goes back to the agency now, the first thing they'll do is ask her to take a pregnancy test. What's she going to do?

There's a bitter smell in the room. Dolly looks down at the iron-shaped burn in Sir Tor's linen shirt.

'Damn!'

She squashes it up and pushes it underneath the mound of crinkly, unironed shirts. Sir Tor appears with a pillow in his hand. He goes into the spare room.

She steps towards the door. 'What are you doing?'

'I'm going to sleep in here. It's just for a while,' he says. His eyes flicker away from her. He puts a hand into his back pocket then changes his mind and laces his enormous fingers together.

There are usually two single beds in here, but she helped Sir Tor move the other one into the master bedroom where Sam is going to sleep beside Ma'am Amber from now on.

'When are you leaving?' he asks.

'Tonight, I guess.'

'I'm sorry, I tried. She's fragile, she . . .'

Dolly turns her back on him.

'But I . . .' he says as she goes downstairs.

She starts pulling ingredients out of the kitchen cupboards: a bag of flour, caster sugar. She makes a cake, something she knows by heart. A Victoria sponge.

She stands there with her backside against the kitchen counter, biting her nails. What's she going to do? The air fills with the smell of cooked sponge. The light changes then, and when she looks up, Sir Tor is standing beside her, folding himself into his smallest version.

'Will you write me a reference?' she asks.

'Of course I will. And you'll find another job. You're good at what you do.'

He tucks his hands into their opposite armpits.

'Can I read to Sam before I go?'

'Yes, and when she's back, I'll run you to the agency.'

Dolly goes upstairs into Ma'am Amber's bedroom. Sam is lying under a white sheet on the spare bed, beside the double one with its cushions and grey silk. There are oak cupboards along one wall, a dressing table with bottles and boxes of make-up in lines. The room smells of perfume. Dolly picks a book from the pile at the end of Sam's bed and he opens his eyes. She smiles and gets under the sheet beside him. He moves, puts his head on her chest. She puts an arm around his shoulder.

'Sammy, my Sammy.'

His head goes up and down on her chest as she breathes, a hairy caterpillar of threads behind his ear. If Tala hadn't been in the car park, he might not be here at all. And now Dolly's leaving. His bare arm is warm under her hand, his white hair soft against her chin. She wants to pull the cover off, take one last look at his little toes. She wants to hug him much harder than she's doing now. She tries to think of some important thing to say, some wisdom that he might remember. 'Oh, the woman who used to look after me, told me this.' Some mantra, some incredible truth. But there's only one thing that she can think of.

'Study well.'

His hair is sweaty, stuck to his head now. His skin is a strange colour – the shade clothes go when you leave a dark sock in the white wash. She touches his scarred forehead and it's hot.

She opens the book, but doesn't read the words. She makes something up to go with the pictures. 'And so Colby passed the suit to Sam.' She puts in Ace's and Marlon's names too. She gets Sam to say the words with her and his voice slurs until he says nothing at all.

She moves his head back onto the pillow and goes to kiss him. His eyes are open, rolling back in his head. It's as if some invisible fishing hook is pulling his face down on one side.

'Sir!'

No one comes.

'Sir!' she shouts again.

There's running. Colby's mouth is an 'O' and his scream fills up the room.

Then Sir Tor is there and he moves quickly, and Sam is hanging in his arms. All of them scramble down the two flights of stairs to the basement. Dolly's bare feet slap the concrete in the underground car park and she climbs into the car, the wheels squealing as Sir Tor pulls away.

'My son,' he mutters. 'My son.'

Dolly hasn't even shut the car door, Sam in the back beside her. She turns and sees the bloody cloud from Sam's accident still there on the ground.

'The door, Auntie,' Colby, in the front seat, says to her. And she reaches over and pulls it shut.

Sam's head is on her thighs and even though she can't see it, she knows he's bleeding inside. And there's something bleeding out in her too; she can feel it twisting her heart and making her belly sore. Her underwear is wet. Those pills have taken their time, but now they're working. Her baby is leaking out of her, just a small ball of cells, but she is going, gone, poisoned by the pills.

She looks down at Sam then presses her nose against the window and it's cold from the air con and she looks at the cars going by. The baby is dying inside of her, but at least it makes way for some kind of chance for Mallie. There'll be another job, other children perhaps.

Sir Tor indicates to turn right and switches the windscreen wipers on instead. Dolly's heart thuds to their beat until Sir Tor's fumbling hands manage to switch the wipers off.

The car turns into the hospital and slows. Sir Tor parks and gets out. He carries Sam, and they are inside, half running through the starched corridors. Then Sam is on a trolley and he looks like a different kid, his face distorted.

'Sammy!' calls Dolly and she stretches out a hand as he whizzes further away from her. Someone has caught hold of her arm – a nurse in blue scrubs, and Dolly stands and watches the swing doors swallow Sam and Sir Tor running along beside him.

Colby laces his fingers through hers, and they sit down on the plastic chairs lining the corridor. And they wait, their hands shaking. And her belly hurts like she's menstruating. She really should go to the Ladies to put some toilet paper into her underwear, but she just sits there, the whole of her aching, her head, her belly, her heart.

The woman from the charity arrives, wide-hipped with a dark mole on her chin. She pushes a carrier bag towards Jules who opens it to see a drum of formula with a name she's never heard of, 'Friso'. There's a bulky block of nappies underneath the woman's arm and a battered buggy beside her.

'This should be enough for a while,' the woman says.

'Thank you. Would you like to come in and see him?'

The woman shakes her head, angling her body towards the lift. 'I have a cab waiting,' she says.

'Oh, right.'

Jules waits with the woman until she climbs into the lift and the silver doors close.

So let me rewind, thinks Jules. No interview, no inspection. It feels unsafe, frightening, that a baby could be handed over to a stranger. And then she remembers the Green Card. She couldn't have got a Green Card with a criminal record, could she? Her knees sink into the woollen rug and she holds the baby's moving feet. She presses her nose against his, his eyes a coffee surprise. He is warm and smooth-skinned, but the truth is, she feels nothing for him; he's a stranger to her.

She walks through to the downstairs bathroom and holds him in front of the mirror. His hair is soft, almost greasy like his skin, and she notices how different they look – his button nose wide and flat, hers thin and slightly pointy.

She whirls him around then stops and says, 'Boo.' He blinks and smiles. She hugs him, and something expands in her stomach, and she hugs him again a bit harder.

⧗

Sir Tor comes back down the hospital corridor towards Dolly and Colby.

'We just have to wait. They're still working on him.'

He taps his mobile phone then hangs up. He tries again then sits and puts the phone on the floor. A doctor comes out; her hair tucked into a bun.

'We need to do an MRI,' she says.

'What's the problem?' Sir Tor asks, standing.

'We'll know for certain in a while,' the doctor says. 'But your son may be having a stroke.'

Sir Tor's hands go to his head. A *stroke*, something gentle like running your hand across fur, and yet what's happening to Sam is the opposite of gentle. Colby sees the shock on his father's face and starts to shake. Dolly touches a hand to Colby's shoulder. He leans forward, crying.

Sir Tor tries his mobile again. 'For Christ's sake. Where the hell are you? Call me.'

There are posters on the wall. 'Give Blood' and 'Beware of Dengue Fever'. The clock ticks. And still Colby holds on to Dolly's hand.

The doctor comes back, high shoes without backs so that they click against her feet.

'The MRI shows that one of the carotid arteries is damaged,' she says.

'What's that?' Colby asks.

'It supplies blood to the brain. We need to give him blood-thinning medication to stop him having a stroke.'

'He'll be all right though, won't he?' says Colby.

'We're doing everything we can.' The doctor goes through the swinging doors.

And they all sit, the air thick like warm custard. Colby gets up then sits and keeps on doing it. Sir Tor paces.

Dolly goes to the Ladies. Her belly is still sore, but the blood is dry in her underwear. Surely there should be more blood than this, she thinks. She sits on the toilet and waits.

Later, when the baby is asleep, Jules pulls out the yellow booklet and reads. 'Nurin Goh', the name typed on the first page. There's an address too, somewhere in Tampines. *Is that who you are, Khalib's mother?*

She raises the screen of her laptop which she's put onto the glass dining table. She types the name that's in the book. A list of possibilities flash up, but there's an exact match. She clicks on the link, Nurin Goh, on Facebook. The girl, sixteen, seventeen at most, has been caught in rain, a mist of water on her navy mac. Twisting, side-on, she stares into the camera with the same open face of the baby, his mouth and cave-like eyes, the picture taken perhaps before her life changed forever. There's an unsure, unsmiling expression on her soft face.

The girl has fifty-six friends. Which ones will put their arms around her, carry her through this disintegration? Jules scrolls through the friends, scrutinising the boys for some connective feature to the baby. She sees none.

She opens the yellow book again – the baby has had the injections given at birth, BCG, Hep B, but there are no more clues about who he is, how he came to be.

Jules combs her hair back with the flat of her hand. So Nurin is your mother's name, she thinks. The living room feels full of the separation. Did she look at him before he was taken? Did she kiss him goodbye?

Jules won't get to keep him either. One or two weeks at most then he'll either go back to the volunteer who dropped him off or to the home of his adoptive parents. She thinks of her little niece and how she cried when Jules read her a story about a rabbit who went back to its magic faraway kingdom and never saw his friends again. For her niece, the worst kinds of stories were ones about separation.

⧖

Much later, there is the pat of feet and Ma'am Amber is running, her hair in her face, a pair of sandals swinging in her hands. When she gets to Sir Tor, she stops and leans into one foot then the other as he tells her what's happened.

She glares at Dolly. 'What is she doing here?'

'She was with Sam when he became unconscious. If it hadn't been for Dolly's quick thinking, well, I dread to think.'

Ma'am Amber sits, pushes on her sandals, crosses one leg over the other. Lipstick has seeped into the cracks over her lips.

'Dolly, I'd appreciate it if you took Colby home,' says Sir Tor.

'No way,' Ma'am says.

'Amber, our son is in there fighting for his life. None of this is Dolly's fault.'

'I want to stay,' says Colby.

'For Christ's sake,' says Sir Tor.

'Colby's staying with *me*, Tor.'

Dolly gets up, looks first at Ma'am Amber then at Sir Tor.

'Go!' says Ma'am.

Sir Tor pushes a note into Dolly's hand. 'For the cab.'

Dolly stares at the doors they took Sam through, shadows moving behind the glass. The moment those doors shut was her last glimpse of him. She knows this. She looks at Colby and he looks back at her. These boys are not hers to help any more. She opens her mouth to say something to Ma'am Amber, but nothing comes out except her own shallow breath. She walks closer to Colby, lifts his hand.

'You're a good boy,' she says. 'You just need a bit of help to be it, that's all.'

He leaps up from the chair and hugs her. She brushes his hair from his face and kisses his forehead. Then she backs away, her eyes welling.

Outside, she walks barefoot, small stones pushing their way into her skin. She stops every now and then to pick them out with the toes of her other foot.

Essential House Rules for Foreign Domestic Maids
Rule 5. Toilets: If you have a small toilet with a showerhead mounted on the wall located close to your kitchen, there's no need for your maid to use any other bathroom in your home.

Chapter 15

Tala sniffs. There's something sickly sweet in the air, floral. Hyacinths meet 7-Eleven.

The cross stands guard over Tala's bed, Pope Benedict's gloomy face too. Tala drags a chair across the wooden floor then climbs on top and feels for her old computer. It's not at the front where she left it, so she reaches her hand further to the back, standing on tiptoes and stretching. Nothing. Her blog; panic flushes through her head.

She feels among the papers at the side. Her logbook of maids' complaints is still there and only one other book. She brings that one down, her yellow bank book. That means her passport is gone as well as her computer. Heat blowtorches her cheeks. Her mouth goes dry like someone has shoved crumpled paper inside it.

She combs her hand over the mottled cover of her bank book then opens it, the grand total of her life now in four figures. She's only a little off her target. She stretches to full height again, and jabs her hand around the cupboard space. Her passport, her computer really have gone, the two things that take her home.

The chair tips sideways, the legs bowing as they bang to the floor. The floral smell is Mrs Heng's; she's been in Tala's room. She's got Tala's computer, so she'll find out that Tala is Maidhacker.

Tala stands there, a lava of anger swirling in her chest, and another emotion too. She lifts her right hand, and looks at it quivering. She doesn't need to see the other one to know that it's doing the same thing. The shell that Marlon gave her catches her eye then, sitting on the table beside the mattress. She can't let this happen.

She doesn't feel herself open the door of her room; she doesn't feel the soles of her feet striding down the hall. *What's going to happen now?* It's like an invisible cord is noosing her because her breath hardly comes at all.

Mrs Heng is sitting in the living room, picking her toes, a little pile of hard skin on the arm of the patterned easy chair.

'Right, lady, where have my passport and computer gone?'

'A well-dressed woman came looking for you a couple of days ago,' says Mrs Heng.

'What are you talking about?'

'She came round here, asking if Tala Pabro Castillo was at home.'

'Who was she?'

'She wouldn't leave her name, but my guess is that the Ministry of Manpower could be onto us.'

'But no one would report me.'

'I wouldn't be so sure about that. Anyway, it's time you paid me the money you owe me. I've been paying the monthly levy to the ministry for employing you and you haven't reimbursed me for more than a year.'

Everyone who employs a foreign domestic worker in Singapore has to pay a levy to the Government, but Mrs Heng demands that Tala pay her back with an inflated sum of money. Tala sinks her teeth into her gum; she's been putting off paying Mrs Heng.

'Since you haven't paid me, I'm keeping your things as collateral.'

'You can't go into my room.'

'My room. My house. You pay me my money, you get your things.'

'My computer – how am I going to contact my family, hey?'

Mrs Heng pushes herself up, her hand agitating the skin desiccations.

'I need my money,' she says.

Tala's hand is tingling with electricity; it wants to smack Mrs Heng's face. She forces herself to stay put two metres away from the old lady.

'Stealing's wrong; whatever you think I owe, stealing's wrong.'

'Don't you dare talk to me like that.'

'You'll get your money, but I want my stuff.'

Tala marches over to the bureau, the conflict of patterns in the room blurring around her. She turns the lock and starts looking through Mrs Heng's papers, a magnifying glass, one of those cheese graters for feet, another of Mrs Heng's amateur paintings on a tile – this one with a cherry blossom tree, its flowery branches spread wide, and petals falling. There's a splodge of pink in the corner where the paint must have dripped. Tala puts it to one side and carries on searching. Mrs Heng is behind her then.

'Pack your stuff and leave!'

'I'm not going anywhere until I get my things.'

'If you don't leave, I'm going to call the police.'

'If you do that, they'll cart you off too, you stupid *tanga*!'

'What did you call me?'

Tala's hand is going numb, like it's daring Tala to slap her. *My God, don't do it, Tala,* some distant voice says, but the voice isn't loud enough because now Tala's hand is in the air, sweeping towards Mrs Heng. It is weightless, breezy. Tala looks at the hand, but it's not doing what she wants it to. It's just pointing, the fat finger stabbing towards Mrs Heng.

'You're a bad woman, the worst kind,' says Tala.

Mrs Heng's shut mouth is a knot of wrinkles, her nostrils opening and closing like the mouths of fish. She turns away, picks up the cordless phone and dials.

Tala walks down the hall. She opens one of the low-down cupboards in her room and pulls out her canvas bag, which is mouldy in places. She puts the photograph frames in first, her sheet, her pillow, her logbook. She pushes her magazine into the bag too then thinks better of it. What was it Russell Grant said about finding happiness?

Face your challenges head-on and you'll go a long way to achieving happiness.

She drops the magazine into the bin with a thud, Russell's mouth so wide the dangly thing at the back of his throat is on display. Tala puts the Pope into her bag along with the cross. She scoops up Marlon's shell. It's cold, untouched by the heat of the room. She pushes it into the pocket of her skirt. She scans the room one more time, slings the bag over her shoulder and heads for the front door.

It's already open; Mrs Heng is standing right beside it.

'I'm still waiting for my stuff,' says Tala, stretching up her five foot four inches, so she looks down at Mrs Heng. Just.

'You bring me the money,' says Mrs Heng.

'I must use the toilet.'

Before Mrs Heng has the chance to object, Tala goes into Mrs Heng's bathroom and flips the lock shut. She dumps her bag down, uses the toilet then goes over to the sink. Her reflection in the mirror above it is pale with shock. She touches her hand to the glass; it leaves a smudge which doesn't disappear. She takes a squeeze of the Jo Malone soap then another and another until her hand is a pond of lime basil. Her passport and computer indeed. She spots a bottle of cloudy pink mouthwash and twists off the lid. She gives her throat a good churn-up like Mrs Heng does every morning then spits once, twice. She screws the lid back on, picks up her bag and opens the door.

Mrs Heng is still standing beside the open front door, her arms folded. She mutters a number.

'That's far too much!' snaps Tala.

'That's how much it'll take to get your belongings back,' says Mrs Heng.

'But I can't afford that.'

Mrs Heng pushes Tala outside and slams the door.

It's airless and some critter lands on Tala's face. She slaps herself and something dies right there on her skin. She starts walking, heaving really since the bag is so heavy. Not all that much to show for the past eighteen years though. She walks and she limps, letting disbelief carry her forward. Then she's on the highway, cars whizzing past.

In the Lion City, you can walk just about anywhere and know that you're safe. Danger isn't in the darkness here, thinks Tala. It's behind the shut-up doors of those pristine condos where employers can half-starve their maids if they so choose.

The numbness recedes. What is she going to do now though? She's not going to Dolly's, that's for sure, nor to any of the other women's places. They look up to Tala; hell, they need someone to look up to, so she's not going to tumble herself down. And she doesn't need anybody else's help anyhow, not Tala.

She passes a five-storey shopping mall, posters across the first-floor windows. The car lights catch a hedge, a bat fluttering. There are flowers in the roadside bushes, their colour bleached by the headlights, which glow bright then disappear. Tala plucks a flower and presses the velvety petals. The truth is, Mrs Heng asked her for that money before, but she'd hoped the old lady might have one of her forgetful moments.

'You *tanga!*' Tala hisses, crushing the flower in her hand and dropping it to the ground.

Since when did Mrs Heng ever forget about money? And then she goes and gets scared by some Ministry official who called at the door. But then if some official came knocking, that means they must be on to Tala.

Tala decides to cross the road. When she steps onto the tarmac, a horn blares, fading to nothing further down the highway.

'Watch where you're going!' She waves her fist about, her chest thudding. She climbs back onto the pavement.

She waits, and when there's a break in the traffic she crosses quickly, her flip-flops kneading a blister into the crevice beside her big toe. On the other side, she kneels down on the grass verge, her bag a lifeless body beside her. The warm night closes around her. She takes the squashed water bottle from her bag and drinks. *My God, it's come to this.* She shakes her head. She could ask Rita if she could stay with her. But then everyone would find out, and most employers don't let the women bring friends back anyway. And it's not as if she can just draw out money and pay for a flight home now her passport's been stolen. *That's it.* She stands. Gravel scatters on the path as the silhouette of a lizard scampers away. She walks on, and there in front of her is another mall, the green letters of a Jollibean branch at the bottom of it. BreadTalk and Heavenly Wang.

She steps over a low wall into the car park with a concrete building to one side. The grey door to the toilets creaks as she pushes her way into the dark. The lights wink on and off with the fall of her feet. Three sinks are spread out underneath smudged mirrors crying out for the vinegar treatment.

Tala pushes open the doors of each cubicle to see whether she's got company. They're all empty. At the middle sink, she presses the tap and a drizzle of water comes out. She leans down and takes a drink from the tap. A long black hair swims towards the plughole. There's an empty metal bracket on the wall where the soap dispenser used to be.

Tala pulls her T-shirt up and around her head, so that it's wrapped around her like a bolero jacket. She spruces water into her stubbly armpits. In the mirror, strands of hair drip around her face; her bosoms sit loose in her baggy brown bra. She's not too bad with her clothes on though, she thinks, and gives the smallest of laughs. A whizz around an underwear shop in Plover Plaza and she might even be the right side of sexy. A roll of lazy skin spills over the elastic waist of her skirt. Even if she didn't eat for a whole week, the hump of her stomach has plenty of storage. She pulls her T-shirt back down.

She pushes open a cubicle door and sees a soggy white mound of toilet roll on the floor, the seat scattered with piddle. She asks herself why people's aims are so bad in this country when all you have to do is sit and let go. A cockroach scuttles in a diagonal across the wall, antennae swaying. She tries another door. This cubicle is larger, drier, with a rectangle of shrunken lavender soap on top of a unit hiding the cistern, and a circular, metal container fixed to the wall, but no sign of any toilet roll. She bolts the door and slides down the wall to the floor, pushing her bag against the space underneath the door. She is wired; her arms and legs twitch while her head fuzzes like an out-of-tune radio. Despite the yellow smell of piddle, her stomach rumbles.

'Homeless,' she says. She pulls Marlon's conch shell from her pocket and gives it a kiss. She hasn't had a place she's called home for years.

She needs to find a way out of this mess. She needs her passport back and her computer with all that potentially ruinous information on there. Her blog. If Mrs Heng opens the computer and logs on, she's bound to discover it. And she probably will given that she's as nosy as Tala. People rarely criticise Singapore, and if outsiders do their work permits might not be renewed. There's no way she'll be allowed to stay on if anyone finds out she's writing that blog.

This could be the end, she thinks, just as all the little overhead lights on the ceiling go off. She imagines Ace's face shining in the darkness, his pockmarked cheeks. The end – she'd thought that once before. She was working in Singapore when Ace fell critically ill with sepsis. She flew out immediately. He lay on the hospital bed, his neck scrawny, a tube up his nose. And Tala sat down beside him and put everything into wishing him better. If his end had arrived, she thought, hers had too. She made a silent threat to rip the cross from around her neck and throw it into the sea if her eldest son died. And she waited, and three days later Ace regained consciousness.

So this isn't her lowest point. She kisses the shell again and
the motion-sensitive lights flicker to life. She tries to sleep, curling
herself into a ball with her head on the knobbly bag. The lights
go off, but when she tries to make herself comfortable, they flash
on again. She is soaked in sweat, her back, her feet, her head, so
eventually she gives up, slumped there, trying to work out what
the hell she's going to do.

⧗

Back at the town house, Dolly stares at the cake from earlier.
Something black is moving on it, its tail curling up the kitchen
wall. The ants have made an S there. She throws the cake into
the bin and the ants turn in frenzied circles looking for it.

She goes down to Sir Tor's study where the computer is still
on, the air con humming. In the printer tray, there's a piece of
paper covered in typed black letters. Her reference.

*Dolly has been an integral part of our family for five and a half
years.*

She finds a small key on top of the desk and turns it in the
lock of the drawers. She goes through the papers and finds her
passport. She knocks against the computer and the screen comes
to life, Vanda's blog. Why would Sir Tor be looking at Vanda's
blog? She uses the arrows and moves the page up.

*The maid, Dolly Pabro Castillo, 35, (work permit number 67894)
was looking after the boy when he ran into the car park and the car
ploughed into him.*

There's Dolly's photograph, a close-up of the side of her face
and all those earrings. She spins, a noise like water in her ears.
Vanda's put her name up there, her work permit number. What
if Charmaine reads this? And, how did Vanda get her name? He
wouldn't do that to Dolly, would he, Sir Tor? But Ma'am Amber
would. Is she the one writing this blog?

Dolly goes upstairs into Ma'am's room. Thick historical books
are piled on the cabinet on Sir Tor's side of the bed. She opens

the drawers of the dresser and looks at the lines of bras and lacy underwear. For a moment, she wants to pull them all out, throw them on the floor the way Ma'am Amber did with Dolly's stuff, but she doesn't.

The notebook that Ma'am Jules bought for Dolly is there amid the underwear, and something shiny. Dolly pushes her hand in and picks it up. A gold brooch glittering with diamonds. It's covered in flowers and twisted leaves. She shouldn't do this. She knows it's wrong, but Ma'am Amber has so many of these jewels, and Dolly needs this. Mallie needs this too. Dolly puts it into her pocket.

She opens Ma'am's wardrobe and pulls a stool towards it. On the top shelf, there's a plastic bin liner stuffed full with something. The bag crinkles in Dolly's hands as she opens it. Bras, faded T-shirts, a red silk nightdress with lace on the chest, all clothes that Ma'am doesn't wear any more.

Dolly pulls the red nightdress out and gets down from the stool. She holds the silk against herself. This could be just the thing to make Gavin part with more money. She could carry on accepting his gifts like the necklace from Tiffany and the silk scarf. She could carry on taking the cash from his wallet while he dozes, oddments that a man like that won't miss.

She goes down the stairs, into her room, and lays the nightdress on the bed, along with her notebook. She pulls the brooch from her pocket. Guilt forms a lump in her throat, but she swallows it down. She has to do this. She'll sell these things and the money will cover Mallie's school fees for a while.

The phone rings in the living room. She walks through the dark to it and puts the plastic to her ear. It crackles.

'Dolly?' says Sir Tor.

'Yes?'

'Sam is out of danger.'

'Thank God.'

She waits for him to say something else, but he puts the phone down. She fumbles around on the island unit for the boys' box of coloured pencils and felt-tip pens, and goes back to her room with it.

She packs the nightdress and brooch into her bag. She takes a glue stick from the box, pulls her loose recipes from the closet then starts to stick them into her notebook. Thoughts float to the surface of her head. Colby eating several spoons of that chocolate cake mixture; Sam decorating those cupcakes with hundreds and thousands that cascaded all over the floor. The book begins to bulge with stuck-down paper, and a collection of memories.

Chapter 16

There's rapping on the toilet door and Tala wakes with a start. The smell of bleach fills her nose, coats the back of her throat.

'Hey! Who's that?' a voice says.

Tala puts one hand on the floor and her fingers come away wet. She puts her hand back down and struggles to standing. Her knees buckle and the shell crashes to the floor. Tala gasps, bends to grab it, and a pain knifes her back. She winces and examines the shell; it's intact.

'Come out,' the voice says.

'Wait!'

Tala puts her bag on her shoulder and fights with the door, squashing herself and her bag through the awkward gap.

A plump woman stands there in a headscarf covered in pink birds. 'What you doing, *lah*?' she shrieks.

Tala rushes past her out through the exit. The door is propped open with a bucket of suddy water. A bird caws in the distance. Tala tries to break into a run, but with her bag on her shoulder, it's a sort of waddle and she duckwalks up the road. A schoolboy in a lemon-coloured uniform is playing football with a stone. Tala passes a woman in sunglasses bending sideways to hold hands with a newly walking child in a crumpled pink dress.

Tala turns back to look. The toilet attendant is still staring, leaning on her mop like she's about to climb Mount Everest.

Jules is lying in the darkness of the spare room, the baby in the bassinet on the floor. She hasn't slept all night and not just because of the baby. David hasn't come home.

She's rung him, texted him, but he hasn't picked up or replied. She's been up twice to feed the baby a bottle, each time playing out in her head the possibilities of David's disappearance. He's been acting like such a weirdo lately. Jumpy; cutting calls short on his mobile phone when she appears.

Where the hell is he? Maybe he's been hiding some health problem; maybe he's fallen and hit his head, or had an accident, a crash in his car.

She looks at the clock again. 7 a.m. The baby is still asleep, eyelids flickering. A key claws the lock. Jules is up and walking down the corridor just as David opens the door. He is pressing both hands to his head. Through his fingers, his face is ashen.

'Where have you been?'

'Oh shit. Oh . . .'

He staggers over to the sofa, lies down. She stands over him.

'David, talk to me, are you all right? You look like crap.'

'Oh God, I . . . Something happened at work.'

'I've been calling you, leaving messages.'

'I should have checked my phone.'

'Look, what's happened? I've been so worried.'

David groans, closes his eyes.

'What's going on? You've been acting all shifty over the past few weeks. Tell me.'

'Please, Twig, get me a glass of water, will you?'

It's been years since David called her that. She remembers the note he attached to that Oasis CD: *To Twig. I miss you loads, love David.* He's never been one for drawn-out messages. David. She's never shortened his name. They met when he asked her to dance at some school disco in Greenford and she cringed that she was a whole head taller than him; at least she'd worn her flats.

She searches through the tubs of medicine in the kitchen

cupboard now and finds the aspirin, the question branching through her again: *where was David last night?*

He swallows two tablets dry then downs the water in one and moans. Khalib starts to cry. David sits up, his half-closed eyes now wide open.

'The baby?' he says.

She almost laughs; his hair is flattened at one side of his head, the other side sticking up at an angle. He is grimacing, criss-crossing his arms over his chest and leaning away from the sound.

'Yeah, the baby.'

'Oh, Jules, I'm sorry.'

She retrieves Khalib from the spare bedroom and goes back into the open-plan living area. David has stood up. She puts Khalib into his reluctant arms.

'Jesus.' He sits.

'It's Khalib, actually,' she says.

He peers at the baby, frowns and swallows.

'Hello, little one,' he says then. His face has softened, his voice too.

She warms the bottle of milk in a pan of boiling water. She takes the bottle from the pan and hands it to David.

'Now, stop fucking around, and tell me what's going on,' she says.

'Oh, God. We went out for drinks – whisky, cocktails, you name it. I didn't hold back and it got a bit messy.

'The cab driver dropped me at the front of the condo and I started walking back to the flat. I fell asleep on one of the sunloungers.'

'You were so drunk you fell asleep outside?'

'Yeah.'

She fixes him with a stare. The man who wakes regularly at four in the morning and goes downstairs for a bowl of cereal and a flick through the television channels with the sound turned down.

He moans. 'My head.'

Khalib is slurping at the bottle in David's arms. She leans forward, tilts the bottle up, so the milk covers the teat completely.

David smiles. 'He's so cute, Jules.'

'Bloody hell, David, you're more broody than I am.'

'Poor little kid.'

'He felt like a stranger when he arrived,' says Jules. 'But already I'm falling in love with him.' She and David look at each other. 'That sounds crazy doesn't it?'

'He's a tiny, helpless baby – who wouldn't fall in love with him? You thought someone was going to adopt him, but why can't we adopt him?'

'Blimey, you're a bit keen.' She smiles. 'I haven't asked about that yet.'

The baby is lying there, gazing up at David, with his sprig of curls and the dimples in his cheeks. It's only been a matter of hours, but the feeling in Jules' chest is real and tugging – she wants to be this boy's mother.

'Are you serious about this?' she says. 'Shall I ask the charity about adopting him?'

David shuffles in his seat, making the baby flinch. 'It's worth asking the question, at least.'

Jules takes Khalib from David and goes upstairs. Khalib's head rocks backwards to see her. How is it that the boy should be without a mother, that she should be without a child and the universe hasn't picked up these broken pieces and rearranged them with easier endings? Then she thinks of that girl who was screaming when they brought her into the maternity unit.

Jules had started to take down the girl's tracksuit bottoms. She'd kicked out, breaking Jules' safety specs. Jules had watched the rest of the labour through a crack in her right lens. By the time the junkie girl's trousers were off, Jules could see that the baby was crowning, a tuft of brown hair emerging then disappearing. The baby was flushed out in one final heaving roar. Jules had seen that baby in the special care unit rigged up to all those monitors. How she'd wanted to carry him away, but it was social services who did that in the end.

She logs on to the internet, the baby pressed against her shoulder and clicks on that stupid Vanda blog again.

'Jesus Christ,' she says, putting her hand against the baby to steady his wobbling head. 'I mean, what the fuck?'

There is Dolly on the screen, the photograph Jules took of her that day. The close-up of the earrings, the butterfly tattoo on her shoulder. How did Vanda get hold of that?

Jules had Instagrammed the photograph, but hadn't named Dolly in the caption. There were no clues to who Dolly was, so how come Vanda worked it out? Some two-day photography course when she first arrived here, and Jules thinks she's Don bloody McCullin. She should have stuck with midwifery. She'd never made a mistake. Her OCD came in handy when giving injections, all that triple-checking.

Taking pictures was just a pastime and now there's a permanent record of Dolly's face and name up on that website. If Amber sacks her, this will reduce her chances of getting another job. Christ, how did Vanda even know this was a photograph of Dolly?

A child is fighting for his life in hospital after being run over by a car on his maid's watch.

Jules puts a towel onto the rug and the baby kicks there. She reads the rest of the opinion piece then sits and types a response.

The photograph you've included here is mine. I didn't give permission for it to be used, and I'd like it taken down immediately. I really object to you using it to accompany this article with its unfounded accusations.

Dolly is none of the things you say. You can't judge someone when you don't know all the details.

She hits 'post'.

⧗

Dolly wakes in her bedroom fully dressed. Her bag is packed and lying on the floor. It's time to leave now. She switches on her phone and it beeps. There's a text message from Tala.

Mrs Heng's thrown me out. Will call later.

Does that mean Mrs Heng's found out about Maidhacker? Dolly turns off her phone; Tala already has problems of her own without having to deal with Dolly's. She should leave the phone here; it's Ma'am Amber's after all. But she pushes it into her bag.

She opens the fridge and the smell of raw meat washes over her. There are two fresh steaks wrapped in plastic on the shelf, a watery pond of blood beside them. She takes a bottle of water from a slot and closes the door.

She walks outside, past the palm trees, the lines of switched-off lights around the bark, the swimming pool blue with tiles. A Filipina walks past her, staring at the rucksack on Dolly's back.

Dolly stops. She can just make out the security guard sitting inside the glass box at the entrance.

Why doesn't she go and ask the man she's been sleeping with for the past year to help her right now, say that she needs Gavin to help her find another job, say that she needs money to tide her over?

She turns around and walks back into the condo, right up to his oak front door. She clenches her fist, raises it, ready to knock.

She looks at her hand then, bunched in the air, the way it stroked and kneaded him. He kissed this hand once then put it tight around himself, and showed her what to do.

She turns and walks away from his door.

At the condo entrance, she drops her bag to the ground. She unzips it and pulls out that sexy red nightdress. She crushes it in her hand and stuffs it into the bin. The silk strokes her fingers and slides away.

She walks past the security guard, her head upright, the sun painting her with light. She climbs the thin path with the big butterflies painted on the slabs, the open drain beside. There is no one at the bus stop, and it takes a long time for the bus to come.

When it does, she scans her card and gets on. Outside, a man with a black and white scarf wrapped around his head is spraying the flowers in the middle of the highway. The pesticide smokes. The sour-smelling chemicals slip through the cracks of the bus. The high-rise buildings are brown, and white, and yellow.

Everything will be okay, Dolly tells herself. But Sam, what sort of state will he be in this morning?

The bus stops, and Dolly gets off and climbs the steps to Lion Plaza.

She goes through the sliding doors. Drums bash from the performing arts place. Purses on strings dangle outside a thin shop. Escalators roll along one side, a glass lift goes up and down on the other. The floor is plastic and shiny, and her flip-flops squeak on it. Then there it is: Maid Easy For You.

A woman is standing in the window holding up a sign that says 'Buy Today and Get Discount'. Dolly thinks she's a plastic model at first, but her smile slips. Dolly steps through the door.

Maids sit in blue aprons, listening to a woman at the front who is pointing to the whiteboard with a stick. A wide black line of fringe, puffy cheeks, shoulder pads in a cream blouse. Charmaine.

'And no boyfriends!' She puts her hand to her ear. 'What's that?' Her mouth hangs open, a red boiled sweet on her tongue.

'No boyfriends!' the women chant as one echoey voice. A few of them giggle.

Charmaine claps her hands. 'Go to your work stations now.'

Dolly walks towards her.

'Yes?' says Charmaine.

'I need a job.'

'You what?'

'I need to find another job.'

Dolly's face is burning hot. Charmaine points her foot sideways.

'You've been here before, a long time ago. I remember your face.'

'You did the contract for my first job. But I can't go back there, not now.'

'What?'

'The woman doesn't need a maid any more. I have a very good reference from her husband though.'

Charmaine looks Dolly up and down. 'I bet you do.' She moves towards a wooden desk. 'Everyone wants cheap, especially when you're damaged goods. Sit down.'

Dolly sits beside the desk and Charmaine pulls up a chair. She asks Dolly questions then taps the paper with her pen.

'The trouble is there're no vacancies at the moment,' says Charmaine. 'The window's worth a try though.'

She points and there in the window is that woman still holding the sign, with her back to them, her hair streaked with grey.

'Here,' says Charmaine.

Dolly looks down at the big piece of cardboard in Charmaine's hand. 'Lowest Pay and Fee', it says. Dolly doesn't take it from her.

'Leave your things over here and go do the pregnancy test in the toilets first.' She hands a plastic stick to Dolly.

'Girl!' Charmaine calls to the woman in the window, who turns around, her wrinkled face sagging.

'You work on the doll now.'

Charmaine points at a big plastic changing station with a doll on the top. Beside it, a Filipina is pushing another woman around in a wheelchair. The woman gets up then and they swap.

The woman in the window puts her sign on the desk and goes to the changing station. She picks up a bottle of brown sauce; it squelches when she squeezes it over the doll's backside.

A woman in a black dress, high heels and fat hair is standing in front of the smiley wheelchair maids now.

She says to Charmaine, 'I take that one. How much?'

'You take her today, and you can have her for $250 a month.'

Dolly heads out of the agency door, down the people-packed corridor. The mall toilets are shiny with black tiles and mirrors. She goes into the cubicle at the end; a hole cut into the floor smells of urine. She crouches and pees on the stick. She waves it around. Someone knocks on the toilet door. 'Are you done yet?' It's Charmaine.

'Yes,' says Dolly, then looks down and sees that there isn't one line, but two pink ones.

What about the blood that was there in her underwear? Should she spit on the stick to make the pink lines disappear? Should she break it in two and say it didn't work? She can hear Charmaine tapping her foot, and Dolly just stands there looking at the plastic stick, the stench of urine up her nose.

Her daughter's name stamps through her head. *Mallie. Mallie. Mallie.* The pills didn't work and now Dolly will be thrown out.

'Girl, I haven't got all day.'

Dolly opens the cubicle door and gives Charmaine the stick. Charmaine tuts and spits her boiled sweet into the bin at the door. It makes a thump as it lands.

Chapter 17

✈

The front door goes. Jules lifts the baby and heads along the corridor. David is gone from the sofa. She pulls open the door.

Tala's hair is a series of bumpy knots. At the side of her mouth, there's a white circle, a crust of sleep in her left eye. A big canvas bag is at her feet.

'What's happened?' asks Jules.

An unsure smile quivers across Tala's mouth. She shakes her head, but says nothing.

'Come in,' says Jules, and Tala follows her, leaving the bag behind on the tiles.

Jules pours a glass of water and hands it to Tala.

'My employer threw me out,' says Tala.

'Why?'

'She thought she was going to get into trouble,' says Tala. 'She's kept my passport, my computer. I didn't get them back before I left.'

'She took your things?'

Tala nods.

'She can't do that.'

Tala nods again.

'Where did you sleep last night?'

Tala shrugs. 'It doesn't matter.'

'What are you going to do?'

'I'll have to find another employer.'

'Well, you've got this job.'

'I need something more than this, ma'am.' Tala gulps at her drink.

'Well, look, you can stay here for now, maybe we could employ you or something.'

'But what about . . .?' Tala points to the baby.

'I'm just looking after him.'

'What?'

'For a charity.'

'You get paid for this?'

'No. It's just I . . .'

'Oh my Gad, ma'am, you're practising.'

'What?'

'For when you have a baby of your own.' A huge smile is about to burst across Tala's face.

'That's not what this is.'

'But soon, ma'am, soon. And babies are the best. Oh, boo, boo, ga, ga, ga.'

Tala's lips pout. More peculiar sounds tumble out as she takes hold of the baby's fingers and bobs them.

'He's a treasure, isn't he?' says Jules. 'His name's Khalib.'

'Oh, you'd be the best mama that boy could have.'

Jules feels tearful. It must be her hormones. She's not a crier, never has been. In her old job, she'd be crying all the time if she was. Her eyes find Tala's. The two women stare at each other. Tala covers Jules' hand with her own then Tala's gaze snaps to the front door.

'Oh, my bag!' she says.

'It's outside, I'll get it,' says Jules.

The women walk to the door as if in a race. Jules gets there first, and drags the bag. Tala takes the other handle and pulls it her way.

'It's okay, ma'am.'

'No, no, I've got it,' says Jules.

'You've got the baby, ma'am.'

Tala pulls the handle; this time it rips free from Jules' hand. The baby starts to cry. Jules picks up her keys and clinks them in front of his face, but the crying gets worse.

Tala is making those baby noises again, her face pressed near to Khalib's. 'Here.' She holds her arms out.

'Oh, no, I can do this.'

Tala's arms stay put in the air. Jules hands her the baby. Tala sits with him face down on her knees and rubs his back hard – too hard, it seems to Jules. He burps loudly.

'Oh, my Gad, boy, no wonder you were crying,' shrieks Tala.

Jules laughs then stares at Khalib, upright in Tala's arms now, struggling to lift his head. Why can't he be Jules' son when she so wants him to be? His vanilla smell, the dimples in his cheeks, the person he'll turn out to be. The memory of that blog and Dolly's photograph snatches her then. Telling Tala about it will have to wait, for now at least.

⧗

Dolly is sitting with her back against the wall, her feet on the brown, scratchy carpet. There are four women around her, sitting, lying with their heads on the floor. One woman is in the corner on her knees, muttering.

The red clock ticks on the wall; she's been shut inside this sweat-filled, windowless room for hours now. Her belly bubbles; too late for the kill-pills now. She'll return here after she's given birth to this baby. Tala has money saved; she'll lend her some and Dolly will be able to start all over again. She gets up, presses the brass handle down, but the door's locked. She slaps her hand against the wood.

'Hey!'

She works the handle again then punches the wood. 'Hey!'

Charmaine opens the door. She has on a black suit, shoulders like shelves.

'I need my bag. I want to call the family who I work for,' Dolly says.

'You don't work for anyone any more.'

'But my previous employer, he'll help.'

'The van is taking you and some of the others to the airport in fifteen minutes.'

'What? But I haven't even said goodbye to my sister.'

'Wake up! Get ready!' Charmaine shouts to the other women. 'Where's my bag?'

Charmaine doesn't reply. The thick air moves. Women get up, yawning, arms stretching, dead things coming back to life. There are coughs, sniffs.

'Oh, God,' says a voice. Someone zips up a bag.

'Please, can I just use a phone?'

'Phone costs money. You got no money,' says Charmaine.

'But Sir Tor has.'

'He the father of your bastard, is he? No phone calls.' She closes the door. The key turns in the lock.

Dolly leans her forehead against the wood. She needs to get in touch with Tala, tell her what's happened and find out how Sam is.

When Charmaine opens the door finally, Dolly takes deep, warm breaths of the outside. Charmaine leads them through the mall to the toilets. They shuffle past people. Someone calls a name, 'Clarissa!', and Dolly turns her head to see a woman in white sneakers chasing a small girl who's running through the crowds with bunches in her hair. The shop signs blaze red and white.

In the toilets, the smell sweeps into Dolly. She throws up into the hole in the floor and wipes her face with her hand. She retches again and again even when nothing comes up. She stands there burping.

'Hurry up!' Charmaine shouts.

Dolly puts her hand against the cracked tiled wall, dirt smudged in the grout. She waits and the retching stops.

She walks back to the agency behind Charmaine and the other women. She could run, but she doesn't. She could hide, but she doesn't do that either; she just walks. Back in the agency, the women sit on the red plastic chairs, the same chairs that were there when Dolly did her training.

Charmaine gives Dolly her rucksack. Dolly pulls out her phone and presses a button on it, but there's no juice on it any more. She goes through her bag, but can't find the plug to charge it. Her bank book and passport are inside the bag. She puts her hand in for the brooch and there it is, the stones in it sharp as shells. The recipe book is there too and Mallie's Minion toy, but the Tiffany box is gone.

The women on the chairs are a line of pastel shorts, a flowery skirt and Dolly in her jeans. There are posters on the wall. 'Cheap Maids'. 'Evelyn Loh Insurance'. And the plastic doll sits in its Pampers staring with one eye blue, the other white in the places where the paint has chipped off.

Charmaine strides to the door, her keys jangling. 'We go,' she says.

The women get up and shuffle through the door. They step onto the escalator and for a moment Dolly feels as if she's about to fall. She clasps the side. The smell is garlic and bleach, one big stinky cocktail of cleaning products and old food. Dolly burps and saliva floods her mouth. She swallows it down and carries on walking, then burps again.

There is a blue van outside. A queue of people, waiting for cabs, stare at the women. Dolly is the last to get into the van; it smells of dust. She pulls at the seat belt, but there's nowhere to slot it in. She presses her head to the glass.

The van roars, and someone bashes the window. The hand is rough with fat fingers and Dolly looks past that to the pretty face.

'Tala!' Dolly puts her hand to her sister's through the glass.

And Tala shapes her mouth, but doesn't make a sound.

'Tala!' Dolly shouts again, but the van moves off and Tala's hand comes away from the steam-patched window. She is shouting and running and reaching out. And Dolly stands and bumps her head on the ceiling of the van.

'Sit down, *lah*!' says the driver.

He goes over a bump in the road, and she falls into her seat, still turning back to look. Tala's face is wet, her chin shaking. She gets further away, smaller, and Dolly tries not to blink.

Then the van turns right and Tala is gone, and Dolly's breath is quick, her mouth dry. The driver switches on the radio. It fizzles then there's a song.

Through the front window, there is a long black road. She pulls her purse from her rucksack and opens it. The photograph of Mallie with her wispy pigtails smiles through the plastic, but the last of the money that she took from Gavin isn't where she stuffed it. There is nothing but loose change. She's getting closer now to her daughter though, closer. She'll be able to touch her skin, her hands, smooth her fingers over her daughter's hair, see how she's changed. And she'll be her mother again even if it's only for a few months more.

The van disappears into the distance, and Tala's chin wobbles. They're taking away her sister, but where to? She swallows down the rest of her tears and strides into the mall. When she knocked on Ma'am Amber's front door earlier, Sir Tor opened it and told her that Dolly had already left for the employment agency.

She tucks her T-shirt into her skirt and pushes open the glass door to Maid Easy For You. The sweaty air travels over her.

Charmaine is standing in front of a whiteboard with women in blue aprons looking up at her. Her fringe is so neat it looks like someone put a ruler against it to cut.

'And sometimes the employer might offer you a mobile phone instead of a day off,' she says. 'It's up to you which one you choose.'

This place hasn't changed much. There's the ironing board in the corner, covered in shiny silver fabric, a white unit with shelved funeral pyres of plastic dolls with nylon hair and chipped eyes.

Tala taps her foot, puts her hand on her hip. Some of the women on the lines of chairs are sticking their hands in the air and asking questions. Tala hasn't got time for this. She stops tapping and starts marching right to the front of the class where Charmaine stands with a pencil in her hand like she's about to conduct an orchestra.

'Ma'am Charmaine, can I have a minute of your precious time?'

'I'm taking a class here.'

'But, ma'am . . .'

'Impatience is not much of a recommendation.'

Tala's nostrils flare in a bid to take in as much air as possible. Shoulders back, chest heaved, she brings herself to full height.

'Where are they taking my sister?'

Charmaine stares. 'Who's your sister?'

'I've been here enough times for you to know me.'

'I don't recall.'

'My sister, Dolly Pabro Castillo.'

'I'm not sure, I . . .'

'You couldn't miss her, she has lots of earrings. She's beautiful too.'

'And loose.'

'What?'

'She's pregnant.'

But the pills?

Charmaine bends and pulls a long plastic stick from a bin. She pushes it towards Tala as if she's about to shove a thermometer into her mouth.

'Here's the test. She's being deported back to Manila.'

'To Manila? But that's more than three hundred kilometres away from our home.'

'The twelve o'clock plane out of Changi. You might just make it.'

Tala turns on her heel. The glass door creaks closed behind

her. She pulls her phone out of her handbag. It's 11.43 a.m., but even if she had time to get to the airport, they wouldn't let her anywhere near Dolly. She uses her mobile phone to ring her sister, but her hands are shaking so much she misdials. She tries again and presses it to her ear. It rings and rings. She sends a text instead: *We'll work this out. Try not to worry. Just call.*

Face your challenges, isn't that what Russell Grant said? But right now, Tala can't think of any way out of this mess that they're in.

Jules goes into the kitchen. The children are in the school playground lining up. A loudspeaker erupts with rousing national anthem-type music. Her mobile phone goes and she picks it up.

'Mrs Harris?'

'Yes?'

'We're moving Khalib on.'

'What, already?'

'The paperwork for the adoption's come through quicker than we thought it would.'

The voice in the receiver doesn't belong to the woman Jules spoke to before.

'When will this happen?'

'Would you be able to drop him off with his new family next week, say Tuesday?'

Consoling words start drifting through Jules' head. *It's better this happens now before you become too attached.* She clears her throat. 'If the adoption doesn't work out, I want to keep him; we want to keep him.'

'Yes, he's a very popular baby,' says the woman. 'Please be at the new family's apartment by noon on the twenty-fifth. I'll email you the address.'

Jules goes upstairs where Khalib is asleep in the bassinet. He's going to be all right, she thinks. She digs her fingernails into her arm to stop the other thoughts rising inside her like floodwater. She doesn't want him to go. She doesn't want anyone else to be this boy's mother. She lets go of her arm then. There are white fingernail marks carved into her skin.

Chapter 18

The windows of Ninoy Aquino Airport are covered in rain. The day looks grey, but when Dolly gets outside she squints away the sun. Men rush towards people. *Two hundred pesos this. Three hundred pesos that.* There is petrol in the air. Two small buses are parked on the kerb, one with a picture of Nicole Scherzinger in a pink and purple dress painted across the side. A man in denims cut off to the knees grabs a trolley and waves at someone. Dolly walks through people speaking into mobile phones.

At the Nicole bus, she climbs the steps.

'Where to?' asks the driver. The chip in his front tooth has turned it into a triangle. His thin moustache runs the width of his lips.

'Tagudin.'

'Six-hour drive to Tagudin. I'm only going as far as Metro Manila. You could get a connecting bus there though.'

'The thing is, I don't have any money to pay my fare.'

People are squashed into the seats. They look at her: a woman, with a ponytail at the side of her head; a man chewing gum. A chicken pecks through the bars of the cage on his knees. The air smells of drains.

'What have you got instead?'

The driver looks at Dolly and winks. She gets off and starts walking away then stops and searches through her bag.

She climbs onto the bus again. 'Here,' she says.

The gold brooch blinks. 'If you take me all the way to Tagudin, it's yours.'

The driver takes the brooch and rocks it up and down in his

hand. He turns it around and smiles. He works his thumbnail at the back of it.

'It's not worth anything, this.'

Dolly takes the brooch. There's a damn barcode on the back of it.

'Listen, I'll take you to central Manila,' says the driver. 'But you'll have to sit in the aisle.'

'What?'

'There's no seats left, lady.'

Dolly gets on and sits on the floor. What a fool she's been. The woman with the ponytail gives her a scarf to put under her backside. Someone eats something hot and spicy and Dolly swallows and breathes deeply. The woman hands her a squashy bottle of water and she drinks, and it is plain and clean and oh so good. The woman passes her an orange-coloured pinaypay then. The fried banana cake is a comfort.

Dolly pulls the phone from her bag and looks at it again. She wishes it wasn't flat. She reaches into her bag and presses the Minion's fatness. A small thing for Mallie. And Sammy? She didn't even get to say goodbye to him. Did she give him enough hugs before she left? What if he dies? She leans her head against the side of a seat and the bus creaks and cracks and jumps. A cockroach scuttles in circles under a seat.

When the bus stops in the middle of Manila, Dolly gets off first, her bag on her shoulder. The dust covers her toes in the flip-flops. Others get off too and they bump and brush past Dolly. She stands there looking up at the big sign of a woman in her lacy, black underwear, her boobies all round and pert. Dolly turns away and another sign looms: 'God Watches Over You'. She turns away from that one too, and the sky is full of wires fixed to tall poles. Cars go all about, white ones, grey ones, buses with big grilles on the front, one of them the brightest yellow with a sign across the top that says 'Mandy'. Horns toot, people call out, men run towards a van.

Dolly opens her bag and takes out her phone. She presses the 'on' button pointlessly. Even if she had some money to use in a public phone booth, she can't recall Tala's mobile phone number or Mama's number either.

Dolly walks for a long time, past people eating banana-Qs on the kerb, a kid selling plastic raincoats, knees scabbed. She gets the smell of carioca and her belly makes a noise. She drinks the last drops of water from the squashed bottle.

Dolly turns off down an alleyway. The brick buildings are close together, blue rubbish bags all along. A black dog sticks its nose into one of the bags then looks at her, its teeth jutting over its jaw, thick drool coming out. Dolly stops. There are bones around the dog's paws and old vegetables too. Up ahead in the alley, something moves, dirty bare feet attached to trousers.

She turns around and keeps to the busy roads after that. Multicoloured buses pass by, one with Justin Timberlake's face on the side, baskets up top tied with string. A nun walks, her big cross swinging against her white dress. Dolly could stick her hand into the traffic and by chance, someone driving to Tagudin might stop. She could hope for another free ride on a bus, but Tagudin is a long way from Manila and she'll have to pay somehow.

There is the bus station, a bench along the outside. A woman with more fringe than hair is sitting on it, her head sinking. A man beside her is leaning forward, his head in his hands. Dolly will be able to take the weight off her feet if she rests on that bench for a while. She sits, puts her head against the bricks behind. A vent rolls air. Her nose is full with the smell of dog shit. It's so strong she checks the soles of her flip-flops. When she looks up again, the woman has gone.

A grey truck with the back uncovered drives by slowly then stops in front of Dolly. A man with angular cheeks, and a scarf tied around his head, leers at her from the driver's seat. She looks away, fiddles with her hair. She hears him laughing. The truck pulls away, then the wheels whine as it reverses, pausing in front of her again. The man lifts a knife to his lips and pokes the steel with his tongue. Dolly starts to hyperventilate. The truck moves away again slowly.

Dolly gets up and starts running, looking over her shoulder at the truck which has stopped again.

'Mallie is safe,' she says to herself, and that's something.

She runs along a street out of sight.

Jules puts the new clothes that David bought for Khalib into a carrier bag, then the old blanket that she's washed, a spare bottle.

Khalib's asleep in the bassinet on the rug in the living room, something catching at the back of his throat as he breathes. The newspaper crinkles in David's hands. He is sitting on the sofa, holding the paper so high she can't see his face. She picks up her camera, lies on her stomach on the rug and takes some shots of Khalib, his bare feet making the shape of the letter V, his scrunched hands. She gets up then and angles the camera downwards, snapping the curve of his chin, his plump cheeks.

There is a faint knock on the front door. When Jules opens it, Tala is stooping there, the bags under her eyes more swollen than earlier.

'What's happened?'

Tala steps inside.

'Before I went to work earlier, I found out Dolly had gone back to the employment agency. I rushed over there, but it was too late.'

'What do you mean?'

'They've deported her.'

'But why?'

Tala bites her lip, looks up at Jules. 'To have to say this to you, ma'am, of all people . . .'

'What?' Jules whispers.

'She's pregnant.'

David puts down the newspaper.

'And they've deported her for that?' asks Jules.

'They give all of us a pregnancy test every six months. If you're pregnant you have to leave.'

'Jesus,' says David.

'She's been so stupid!'

Jules' heart speeds up. *It must be Gavin's baby.* Both women look at Khalib.

'What's Dolly got to say about all this?' asks David.

'I've tried her phone; there's no reply. I don't know where she is,' says Tala.

'I'm sure she'll get in touch. She's probably still travelling,' says Jules.

Tala nods. The baby snuffles, his eyelids flicker open then close again.

'Tala, you know you can stay here as long as you need, don't you?' says Jules.

She hears David swallowing hard.

'Would it be okay to stay just for a couple of weeks while I try to find a new place to live?'

Jules' eyes snap to David. She opens her mouth to speak, but David snatches the moment. 'We'd be happy to have you,' he says.

'Oh, thank you.' Tala is slightly breathless. 'I'm sorry to rush off like this, but I've just come back to get something,' she says.

She delves into her canvas bag, still lying on the floor, and grabs a yellow book then pokes it into her handbag.

'Here,' says Jules, handing Tala a key. 'I'll make up the bed for you in the spare room at the end of the corridor.'

'I'm so grateful, ma'am. Thank you. And I'm sorry, but I really do need to go out again.'

Tala belts through the front door, and Khalib stretches his leg and starts to wake.

Essential House Rules for Foreign Domestic Maids
Rule 6. Respect: Your maid must treat you respectfully and carry out her duties as instructed. She must be co-operative, quietly spoken and never rude.

Chapter 19

The bank teller sandwiches the notes inside the bank book and pushes it underneath the glass towards Tala. She's drawn out most of her money to give to Mrs Heng. Tala can still claw it back though, can't she? Pay Mrs Heng and carry on. But what if Mrs Heng finds out she's Maidhacker? Maybe she'll ask for even more money to keep her trap shut.

Tala stuffs the money into her bag and pulls out her phone. She checks it for what feels like the hundredth time. Nothing. Dolly can look after herself though. Underneath all that quiet, there's a will of iron. That's who Mallie gets it from.

Tala goes down the steps of Plover Plaza and walks along Orchard Road. She clutches the bag and its booty to her chest, the handle dangling. The street is so spotless, it's like it's been cleaned by a whole bunch of Pinoys; then again it probably has.

Blue cabs wait in lines behind the lights, the mirrored rectangles of their windows hiding the drivers inside. A man leans out of a side window, holds a nostril closed and blows a string of glue through the other one. How disgusting, though sometimes Tala thinks her life is all bodily residues – skid marks down toilets and so much dust.

A woman strolls by in a pink baby-doll dress so nylon that if you set a match to it she'd go up in flames. She looks as lacy as Mrs Heng's daughter. Tala walks behind her then the woman stops abruptly and Tala bumps into her, her hand tangling in the woman's swish of long hair. The woman tuts and checks the zip on her bag. Tala passes and looks back. The woman's face is different to the Heng daughter; the false eyelashes are just the same though. Something tickles Tala's hand; there's a clump of nylon hair in her fingers – that's just the same as the Heng daughter, too – and Tala pinches and whips until the strands fly to the ground. *And those women complain about all the hairs us helpers leave behind . . .*

Tala pushes her hand into her bag to check the money is safe inside, and on she walks, past rectangular planters spiked with palms. This won't be the first time she's thrown money away. All those school fees for Ace, paying it into Bong's bank account first. A phone call came from the school to say Ace had been skipping lessons and the fees hadn't been paid for the past three months. When Tala phoned the village shop, Bong didn't call her back. She paid for a flight home and marched on into the house. Marlon came back from a day selling with the guavas around his neck, an HB pencil pushed behind his ear. The house was dotted with barely hidden empty bottles: a flat one shoved between the cushions of the sofa; in a cardboard box beside the sink; under one of the coiled mattresses beside the wall. The smell of stale alcohol had seeped into the warmth of the living room. A cockroach escaped through a hole in the wooden wall.

Tala and Marlon loaded the glass into an old trolley, and Marlon pushed the chinking bottles up the dirt track and along the tarmac road. The music of the glass was cheerful and put a smile inside Tala despite everything. Despite all that wasted money, despite her son having wasted his big opportunity.

Back in the house, she sprayed and tidied. She looked through a stack of papers rippled with Marlon's painted pictures. A child with a beaded sash over her face, a brown image of a nipa hut with a blue bird on the roof. She hadn't thought to bring Marlon more art supplies.

Bong didn't make any noise when he came up the path, but when she looked through the glass, there he was swaying on the hammock tied between two palm trees. She looked up into the leaves with hope, but there were no coconuts to come crashing onto his head. Tala closed her hand around the bottle of Ajax on the counter and pulled open the door.

Bong was sleeping, lips glistening. Tala unscrewed the lid and poured the Ajax into his face. He sat up, the hammock going this way and that.

'What did you do that for?' he shouted, soaking, spluttering, more pine fresh than White Castle Whisky.

'For you, you idiot. For wasting my money!'

He went inside, put his head under the tap then fell asleep for the rest of the day, and there was no budging him. And all that time she'd thought he had another woman. But the temptation she'd imagined with pert bosoms and curvy lips was 40 per cent proof with a screw top.

When Ace walked in, Tala started simmering all over again. He kissed her on the forehead, and she pushed her hand into the pocket of her shorts to stop herself slapping his pitted cheek, and her who hadn't hit her children, ever.

'Why the hell have you been missing college?'

'Oh, give it a rest,' he said.

'If you don't go, what do you think is going to happen?'

He shrugged.

'You're going to end up like your mama, that's what!'

He went back to school for a week after Tala left then he fell in with this now-pregnant girlfriend of his, Alice. Tala didn't hear from him for years in-between. The truth is she gambled on the wrong son. Ace doesn't work, but Marlon does, selling guavas, driving a scooter, working in the warehouse of the local super-market. It leaves little time for his art.

Tala considers how she might love one son more than the other, but no, there's an equal swell of love for both. She keeps on walking, people passing with their ribboned paper bags. The air's like holding your hands too close to an electric dryer. A tune pounds from a kiosk selling food, breaded prawns on sticks, boxes of chicken rice. She passes one towering shopping mall after another, metal columns and glass glinting with light. Cars roll down the road. Crossings beep. A tambourine shimmer of music sails through the heat.

The last people in the bus queue climb onto the 123, and Tala runs and *ay nako*, she has to dodge a young boy on a blue scooter zipping along the pavement.

The back doors of the bus start to close, but she makes it to them just in time and they slam with her head in-between, her body and feet still on the road outside. She shimmies sideways as the bus pulls away, her head jammed between the rubber door seals.

'Uncle!' shouts a woman on board the bus, but all Tala can see is the grey plastic floor.

The driver must notice her then because the brakes squeal, and there's a cacophony of hooting car horns.

The doors open and Tala stands upright, closing her hands around her neck. With everything still attached, she steps on, seven people looking up at her. One woman is covering her mouth with a hand, and when she sees Tala staring she looks away.

'Sorry, *lah*!' the driver shouts.

Tala nods in his direction, and sits in a free seat. Talk about losing your head. Her heart's still thudding, her neck sore from the doors. They slide on by the university on the highway, picking people up at every stop. The road is lined with shrubs, a strip of velvet grass running down the middle. A big sign with a sunflower on it.

When the highway widens into three lanes and Tala sees the roundabout rising like a miniature hill, she pings the bell. She gets off, mosquitoes buzzing over water in a dip, clods of broken concrete. She steps over them and walks across the carpet grass towards the yellow HDB flats. There's that poor caged bird, but Tala won't be poking any bread through the bars this evening.

She feels for the money in her handbag. She might as well

throw it into the air because will Mrs Heng even give her things back when Tala hands over the money? But she doesn't have a choice; she needs her computer and her passport, and she needs to know whether Mrs Heng has found out about the blog.

The budgerigar chirrups on its perch. She walks on past, its gentle song in her ears. She catches hold of the banister, pulls her bulk up the stairs. She gives a little ding-dong. She starts tapping her foot faster and faster, her eye on the scratched brass *92H*. She counts and gets to triple figures before Mrs Heng pulls open the door in a lavender shirt and trousers. A dry birthmark of tissue paper is stuck to her chin.

'I've got your money,' says Tala.

Mrs Heng pulls Tala inside by grabbing at her T-shirt. Tala gives her hand back to her and takes out the notes. Mrs Heng snatches them, fans them and counts, her lips twitching, her mouth ponging coffee. And Tala stands there not knowing what to do with her now empty hands, fevered words clogging in her throat; there are so many of them she needs to speak.

'I get your things,' says Mrs Heng.

Her pink elasticated slippers pad down the corridor. There's a distant sound of doors opening and closing. Tala smells something burnt. Mrs Heng is an even worse cook than her. There'll be overdone binned chicken, and rice permanently scabbed to a saucepan. She must have cooked at home for once instead of heading down to the hawker centre.

There she is now, her slippers squeaking on the marble-tiled floor.

'Here.' She gives Tala a heavy plastic bag with a tear in it. The wad of money is gone from her hand.

Tala feels inside the plastic bag, touches her computer then her passport. She needs to get out of here and fast. As soon as she's out through the front door again, Mrs Heng slams it, so that Tala's blinded by the swish of her own hair. She untangles herself and doesn't look back. Mrs Heng can't have discovered the blog, otherwise she would have said something. The air beyond the open side of the corridor is dark now. She passes a blue door with a fat black bin liner outside. The bag sends out its durian stink. Tala covers her nose, clutching the computer to her chest like she's hugging a baby. Not that she's in the mood for making goo-goo sounds.

She sashays, pumping her fists like a bulging speed walker. The cars drone by on the distant highway, a bird tweets. The budgerigar? She's already passed the cage; she keeps going, but then she stops.

She walks back to the cage and undoes the bolt. She watches the budgerigar for a few seconds, but it just carries on fluttering around the cage.

'Come on, you stupid article!' she calls, shovelling her hand inside.

But still the bird ignores her. She leaves the door open anyway, and walks on.

Her bank book's almost empty now she's given most of her savings to Mrs Heng, and Dolly is gone. She puts her free hand to her mouth as if that can stop the thoughts coming. Then all those words in her throat go rising into her head, and she knows that she is never going to be silenced.

⧗

Dolly watches as a woman comes out from a shop, a sign up top that says 'Raymundo Food'. She pulls down the shutters. She is an old woman with gold in her teeth. She sees Dolly, and looks one way then the other.

The smell of pork adobo comes into Dolly's nose and her belly starts to dance. She vomits and spits the last of her stomach contents to the ground; there's nothing much. The woman's footsteps in her clogs make a sound like beating bamboo as she approaches Dolly. Her dress is orange with thin little straps and she has lines on her face. It could be Tala's face, put together in a different way; the nose thinner, the chin not so wide. Her teeth look like they have been covered in grey felt-tip apart from the gold bits.

'You can sleep in there,' she says.

'In your shop?'

She laughs. 'I can open it back up again.'

Dolly swallows. 'No.'

'You've been walking a long time. I saw you earlier. And it's dark, and well, it's safe in there.'

Dolly thinks about the man in the truck leering at her. 'You'll come back in the morning?'

'First thing.'

She hands Dolly a can of Calamansi Soda, and Dolly drinks. It'll only be for a few hours until the bank opens, then she'll be able to withdraw her savings.

The woman pulls up the shutters and Dolly goes into the shop. It is dark and she bumps into something. She takes her bag from her shoulder and puts it onto the floor.

The woman closes the shutters behind her then with a shake and rattle. And Dolly stands there in the black, gloopy air.

She lies down on the floor and reaches for her rucksack to put under her head, but it's not there. She crawls and pats about the smooth floor, but feels nothing except boxes.

The woman has taken her bag. Her passport is gone, her bank book too, her recipe book, and everything else.

She goes towards the shutters and pulls them up, then she's outside in the half-light again, looking down at the padlock in bits on the ground. The woman must have broken in.

Dolly goes back inside the shop where a gecko is clicking. There's barely enough light from the street lamp to see, but she searches around the cash register, the drawer of which is open and empty.

She clambers to her knees, pushes her hand beneath the counter. She pulls out dust, what feels like hard kernels of dead beetles, and something else. Coins, a note. She puts them into her pocket.

Over at the shelves, she grabs a packet of Magic Melts, and puts two biscuits into her mouth at once. The crumbs catch in her throat and she coughs.

She goes outside and walks towards the lights. There is a skeleton of metal on the roof of one building. Three men sit in front of another, one of them making a roll-your-own. A jar on a table is full with ash. And on she walks, the mud making patterns on her legs, threatening to sink her.

A lit-up sign looms, The Pink Lady; the light is out on the L. Through the open door, Dolly watches the women in spangly bikinis twist around silver poles. The heels of their shoes are thin and gold. One of them wears a metallic red bra; the bare nipples of the other woman tip themselves to the ceiling. The music drums through Dolly.

She looks down at her hands. Her bag has been stolen, but finally she knows just what to do.

Tala breaks into a waddling run as she nears the condo, her computer making her list to one side.

She bounces along the pavement, her breath fast and gasping. The lift comes and she glides up, uses the front door key that Ma'am Jules gave her. The apartment is in darkness; they must all be in bed. She tiptoes through the corridor and switches on the light in the spare room.

Jules has put Tala's canvas bag on top of the double bed, pushed against the panelled wooden wall. There is a thin wardrobe in the corner, and an air-conditioning unit over the door. Tala sits on the bed which is covered in a crisp white sheet. She presses her hand into the plump pillow. Relief settles on her for a few seconds, but then the memory of the mess that she's in dawns on her all over again.

She switches on her computer and while she waits for it to boot up, she examines her hair. It's getting as grey as cement. She snatches at the offending strands and yanks them out – at least this is one battle she might win. *Because I'm worth it.* Humph, she's worth nothing at all. Just $150 left in her bank account.

She tries to log on to her hotmail account, but the internet won't connect. She fishes through her bag for her glasses, perches them on her nose. When she cleaned here the last time, she noticed that Ma'am Jules had written the Wi-Fi network password on a piece of paper stuck to the fridge. Tala tiptoes down the corridor now, gets the piece of paper and goes back to the spare room.

She sits, types the password in and the computer connects with the internet. Oh, but there's still no word from Dolly. She logs on to her blog instead. Maidhacker. Tala brings up the site stats then and squints; that can't be right. She must be reading it wrong. She touches her finger under the numbers and trails it along, saying them out loud. Has Rita been sitting there clicking on and off Tala's blog just to cheer her up? More than 5,000 people have looked at that post about Dolly.

This must be some mistake. Tala clicks onto analytics and her eyes pop out of her head like they're on springs. More than 19,000 people have looked at her blog since she started it. There's a little creak beyond Tala's door. She goes still and listens then creeps towards it and whips it open, but no, there's no one there.

She logs out of her blog and clicks onto Vanda's. There are more comments underneath that post about Dolly. *Brilliant post, Vanda!* Oh, and listen to this: *The girl clearly wasn't doing her job properly. I hear she's been thrown out of the country, and quite right too.* Three comments down, someone else has put the boot in: *Deported? They should have charged her with neglect.*

Tala takes her conch shell out of her pocket.

'What am I going to do?' she whispers.

She holds the conch to her racing heart, willing it to give her some answers. No sign, no sound comes back. Then she stretches out her restless hands and starts typing. She knows this is risky, especially now Rita has found out she's Maidhacker, but her fingers keep stabbing the keys. *20 Ways in Which Employers Abuse Domestic Helpers.* She lists things: *Wage theft. Not being allowed out of the apartment. Forcing a maid to sleep under the dining-room table.* She expands the piece with newspaper reports of court cases.

She hits 'post' and within a minute three people have starred it. Maidhacker is back in business, she thinks. She shuts up her laptop, thinking that what she really needs to do is shut up Vanda. She puts her laptop into her big canvas bag and zips it. If only she had a padlock.

She pulls off her clothes and curls her exhausted body on top of the bed, her mind pumping with thoughts of her sister, and poor little Sam.

Chapter 20

The noise of the diners rises around Jules and David, but Khalib sleeps through it in the buggy, his head bent, doubling his chin.

'I can't believe we've got only a few days left with him,' Jules says, moving her uneaten corn fritter around the plate with a fork.

David leans towards her. 'Neither can I. God, I wish we could keep him.'

She nods, puts down her fork and forces a flat kind of smile.

'What are we like?' she says. 'Head over heels in love with a baby we've only been looking after for a few days.'

'He's shown us, though, hasn't he?'

'What?'

'What you've been worried about all along. That you might not be able to really love a child that wasn't yours.'

She looks at the sleeping baby. She wishes the parting moment was over with, so she can start mending all over again.

'Well, at least the alcohol and healthy-diet police have gone for good,' says David and takes a swig of his beer. Two inches of it disappear down his throat. 'At a time like this, I need to keep eating.'

A waiter passes, and David asks him for the dessert menu. In crisis moments, like when his pub-dwelling builder dad died of a heart attack seven years ago, David went up two trouser sizes, but the last thing Jules feels like doing when she's upset is comfort eating.

She turns to look at the stretch of bench tables full with people, the brightly coloured dresses, the crisp shirts, the wooden shelves lining the shop. On them are plastic bags with macarons inside, novelty-shaped pastas and patterned tins.

'How is Sam doing?' asks David.

'Well, he's stable now. Amber seems to think he might be allowed home soon. Not that the hospital is in any rush to let him go after what happened the last time.'

She can feel it rising up her throat: Khalib, the IVF, Sam, and that bloody photograph of Dolly on Vanda's blog. Just who the hell is Vanda? So many of the women here have odd ideas about their helpers – as if they've stepped back in time – that it could be any one of them: Maeve, Jemima, even Amber, though with what she's going through at the moment, it seems highly unlikely.

The waiter returns with a menu. David takes one look and orders the tiramisu, his cheeks already swelling with sugary anticipation. The waiter takes away their empty plates. Jules can feel David's restless legs jigging against hers; he bites at his nails, his eyes darting.

She pulls his hand from his mouth and lays her fingers over his.

'There's something up with you, David, and it's not just the baby or the IVF, is it?'

He bites his lip. 'I've been waiting for the right time to tell you, but . . .'

The waiter returns and puts the tiramisu on the table. Jules takes back her hand. It feels like a spider is inching its way up her spine as she waits for the waiter to walk away.

'Oh God, I wish I didn't have to tell you this.'

'David, for Christ's sake, just say it.'

He reaches out and takes her hand. 'I'm going to lose my job.'

'What?'

'They've given me three months' notice.'

'But why?'

'Cutbacks. They're getting rid of loads of us.'

He smoothes his hand over the wooden table.

'How long have you known?'

'For weeks. I didn't want to tell you, what with the IVF. I didn't want to stress you out.'

'And the night you were out, what was that?'

'A bunch of us, well, we were drowning our sorrows.'

She leans her elbows on the table, puts her chin into her hands.

'It means we have to leave,' he says. 'We have to get out of the country.'

'Why?'

'Because they turf you out when you haven't got a job.'

'What about my job?'

'Well, maybe, but it's expensive to live here. I'm not sure we'll be able to afford to stay on.'

'Well, summer in London, here we come. Christ, I don't think I can face going back yet.'

'You can't run away any more.'

'Running away. Maybe you're right, that's what I was doing, but coming here, it's rubbed my face in it. All these huge families everywhere, all these pregnant women.'

'It's a bubble here, not real life.'

'I'm going to miss this heat.'

'And that pool.'

'And this baby,' she says, looking at Khalib.

'He's a good kid.'

'He's a great kid.'

David squeezes her hand.

'So why don't we do it?'

'What, adoption?'

'Come on – we'd be all right at it, you and me. We've talked about it often enough.'

'He felt like a stranger to me, Khalib, but it hurts that we have to give him back. Stupid really, but I feel like I love him.'

'It's not stupid.' David looks down at their linked-together hands. 'I feel like that too.'

He picks up the spoon and starts to shovel the pudding into his mouth.

Khalib is wearing a stripy T-shirt and shorts that David bought him from babyGap. They'll never see Khalib again after he's adopted. She gulps the thought down, rubs her fist at her eye. The minutiae of their lives will close around them like water soon enough, and Khalib will settle and grow with his new family, she hopes.

The pudding disappears in record time.

Chair legs screech as if someone is scoring their fingernails down a blackboard. At one of the bench tables, a man has stood up. Jules sees his scalp shining through his gelled blond hair. It's Gavin.

'I'm just not having it!' rails a broad cockney voice. Maeve. Her hair is unfurling from the spongy bun ring fixed to her head. She picks up her glass, stands and hurls her white wine over Gavin.

Silence descends on the restaurant. Gavin turns and sees Jules, his overlapping teeth gritting, his sodden white shirt sticking to his muscular chest. He pulls the fabric away from his skin and heads for the loos; all the diners are staring at him.

Maeve dabs her serviette at her cheeks. She's shaking. A waitress rushes over to her with a cloth to wipe up the mess, and the silence pervades.

'What the hell was that about?' murmurs David.

'She's probably found out he's been having an affair with Dolly.'

'Dolly? Tala's Dolly?'

'The very same.'

The bill arrives. David pays and they head back to the car, the grey Toyota, safe and reliable unlike their old London sports car which has to be driven around the block for a warm-up before they can be sure it's up to doing a longer distance. Jules' brother Steve is looking after it for them while they're away. Jules straps Khalib into the back then climbs into the driver's seat and starts the engine.

David switches on the sound system. A mash-up of drums and electronic riffs surges through the car as he clicks through the compilation CD. Making a decision isn't something he finds easy. He settles on a bit of Coldplay as Jules turns into the lane that leads to Greenpalms, the silver sign on a slab of concrete. There's a woman with a red handbag on her shoulder standing beside one of the cream pillars waiting for a cab. The security guard in the glass box nods his head at them.

Jules parks in the underground car park then pulls at the door handle of the car. David puts his hand on her thigh to keep her there a moment longer.

'We're a family, you and me,' he says. 'Whatever happens. We don't need a child to make us a family.'

⧖

Dolly walks, a shredded blister on the sole of her foot. She trips and smacks to the ground, small stones grinding into her knees through the jean holes. She wandered the streets throughout last night. Now she's sleep-deprived and desperate. She gets up, passes tower blocks and buildings, overgrown patches of grass.

The coin is sticky and dusty in her hand. She used the rest of the money that she found in the shop to call Gavin from a telephone booth. The receiver buzzed intermittently at her ear then clicked to voicemail. She didn't leave a message. She's tried him five times in all, but he hasn't picked up. She wanted to call Tala too, but couldn't remember the order of the digits, and wasted yet more money on three wrong numbers. Now there's not enough money left for a call from a booth.

A street vendor sits on a stool beside basins of garlic, green chillies and potatoes. A sign saying 'Kamatis 10' is stabbed into a tomato. A yellow bus clanks by. Dolly goes sideways to avoid the pick-ups parked bumper to bumper along the pavement.

Underneath awnings, there are lines of food stalls. Women in aprons poke steaming woks. A man in a beige shirt, with a name badge hanging around his neck, stops momentarily to look. There's the whiff of mechado. He pulls out his mobile phone and speaks into it, moving away. She walks faster to keep pace.

'Please can I use your phone?' she says.

'Piss off!' he snaps.

There are people sitting on small stools on the pavement near a stall, forking food into their mouths from polystyrene plates. Garlic wafts; fried things and petrol too. People mill, point and pay.

Dolly walks up to the sweat-soaked stallholder whose thin black hair is tied up, wisps of it over her ears.

'Please, ma'am, I need to call someone. Do you have a phone I could use?'

'A local call?'

'Overseas.'

The woman shakes her head.

'Please,' Dolly says again. She opens her hand, the mottled coin in the centre of her palm.

The woman flicks her head to the side for Dolly to come behind the counter. 'What's the number you want? I'll dial. One minute only, okay?'

'Okay.'

'And don't let these bandy legs deceive you; I'll catch you if you try to run off with my phone.'

'Hey, hurry up!' shouts a man in steamy glasses.

Dolly hands the woman the coin and says the number. The woman types it in and hands the phone to Dolly. Dolly presses it to her ear, blocks her other one with a finger. A pan sizzles, paper plates piled high with noodles are passed to people. Dolly turns away and the phone beeps in her ear.

'Hello?' It's Ma'am Maeve's voice.

Why has she picked up Gavin's phone? Dolly doesn't say anything.

'Who's this?'

'I'd like to speak to Gavin, please.'

'What?' Ma'am Maeve spits the word.

'I just need him to come to the phone.'

'Who is this?'

'Please.' The word 'ma'am' is about to slide off Dolly's tongue, but she stops herself. 'I just need to speak to him, that's all.'

'Why are you calling my husband?'

Muffled words then. Dolly listens hard.

'Give me my bloody phone!' It's Gavin's voice in the background.

'I'll do no such thing.'

A crunch, a clatter.

'Hello?' says Dolly.

A far-off voice. 'My bloody face, ow! You bitch.'

'How many fucking women have you got on the go? You bastard! You lying cheating bastard!' Ma'am Maeve shouts.

'Who is this?' Gavin says loudly into the phone.

As if he didn't know. 'It's me, Dolly.'

'Ow! Get away from me. Stop it!' Gavin shouts.

Thuds. Heavy breathing. A slammed door.

'Why are you bloody calling me? Oh, Jesus, my eye.'

'The pills didn't work. They threw me out.'

'I don't understand.'

'I'm still pregnant; I've been deported.'

'Hurry up!' says the stallholder to Dolly, holding out her hand.

'If you think I'm going to pay for this . . . for your . . .' says Gavin.

'Have you heard anything about Sam?'

'What? Oh, that kid, he's . . .' His unsure voice drifts away. 'He's on the mend. Still in the hospital, though. Look, what do you want from me?'

'I just need your help. I'm stuck in Manila. My bag's been stolen. I need you to phone the bus station, buy me a ticket back home. A one-way ticket to Tagudin, that's all.'

'Oh, for fuck's sake.'

The line goes dead. Dolly clicks off the call and hands the phone back to the woman.

'Bad news?' asks the stallholder, stirring vegetables in a wok.

'I hope not,' says Dolly.

She walks away, the smell of cigar breezing over her.

Gavin is no longer part of her. There's a baby inside her – she touches her stomach – but it's not really his baby; it's hers.

There it is, the bus station; lots of people sitting on the bench outside now, smoking, sleeping, the cars zooming along each side of the road. She finds a space, squashes herself in and waits, hoping that Gavin will phone the bus station soon.

Eventually she walks up to the kiosk.

'Someone was going to buy a ticket for me; did they?'

'Name?' The man with a blue cap on his head reaches for a small plastic box.

'Dolly Pabro Castillo.'

'There's a ticket here, marked for Dolly, just Dolly. Is that you?'

Relief surges through her. Her rigid body loosens, her knees go from under her. She stumbles and rights herself and stares at the man through the glass.

'Tagudin, yeah?' the man says loudly.

Dolly nods and the man pushes the ticket under the glass.

Chapter 21

✈

Jules looks out of the window as David drives. She watches a girl with beakers of tea-to-go in each hand walk from a branch of Coffee Bean. Jules turns to take a look at the car seat criss-crossed with straps, the baby facing the back seat so that she can't see his face. Why did she think looking after this baby was a good idea? The fallout is coming. The charity emailed Jules with the address and the name of the couple who are adopting Khalib; David is driving there now.

She can handle this, can't she? It is nothing compared to what poor Sam has been through, and Amber for that matter. The outcome could have been so horribly different. Giving this baby up is going to be hard, but then how hard must it have been for his real mother watching someone else carry him away?

The car passes houses with flat roofs, barred gates, palms peeking through. There are open drains and thin uneven pavements. A long-beaked bird with a yellow chest flutters into a bush peppered with pink flowers. The air conditioning in the car whirs.

They stop outside number 24, a double-fronted white cube of a house. There are three pairs of shoes lined up outside the front door. The tiles in the courtyard are shiny, the flat roof skewered with silvery aerials.

Jules scoops up the plastic bag full of Khalib's clothes and bottles. With her other hand, she lifts Khalib in his car seat. As she rings the buzzer and speaks her name into the intercom, the metal grilles glide sideways. She thinks she should make some gesture to the baby in this, their last moment alone. She should whisper something important into his ear, but she doesn't.

She walks towards the front door that's already open. A woman is standing there, looking at the car seat in Jules' hand. Her earrings are silver teardrops.

A man with frameless glasses rushes to the door behind her, standing on tiptoes to see.

'You must be Jules,' says the woman.

'Mrs Lim?'

'Yes.' The woman's smiling widely now and staring at Khalib.

Mr Lim puts his hand on his wife's shoulder and ushers Jules inside, taking the plastic bag from Jules' hand.

'Please, come in,' he says.

Jules steps in and they follow.

'Well, this is Khalib,' says Jules, putting the car seat onto the floor.

A wooden staircase runs down the side of the open-plan living room.

'He's beautiful,' says Mrs Lim.

'And so cute,' says Mr Lim. He looks at the baby then at his wife.

Mrs Lim has sparkly eyeshadow on; Mr Lim's in a pressed blue shirt. They've dressed up for their big day. How long have they been waiting for it?

Jules clears her throat. They stand there looking at one another with all the awkwardness of silence between strangers.

'He'll be going through the night before long,' Jules says.

Mrs Lim's face folds into a momentary frown of confusion, then her eyebrows arch with surprise and she bursts into a slightly hysterical giggle.

'Oh, before I forget . . .' says Jules. She pulls an envelope from the plastic bag now on the floor, and hands it to Mrs Lim. 'I got these developed for you, just a few photographs I took of him.'

'Thank you.'

Jules bends and caresses the baby's face, tries to commit his brown eyes, his dimples to memory, already knowing that soon after she walks off she'll forget, in the way that it's impossible to conjure up the perfect faces of those you've loved. At least she's taken lots of photographs of him. She smiles to herself; he's fallen asleep. What a blessing, she thinks, that he'll remember nothing of this time.

'Goodbye,' she says.

A tear snakes its way down Mrs Lim's face as she looks at Jules.

'Thank you for bringing him to us,' she says.

Jules touches her arm. 'He's, well . . . you're going to love him.'

Jules turns away then and walks out to the car, the heat blanketing her. She stares at the pavement, her chest cleaved in two. The driver's door opens, and David gets out and hugs her so hard that it hurts.

Sitting on her bed in the spare room, Tala opens the email that Dolly sent a few days ago, saying that she'd made it home.

The pills didn't work. Charmaine gave me a test at the agency and it was positive. I'll find a way to get back there, Tala. I promise you. But tell me, how is Sam now? I'm so worried about him.

Tala takes off her glasses and picks up her conch shell, then she hears a noise coming from the living room. Someone is crying. She treads slowly down the corridor and sees Jules sitting on the sofa. The conch is still in Tala's hand as she sweeps in front of her. The baby has gone.

'Oh, ma'am,' says Tala.

Jules sniffs again, wipes her eyes with a fist. Tala sinks into the sofa beside her.

'Just being stupid, don't mind me,' says Jules.

'They should have let you keep him. Such a lovely baby. That face, oh.'

The sun goes in, draining the room of colour.

'Isn't there a chance you can adopt him?'

'No.'

'But you'll try again?'

'What, fostering?'

'The fertility drugs.'

'What? How did you . . .?'

Jules peers at Tala. Tala bites her lip.

'I saw a syringe, ma'am. That first time I cleaned for you.'

'Oh. Oh, right. Well, no, I'm not going to try IVF again. We tried three times. It wasn't three times lucky.'

'It seems like everything when you can't have that one thing. It's agony, just like grief.'

Tala looks down at the conch shell shut now into her hand, the beige of it between her fingers. The woman in the opposite apartment comes onto her balcony to water her pot plants with a hose. The sun comes out again then, pouring jaundiced light over the women.

'How is Dolly doing now she's home?' asks Jules.

'She's okay, I think.'

Tala pats Jules' knee then heaves herself out of the chair and goes back down the corridor holding the conch to her racing heart.

Jules is jogging down the hill towards the market, but keeps glancing at her watch. When she's been running for only ten minutes she about-turns and jogs back up. Her skin is bursting with moisture in the mid-afternoon sun. Her backside aches, but with every thud of her feet the feeling that she's forgotten something, left the baby somewhere, evaporates. He's not coming back.

She's tired. She had a fitful night's sleep again. She slows to a walk and turns the bend. There's a crowd of mothers waiting to greet their children from the school bus, along with several maids. One group the colours of their clothes as sharp as tropical fruit, the other group a little washed out. Maeve is there, two women huddled around her.

Amber stands on the grass verge metres away from both groups, pushing a stone around with the toe of her sandal, her arms folded. Even from here, Jules can see that Amber has made no effort with her appearance. She is braless, in a vest top, her nipples piercing the baggy fabric.

Jules walks slower to take them all in. The scene doesn't look right with its distinct groups. Jules picks up her pace, so Amber doesn't have to stand alone.

'How are you?' Jules asks.

She takes Amber's fingers in her palm, but they slip away.

'I'm fine.'

Amber's face is all pink patches, broken veins on her cheeks and around her nose. Some of the hairs in her eyebrows stand to attention. Gone is the usual slick of foundation, everything combed and glossed.

'And Sam?' asks Jules.

'He's lost some hearing in his right ear, but the doctors say he's still on course to come home again next week. I just hope he doesn't have to go back again.'

'How's Colby doing?'

'I kept on thinking he was fine. Fooling myself, I suppose. Tor tried to speak to me about it. Since he was hardly ever there, he was easy to ignore. But Dolly, she was the one who tried the hardest to tell me. The doctors think he may have ADHD.'

There's a single orange stem of Heliconia in a shrub on the other side of the road. The air is swollen and still.

'He'll get the help he needs now, Amber,' says Jules.

When she glances at the other women, she notices that Maeve is looking only at her; it's as if Amber isn't there. Maeve's kitten heels stab the grass as she walks over.

'I heard about what happened with that baby, looking after

him then having to give him up. I'm sorry you had to go through that. How are you coping?'

'What?' asks Jules.

'And you're leaving too. Oh, dear, I'm not sure I could face going back to Chelmsford.'

She is pinching Jules' arm with what doesn't feel like concern. Maeve's other hand hangs. Each of its knuckles has a livid purple circle on it. Jules fights the urge to suggest a bandage. She takes her arm back.

'I'm absolutely fine,' she says.

Amber is bowing her head.

'It's terrible,' adds Maeve, her mouth hanging open a little. 'I just wanted to say, well, I hope you're okay.'

Amber takes a step backwards, but Maeve doesn't seem to notice.

'Right. Thanks,' says Jules.

Maeve glances at Amber and walks away. She takes up her place among the women again. All of them look over briefly.

'What was all that about?' asks Jules.

'What do you mean?' says Amber.

'Maeve, all those filthy looks, not speaking to you.'

'I wouldn't speak to me either.'

'What?'

Amber's voice lowers to a whisper. 'I've been seeing someone.'

Jules' question comes out with a small laugh, 'What?'

The bus is sliding to a stop before them. Its doors sigh open and the children descend in their navy and white uniforms.

'Hello, honey,' says Amber. Colby smiles, but doesn't reply. He walks in front of them heading under the glass canopy of the condo entrance.

Jules and Amber hold back. Maeve veers right with the other women; the maids disperse in different directions.

'It was Gavin. I've been seeing Gavin, Maeve's husband,' says Amber. 'Everyone knows, even Tor.'

Jules feels the urge to swear loudly She looks up and down the lane to make sure no one can overhear.

'Why would you do that?'

'I love Gavin.'

Jules stops herself from saying, *ugly bastard*. No, make that *lecherous, ugly bastard*. How would Amber feel if she knew he'd been sleeping with her maid too?

'When did it start?'

'At the party I threw. I went outside for a cigarette. Hate the things, only touch them when I've had too much wine. He pushed me up against a wall and started kissing me.'

'He was pissed. Everyone was.' Apart from Jules, that is.

'It wasn't the drink. There's something between us, has been for a long time.'

'But he's—'

'Tor saw us kissing at the party. He threatened to leave me if I kept seeing Gavin. We carried on anyway. He'd come round after the kids had gone to bed, when Tor was out. It went on for days.'

'Not long then,' says Jules. At least that's something.

'He ended it with me, said his family meant too much to him. He even told her about me – Maeve, I mean. Confessed it all. He said I'd pursued him, though he seemed as eager as I was.'

'What did she say?'

'To stay away. It was awful. She came round one night, snarling at me. She was such a bitch. She texted Tor, told him everything.' She folds her arms then unfolds them.

'After that, I didn't go near Gavin. Then Sam's accident happened. I was so low. It was like Tor blamed me. He wouldn't talk to me. Christ, I needed someone. I texted Gavin, asked to meet.'

'And he did?'

She nods. 'Yes, stolen hours away from the hospital. My son was fighting for his life and I was having sex with Gavin in some ten-dollar-per-hour hotel. As soon as Sam was out of danger, Gavin told me it was a mistake, he didn't want to carry on. But I still love him.'

Jules puts her hands on her hips. 'Oh, Amber, you feel like that now, but . . .'

'There's a magnetism there; it's not easy to walk away from that.'

'Oh, for goodness' sake, Amber. He was shagging Dolly too.'

'What?' Amber's chin quivers.

'Oh, shit, I'm sorry, I . . .'

'Why would you say something like that?'

'The night of the party, I saw him coming out of Dolly's room.'

Amber looks down at the concrete. The women start walking slowly. There's no sign of Colby ahead of them now.

'You're sure?'

'I'm sure.'

Amber sags, every part of her loose, her shoulders, her breasts, her jowls.

'I thought that Gavin, he . . .' Amber's voice breaks. 'Is he still seeing her?'

'Not unless he's conducting a long-distance relationship.'

Amber stares at Jules, her mouth gaping. 'What do you mean?'

'She's been chucked out.'

'What?'

'Dolly's been deported.'

Amber stares at the ground, her eyelid twitching. She pulls her hair to one side and starts braiding it frantically. 'She's been deported? But why? Is it because of the accident?'

'It's because she was . . .' Jules clears her throat. 'Because she's pregnant.'

Amber stops. She squeezes her watery eyes shut. A strangled noise slips from her mouth. She starts walking away.

Jules follows. 'Wait!'

She catches Amber up. Amber's shoulders are rounded, her expression stern.

'You don't think it was his, do you?' asks Amber.

'Well, it's possible.'

'My God, what an absolute sleazeball.'

They keep walking then Amber stops and stares at the largest of the empty swimming pools. A man stands on the edge, pulling a net through the water, gathering leaves.

'My mom was right,' says Amber.

'What?'

'I was a teenager when she told me I wasn't all that attractive.'

'She what?'

'That's what she said: "You might as well accept this now, but you'll always be last in the queue where men are concerned."'

'That's not who you are, Amber. Look, you're better than that creep. Just . . . Oh.' She lays a hand on Amber's back. 'There's something else.'

Amber turns and looks at Jules then. Snot leaks out of Amber's nose; a wet pellet lands on the concrete.

'Tala's staying with me at the moment. It's complicated,' says Jules. 'But, well, she's lost her job, and what with Dolly leaving, I think they're broke, Amber.'

Amber sniffs hard, pulls a tissue out of the pocket of her shorts and starts dabbing at her nose. Her bare fingernails are bitten, the skin around them ragged.

'I just kept thinking, if Dolly hadn't been there, Sam's accident wouldn't have happened,' says Amber. 'I couldn't look at her. Every time I did, I saw him under the car again, but she had been trying to tell me about Colby for months.'

The women start to meander along the pathway again.

'Do you think I should go and speak to Tala?' asks Amber.

'Well, I'd leave it for a while, maybe.'

'I'm cringing about Gavin. He's made such a fool of me.' She starts plaiting her hair again.

'It's not too late to patch things up with Tor though,' says Jules.

'Tor wants a divorce. But I've told him if he divorces me, I'll take the children.'

'You'd do that to him, be vindictive like that?'

Amber tosses her plait towards her back. 'A mom should always get to look after her own children, Jules. And there's no way I'm staying in a loveless marriage just so Tor can see them every day.'

'Loveless? You mean you don't love Tor at all?'

'I followed him here. I've given up everything for him. All I have are his snide comments about how uptight I am – that, and my children.'

Jules remembers that day at the pool; Maeve across the water from Amber. She thinks about the way Amber launched herself at her, how it had made her back off. Had Amber done it because she no longer had any friends? Amber links her hands around Jules' arm as they walk.

'Anyway, all this talk about children . . .' says Amber. 'But how are you feeling about everything?'

'I'm fine.'

'You've still got time.'

'I can't keep doing that to myself.'

'If you put enough energy into something, you'll get it in the end.'

'I don't think it's that simple, Amber.'

'What about adoption? I mean, you looked after that baby?'

Jules shakes her head. 'Like I say, I'm fine.'

They've reached Amber's front door now. Jules looks at Amber whose nose is red, her eyelid still flickering.

'Are you coming in?' asks Amber.

'I'd better not; I'm doing an evening shift at the surgery,' says Jules.

She walks away, turns around and Amber is still standing there, stooped and staring. Jules blows her a kiss. Amber's mouth stretches a little wider and for a moment, Jules thinks she's smiling.

But Amber's shoulders are shaking and she blows her nose as she goes into the town house.

Jules fights the urge to follow her in and climbs into the lift, which rises. Inside the apartment, she kneels and pulls a dusty book from under the sofa. *Natural Ways to Boost Your Fertility.* She strides to the back door and unlocks it then heads out to the landing with the book still in her hand.

She opens the metal door to the rubbish chute then slings it inside. It disappears and scrapes its way down. There's a thump as it hits the bin. She slams the chute door shut, goes back inside and pulls on her receptionist's uniform.

Essential House Rules for Foreign Domestic Maids

Rule 7. Doors: Maids should use the back door to exit and enter your apartment, except when accompanying your children or your dog.

Chapter 22

Tala paces the floor in Ma'am Jules' spare bedroom. She has already asked most of the people she works for whether they'd consider employing her as a live-in helper. All of them have said no. There's only two of them left to ask – Ma'am Jules and Ma'am Jemima. Tala boots up her computer, so she can make sure the photograph of Malcolm's poop hasn't appeared on Vanda's blog.

She waits, then there on the screen is the photograph of Tala, the sun behind her so her face is a black patch, the dog lead in her hand, and blind old Malcolm at her side.

> This is just more evidence of maids misbehaving in our country.
> This girl was caught allowing a dog to foul the pavement and
> refused to pick up the faeces.

Malcolm canters through Tala's head like a battery-operated toy. If Ma'am Jemima sees this she'll sack Tala, and Tala can't afford to lose any of her jobs.

Tala hasn't blogged for days, but her fingers are tingling now with the need to type a response. She logs on to Maidhacker and stares at the statistics. 27,801 people have looked at her blog now. She gulps, pulls her hands off the keys. But what the hell, she starts to type.

MAIDHACKER'S BLOG:

What It's Like to Be a Domestic Helper

Dog Versus Helper

You may break into a smile when your employer gets a pet pooch. You may go as gooey as wet mud, but pretty soon you and Fido may be less than the best of friends.

There must be some scientific explanation for this, but ma'ams always choose dogs with features that resemble theirs. Ladies who spend a lot of time in the bathroom dyeing their moustaches (that white stripe over their lips isn't coffee froth), well, they'll plump for Welsh terriers. A ma'am who always dresses in pink net or lace will go for a chihuahua that she can fit into her Fendi. And for a ma'am with fat jowls and an attitude to match, it's got to be a bulldog.

You know how you have to walk three steps behind your ma'am carrying her shopping bags? Well, now you'll be expected to clasp your fingers around a bag of another sort, one with a warm soft centre.

Watch out for the big dogs. Because the bigger the dog, the bigger the poop. What you want is a dog that rarely goes – take it from me, its pain is your gain.

I've looked after all sorts – Archibald Terence with his halitosis, Skittles with his high-pitched yelp, and Custard Cream the ageing Labrador who only had three legs. Should have called him Tripod. I've walked them miles through raindrops the size of pebbles. I've scooped enough poop to fertilise the Banaue Rice Terraces twice over.

Believe me, it may be love at first sight for the new addition to the family, but when Ma'am locks away your passport while propping poodle's own little ID on a shelf for all her friends to see (yes, pets really do have passports), you may start to feel the distance growing between you.

And when Ma'am tells you it's a tin of chicken luncheon meat for your dinner again tonight, all while little Dixie is sat in her lap, ears back, eyes closed, Ma'am's nail-varnished hand endlessly stroking his fur, you'll start to wish you had four legs too, and enjoyed sniffing other dogs' undercarriages.

Beware of the dog, ladies.

Tala hits 'post', takes off her glasses and tramps towards the open-plan living area.

David is washing cups in the sink.

'Shit,' he says as he bumps his head on the drainer over the sink.

'Hello.'

He turns, drying his hands on a tea towel. He takes two steps backwards. Tala reads his T-shirt: Superdry. He looks anything but, big fat sweat clouds under his arms, a droplet on the end of his nose.

'I'll make dinner for you,' says Tala.

'I'm just going to have a sandwich.'

'No, no. Let me make something for you. I bought some food.'

'I can't let you do that. You've been out at work. Besides you don't have to.'

'Sir, I insist.'

'Just call me David.'

God, she keeps on getting it wrong. And her cooking may be terrible, but she needs to pull out all the stops because her situation is shaky here.

'I must!' she says, but it comes out louder than she meant and her voice echoes.

The door rattles and in walks Ma'am Jules in the white top and trousers she wears at the surgery.

'Hi, Tala.' Her face is a large frown.

Tala throws a laugh out. 'I'm making food; sit down, sit down.'

Jules flops onto the sofa beside David and the pair of them start talking in low voices. Tala pulls out pans, spoons, with a clatter and bash. She drops a cup onto the floor and it shatters. *Settle down, Tala,* she tells herself, but it doesn't help. She picks up the sharp pieces and puts them into the bin.

The mashed potato browns in the pan. No matter how much she stirs it, she can't get the lumps out. In another pot, there's drained pasta filled with some sort of cheese. She puts dollops of mash on the plates and arranges the wilting pasta around them in a circle.

'Dinner is served!' she shrills, and Jules and David take their places sheepishly at the table. She sets the plates in front of them.

'Oh,' Jules says then adds in a rush, 'Aren't you going to have any?'

'No, I . . .'

'You must,' David says, pulling out a chair.

Tala goes to the kitchen and slaps a small amount of potato and four squares of pasta onto a plate. She sits and chews, trying to ignore the watery consistency. Soft, tasteless cheese spurts onto her tongue. Why would anyone want to eat this stuff? David shakes the salt. He swallows like he's having difficulty.

'Well, it's certainly different,' David says with a smile.

'I have a very small appetite.' Tala waves her fingers in front of her mouth and laughs. 'So full already.'

'Me too,' Jules says, putting the fork down.

'It's good?'

'Oh, yes.' David pats his stomach. He doesn't look like he ate all that much. Neither does Jules.

David clears his throat. 'We've got something to tell you, Tala.'

'David!' says Jules. 'We were going to wait.' She tilts her head to one side.

'The thing is . . .' says David. 'I've lost my job, so we might only be here for a few more months.'

'But you've only just got here,' says Tala.

'I know, but, well, it means we won't be able to offer you a job long-term,' says Jules.

'I'm sorry to hear about your job, sir. I mean, David.' Tala looks at the congealed potato on the plates. She takes them to the kitchen and scrapes the leftovers into the bin.

When she goes back to the table, David is kneading his brow. Jules is staring at the table.

'Tala, sit down,' she says.

The faint sound of a Skype call chimes into the room. Tala listens; it's coming from her laptop. She rushes through to the spare room. It's Mama. Mallie is there in the background sucking her thumb, and making her Minion toy jump.

'Can you hear me?' shouts Mama, the screen full of just her nose, she's that close.

'Yes!' Tala shouts back.

'Dolly wants to speak to you!'

The camera slides sideways and focuses on the table, so that all Tala can see is a blackened banana and a guava along with a plastic cup half full with liquid.

Dolly's voice comes from the side. 'I feel so awful that you're stuck there, Tala. If I hadn't been so stupid . . .'

'Oh, everything's fine,' Tala says in a voice so high it's like she's auditioning for an opera.

'And Sam, how is he doing?' asks Dolly.

'He's getting better; he'll be home any day now, apparently.'

The camera angle shoots sideways again and there is a close-up of Mama's mouth.

'Alice had a baby girl!'

'A baby!' Tala says in the squeaky lilt she reserves for people under the age of six months. 'Oh, but is everything okay?'

'Well, the baby's okay. But she was 10lbs 3oz, so Alice, that girl is going to have to do pelvic floor exercises like it's an Olympic event.'

Tala crosses one leg over the other.

'They've given her a name. Bunny,' says Mama.

'Bunny?'

'It's just ridiculous, Tala; you need to talk to Alice. Maybe she will listen to you. It's such a terrible name for a baby, a cruelty.'

Bunny. Of all the names they could have chosen, they've gone and named her after a fluffy breeding machine.

'But as for this one,' says Mama. 'Another pregnancy and still not married!'

'Mama!' says Dolly.

'I mean, what are we going to do, Tala?'

'We'll work something out, Mama.'

'Well, one mistake, I can just about understand, but another . . . I mean, I said to your sister . . .'

Tala puts on the electric fan and turns it up to the high setting. 'What's that, Mama? You're breaking up.'

'I was just saying, your sister's made yet another mistake in the men department.'

'It's no good, Mama, I can't hear a thing.'

Tala hangs up. She needs to find a new job, and soon. She stands and does a series of waist-bends from side to creaky side as if limbering up for the enormous task ahead.

Chapter 23

Tala is sitting on the packed bus, concentrating on how she's going to persuade Ma'am Jemima to give her a full-time job. Tala opens her bag and closes her hand around the conch shell. *Please*, she thinks. She has a little practice by talking to the glass.

'Oh ma'am, I'm such a good cleaner. Just think, I could do your dusting every day,' she whispers and smiles. 'Oh, sweet Malcolm, my darling.'

A woman at the front of the bus stares at Tala, her mouth revealing metal braces.

I'll fold myself up like an envelope, thinks Tala, the sharp edge to my voice gone, the purse to my lip. I'll be serene like my sister and keep my trap well and truly shut.

But then Ma'am Jemima's no fool. She short-changed Tala once and Tala shrieked, 'You're five dollars short!' The way Ma'am Jemima's lip liner scrunched, she already knows that though Tala may have many attributes, serenity isn't one of them.

Tala dings the bell and gets off, crosses the road and sweeps towards the condo with its circular towers of apartments, palms billowing in the miraculous breeze. She points her nose at the sky.

'Yes?' The security guard, in his little box, leans sideways out of a plastic sliding window.

'Flat C53,' says Tala in the best English voice she can muster.

'Who are you servicing?'

'What?'

'Who do you work for?'

'A person.' Tala doesn't want to give away any of the people she works for in case they get into trouble for paying her cash in hand.

'The name?'

Tala flattens her hand to her chest and smiles. 'Well, it's, er, Ma'am Jemima I've come to see,' she says quietly.

The security guard waves her on. She doesn't dare look back at him, hot in the knowledge that he's still leaning out of the window gawping at her.

There she goes, into the condo reception, past the fountain and the painting of the woman in the swirly dress, the sign above her that says 'Livia Luxury Apartments'. Tala goes into the lift, turns her key in the lock and presses for floor four. She pops into the wooden expanse of the flat, Malcolm doing his high-pitched barking. He doesn't go for her like he often does, but scrapes his fundamental along the pink rug.

Ma'am Jemima walks towards Tala in white silk trousers.

'Such a good trick, Malcolm bubba,' says Tala and gives this laugh to make Ma'am Jemima think Tala's in love with Malcolm, just like her.

Ma'am Jemima has never been cross with Tala before, but she looks it today, her mouth turned down on either side.

'You can do the living room first,' she says. 'I'm on a conference call.'

Tala goes into the utility room and unravels her skirt, slings on her uniform as she calls it. She rolls back the furry rug and brushes the marble floor, then mops the whole place down. In the kitchen, she buffs and shines and even takes the dishes out of all the cupboards and wipes inside.

She stays half an hour longer than she needs to, then Ma'am Jemima emerges from her study looking at the gold watch on her wrist.

'You're over your time,' she says.

'I hadn't realised,' says Tala. 'But ma'am, I've been thinking.

I'm looking for another job, well another sponsor really, and I like working for you.'

'I don't need a live-in.'

'But ma'am, you'd hardly ever see me. I'm very good at—'

'There's something I need to talk to you about.'

She sits on the sofa, pats the space beside her. Tala sits too and looks at Ma'am's high heels lost in the deep strands of the rug, her back straight.

'I can't have Malcolm fouling the pavement,' says Ma'am Jemima.

'What?'

'You let Malcolm foul the pavement, didn't pooper-scoop.'

'Oh.'

'Vanda's blog. I saw my Malcolm's photograph up there. I could just make you out.'

'I forgot the poop bag.'

'You must always take bags with you when you're taking Malcolm for walkies.'

'But ma'am . . .'

'No buts, Tala. And it's not the first time it's happened either.'

A tiny poop from a tiny dog. *Oh, my God, she's not going to sack me, is she?* Tala does the thing she's best at and starts talking.

'I've cleaned all your cupboards out today, ma'am, with disinfectant; the dishes are all stacked.' Tala kisses her fingers and throws them into the air then gets up and opens a kitchen cupboard with a huge grin on her face. An empty Pledge spray and a finished Ajax bottle poke out of the bin.

'Well, yes, and I thank you, but—'

'And your taps, ma'am – you could see your pretty face in them, they're so shiny.'

'Yes.' Ma'am pouts and smiles.

'So you'll think about it, ma'am, being my sponsor?'

'No, Tala, I won't, I'm afraid.'

Ma'am Jemima picks up her handbag from the floor and fishes around in her purse. She gives Tala two $50 notes.

'Ma'am, you've given me too much.'

'That's overtime,' she says and there's a crease of sympathy in her forehead.

Tala gets up and puts one of the $50 notes onto the glass coffee table.

'Take it,' says Ma'am Jemima.

'I don't need handouts, Ma'am.'

Tala walks out of the front door, Malcolm clawing at the wood as it closes.

Jules reaches to the side of the sunlounger and tries to tilt it further back. She fails and it clatters backwards. She cleans her sunglasses on the towel and lies down, flat out, turning to watch David beside her, reading some book about conspiracy theories, his nose white with factor 50.

Her legs are hairless, shiny, her knees bright red. She reaches for her own book; just twenty pages to go. She touches her nose and feels the hole there, that tiny badge from her past.

Gavin is coming this way in his khaki cut-offs, a pea green Ralph Lauren T-shirt stretched around his muscles like a super-hero's. And hang on a minute, isn't that a black eye? As he gets closer, Jules sees the purple bloom of it across the left side of his face, the edges yellow. His nose has taken a battering too; then she remembers Maeve's knuckles.

Gavin, who's clearly spotted David and Jules, struts faster on his skinny legs, his attention absorbed by the flowerbeds lining the pathway. When he passes Amber's house, he puts his hand to his head as if trying to shield himself from the sun.

Jules stares up at the blue sky. How she misses Khalib. She wonders what he's doing now.

'Are you okay?' David asks.

'It feels a bit empty without Khalib, but I'm getting used to it, I think.'

'Shall we do it again?'

'The fostering? I'm not sure I can face the heartache really. Besides, we'll have to leave soon. Like you said, there's no way we'll be able to afford the whopping rent on the apartment on my salary.'

'Actually, I've just found out the company has to honour the contract; they've had to pay the rent until the end of the year even though they're getting rid of me.'

'So we could stay?'

'Well, I could do with going back, applying for jobs.'

'Yeah, but you could apply for stuff here, go back when you get an interview. My job'll tide us over.'

'Do you really want to stay after everything that's happened? I mean it's been pretty awful so far.'

He turns on his side to look at her, but she can't see his eyes through his Ray-Bans.

She'll have to face everyone if she goes back: her friends, her work colleagues, her family. She'd rather stay than have to do that. Just a few months more. It'll give her time to weigh up what she's going to do now her last chance for a baby has gone.

'I know it's been bad, but I'm not done here yet.' She gives a half-smile.

'Really?'

'It's probably a bit bonkers, but I just want to stay longer, that's all.'

'Well, if you feel like that, then we will for the next few months anyway,' David says.

He takes her face in his hand and kisses her, the lenses of his glasses full of her reflection. There's a splash as a child jumps into the pool. David picks up his book again, and Jules carries on looking at him, his rosy cheeks, his spiky hair.

She puts down her book, pulls her goggles over her face then walks over to the swimming pool and lowers herself in.

Someone knocks on the front door of Ma'am Jules' apartment and Tala jumps so high her backside leaves the bed and bounces down again like it's on a trampoline. Have they come for her? She carries on sitting, and there are three more knocks. She's not answering; she's just a guest after all.

Knock-knock-knock. Harder this time. Her heart's knocking too. She gets up and looks through the spyhole. It's Ma'am Amber, her distorted head and body with the proportions of a Chupa Chups lollipop. Tala opens the door.

'Jules told me you were staying here.'

One of Tala's hands keeps the door open, the other's on her hip. 'You didn't have to go and sack Dolly.'

'I couldn't have her in the house after Sam.'

'But ma'am, it wasn't her fault.'

Ma'am Amber is puce. 'Have you heard from her? Is she okay?' she asks, fiddling with a button on her black shirt.

Tala sniffs. 'Yes, she's okay.'

'Well, good, I'm glad. Oh, Tala, I'm sorry I sacked Dolly. The accident wasn't her fault, I know that now. I've always known it; it's just I wasn't thinking straight. I was so worried about my son.'

'Well, I . . .' Tala narrows her eyes, then she can't help herself: she reaches out her hand and touches Ma'am Amber's shoulder. 'Well, don't you go upsetting yourself all over again, ma'am.'

'I came to see you before, by the way. I went to Queenstown.'

'What?'

'I spoke to the lady you live with, Mrs Heng.'

A pulse starts in Tala's neck; she wrings her hands together. So Ma'am Amber was the well-dressed woman Mrs Heng meant, not some Ministry official.

'I went there to say thank you; if it hadn't been for you, I would have kept on reversing that car.'

Ma'am Amber throws her arms around Tala, and Tala just stands there on the doorstep, eyes popping, hands hanging by her thighs. Tala's lost her place to live because of Ma'am Amber; her chest contracts with anger. Ma'am Amber's got BO, but she's also got a child in the hospital. Tala puts her arms around Ma'am Amber and hugs her back. Ma'am Amber sniffs and pulls a tissue from the sleeve of her shirt.

'And your son, how is he?' asks Tala.

The digital panel above the lift, just behind Ma'am Amber, goes from 4 to 1 then B.

'We're bringing him home from the hospital tomorrow.' Ma'am Amber steps backwards. 'You'll say no, I'm sure of it. But the thing is, well, Jules said you need a job and my husband and I, we're separating, and we both need someone and I just feel so bad about what I did to Dolly.'

Oh, they're getting a divorce. Is it because of the accident? But if they're splitting up, this could mean there might be a job for Dolly with Sir Tor eventually.

Ma'am Amber is trembling slightly. She bites her lip. 'And I should just mention something else. I wouldn't expect you to sleep in that cupboard. If you say yes, I'll make up the bed in the spare room for you myself. The window looks out onto the patio.'

'I'll do it,' says Tala.

That way Tala might even find out if Ma'am Amber really is the woman writing Vanda's blog.

'Can you start tomorrow?' Ma'am Amber asks.

Tala nods and watches Ma'am Amber turn to call the lift. My God, Tala would have started today if Ma'am Amber had suggested it.

Essential House Rules for Foreign Domestic Maids

Rule 8. Curfews: It is advisable to give your maid a curfew if she has a day off. After all, you won't want her to be tired, or worse still hungover for work the next day.

Chapter 24

Tala's got the whole place to herself down here in the basement of Ma'am Amber and Sir Tor's town house – the big bedroom with its wooden floor and glass doors that open on to an enclosed patio with a red flowering plant poking from a square in the centre of the tiles. There's a little hall and beyond that a window-less bathroom with a proper shower cubicle done out in beige marble tiles. Ma'am Amber and Sir Tor have remained living together while they looked for separate apartments. They have less than a week left before they go their separate ways. Tala kept expecting Ma'am Amber to say that her being down here wasn't working, that she'd have to move into the bomb shelter after all, but that hasn't happened. Tala hasn't unpacked her stuff though. All her clothes are still neatly folded in her bag, her toothbrush and soap and hairbrush wrapped in a flannel at the side of the bathroom sink. Her laptop is lying on her bed. She's only posted once since she's been here. *Curfews or Quit*, the post was called. All about how employers tell domestic helpers that they must be back home by a certain time on their days off. 'It's meant to be a day off, not just ten hours,' Tala wrote. It was risky, but only Rita knows that she's Maidhacker. Just so long as she keeps quiet about it.

She looks at the digital clock beside the double bed. It's time to meet the children from the school bus. Tala goes upstairs and opens the oak front door. She slips on her flip-flops, which she always leaves outside for airing.

She curves along the pathway, some unseen creature crinkling through the leaves of the sideways plants. Women are gathered at the front, three domestic helpers sitting on the low wall underneath the glass canopy. Behind them, a spray mists the lilies and purple orchids with water. Two Western women stand facing one another. One of them has kicked off a bronze Birkenstock and is grinding her bare heel into the stone.

Tala flip-flops past all of them and heads out into the road where the bus will stop. Here it is now, the single-decker, fuzzy faces in its windows. It whines to a stop, the bus uncle waving to each of the children as they descend the stairs. Tala feels like telling them all to say thank you. Then, as if one of them has heard her silent scold, a girl with two fat plaits says, 'Thanks!'

Sam is the first of her charges to come off. He sees her and smirks, that scar still pink on his forehead, but then it's only been two months since the accident happened. This is his second day back at school. She puts her finger into the air and raises an eyebrow.

'Oh!' he says and turns. 'Thank you, man!'

Tala and Sam stand there holding hands, their skin a sticky sandwich of heat. Maids and mothers are huddling, some holding hands with children dressed in uniforms with green squares on. One maid looks at Tala then snaps her gaze away. Another, Lydia, can't stop the looking, and the smiling. She makes her hand into a fist and gives Tala's arm a gentle punch as she passes.

'You're so angry about everything. I love it.'

Tala's eyes open very wide; she glances down at Sam who is dragging on her arm and scraping the tip of his sandal along the concrete.

'What do you mean?' Tala whispers in Lydia's ear.

'It's you,' she says and not quietly. 'You're Maidhacker.'

'What the—?'

'Rita told me; it's the worst-kept secret ever!'

Tala gasps and covers her mouth. She looks around and the other Filipinas are staring at her, all of them with these silly smiles. Tala opens her mouth behind her hand. It's only a matter of time before the Ministry finds out, and, oh please, oh no.

Tala taps her foot. Just where is Colby? Not that he needs ferrying the few metres from bus to front door, but Tala is pulling out all the stops so she can hold on to this job. If everyone knows she's Maidhacker though, there's a good chance Ma'am Amber will find out too, and all that stuff Tala wrote about her and the way she treated Dolly . . . Tala holds tighter to Sam's hand.

'Ow, you're hurting me!' says Sam.

'When's that boy coming off?' Tala snaps to no one in particular.

All the maids are wandering away now, still looking at Tala.

'Boy, hurry up, *lah*!' shouts the bus driver.

Colby comes down the steps, brow furrowed. *Ay nako!* He needs some discipline to iron out this touchy personality of his.

'I'm so sorry,' Tala calls out to the driver, a hand on her hip.

'It's not your fault, Auntie!' He smiles as the door closes.

Auntie? The man's around the same age as her and he's calling her Auntie? All this to-do must have given her more grey hairs than she thought.

'Why can't my mom ever come and meet me?' whines Colby.

'I don't know.'

He catapults his bag to the ground and walks off. It's a blue bag, slashed with a green tick. Tala stops in front of it and folds her arms.

'Boy, pick that bag up!'

He doesn't look round.

'Boy!' Her voice catches and multiplies in the balconies.

Colby stops.

'You pick it up,' he says. 'You're my maid.'

'If you don't pick the bag up, it will stay there.' Tala unfolds her arms, and strides with Sam running along beside her like someone has pressed his fast-forward button.

Colby's mouth has fallen open. Tala smiles and walks on, knocking aside the web of a stinging caterpillar lowering itself

from a tree. She turns back to see Colby putting the handles of
the bag in the crook of his arm, a pained expression on his face,
his chin wrinkled in complaint.

She slows up, so that by the time she reaches the door, Colby
is only a metre behind. Sam steps inside followed by Colby who
glares at her and drops his bag onto her toes.

She tuts loudly then goes into the kitchen to prepare dinner.

Ma'am Amber watches Tala load the coriander over the coconut
concoction and serve it onto plates. It smells of cooked chicken
and limes. The family have already lowered their culinary expec-
tations, especially Sir Tor, since she turned his favourite meal of
sirloin steak into a charred biscuit the other day.

Who knew chicken could spit so much? thinks Tala, wiping
the grease speckles off her forehead with the back of her hand.
She threw the pieces into the pan and the oil hissed out a vapour
that has covered the cooker hood, the worktop, even the trolley
at the furthest end of the kitchen with a layer of grease. There's
been lamb the texture of tyres, burnt fish, tooth-shattering pork
chops. Tala is an appalling cook and at almost fifty – my God,
she can't bear to think of that inflated number – she is never
going to change.

'I guess it's chicken for dinner,' Ma'am says, and Tala follows
her eyes to the oily pool in the frying pan.

The two children and their parents sit around the table like
the Last Supper. Ma'am Amber screws up her nose. Colby looks
like he's grinding his teeth on rubber. He might be about to
dislocate his jaw. He pulls a morsel from his mouth, pushes it to
the outside of his plate. Sir Tor eats around it all, scooping up
rice which falls from his fork.

'So have you heard the news?' asks Sir Tor.

'No,' says Ma'am Amber.

'Gavin and Maeve are moving to Malaysia.'

Ma'am Amber's fork starts to shake and a lump of chicken falls back onto her plate with a splash of sauce.

'Good riddance, wouldn't you say?' says Sir Tor.

Ma'am Amber's chest rises and falls.

'What's riddance?' asks Sam. His hearing has definitely improved.

'Eat up,' says Ma'am Amber.

'It's horrible,' says Colby. 'I wish Dolly would just come back.'

Sir Tor and Ma'am lock eyes. 'She doesn't work for us any more because I got cross with her,' says Ma'am.

'But why?' asks Sam.

'Because . . .' She puts down her fork with a hollow echo. 'Because I was wrong about something. She left because of me, and I'm sorry for that.'

'The employment agency has sent us the bill for her flight home, by the way,' says Sir Tor.

Amber hangs her head. When Sir Tor sees Tala approaching, he clears his throat.

Tala pretends she hasn't heard. She is beside them now with a rectangular tray of drinks balanced on her arm. One of the wobbling drinks falls on its side, tipping red wine over Sir Tor's trousers. There's a scrape of chairs and Sir Tor is up examining his lap, Ma'am Amber too.

'Please don't worry,' Ma'am Amber says.

Colby freezes, the fork poised halfway to his mouth.

'Everyone has accidents,' Ma'am Amber says, mopping at Sir Tor's crotch with a paper serviette, which leaves splinters of red on the fabric.

'Look, Dad, you've got your period,' says Colby, sniggering.

Ma'am Amber slaps Colby's hand away from his face, so that the elbow he is leaning on slips off the table with a crunch.

'So sorry, sir,' says Tala, then remembers that Ma'am Amber told her not to call them ma'am and sir. 'I mean, Tor,' Tala adds, before rushing to the kitchen with the flooded tray.

'It's not a problem,' says Sir Tor, clearing his throat.

They all sit down again as if nothing's happened, no one commenting on the overdone curry that Tala has spent three hours in the kitchen creating.

'I can see why she didn't have a live-in job before,' says Sir Tor under his breath.

Ma'am Amber turns away, covering her mouth. She's laughing and for a moment it's as if the hushed arguments between her and Sir Tor have been resolved. Then the spell is broken.

'Is that the time?' Sir Tor says, glancing at his watch. He stands abruptly. 'I've got some work to catch up on.'

He rushes downstairs to his study. Ma'am sits there, her pink nail-varnished hands flat on the table. Tala peers at her from the open-plan kitchen. The only sound left in the room is Colby pinging his fork against a glass then Ma'am Amber lays a patient hand on his fingers, and all is silent.

Chapter 25

Four months later

The white cotton hugs Dolly's enormous bump. Mallie sits in the corner of the room staring at it. The fan on the table whirs. There are kids' books all over the stone floor, and a silvery painting on the wall, thin tree trunks with blue lines running behind them like sea. Marlon painted it on a piece of wood. The midwife, Cassandra, presses her hand into Dolly's belly.

'Feet first,' she says.

Wayward hairs stick out of her chin. 'You'll need a hospital for this if the baby doesn't turn.'

'There's a month to go. She'll turn,' says Dolly.

Mallie's red football shirt is two sizes too big. Dolly opens the door for Cassandra and the midwife goes through, Mama bumbling along behind. Mallie rolls a ball across the floor with her foot.

'Are you happy about having a sister?'

Mallie shrugs. The baby will turn, it has to. Dolly won't need to go to hospital. Mallie goes out of the door and it slams behind her.

Ma'am Amber wired 60,000 pesos into Dolly's bank account four months ago. She also sent a letter telling Dolly how sorry she was about treating her so badly; all that shouting, all that blame. Thankfully, Sam has no lasting damage from the accident except for some hearing loss, and a scar on his forehead and behind his ear. Dolly wrote back to Ma'am Amber and enclosed a short letter for Colby and Sam. How she misses them both, Sam's little voice and Colby needing her the way he did. Ma'am Amber mentioned that he is seeing a doctor now, so she must have finally stopped lying to herself. Dolly is using the money to buy ingredients for cakes which she sells at the side of the road. She's trying hard to keep her stall going; she still hopes to open her own bakery, but she doesn't make much of a profit. She's not going to throw that money away on a hospital; she can't.

She goes outside. Mama is hanging clothes on a line tied between the roof of the house and a palm tree. Mallie hands Mama pegs. Dolly steps across the square terracotta tiles and out to the dirt track.

'Girl, where are you going in your condition?' calls Mama.

'To buy some more baking ingredients.'

'You should be sitting down, resting.'

Dolly holds out her hand to Mallie, but she just tilts her head and smiles.

'Do you want to come?'

'I'm staying here,' says Mallie and waves.

So Dolly keeps walking, her feet swollen, her flip-flops sliding. There are steps sliced into the hills. The sky is dark blue.

Footsteps tap behind her and she turns and Mallie is beaming at her. Then Mallie's fat fingers are bendy in Dolly's. They walk. Mallie glances up at her mama. They cross the thin track, the water dark green through the trees. A man stands on a raft pushing himself along with a wooden pole. The branches scrape at Dolly; she keeps holding on to Mallie's hand.

When they get to the road, wires are tangled overhead. They pass the white church with its pillars and the grilles in the walls. A monitor lizard wiggles along the road. A man on a red motor-bike with a sidecar rumbles by.

Women walk along in different-coloured vest tops. A man in a brown shirt pulls it up and scratches his round belly. They pass an abandoned, empty trolley with a blue sign that says 'ICE', and a wall made from breeze blocks. There is a boarded-up shop, and a girl, her arms folded in front of a blue quad bike. Then they get to the supermarket with its trolleys and a basketball post outside.

They go into the lights and the electronic music. Dolly points to things on the shelves – a big slab of bright yellow butter and a bag of flour. Mallie puts them into the plastic basket.

They walk home along the road busy with people walking, mumbling, laughing. The tarmac turns to stone then sand. Their feet make dust.

At home, they work at the table outside, round with metal leaves. And soon Mallie's hands are covered in butter and flour. She has yellow blobs of it on the end of her nose, her chin, her hair. They put the tin into the oven and the smell seeps out, and Mallie keeps licking her lips.

'Let's open the door to look,' she says.

But Dolly shakes her head and trusts that the cake is doing its rising. Their oven doesn't have a glass door like Ma'am Amber's.

Tala has to stay there until Dolly makes decent money from this venture, or leaves for an overseas cleaning job again. Tala's still writing that blog though, post after post about all sorts of subjects from how to beat homesickness to busting the myth of the happy maid. Dolly suspects Tala is becoming more identifiable in her posts. And if she's found out, she'll be deported, which is even more reason for Dolly to be frugal with that money Ma'am Amber gave her. It's a small thing giving birth. Dolly can do it without expensive medical care.

She opens the oven door and hands the knife to Mallie. Mallie stabs the cake and the knife comes out clean. Dolly turns the cake upside down onto a plate. The steam curls.

'It smells good,' says Mallie. 'Can I eat some?'

'Too soon and it'll give you belly ache.'

But Dolly cuts a slice anyway and hands it to her daughter. She pulls Mallie into her arms then and they stand there rocking, Dolly and her daughter, the baby in the belly pressed between them.

Jules climbs to her knees and adjusts the settings on her camera. She pans sideways as Sam scrapes past on his blue scooter, with a look of determination on his face. She examines the shot. The wooden twists of the Henderson Waves bridge are blurred in the background just like she wanted them to be. They are more than 30 metres above ground, standing in the curved slats of wood which undulate into the distance. The bridge is punctuated by alcoves with ribbed roofs and timber seats. Over the side, Jules can see a canopy of trees. Sam's beside her now, his warm breath on her ear.

'I like that one,' he says.

She looks down at the little screen and flicks through the rest of her pictures. She's trying to master movement, but street photography is still her favourite, catching people unawares. She stands, points the lens at Sam who is daydreaming.

He climbs onto his scooter again and turns in circles. The slatted wooden boards of the bridge curve up one side to form a wall, and she leans her back against it. The tops of the leafy green trees dance behind her. Cream high-rises loom in front of her. The bridge snakes on and on.

Colby and Amber are approaching. Colby is rollerskating and holding his mother's hand. He teeters backwards, jerking Amber who pulls him upright again. Jules captures them as they get closer. Amber has on flat bejewelled sandals, and a belted short green dress. Her hair, cut short now, is curly and fat around her head like an old-fashioned microphone. Wet tendrils are stuck to her forehead. Colby takes off and Amber picks up her pace. He whizzes past Jules, and Sam starts scooting after him.

'Don't go too far ahead!' Amber shouts.

'How are things between you and Tor?' asks Jules.

'Okay, I guess. For a while, I was thinking about moving back to Chicago. Things are better now that I've moved out. You were right, Jules, I couldn't take them away from Tor.'

The women carry on walking.

'I'm just so relieved that Gavin and Maeve have left,' says Amber. 'I acted like a fool over him. I'm mortified about it all. I thought I was in love with him, but really I was just bowled over by the fact someone was attracted to me.'

'You were really fragile back then, Amber. But what about now?' asks Jules.

'Well, coming off those antidepressants was kind of scary, but hey, I'm not falling apart. I'm actually feeling more level-headed, less shaky. But God, I really needed to be on the pills before. I was a basket case when the accident happened and I was such a bitch to Dolly. I can't begin to imagine how much worse I would have been if I hadn't been medicated.'

Jules clears her throat. 'Have you heard anything more from the police?'

'About me being over the limit, you mean? Well, they told me I might have to go to court, but I haven't heard any more about it yet.'

'What will you do with yourself now?'

'I've got my routines. The charity functions, the children. I might even try my hand at a bit of teaching. I need to do some work again.'

'Oh?'

'They're crying out for math teachers. One of those Kumon schools would snap me up.'

'And Colby?'

'We've got another meeting with the specialist next week.'

'He seems to be doing well.'

'So far . . . Oh, Jules, I wish you could stay. I spend my life saying goodbye to people.'

'Well, I'm not going just yet.'

Amber smiles, touches Jules' arm then breaks into a jog. She stops beside her boys and the three of them look out over the cramped treetops.

Jules gets closer, presses her camera to her face and shoots. Shielding the screen with her hand, she looks at the picture she's taken. There's a faint smile on Amber's face. Her cheeks are red and shiny, and completely make-up free.

'Come on, Jules!' Amber shouts. 'We've still got miles to go.'

With that Amber crouches, unbuckles her sandals and pulls a pair of battered black trainers from her bag. She forces them onto her feet and starts to pound after Colby and Sam who are wheeling away. Jules breaks into a run too, the camera banging her chest like a heartbeat.

Your Maid: 20 Signs of Laziness

Blogger Maidhacker says she's giving a voice to the thousands of women who work as maids in this country. She says they don't have many rights despite being such good workers. Well, in my experience, most of these women are lazy like sloths!

Chapter 26

Ma'am Amber now lives with Tala and the boys in this old condo with fans on the ceiling instead of air con. There are faded pillars down there in the grounds, peeling blue paint and a swimming pool shaped like a shell. Tala is back in a bomb shelter, a narrow bed squashed between the close-together, windowless walls. The walls are crowded with Tala's things. Her posters, her cross, a huge frieze of photographs.

Sitting on top of her bed, Tala switches on her computer, her feet on the tiled floor. Phew, it's so hot. She logs on to her blog. She knew it was better to keep quiet after so many of her friends found out she was writing it, but her old laptop stared up at her every night, containing all that misguided rubbish that Vanda spouts. And she felt compelled to carry on. Most of her friends have shared their personal stories of working as maids, and Tala has featured them all anonymously on Maidhacker. She's blogged about the millions of domestic helpers that face conditions of slavery worldwide, and run an article about Aidha, an organisation in Singapore that specialises in teaching maids money management skills and how to start their own businesses.

She looks at her home page now – all this stuff about why she's writing this blog in the first place. She examines her stats page. As she hunches over the screen, the numbers start going up: *97,501, 97,502*. Has her blog got some sort of virus?

What's Vanda got to say about all this? Tala brings up her website. Vanda's changed her masthead – a painted stretch of amateur pink cherry blossom branches that look vaguely familiar. Oh, but just listen to her calling domestic helpers sloths.

Hang on a minute. *Lazy like sloths?* Hasn't Vanda written that before? She sounds a bit like Mrs Heng. Tala stares at that masthead and thinks of the terracotta tile with a cherry blossom tree on it that she came across when she was searching for her passport and computer in Mrs Heng's bureau. There in the corner of the masthead is the splotch of pink paint that Tala saw on Mrs Heng's hideous attempt at art.

Tala gasps, her heart hammering. *Mrs Heng?*

Tala hasn't been cold in the whole fifteen years she's been here, but this shiver goes through her. The Illy coffee Mrs Heng put on the top shelf; doesn't Vanda drink the same stuff? Why didn't Tala think of this before?

The logbook Tala kept, containing all those details about her friends, their names, their work permit numbers, all that evidence, so she could help them should they ever need her help. It dawns on her that if Vanda is Mrs Heng, it's Tala she got all the information from. *Ay nako!* It's not just Vanda who ruined those women, it's Tala too.

Some rescuer she turned out to be. She puts her head into her hands. Some of those women had to go home because of Vanda, because of Tala. Mrs Heng must have been going through Tala's things long before she took the computer.

Tala logs on to WordPress, clicks on that pencil in the corner and starts to type a post. It takes a long time to say what she's got to say, especially with the one-fingered typing, but it comes out, all of it. The way Mrs Heng let Tala work for other people and pretended to be Tala's sole employer to the Ministry, the way she took Tala's computer and bribed her. Tala puts in every last detail – the way she picked her feet and her teeth, all the bad things her daughter said about her behind her back. Tala puts in Mrs Heng's full name and address too.

Tala reads the post back, her chest boiling like a kettle. She knows she shouldn't do this, that this will get her into even more trouble, but the whole thing is Tala's fault and Mrs Heng's and now it's payback time. Tala gives the thing a title:

Veronica Heng Revealed as Vanda.

She hits 'post' and waits, and oh my, on the screen even more stars appear beside what Tala's just written. It seems the post is being liked all over the world.

⧖

It starts in the night. There's no water gushing between Dolly's legs like the first time she gave birth, just waves of something pulling her down. Mama comes to the side of the bed with a cup of something hot in her hand and Dolly turns away.

It is only when the waves get closer together and the sheet is bloody that Mama starts to pace.

'Oh my God,' she says and blesses herself. 'This isn't right. What are we going to do?'

Mallie has pushed a fist to her mouth and looks up at her *Lola*. Through the sweat and the feeling like Dolly's drunk too much Red Horse, she tries to smile at her girl.

Mama looks at Dolly. 'Oh no, this is not right, not right at all.'

Mallie sits on the bed beside her and covers up the blood with a towel.

'You'll be fine, Mama, you'll see,' she says.

Dolly tries to smile again, but the pain pulls her in, wraps her, covers her face, swallows her breath.

'Mallie, you go into town and get Cassandra,' says Mama.

'No!' Dolly shouts.

'Yes,' goes Mama.

Mallie leaves and Dolly keeps looking at the door. It takes a long time for Mallie to come back, but when she does Cassandra is beside her. Cassandra puts her hand between Dolly's legs.

She looks behind her at someone – is it Mama? – and she says, 'She needs to go to the hospital.'

'I'm not going to hospital.'

'This baby has got to come out, but it can't do it on its own.'

'I can do it!'

'You have sixty thousand pesos in your account. That's enough for the hospital bill,' says Mama.

But the money that Amber gave Dolly is for the bakery. Inside Dolly's head, there are cakes on shelves, a floor dusted with flour. The image dissolves then. The ceiling starts to spin. And she's going down and down, and the pain is pressing her. All she has to do is push; it should be simple.

'You want to die here in this house?' Mama screeches.

'I can do this,' says Dolly.

'No you can't,' says Cassandra.

'I damn well can.'

Another contraction sucks her in. She puts her head back, her mouth open, but no scream comes. There is the sound of a bike outside; it is close and it revs. The women bundle Dolly up, pull her to her feet. And the last thing she sees before she goes outside is Mallie, her hands together like she's saying a prayer.

Dolly climbs onto the back of the quad bike and holds onto the person with long black hair. Her hair goes into Dolly's mouth; it smells of shampoo, some clean kind of comfort. Dolly's head rocks and bumps against the person's back, her hands hurting she holds on so tight.

A nurse, with a white Alice band flattening her hair, walks Dolly to a trolley. There are other women in the room, legs splayed, one on all fours, and the nurse looks at Dolly, into Dolly, then the trolley is moving and there are lines of lights on the ceiling, and quick signs she can't read. She tries to get up from the trolley, but an arm pins her down and the pain heats her up, splitting her, skinning her. She tries to fight it. She tries to push, open herself, but all there is is the pain filling up every one of her spaces. And the blood pounds in her ears and something is over her mouth, and there's a stab to her arm.

Mallie and her knew each other for just a few months, months of cakes and playing in the dust, months of Dolly writing down sums for Mallie to solve. And now Dolly feels as if she's about to die. She doesn't hear a baby crying. She doesn't hear anything at all except the faint, slow beat of her heart, then there is nothing at all.

Chapter 27

The next day, the smell of burnt stir-fry hangs in the apartment air. Tala's cooking has improved slightly since she's been working for Ma'am Amber, but she still has the odd disaster even now. Tala has already packed her bag. She is already thinking about how stupid she was to reveal that Mrs Heng is Vanda. 'You always have to have the last word, Tala, always!' Mama's voice hisses in Tala's head.

Tala peeps out through her bedroom door. The children are squished together on the sofa watching a film about a boy in round glasses riding on the back of some big bird. How Tala wishes some big bird would fly in and carry her away; she's been such a *tanga*.

Someone shouts from outside. 'Get away from there! This is private property!'

Tala does up the button on her red shorts, goes out of her room and stands behind the net curtains. There are people jostling down there, glasses poised on noses, notepads in hands. A security guard is pushing them back from the stairs of this building. One of them is far too close to that swimming pool; maybe he'll fall in and soak that shirt and blue tie.

'Get away!' the security guard shouts. He looks like he's enjoying himself.

Tala makes sure the front door is locked.

Someone's right outside it. They knock on the wood. 'We want to talk to you. You're Maidhacker, aren't you?'

Tala's heart splits itself into two and starts thudding in both of her ears.

Of course, she knew Mrs Heng would phone the newspapers after she read the Maidhacker blog post; it must have been her that told them Tala is Maidhacker. Mrs Heng would have guessed it was Tala who wrote it since no one else apart from Tala could have known so many tiny details about the old lady. Mrs Heng probably claimed the reward from the newspaper too. God, all that time Tala was reading the Vanda blog not realising it was Mrs Heng who was writing those poisonous posts. Tala wanted her to feel what it was like to be exposed, like she exposed Tala's friends. Tala wanted her to feel the shock of it. And now it's Tala's turn.

There is a low-down bump on the door like someone has kicked it. Someone from the Ministry is bound to arrive and escort Tala to the airport after those bad things she said. It's just words strung together on a page, opinions, so how come everybody is going so crazy about it? Oh God, just what the hell is Tala going to do?

Colby, who has been lying on the sofa, sits up now, frowning at the door. Sam stays glued to the television, his good ear angled towards the sound. The net curtains billow at the half-open sliding window. The blades of the ceiling fan whir and spin. The sun shines a light on the bookshelves, which stand at a right angle to a wall.

Ma'am Amber comes into the living room with a new dress on, sleeves like wings with lots of sequins at the end of them.

'I'm going out,' she says.

'Oh, you look lovely, ma'am. I mean, Amber. So pretty, so new, so . . .' So help Tala, just keep talking, so Ma'am Amber doesn't hear all those reporters outside.

'So fat!' says Tala.

'So what?' says Ma'am Amber, her mouth falling open.

'So fat. But really, you should go for your dinner dance now, and oh, have such a wonderful evening. Don't worry about anything, and, well, maybe you should go out the back way because there's some bad business going on down there.'

'What bad business? What's happened?'

Ma'am Amber moves towards the window, so Tala steps out in front and they bump. Tala looks up at her.

Think, Tala, speak. 'A spitting cobra. It's gone and killed some-one's cat, swallowed it whole. They're trying to catch it, said not to go down into the grounds.'

'Maidhacker!' someone shouts from outside.

'Who's that?' asks Ma'am.

'Snake control. They must have got it, hacking it, hacking it to pieces. And you in that white dress – oh, it doesn't bear thinking about.' Tala shakes her head.

'Oh, my God, I hate snakes. Watch over the children, won't you?'

'I will.'

Ma'am Amber presses her mobile to her ear. She's calling a cab. She goes out the back door. Tala thanks her astrological stars for that.

She goes back into her room and opens up her computer. My God, she's all over the internet:

Secret Maids' Rights Blogger Exposed

Her name's up there too – *Tala Pabro Castillo* – and a photo-graph of her in her sunflower dress. Wasn't it Jules who took that photograph, come to think of it? How did they get that? But it's not just *The Globe* that she's featured on. She's front-page news on the *Salamin* website too.

She clicks onto Vanda's blog, but the computer says 'The website cannot be found'. She tries again, but no, there's some problem. Vanda's blog doesn't appear.

She goes into the living room again and looks through the window. There are more reporters out there now. The knocking on the door starts all over again.

'Who is that?' snaps Colby.

'Just ignore them,' says Tala. 'Snake on the loose.'

He picks up the remote control and turns the volume up. The phone starts to ring.

Jules looks up at the square modern light in the living room, a pane of glass with four bulbs underneath it. It is dusty with moths and mosquitoes, dead and crumbling. The fridge shakes. The megaphone on an outside wall of the nearby school blares a tune, but it's quiet, too quiet.

She sits at the table and lays her head there. She's going back. This so-called adventure's come to an end, none of the countries ticked off because they've run out of money. But at least she knows now; the future she imagined isn't to be.

She looks down at her name badge and opens the pin. *Jules Harris, receptionist.* The surgery job, it wasn't much of a job, not in comparison to the one she used to have.

In the kitchen area, she switches on the kettle. She lets a cup of tea stew then takes it upstairs, the bag still in the cup.

She switches on her computer. There's no notifications on her Instagram account, but then she hasn't been posting any photographs lately. She clicks onto *The Globe* next, and Tala's shocked, rabbit-in-the-headlights face is on the screen. The sunflowers glaring on that dress, the hair straying across her face. The big silver fridge is in the background.

'Oh, Christ,' says Jules.

Not again! Isn't there a law against this? That's her photograph up there, the one she took of Tala.

Secret Maids' Rights Blogger Exposed

Popular blogger Maidhacker has been unmasked as Filipino maid Tala Pabro Castillo. The 48-year-old disgruntled mother of two blogs about the way employers treat their maids in Singapore, as well as migrant workers' lack of rights.

Pabro Castillo's latest blog post revealed the name and address of the infamous Vanda blogger. Vanda has been featuring the names and work permit numbers of 'bad maids' for the past three years. According to Pabro Castillo, Vanda is, in fact, Veronica Heng, 67, a retired data centre operator from Queenstown. Pabro Castillo claims she had been working for Heng, and that Heng flouted strict Ministry of Manpower rules by allowing Pabro Castillo to be employed in other homes.

Jules clicks off *The Globe* and googles Tala's name. The search leads her to a Filipino paper whose words she can't understand, and there it is again: the photograph that Jules took. The photograph is in the *Singapore Mirror*, too, with details about how Tala had been working illegally in Singapore. Tala, a blogger? Jules shakes her head. She brings up Maidhacker, scrolls down. She reads snatches of it.

Tanga! Disgusting.

Tala's there in the words, in the indignation. How did Jules not notice this before? Jules had no idea Tala was a writer. 'These hands are made for cleaning,' said Tala, smiling. But those hands were made for much more than that.

Jules scrolls down to another post, an early one – there are pages and pages of comments.

How did the newspapers and Vanda know that the photograph Jules took was of Tala? She didn't name Tala when she Instagrammed the picture. She didn't name Dolly either and yet Vanda had put a name to that photograph too.

She logs on to her Instagram account – could it provide a clue? She clicks onto Dolly's photograph. It has been liked thirty-four times. She looks at the people who've liked it – all of them names she doesn't recognise. *Rita Rivera. Marifé Mendoza. Lydia Ramos.* There's even a comment that she hadn't noticed before, from someone called Veronica378. *Maids use this country as a free and easy holiday destination.*

Back-to-back jobs and still Tala found time to write. Good on you, thinks Jules, but then it's not good, is it? The *Singapore Mirror* is saying that Tala could be deported.

Jules deletes both photographs from her Instagram account then closes the laptop lid as if that can make the whole thing disappear.

Chapter 28

The sun streams through the windows of Ma'am Amber's apartment. There's no one outside now. The condo has settled into its usual quiet, leaves swishing through the shell-shaped swimming pool. The children have gone to school and Tala is on her knees rolling back the rug for vacuuming. Ma'am Amber is lying on the sofa reading some magazine, her feet on the arm of the chair. The door goes, three hard knocks, and Tala lets go of the rug and it starts uncoiling, fluff from it flying off into the light. Ma'am flings down her magazine.

'That's a bit much,' she says.

Tala kneels there, her heart full of those knocks, her ears bursting with the shock of them, but then she knew they'd come. She can't believe they've left it this long.

'Aren't you going to get that?' asks Ma'am.

Tala shakes her head. *This is it; it's over.* There's a big crease down Ma'am's forehead; she's glaring at Tala.

'What's wrong?' Ma'am snaps, her lip up on one side.

Tala can feel Ma'am Amber thinking it, that Tala is the paid help, that she can't refuse to do anything. The knocks come again, and Ma'am Amber just stares at Tala, her face one big question mark.

She gets up and so does Tala. Tala rushes into her room and leaves the door open behind her. She pushes her toothbrush into her big bag, double-checks her shell is still there in a side pocket. She's packed everything except her computer. They'll take that for sure. She touches the thick, cold metal of the cupboard-room door and listens.

Ma'am opens the front door and someone speaks to her in a low voice. The voice is a woman's, but Tala can't hear what she's saying.

'She's not here,' says Ma'am loudly.

The voice again, mumbling.

'I had no idea. My gosh, really? Well, yes,' says Ma'am.

The door closes. Is the woman inside? There's a tap on Tala's door.

'Tala, come out, there's no one here.'

Tala opens the door, her nose in the air.

'You've been busy,' says Ma'am. 'I had no idea that blog was you, no idea at all.'

Tala opens her mouth to speak, but doesn't say a thing. She feels too guilty. Just after Vanda had posted Dolly's photograph, Tala had blogged about the car accident and how it had all been Ma'am Amber's fault.

'You better get your belongings together,' says Ma'am Amber.

'I'm already packed.'

A wry smile is spreading across Ma'am's face. 'Someone needed to say those things,' she says, surprising Tala.

Tala's mouth hangs.

'Look, that wasn't a reporter, it was an official from the Ministry and she's coming back. Do what you have to do – go say your goodbyes, Tala, because I'm pretty sure she'll be back to take you to the airport.'

Tala trudges through Greenpalms condo in her poppy-patched skirt. She pushes the sunglasses high up on her nose. The panel above the lift shines: Out of Order. It could be the caption to her life. She takes the back stairs and passes a Filipina lifting a shopping trolley down. Tala sticks her nose in the air, but it doesn't make a difference.

'Tala Pabro Castillo,' the woman says. She's no woman Tala ever helped out in her rescuing days.

'You've got the wrong person, lady.'

'I'm just waiting for you to write another post on that blog again. Oh, it made me laugh. You said all the things we were thinking.'

Tala hightails it past and gets to the fifth, all out of puff. She knocks and Jules comes to the back door.

'I don't know why I didn't realise that blog was yours from the very beginning. It's got you stamped all over it!'

'Such a load of old rubbish,' says Tala. So help Tala, she points that finger of hers at Jules, who's standing there in ripped denim shorts.

'You gave them that picture.'

'I didn't give anyone that photograph, I swear.'

'And now they're throwing me out.'

'What?'

'The Ministry's looking for me.'

'But I thought you didn't have enough money to go home.'

'I don't.'

'Oh, Tala. I didn't give the newspapers that picture; they just copied it off my Instagram account. I'm so sorry.'

'Why did you put it on Instagram?'

'I'm not sure really. I've just been posting some of my photographs, that's all. But I didn't give it to the newspaper. Look, come in.'

There's cardboard everywhere, on top of the sofas, flat on the marble floor along with a tangle of string. A man in a woolly hat and a tattoo of joined-up diamonds twisting up his arm walks through with a roll-your-own in his hand.

'Better use the back,' says Tala. 'The lift's not working.'

He retraces his steps. 'When do you leave?' Tala asks Jules.

'Tomorrow. Night in a hotel then we're off.'

'This isn't the way I thought I'd leave.'

'It's not right, that they're throwing you out.'

Tala pulls something out of her handbag and looks at Jules.

Another man comes into the room, gets down onto his knees and starts bashing the cardboard, turning it into a box. Tala's stuff is packed except there are no boxes, just her old bag, and a bank book as empty as when she first arrived.

Tala stands there staring at Miss Branch of a Tree and thinks of that day in the underground car park just over six months ago when all the distance between them disappeared. Now Jules is going in one direction, Tala in the other.

'I'm going to miss you,' says Jules.

The air conditioning judders. There is the sound of books being piled into cardboard.

'Sometimes you have to let things go, then life will give you other gifts,' says Tala.

She moves closer to Jules, takes hold of her slim fingers and squeezes them. Jules' pinched face softens. She tilts her head, and Tala leans in and hugs her, the smell of Jules' perfume up her nose, her freshly laundered clothes.

Tala pulls away and presses something cold and smooth into Jules' hand.

'It doesn't look much, but it's my best thing,' says Tala.

Chapter 29

☒

Edward is tied to Dolly's side and she walks, slow and sore from the stitches. They told her not to carry her baby for six weeks. The cool box is empty and light in her hand. They sold every last one of the mamons today. She touches the coins in her pocket, Mallie in her too-short blue school dress walking beside her and squinting in the sun.

Dolly's managing, but only because of that money Ma'am Amber gave her, and Tala's job. If it wasn't for them, Dolly wouldn't have enough to keep Mallie in school. Mallie needs a bigger school dress, and some new shoes.

Dolly takes a book from her bag, pushes it into Mallie's hands, and they walk, Mallie reading as she does. After a while, she trips onto her knees in the dust, the book crashing to the ground.

'Are you okay?'

She nods.

Dolly tries to bend to get the book, but her caesarean scar hurts. Mallie gets there first.

'The book's good?'

'Three pages left.'

She shows Dolly the cover, a boy with a ticket in his hand.

'He won something?'

'He's going to live in a chocolate factory.'

'Oh, his teeth!'

Mallie smiles her spaces.

'Will you have to go away again?'

'Oh, darling, I hope not.'

'I don't want you to go.'

Dolly takes Mallie's hand in her own and squeezes it. Mallie takes it back again.

'Will I go away one day, get a job like you?'

'That's why you go to school, so you can get a really good job.'

'What will I do?'

'Anything you want.'

'Be an astronaut.'

Dolly smiles.

'Or build a chocolate factory,' says Mallie.

'Will there be room for me?'

'Yes, and I'll buy you toothpaste.'

Dolly squeezes Mallie's nose where there are droplets of sweat. There's a brown stain on the collar of her T-shirt dress.

'Have you already started making the chocolate then?' asks Dolly.

Mallie looks at the collar. 'Don't be silly, Mama. That's mud.'

They walk along the road. A bright green bird sits on a roof. There's a quad bike outside the old wooden barn, perspex over the windows, the painted letters on the sign, 'E-Cafe'.

They go inside where a man stands behind a tall wooden counter, a red ribbon tied around his wrist. There are tables in the room with big fat computers on each one, chairs small enough for kids.

'Fifteen minutes,' says Dolly and pushes some coins across the wood. The man's fingers brush hers as he takes the money. She pulls her hand back. His eyes make her think of praline. He smiles, looks away.

She sits, her belly hurting.

The Globe is the home page. And there is Tala's shocked face. Is she dead?

Maid Tala Pabro Castillo has been unveiled as mystery blogger Maidhacker.

Tala, what have you done? Dolly knew Tala was still writing the Maidhacker blog. Dolly had said things over Skype like, 'You need to stop writing.' 'What writing?' Mallie had asked. And Dolly had replied, 'Oh, nothing.' But Tala didn't stop, and now look. She could lose her job, her work permit.

'Mama, what is Auntie Tala doing on the internet?'

Dolly's mouth is dry; her chest fizzing. Every day she sets up her cake stall at the side of the road, and every day, the manager of the supermarket comes out and waves her away. People buy from her anyway. But Tala needs a job to support Mama and Mallie until Dolly can make proper money. Why couldn't she have just stopped? That constant chatter, the hand slapped to her chest. Keeping quiet isn't who Tala is.

'Let's email her,' says Mallie.

But Dolly just sits there staring at the screen. Mallie starts typing: *Auntie, you are famous.* Then with one finger, Dolly types: *I guess you're coming home then.* Dolly hits 'send' and they walk out into the dazzle of the day.

'I'm hungry,' Mallie says.

Dolly pulls the lump of squashed cake from her bumbag. Mallie undoes the paper and bites into the cake.

'Maybe we could open a cake factory instead of a chocolate one,' says Mallie.

'Who's going to bake the cakes?'

She pushes against Dolly's hip. 'You, of course.'

Dolly looks down at her daughter; it seems as if Rita is right, people like them don't do things like open bakeries.

'Mama, why are you sad?'

'I'm not sad.'

'Stop pretending.'

Dolly touches the back of Mallie's silky long hair and thinks about how she's been pretending for the past six years, pretending that she's invisible.

She looks at her fingers in Mallie's hair, the skin rough, the nails torn. She touches her other hand to her sleeping baby. She can go on pretending just like before, be the girl who lives in a cupboard because somewhere down the line, one of them is going to make her own rules, one of them is going to live out her own possibilities.

They walk on, over grass flicking at their ankles, over puddles, past the up and down earth and lines of palms swaying in the distance. A boy rides his bike past them too fast and Dolly presses Mallie into her. Then there are pins of rain in the air and it gets heavier and the sky goes dark.

She thinks of the day that Ma'am Amber knocked Sam over and how she'd screamed that it was Dolly's fault. She thinks of the way Sir Tor spoke up for her, and how Colby thought he'd seen Sir Tor in her room. There was never anything between her and Sir Tor. Edward has a squashed nose just like Gavin, though she tries not to think of Gavin. 'Make the father pay!' Mama has said more than once, but Dolly has not been in touch with Gavin since the day she took the bus back to Tagudin.

Edward starts to cry now, and Dolly bumps him up and down. They're close to home, so there's no point in stopping.

The rain runs off the end of Dolly's nose, and Mallie's hair is wet and shiny like black patent shoes.

They look at each other, Mallie and Dolly, both frowning at first then Mallie's mouth stretches into a smile and Dolly smiles too. And even though Dolly's not supposed to lift her, she pulls Mallie onto her free side. She bounces them, her kids, Edward crying into one ear, and Mallie laughing into the other.

And that's all there is, Dolly and her kids and the pelt of the warm rain coming down and soaking them.

The slice of yellow cake in Mallie's hand is mush now and it falls apart on the ground. And the words start pumping through Dolly. *I can do this. I just need to find a way.*

Singapore Mirror

Breaking News

A Queenstown resident who allegedly made anti-Filipino comments on her now defunct blog was yesterday charged with sedition.

Veronica Heng, 67, of Queenstown, wrote her anonymous Vanda's Blog – Life as the Employer of a Foreign Domestic Helper *for three years. Her identity was revealed by her former employee Tala Pabro Castillo, 48, in her counterblog Maidhacker.*

In an October post, Heng allegedly made disparaging comments about overseas migrant workers. According to the charge, Heng's post could promote feelings of hostility between Singaporeans and Filipinos.

Under the Sedition Act, anyone found guilty of promoting feelings of ill will and hostility between different races can be jailed for up to three years and face fines of up to $5,000.

In addition to the sedition charge, Heng has also been charged with illegally deploying a foreign domestic worker. Heng allegedly allowed Pabro Castillo to work at eleven other places of employment for a period of six years, flouting Ministry of Manpower rules. This further charge attracts a maximum penalty of $10,000.

Chapter 30

The Ministry has come for Tala. Her canvas bag is already packed
and at the door. The children stand there looking. She shakes
the hair from her face, and when she bends down to kiss him,
Sam takes her hand and doesn't let go.

'Everyone keeps leaving,' he says and his chin wobbles like
he's going to cry.

He looks at his mama then at Tala. 'Why do you have to go?' he wails.

'Because it's the way of things,' says Tala.

She walks through the front door behind the woman from the
Ministry in her navy blue stilettos and narrow grey skirt. The
woman told Tala that she'll have to face the consequences of
working illegally while living with Mrs Heng. Sam keeps pinching
Tala's fingers, pulling her back. Tala takes four steps then Amber
yanks Sam's hand away and closes the front door behind her.
When Tala turns back, Amber is still standing there. She stretches
an envelope towards Tala.

'This came for you,' she says.

Tala takes it from her, and stuffs it into her bag.

'And this is from me.' There is a stiff white envelope in Amber's
other hand.

'What's this?'

'A gift.'

Tala takes it, pushes her fingernail under the stuck-down flap
and tears it open. The card has a printed pink bird on the front.
There are looping words inside, but Tala can't read them all
because in the way is a wad of $50 notes.

'Oh my Gad, you know I won't accept this.' Tala thrusts the whole thing back towards Amber.

'I insist.'

'I don't want your money.'

'Everything you've done for us . . .'

'I don't need your help, Amber. I don't want your help. I'm more than capable of sorting this whole mess out. This is a temporary to-do.'

'This isn't just for you, Tala; it's for your new grandchild.'

The card and the notes stay wafting in the air between them. Tala doesn't say a thing, just stands there with her mouth open, her body shaking so much it's like she's on one of those vibration plates in the Greenpalms gym.

Amber has tears on her face. 'Just take it, Tala. Put your pride aside, and take this. It's the least I can do.'

'Hurry up,' says the woman from the Ministry.

Money won't be a lot of good in prison, thinks Tala. She sags, her shoulders rounded, her 38F bosoms going further south. She pushes the envelope into the bag on her shoulder.

She reaches her hand out to shake Amber's. Then Tala is wrapped up in Amber's arms and Amber is pressing her tight. Tala pats her back a few times and whispers into her ear. 'Thank you.'

Tala goes down the steps beside the female official with her crisp white shirt. The bag slices Tala's shoulder.

The car is an old blue thing. The woman puts her hand over Tala's head when she bends to get into the back.

The car is oven-hot; the blacked-out windows give a grey tinge to all that they pass. A man holds a long thin nozzle spraying jasmines planted at the side of the road, a scarf wrapped around his head. A Filipina is pushing a boy in a wheelchair, his head lolling to one side. They overtake a pick-up truck with an open back, lots of dark-skinned men squashed in there, bumping up and down along the road. It's the same for all of them – constructing those grand buildings and condos, keeping them clean, working for the people inside. Tala thought she could change some of it, but she hasn't changed a thing. Still, at least this woman isn't carting her off to court; this is the way to the airport.

They pass straight flowerbeds, and shiny cars, palms nodding their heads, a spiral staircase up the side of a white condo. Tala rests her head on the glass. She's leaving; not the way she wanted, but she's leaving anyway.

The car stops and the woman gets out first and opens Tala's door, and they walk towards the tall glass airport building. Inside, the woman keeps holding on to Tala's arm, but Tala shrugs her off and grabs a small thin trolley, dumps her bag in there.

The woman walks beside Tala, down slopes, through the huge carpeted corridors, quiet despite all those people striding and talking, drinking coffee in cafes, pulling books from shelves in stores.

Tala walks past benches, and pots stuffed full with purple orchids. Tala tests an orchid out, but it's not plastic. She smoothes her thumb along a velvet petal. Then she is handing her ticket to a man in a blue uniform who says, 'Have a nice day,' though there's nothing nice about it.

A woman asks Tala if she has anything electrical in her bag and Tala nods. She pulls out her computer and lays it in a tray, expecting someone to snatch it up and take it away. Tala walks through an arch that beeps, so she has to walk back and put her sandals into a box, then she walks through again, her sweaty feet sticking to the floor. This time the arch is as quiet as that whole clean airport out there.

She's in a big glass room now, her computer stuffed back inside her bag. Through the glass, that Ministry woman keeps a watch on Tala. A plane taxis in the distance. Another stationary plane, with a red tick along its side, looms nearer to the glass. Tala is surrounded by Filipinas splitting the air with their excited voices. It's not so quiet in here with all of those women. The women's laughter and words are all mixed up and the noise gets louder and louder still.

Chapter 31

Jules strides down the corridor of the birth centre at St Thomas'
Hospital, the beige linoleum scuffed with wheel marks. At the
nurses' station, she scores through some of the things on the
whiteboard list. She's taken the woman in bed 7 off her drip, and
the baby alongside the woman in bed 14 is doing well now despite
being bruised by a difficult forceps delivery. Jules has delivered
four babies without the intervention of an obstetrician today, and
her feet are killing her.

She pulls off the plastic gloves and digs into the Lindors –
sustenance. There are two red ones left. She unwraps one of
them and shoves it into her mouth.

Isobel's in front of her then, a stubby pencil behind her ear,
hair falling from her ponytail.

'She's been pushing for two hours. It's straightforward, but
she just won't let it come.'

Jules nods, stuffs the other chocolate into her mouth alongside
the melted leftovers of the first one, and washes her hands. The
midwives walk along the corridor. Inside the delivery room, the
woman is on all fours.

'God, I feel stupid,' she says.

She climbs onto her bottom with her legs open and gives a
half-hearted push.

'This is Jules,' says Isobel.

'Hello there. Let's have a gander.'

The baby's crowning, a tuft of hair appearing then vanishing
back inside.

'He or she'll be out in a few seconds,' says Jules. 'I'm just going to give you a little cut first though.'

Fear spreads across the woman's face. 'Oh, no!'

The husband touches his wife's forehead.

'It's better than ripping,' says Jules. 'And I'm going to give you an injection; you won't feel the cut.'

'Thank God.'

Jules pulls the syringe out of the plastic.

'Deep breath in now,' says Jules.

She gives the injection, and they wait.

'Would you credit it?' says Isobel. 'I'm with you the whole way, then this one comes in to claim it as her own.'

Jules laughs. 'Yep, I'm notching them up tonight all right. Can you feel that?'

'No,' says the woman.

'And this?'

The woman shakes her head. Jules readies the stethoscope in her ears and cuts. The woman's face creases up as another contraction takes her then the baby slides out, squashed up and bloody and lardy with vernix. Jules presses the end of her stethoscope to his chest. His heart beats loud in her ears. She puts a towel around him and rubs. She lays him on his mother's stomach where he squirms, blinking wild eyes that seem too big for his body.

'Hello,' the new mother says to her son. 'This feels so weird, like I've always known you.'

The dad touches a bent finger to the boy's face. Their joy flares out and catches hold of Jules. Her stomach is looping like she's on a plane that's just taken off. Maybe she's looking forward to that large glass of white that she's going to have when she gets home. Her twelve-hour shift is almost over then she has four days off. Four whole days.

She's going to change the settings on her camera and try to capture a raindrop hitting a slab on the patio. She and David are trying that new restaurant on the high street, and she's looking after her niece and nephews for a few hours because the child-minder's on holiday.

'Thank you so much!' the new mum says to Jules.

The woman's eyes are blurry with elation, and it's not drug-fuelled. She's done it with no pain relief apart from a couple of paracetamol.

'I'm off now,' says Jules. She smiles and waves at the little family.

Isobel is threading the needle to mend the episiotomy. She looks at the clock. 'Not too bad then, only an hour over your time,' she says to Jules.

'Yeah,' replies Jules.

She goes back to the midwives' station, and hands over to the other senior midwife who's just come on duty. She points at the whiteboard and brings the midwife up to speed about all the women who are yet to give birth.

'See you next time,' says Jules. 'And sorry about eating all the red Lindors.'

'Oh, God, would you listen to her?' a voice goes. 'We'll have to open the Terry's All Gold to compensate.'

She's done them a favour eating all those chocolates since they didn't taste that good anyway. Jules walks through the corridor, past the windows of each ward room. The wheels of a tea trolley squeak. A baby cries. There is a woman's distant scream.

Jules goes into the locker room where there are lines of benches and hooks, a denim jacket sagging from one of them, a pair of battered red Converse plimsolls on the linoleum floor, and beyond all that the shower room. She hears the sound of hissing water.

She pulls off her top and looks down at her stomach; it's not as flat as it was, the flesh bulging slightly over the waistband of her knickers. Has this body failed her; have the inner parts of it let her down? That time has passed now, the grief of it still there, but somewhat diluted. She feels the piece of paper folded in her pocket, pulls it out and sits down.

They are only in the early stages of the adoption process, but she flicked through some of the literature the adoption agency sent to them, including a brochure containing photographs of so many children without permanent homes. She ripped out this photograph – two children in their red school uniforms, the five-year-old sister with her silver-rimmed round glasses, her strawberry blond hair in plaits, and her younger brother, now nailing Jules to the bench with his confused brown eyes.

Anya and Kyle. They've been in the system for years, their mum incapable of looking after them. And they've been separated from their two teenage brothers.

Jules wants to see into the fringes of the photograph. She wants to know how Anya got the blue ink stain on her collar and why Kyle has a small cut on his right cheek. She wants to know what their favourite foods are and what games they like to play. They look a little like she and David, don't they?

She fishes around in her bag and pulls out the conch shell, smooth, and swirly, and cold. It was Tala that pushed it into her hand. Jules runs her thumb over it. *It doesn't look much, but it's my best thing*, Tala had said. Jules presses it against the torn-out photograph.

She tries to keep the thought at bay, but it comes anyway, thumping through her head like the line of a song. *Just this one small thing.*

She changes into her civvies then stares at herself in the mirror. Her hair is longer and the tiny hole is back in her nose where she wears that ruby stud on her days off now just like she used to.

She folds the page and pokes it into her pocket. She pushes the conch shell in beside it and steps towards the locker-room door. 'Anya and Kyle,' she whispers, her chest hardening with determination.

She goes down in the lift and steps out into the noise of the dark, damp street, the hum of the cars, the tap of footsteps, the drift of people's voices. Everything falls away then, and all she can hear is the rush of hope through her ears. She picks up her pace, plunging her hand into her pocket again just to make sure it's all there.

Chapter 32

The walkway is lined with people, a man holding a placard saying 'Vinegas', another holding one that says 'Garcia'. Tala's heart beats quick, but there is no one here for her. She didn't expect there to be. Amber has given Tala a lot of money, but it won't last forever. Tala will probably have to use it to pay for a flight to Hong Kong to work, or some place where no one knows her name.

She collects her holdall from the conveyor belt and throws it over her shoulder. She joins the suitcases, bloated bin liners, girls and cigarette butts at the bus stop. When the little blue bus pulls in, it's so full that Tala can't get beyond the steps of the entrance.

'No, no!' says the driver, waving her back.

It's another hour before the next one leaves. She climbs aboard and pushes herself into the shoulder of a woman who tuts.

Then she sees Tala and shouts, 'Ehhhh, make way for Auntie.'

Tala pulls the envelope stuffed full of cash from the bag. She takes a note from it and hands it to the driver. The crowd gives a little and the doors puff closed behind her. Diesel fumes rise at the window as the bus leaves the airport behind. The hours grind by. Tala's feet start to hurt. She rests them by standing on one foot then the other.

She takes the other envelope that Amber gave her from the pocket of the holdall and opens it. Embossed with some gold motif, it's from someone called Priscilla. Tala doesn't know any Priscilla, so what's she got to say for herself? She reads.

Our newspaper includes daily stories that appeal to a tabloid readership.

Readership? What's she talking about? Tala scrunches the letter into a ball and pushes it into her pocket.

A child outside with a pinched nose, riding side-saddle on the back of his mother's bike, breaks into a smile. Three emaciated goats canter into the road and Tala holds onto the dashboard as the bus grinds to a sudden stop. A woman walks, a basket of oranges on her head. Then the road dies away, and they shimmy on gravel for miles. Shacks with iron roofs, washing lines pegged with clothes and waterlogged fields.

'Girl, you're going home,' whispers Tala to herself. Some home-coming, this.

The bus smells of diesel. The elderly man on the seat nearest her has a hacking cough.

They roll on for hours then there's the sign for the town. 'Welcome to Tagudin'.

'Hey!' Tala shouts at the driver who pushes a finger into his ear canal.

The brakes shriek and the doors open. She edges forwards and pulls herself and her bag free.

She waves as the still-crammed bus drives away, and the woman who she was standing beside waves back with both hands. The woman's smile is so wide she must be celebrating the ability to breathe again.

Tala's face is shadowed with the overhead cables across the street. Oh, that stupid marketing letter – it is jabbing right into her hip. She whips it out and balances it on top of a bin already overflowing with rubbish. She walks away, wiggling up the road with her holdall making her tilt sideways. And then she doesn't know why, but some space in her chest starts opening and making a strange shape, and she stops and turns around and looks at that messy bin.

She walks slowly back towards it, picks up the letter and reads, then stands there swaying like a Tala-sized spinning top. She makes herself read the words again and again to make sure that she's seeing them right. But yes, there's no mistaking it.

Dear Ms Pabro Castillo,

I am impressed by your popular blog, the no-holds-barred way in which you write, and I would very much like to meet you to discuss the possibility of you writing for Salamin. *A large part of our readership is made up of foreign domestic helpers and we are inundated with their emails about the challenges they face, and requests for advice.*

There's a telephone number at the bottom, along with a name: Priscilla Espiritu, Managing Editor.

Tala doesn't let herself smile because maybe this is some kind of joke. She switches on her phone and dials the number. A lady picks up and says something, and this classical music, like the kind Sir Tor used to listen to, starts tinkling in her ear. Then a woman with a loud and certain voice says her own name.

And when Tala introduces herself too, the woman says, 'I'm so glad that you phoned.'

And Tala doesn't say a thing.

'We're struggling to cope with all the emails we're getting from overseas domestic helpers, and we're thinking you might be able to help. We want you to run an online forum where you can offer advice and answer questions. We want you to write a column too. What do you think, Tala? It's clear from your blog you've got so much to say.'

Well, it seems Tala has nothing to say at the moment; she coughs and somehow finds her voice again. Questions spill out of her mouth. 'What sort of forum?' and 'How much money will I earn?' She gets the woman to repeat the numbers and stands quite still, her eyebrow arched in disbelief.

The silence crackles.

'Well?' the woman asks then.

'I'll start tomorrow,' says Tala.

The woman gives her the address of the newspaper offices in Manila then hangs up.

Tala keeps on walking. There's the graveyard, and somewhere in the far corner, Bong's plaque, his name scored into the wood. He was forty-five when he went. 'Complications arising from alcoholism,' the doctor said.

A person in yellow and green sneakers, and a pair of stupid-looking jeans that are just about falling down around his ankles, well, he's walking towards Tala. And there's a woman with a baby in her arms and even from here, that face looks like some sort of statue. A girl in a little red dress pulls her thumb from her mouth and runs towards Tala, her arms outstretched.

'Auntie Tala,' she says.

And Tala drops her bag with a burst of dust, and lifts Mallie and turns her, and they stare into each other's faces, Mallie with the dimples in her cheeks and Tala with all the lines.

Tala puts the little girl down, then Tala is like one of those Mexican wraps with their arms all around her, Mallie's, Marlon's and Dolly's, and the new baby squished against Tala's chest. Oh, he smells so good.

They start walking and Tala starts laughing like a crazy person. And Dolly's all quiet and thoughtful, looking down into the dirt.

'Carioca,' says Mallie, pointing to the cool box in Dolly's hand.

'You've already had two today,' says Dolly.

'It's a special occasion,' says Tala, grinning wide.

Dolly doesn't smile back, her forehead pleated like a curtain. She opens the box and hands each of them a stick of doughnut rings. They walk and they eat, and Marlon puts his arm around Tala. There's a stubby orange pencil pushed behind his right ear. She starts laughing again.

'Mama, I know things are bad, but are you right in your head?' he asks.

'What's that there?' Tala points at an old shop along the drag, a sign that says 'Oriam' slanted across the top, a padlock on the door. The windows are boarded over.

'Shop gone bust,' says Marlon.

Tala sniggers so much she's just about wetting her knickers.

'Are you going to let me in on the joke?' asks Dolly.

'My God, these doughnuts are fantastic!' says Tala. She walks some more. 'I'm thinking we could buy that place, there.' She looks towards the Oriam shop again.

'With what? We've got nothing apart from what I'm earning from the guavas and the supermarket and Dolly's cakes,' says Marlon.

'We could turn it into your bakery, Dolly.'

'Don't,' says Dolly. She looks away from Tala.

'Paper bags on a hook on the wall, cakes on the shelves,' says Tala.

'Tala, it's going to be a long while before I can afford an actual shop.'

Tala takes out her letter and smoothes it on her stomach.

'Well, maybe you should start planning because I reckon I'm going to put a deposit down on that place.'

'What are you talking about?' asks Dolly.

Tala tries it out in her head before she says it; it doesn't sound right at all.

'I've got myself a new job,' she says. 'I'm going to be a writer.'

Writer. The word tastes as strange as chocolate with chilli in. Marlon smiles and shakes his head at Tala. Tala opens her mouth to speak again, but nothing else comes out, which is strange.

Mallie puts the last of the carioca into her mouth and chews. Tala passes her the rest of her doughnuts and Mallie's smile gets even bigger.

Dolly stares at Tala, and Tala walks towards that boarded-up shop, leaving them all standing there on the dry mud.

The birds *whoop-whoop* in the trees. A tuk-tuk rattles by. There's the smell of citrus.

Tala presses her nose to the wood; it's all dark in there, but a thin shaft of light finds its way through. Tala starts to put things into their places. The chairs, and the shelves with loaves on them, the chiffon cake and Dolly's chocolate one, all sliced up.

This could be our best thing, thinks Tala. Yes, this could be our best thing.

Author's Note

When we arrived in Singapore in 2009, I absorbed all its rich detail from the pristine streets to the clouds of pesticide fogging the humid air. We began looking for a place to live, and an estate agent showed us around a flat. She flung open the door of a windowless 12ft by 5ft bomb shelter just off the kitchen. 'Your maid will sleep in here,' she said. 'But there's no window,' I replied. 'They don't need things like that,' she said.

We moved into this flat which was part of a condo, populated by families and the domestic helpers who lived with them. Blocks of flats sat around two swimming pools and everywhere there were palms, orchids, and carpet grass.

I didn't know a soul. I reached out, talking to people, including many domestic helpers who began to share their stories with me. I have worked as a newspaper and magazine journalist for 20 years, and back then I realised that if some domestic helpers agreed to be interviewed, I could write a feature reflecting the low-wage experience of the then 201,000 female domestic workers in Singapore.

Some of the women didn't want to talk, but others opened up about their lives back home in the Philippines, about their lack of rights in Singapore, about their relief in finding employers who cared about their welfare. One woman told me how she hadn't earned any money for a year after she arrived in Singapore because her wages went towards paying back the employment agency for training expenses and other fees.

Another woman told me how she wanted to get fit, but when

she went for a swim in the pool of the condo where she lived with her employers, a security guard demanded she get out because domestic workers weren't allowed to use the facilities. I mentioned this to one British expat I was getting to know. 'Too right,' she said. 'I mean they're staff.' This kind of attitude from employers abounded. 'Oh, they're village girls from the middle of nowhere,' one woman, who employed a maid, said. Others told me how they locked their maids' passports away and gave them curfews.

Some helpers described how they were banned from using any toilets in the apartments they worked and lived in, apart from the one assigned for their personal use beside the kitchen. One helper explained how she wasn't allowed to use any of the apartment toilets at all and was forced to go downstairs to the communal toilets in the grounds of the condo. Other women talked of sexual abuse and bullying.

Most apartments in Singapore have a bomb shelter just like the one in the flat I was renting. Many helpers slept in these, but none of them complained about this to me. 'Oh, it's fine,' said one woman. 'I used to sleep on the floor under the table in the living room in one place I worked.'

Some of the women talked about the hours that past employers had made them work - 14 hour days, seven days a week. Indeed, it wasn't until 2013 that domestic helpers in Singapore, who earn around 550 Singapore dollars, (the equivalent of 305 pounds) per month, were given a legal right to one day of rest per week. By 2015, Transient Workers Count Too estimated that 59 per cent of foreign domestic workers in Singapore still didn't get a weekly day off. Today, there is still no statutory minimum wage for domestic workers, and they are not covered by Singapore's employment act.

I came across a now defunct blog by an anonymous writer who called herself Tamarind. On it, she listed 'house rules' for helpers including washing hair daily, and not scolding the children.

She also spoke of using secret cameras to spy on maids. It was then that I realised that the plight of female domestic workers was more than a feature; it was a book, and I started to write it.

I had a personal motivation too. My Irish father had moved to London in 1957 to work in an ice cream factory and had battled prejudice. Many times when I was growing up, I heard people make offensive jokes about the Irish in front of him. Those comments stung and stayed with me. In Singapore, I felt a similar outrage as I noticed people not just making disparaging comments about domestic helpers, but also subjecting them to degrading treatment.

I didn't employ a live-in helper while in Singapore, but I did have a cleaner called Gina*. Like Tala, she made her living doing part-time jobs, and poverty had forced her to leave her sons to work overseas. 'After I left the Philippines, I didn't see them for three years; imagine that,' she said and began to cry.

Even though I had started to write *The Maid's Room*, I was still battling my own grief at not being able to have a second child after going through IVF.

I read an article in a magazine about a charity called Sanctuary House whose volunteers fostered babies. I rang the charity and volunteered.

A couple of weeks later I was given a six-week-old baby boy to look after for just one week. Surprisingly, no one from the charity came to have a look around our apartment and we weren't interviewed. Nevertheless looking after this young child was an absolute privilege - all of us fell in love with him. Even though we weren't able to adopt him because he was being adopted by someone else, fostering helped me to move on from my inability to have another child. It also provided the colour and depth for Jules' fostering of baby Khalib.

During the two and a half years I lived in Singapore, I continued to research and write my book. Most of the helpers I spoke to were from the Philippines and they sent much of their money home to pay for their children's educations and help out other members of their families. Their wages in Singapore exceeded their earning potential in the Philippines, so it seemed as if they were locked into overseas servitude, that this would be their lot for years to come.

I wanted to know if there was some way out for the women. A friend of mine told me about Aidha, a college for the low-paid in Singapore which teaches money management and entrepreneurial skills. Her helper Alice* attended classes there every week. Aidha's motto is, 'Talent is universal, opportunity is not.' My friend was determined to give Alice an opportunity, and Alice took that opportunity and turned it to her advantage. She now runs her own small business back in the Philippines hiring out motorcycles. And she's answered many of my questions about life in the Philippines.

One of the best known examples of a Filipina woman getting a break is the story of street photographer Xyza Cruz Bacani. She was part of the 300,000-strong female domestic workforce in Hong Kong when her employer lent her money to buy a Nikon D90. She began snapping everything from women riding the MRT to abused helpers hugging each other for comfort in a women's shelter. She put her photographs on Facebook, and other photographers began to notice her talent. Xyza went on to become one of the BBC's 100 Women of the World in 2015 and is now one of the Magnum Foundation's Human Rights Fellows. While Tala's character is loosely based on Gina, a woman with such dignity and charm, Tala's blog journey was very much inspired by Xyza's story.

The influence for the scene where Dolly watches a woman standing in the window of an employment agency, with a sign that says *Lowest Pay and Fee,* came from a 2014 investigation by *Al Jazeera.* It found that some maid agencies in the Bukit Timah Shopping Centre in Singapore sold women as if they were commodities by having them sit beneath signs advertising 'super promo' rates and 'special discounts'. Tala's fears about going to prison are rooted in the Alan Shadrake case. Shadrake wrote the book *Once a Jolly Hangman* which explored Singapore's judicial system. As a result, he was found guilty of contempt of court in 2010 and served five and a half weeks in Changi Prison.

While writing this book, I wrote short stories too. The setting for my prize-winning story *Plenty More Where You Came From* is again Singapore, this time focusing on the forced repatriation of migrant shipyard workers, inspired by a series of articles on the Transient Workers Count Too website.

That story and *The Maid's Room*, indeed much of my fiction, is about people exposed to exploitation, but at the centre of all my stories is how, even in the harshest of circumstances, there can be joy.

In real life, there are rarely neat endings, but at a time when an estimated 67 million people are working as domestic helpers across the globe, and a quarter of these are afforded no legal rights at all, perhaps my novel might just be a small symbol of hope.

* Names have been changed.

Acknowledgements

I am indebted to the many women working as domestic helpers in Singapore who shared their stories with me. It all started with you, and I am so very grateful.

This book has been an epic journey and my husband Mike has weathered all the blows with me along the way. Thank you for being my biggest champion and such an honest critic.

So much gratitude and admiration to Rowan Lawton, my fantastic agent, for believing in this book and taking it forward. Thank you Liane-Louise Smith and all at Furniss Lawton for your hard work.

Heartfelt thanks to Kate Howard at Hodder – you really have made my dream come true. Thank you to the other members of the Hodder team for all that you have done to support me, especially Ruby Mitchell, Amber Burlinson, Sharan Matharu and Thorne Ryan. Thank you to my international publishers too for taking this story to readers around the world.

To Sara Sarre, who taught me the importance of turning points – you were mine, Sara. Eternal thanks. To my friend and fellow author Claire Douglas, thank you for keeping the faith in this book, for your stellar advice and for knowing just how it all feels.

Thank you to my parents, June and Michael, for fostering my love of books in so many ways, including all those childhood trips to Barham Park Library where my imagination came alive. Thank you for giving me the space to write, and for so often seeing the funny side of life.

Particular thanks to my kind and clever friend, Anna, who has steered me through many a sticking point. I am so blessed to have you in my life.

Huge thanks to my fabulous and faithful friends who have cheered me on, furnished me with ideas and listened to me talk incessantly about this book, especially Ruth Hughes, Lindi Reynolds, Emily H, Toni Langmead, Emma-Jane Beer, Lucy Hunter and Lizzy Leicester.

Thank you to Joe Melia at the magnificent Bristol Short Story Prize – your generous words kept me writing. Thank you Emma Hibbs, Jennifer Small and Sian Clarke for reading early versions of this book and sharing your thoughts.

Finally, to my daughter, Olivia. Endless love and gratitude for your wisdom and for so often making me see things differently. Thank you for being you, wonderful you.